Rivers of Babylon

by the same author

Rivers of Babylon Bratislava: Archa, 1991, Champagne Avantgarde, 1995 and Koloman Kertész Bagala, 2003

Mladý Dônč (*Young Dônč*) Bratislava: Slovenský spisovateľ, 1993 and Koloman Kertész Bagala, 1998

Rivers of Babylon 2 alebo drevená dedina (*Rivers of Babylon 2, or The Wooden Village*) Bratislava: Champagne Avantgarde, 1994

Skazky o Vladovi pre malých a veľkých (*Tales about Vlad for Young and Old*) Bratislava: Filmservice Slovakia, 1995

Nové skazky o Vladovi (*More Tales about Vlad*) Bratislava: Filmservice Slovakia, 1998

Sekerou a nožom (*With Axe and Knife*), with Dušan Taragel, Levice: LCA, 1999

Rivers of Babylon 3 alebo Fredyho koniec (*Rivers of Babylon 3, or The End of Freddy*) Bratislava: Filmservice Slovakia, 1999

Posledné skazky pre malých a veľkých (*Latest Tales for Young and Old*) Bratislava: Fenix, 2002

Traktoristi a buzeranti (*Tractor Drivers and Queers*) Bratislava: Slovart, 2003

Recepty z rodinného archívu alebo všetko čo viem ma naučil môj dedo (*Recipes from the Family Archive, or Everything I Know My Grandfather Taught Me*) Levice: LCA, 2003

Peter Pišťanek

Rivers of Babylon

translated by Peter Petro

GARNETT PRESS

LONDON, 2007

first published in Great Britain in 2007 by

The Garnett Press,
Dpt of Russian (SML)
Queen Mary (University of London),
Mile End Road, London E1 4NS

© Peter Pišťanek
this translation into English: © Peter Petro
this edition: © Garnett Press

typeset in Times New Roman by Donald Rayfield
1000 copies printed and bound in Turkey by Mega Basım, Yeni Bosna

ISBN 978-0-9535878-4-1

Introduction

Peter Pišťanek (pronounced *Pishtyanek*) is one of the most talented prose writers to appear after the fall of Communism in Slovakia. He is also a colourful and controversial personality whose many-sided activities were unthinkable in the Communist era. He was born in 1960 in Devínska Nová Ves, a village now swallowed up by Bratislava, the capital of Slovakia. He enrolled in Bratislava's Academy of Performing Arts, but did not graduate. He was also a drummer in a very well known rock group. At the end of the 1980s he began to publish in the literary monthly *Slovenské Pohľady* (Slovak Views). His breakthrough came with *Rivers of Babylon* (1991), a novel that caused a sensation and catapulted him into fame. This novel is the first part of a trilogy, followed by *The Wooden Village* and *The End of Freddy* (which the Garnett Press hopes to publish soon in English). Since the end of the 1990s Peter Pišťanek has worked for advertising agencies and edited an influential Internet magazine *Inzine*. He has also become something of an expert on brandies and whiskies.

Pišťanek's reputation is assured by the originality, fine craftsmanship and imaginative inventiveness of *Rivers of Babylon* and the rest of the trilogy. Perhaps this, the first volume, is Pišťanek's greatest achievement, not least because of the mesmerizing presence of one of the greatest characters introduced to Slovak literature, Rácz, a vulgar, unstoppable idiot of genius, a gangster with no conscience, but his own rules of conduct. Rácz appears in the autumn of 1989, just when one world, "Socialism", a corrupt system run by cynical administrators, is crumbling and another world, of rampant robber barons' capitalism, is born.

Better than any historian or novelist of the last fifteen years, Rácz and *Rivers of Babylon* tell a story not just of Slovakia, but of much of Central and Eastern Europe, where an alliance of criminals, intellectuals and unemployed secret policemen has infiltrated the new-born 'democracy'.

Today's Slovak readers acknowledge Peter Pišťanek as the country's most flamboyant and fearless writer, though many are shocked by his iconoclasm. A literature that once showed the Slovaks as a nation of wise bee-keepers and virtuous matriarchs now presents the nation stripped of its myths and false self-esteem. It is high time, however, for the world to read one of the most vibrant and original 'rogue' novels ever written. Peter Pišťanek's Rácz will prove as immortal a rogue as Fielding's Jonathan Wild, Gogol's Chichikov or Thomas Mann's Felix Krull.

Some guidance for the British reader...

Time and place

The novel is set between August 1989 and spring 1990, when the Czechoslovak communist government crumbled and fell in what the Czechs call the 'velvet', and the Slovaks the 'gentle', revolution. Most of the action takes place in Bratislava, then the capital of a Slovakia which was still part of Czechoslovakia. Two scenes of the novel are in the Hungarian-speaking countryside south-east of Bratislava, from where the anti-hero Rácz originates.

Currency

Currency-dealing plays a part in the novel's plot. Before the advent of the euro, there were German *deutschmark*, worth a little under 3 to the pound, Austrian *schilling*, worth about 20 to the pound, and the Czechoslovak crown worth between 40 and 75 to the pound, depending on who exchanged it, and where.

Some characters and how to pronounce their names

We have decided to keep Slovak spellings of characters' names, but here is a guide to pronouncing the more problematic and important ones. All names are stressed on the first syllable:

Rácz, the (anti-)hero	*pronounce as*	Rahts
Ďula, Rácz's sidekick		Dew-lah
Kišš, the village butcher		Kish
Eržika, his daughter		Air-s[*as in pleasure*]ika
Bartaloš, Eržika's suitor		Bartalosh
Šípoš, a gypsy hustler		Shiposh
Mozoň, ex-secret policeman		Mozogne [*n as in Boulogne*]
also known as Ščepán		Shchepahn
Šolik, ex-secret policeman		Sholik

Peter Petro and Donald Rayfield

For Rudolf Sloboda and Tibor Rencés

In the morning the boiler-room stoker wakes up with such hatred in his soul that he doesn't even feel like eating. He just slumps onto his wooden bench, scratching his itching skin, which clings to his sunken ribs, and looks around blankly. He doesn't even try to think about the source of his hatred. The boiler-room is dark, with washed-out peeling walls, but the outlines of the cold boilers are still visible. The wind whistles inside the boilers.

Finally, the stoker gets up. He stokes the furnace that supplies hot water to bathrooms and kitchens. He watches the flames for a long time. The red glow radiating from the open muzzle of the furnace damps down his morning anger and brings him back to life.

All those years stoking in the Hotel Ambassador have wiped out any thoughts about the meaning of life. To his mind a life-style consists of just keeping the fire alight under the boilers and making minor repairs to the heating system.

The stoker lives with no significant human contact. Feelings and emotions that used to determine his relationships with people, animals, things, and opinions have atrophied after many years of isolation. The meaningful world has shrunk to that of his boiler-room. Heating the Hotel Ambassador and other buildings supplied by his boilers is all that he's interested in. As a result of this deliberate mortification, the stoker is subject to periodic outbursts of ferocious rage. They occur pretty regularly. They come as the climax of a period when the stoker tries very hard, like a sheepdog, to gather in the unruly herd of thoughts which have scattered to all corners of his uncomplicated soul. Every time he has thoughts, they start to lick his brain with their rough kittenish tongues, as he sits there crestfallen. With his head in his hands, he seems afraid that the seething flow of unarticulated, truncated, and feverish ideas might burst the bones of his skull. Thoughts combine, bubble, and push the stoker's eyes out of their sockets. They are followed almost at once by thick, inextinguishable fury. It almost takes his breath away and his eyes dim.

This rage is now torture for the stoker. It's not channelled into anything in particular. He can, and often does, turn it on himself. Once his rage gains the upper hand and he needs to release it, he slaps his face until he sees stars. Or he might hit the sharp edge of the table with his withered fingers. Searing pain takes time to come. Waiting for it always makes the stoker rational and sad. He humbly sits back and waits for his dose of painful ecstasy. Pain explodes in the centre of his skull, as soon as the impulses unerringly and mercilessly navigate the nerves of his withered body. The pain is sharp and shattering, forcing him to put his aching fingers deep into his mouth. There, soothed by the warmth of his feverish breath, his pain subsides. It spreads into his skull bones and disperses into the aspic of brain cells. And so does the rage. The stoker suddenly feels hungry and takes immediate steps to satisfy his hunger with a bit of bread, a piece of bacon, and a bulbous red onion.

For Donáth the heating season doesn't begin until the end of summer. Something in the air forces the old man off his rough-hewn, squeaky wooden bench. Nobody in the city suspects yet that the demon of decay has begun its work. People walk about dressed lightly, the swimming pools are packed with swimmers, and the vendors of cold drinks and ice cream are doing brisk business. But Donáth's eyes betray a humble acceptance of the way things are. He sees what the others don't: the colour of the sycamore trees in front of the hotel is a shade dirtier; the dead insects at the edge of the lawn; the changed behaviour of the sca- venging birds hopping about in the back-yard skips.

Donáth purposefully strides the length and breadth of the boiler-room. The mornings are foggy now and the sky is leaden more often than not. Autumn is knocking on the metal door. Only now can everyone see it, but Donáth awoke from sentimental summer daydreams a long time ago. He's forced his fire-toughened body to perform its stiff practised movements. All the equipment has to be got ready for the winter. At this stage he goes without food.

Slimmed down, he works, or stands at the door and makes a low mooing sound meant to convey his diligence, stabbing his chest with a crooked, hardened index finger. In a moment he will explain to all the hotel staff that he's hard at work. Now he'll have to heat the water. A lot of it will be needed. The guests take a lot of baths and they have to be kept happy. Donáth doesn't mind. In winter he stokes all the boilers. There are six of them. Donáth can manage. He clicks his heels like an old waiter. Come and take a look if you don't believe him, but they all seem to believe him. Everyone gets on with their work. From the open ventila- tors of the laundry room billows thick steam, pleasantly smelling of soap. Gypsy women, wearing only full-length aprons, smoke in the yard. They laugh at Donáth and scream as they let themselves be chased round the heaps of coal in the yard. Now and then they lift their aprons and show him they're not wearing knickers and shout "Bugger the Virgin Mary" at him in Romany. Who could stand that heat? But Donáth is only interested in the gypsies when they do as he tells them. Six boilers. Donáth counts them with his eyes closed. Number one, number two, and so on. Number four is out of operation. Donáth can prove it. It's not allowed. It's a safety hazard. A hazard! Donáth pronounces that word with relish, feeling it makes him important. It gives him the indefinable charisma of people who look death in the eye every day. "Hazard." Here they use coal. All the other boiler-rooms in the neighbourhood have switched to oil or gas. This one, Donáth insists, is a classic. Another word. "Classic." How much meaning and charm can be found in a single word!

* * *

It seems as if time stands still in Donáth's boiler-room. In the winter, the gaping red-hot muzzles of the furnaces whine hungrily. In the darkness, illuminated now and then by nervous flashes of fire, the heaps of greasy black coal glisten. The boiler-room supplies heat to almost an entire side of the street, from the Hotel Ambassador to the crossroads. There are only shops there. Shops selling household goods, a chemist's, a car parts shop, and a leather goods shop. The old stoker has to keep the fire going in five boilers. One is out of order. Winters are bad here. The furnaces have to be fed every hour with black fodder, day and night, ceaselessly. That doesn't bother Donáth. He divorced his wife a long time ago, he has no home and he won't sleep in a dormitory. He's been working here for many years. His shelter is a little room behind the boiler-room, but he's never to be found there. He's mostly in the boiler-room. He also sleeps there, on a bench behind a solid, rough-hewn old table. He lugs coal from the coal-room in a wheelbarrow, feeding the roaring furnaces by shovelling it in. He keeps the ashes in metal drums, hosing them down with water and lifting them up to the yard in a special lift. Mounds of grey and black ashes stay there all winter. A truck comes in spring and takes the ashes to a nearby brickworks.

Donáth is completely alone in this work. Four men used to work there in shifts. But now people use oil and gas, nobody wants to mess with greasy heavy black coal. The boiler-room is obsolete and there's a lot of work. Donáth has let his superior, the manager of the Hotel Ambassador, know that he's really tired and exhausted and that they should find someone new, although he will try to stay on for the summer. Donáth has a place to go to. The manager has tried to talk him into staying, but the old man won't hear of it. He was meant to retire seven years ago. He needs to live a little, to relax, and take it easy.

Donáth has checked the furnaces and is now sitting in the basement. He is waiting for someone to take his place. No one is coming. Donáth has been working in this hotel for over fifty years. The work is heavy and demanding, but he doesn't complain. He likes it, and so on. True, he should have retired a long time ago. But he is still working. They respect him. They couldn't find anyone like him. Lately he's been getting tired. Sometimes he gets drunk; sometimes he gets a headache. Donáth doesn't complain. It's all part of life.

It is only the end of August, but the wind is blowing through the city streets. The time has come to put the boiler-room in order. You have to work systematically and not overdo it. After you hit thirty, you're not Mr Muscleman any more. He's alone; he lives here. He works all the time. There used to be four men taking alternate shifts here. Only Donáth is still alive. Years go by and you can't stop time. The gentlemen upstairs in the administration are still fiddling the books to make it look as if four men still worked in the boiler-room. Two salaries and all collective bonuses go to Donáth. Even the bonuses for socialist competition go to him. This means he's competing against himself. He's a one-man collective. Two salaries stay upstairs in the office. The gentlemen will share them.

Donáth knows every nut and bolt here. He is old school. Not long ago, anyone who tried to take over his work would be asking to be killed. But years pass. He's not the same any more. He used to threaten the people upstairs with quitting, but he never meant it seriously. Old age has put him in a quandary. And so has love. Love, in his old age! The people upstairs will have to find out one day. He can imagine how they'll react. But who'll do the work in the boiler-room? There's the question. Donáth paces up and down and sweeps the floor.

The manager enters with the hotel lawyer. The manager is stupid. His father-in-law helped get him through Hotel College and then found him a job in the Hotel Ambassador. Without the lawyer, the manager can't even tie his shoelaces. The lawyer is full of bitterness. He's heard that Donáth wants to leave. He considers this a betrayal. Isn't Donáth, after all, going to miss all this? They gave Donáth a nice shelter. All he had to do was to bail out the water. They even gave him a radio. It's a nice radio. He doesn't spend a penny on food. Behind the lawyer's back he eats in the hotel kitchen, but the lawyer knows everything. And yet he knows nothing, since he turns a blind eye. There's hot food, a little room, a radio, and two salaries. That's not bad. Most people aren't that lucky.

But Donáth has made his mind up. He won't be here by winter. Someone else can work in the boiler-room, if he may say so.

The manager has his say too. He does not look either Donáth or the lawyer in the face. Quietly he notes that he tries to be a good but strict supervisor to his employees. Maybe not all of them can see that what he does is only for their own good. But he doesn't discriminate. What would become of us, if everyone discriminated? Systematic and people-oriented work will bear fruit one of these days. "Today only I understand it," says the manager, "tomorrow others will understand as well. And the day after tomorrow, even a hopeless idiot will understand." In the manager's opinion, one has to set oneself ever-higher goals and not rest on one's laurels. And prove it not merely with words, but with honest work. Aim ceaselessly higher. That's the slogan of the day. Not least of all, of course. Enough empty words and grand statements!

Donáth nods his head. He's got to know a woman here. An old man needs love. They all know her; she washes dishes in the kitchen. Etelka Tóthová. They want to get married and to move to her house in the country. The house is nothing special: four walls, a roof, a window here and there, a door, that's how it is, nothing fancy. There'll be a pear tree in the front garden, and a pig in the back yard.

The lawyer understood. But it'd be a dirty trick of Donáth's not to look for a replacement, someone young and simple-minded. After all, the Hotel Ambassador has fed him for fifty years. To find a replacement is the least Donáth could do for the hotel. Let him train the new man and initiate him into all the secrets. And then, fine! By winter he'd be free.

They both leave without waiting for his answer.

Donáth doesn't mind. Donáth is not sex-crazy, he shouts after them. He's lost his hair, his teeth, his eyes are bad, and his hands tremble. Donáth is happy to get a little bit of love and a bit of conversation. Just to have a bit of life. Other people are having a ball. People own all kinds of things nowadays. Like briefcases, spectacles. They just buy anything they like. And what does Donáth own? A radio and this burrow where he has to bail out water every time he wants to lie down and sleep in a soft bed. Donáth has become more demanding. What used to satisfy him no longer does. The Russians will soon reach Mars, but he's still here. In winter he's stuck to the furnaces. These two know nothing about it, these people from upstairs! The hotel manager is an incompetent idiot. He spends his days playing childish games. And the lawyer wears his shoes out, running about doing deals.

Every hour or two Donáth has to stoke each of the roaring muzzles. In addition, he has to adjust the valves, bleed the air from the radiators and fix other minor malfunctions. The stoker also services the heating system. It's better in summer. He only has to heat water and produce steam for the kitchen and the sauna. He can go for a walk. But he does not venture far. He keeps to the hotel surroundings. He observes the bustling cars in the guarded parking lot in front of the Ambassador and then goes to the supermarket for a few bottles of beer. He always hurries back to the boiler-room. He turns on his radio and sings with the singers. Or he goes out to the yard and jokes with the gypsy women from the laundry room. Life passes by without him noticing it.

* * *

The manager is sitting in his office among all sorts of junk that he has brought in from all over the hotel, and is talking out loud to himself. He can't get it into his head that Donáth could ever leave. He was certain that after fifty years the stoker had become the legal property of the hotel. He has always done his utmost to avoid dealing with any problem, but not even in his dreams did he think that the day would come when he'd have to solve *this* problem. The lawyer told him that it wasn't possible to keep someone against their will. There were, unfortunately, laws against it.

"Laws!" the manager recalled, and his fat hand hurled a paperweight at the wall. He didn't like the fact that the hotel management depended on Donáth's whim. If Donáth finds a replacement, then he will. If not, he won't. The manager begins to hum a sad tune. Why did he have to push his way into the city? He'd have been better off sitting on a tree stump, back home in the country, and just staring. Life is a bitch!

* * *

Mr. Kišš, a proud village butcher, is sitting in his living room smoking, one eye half-closed with delight, when the suitors come to call. It's young Rácz and his Uncle Endre. They gallop into Kišš's yard, get off their horses, which are trampling the lawn and the chickens with their giant hooves, and boldly enter the house. Rácz is a bit pale and his bluish shaved face with hurriedly treated shaving cuts gives him a dignified and grave expression.

Mr. Kišš calmly hears the men out. He nods, as if he's just heard something he already knows. Then he coughs. Kišš is filthy rich, so to speak, he says. You can make good money. It's unbelievable what people will eat nowadays. Nothing is too revolting for them. So young Rácz would be interested in marrying his daughter?

Rácz senses that he ought to reply. Yes, indeed, he would be interested. Rácz loves the butcher's daughter and she loves him too. Rácz is a soldier in the reserve and is in good health. He has some property. He's not rich, but neither is he poor. There's a pig, a cow, as well as a horse. The horse is used both for riding and for draught; it's freshly shod, and good for a saddle, a carriage, or even a plough.

Endre interrupts him. He emphasizes to Kišš that the boy will make an obedient son-in-law. He was brought up that way; he used to get hit for the slightest thing in his family. His parents choked to death on money.

Kišš remembers. Yes, it was a sad event. Big funeral.

Rácz can't confirm that. He was doing his military service at the time with an artillery battery in a little village between Prague and Benešov. There were three military divisions: they were the 3289th, the 5963rd, the 1746th regiments. He liked doing his military service. Rácz did his duty and was left in peace and quiet. He missed the funeral. He boarded the wrong train and in the border town of Aš the customs officers kicked him off the train.

"What about the cash," Kišš wanted to know, "the money your parents left? What happened to it?"

"The money's hidden somewhere in the house," Uncle Endre added. "They didn't put their money in the bank. They didn't trust anyone or anything."

Rácz mentioned that he did two years at agricultural college. Let everyone take a look at his big hands! These hands aren't afraid of any kind of work.

"Well, did they search for the money?" asked Kišš, pulling out a bottle of moonshine.

Endre is sure the money is hidden in the house. As long as it's hidden, it's as safe as in a Swiss bank.

Kišš shakes his head. He knows that they took the whole house apart and found nothing.

Endre hasn't lost hope. Maybe it was hidden in the cellar or the foundations. Nobody's looked there yet. Now that Endre thinks about it, he's more certain than ever that the money is definitely there.

Kišš shakes his head. He's heard something quite different: they say the money was found, but the relatives quickly divided it among themselves, while Rácz was roaming up and down the country.

Endre got angry. He's never heard such a filthy lie. Let Kišš tell him who's been spreading such bare-faced lies in the village and he will personally shut their mugs for them.

Kišš pours the drinks. After Endre downs two shots of moonshine, he warms up and calms down.

"The boy's nobody's fool," he says. "Yes, he may be simple and direct. He doesn't say much, either. But, man, he's got his wits about him!"

Rácz senses that he ought to say something as well. Rácz has a nice bit of land. It needs a woman's hand. Someone who would wash and cook for him, and caress him. And feed the pig.

Kišš understands it all. Love is love, but health, on the other hand, is health. But still, money is money. He could give Rácz a piece of advice, as he is older and wiser. Without cash in hand, Rácz is no good, no matter what. He won't get a foot on the ladder. Kišš has been a butcher for many years. He knows what's what. They screwed everything up with that packaged meat, those bastards. That's the end of the butcher's trade. He's just surprised at Rácz. Why is he hanging around the village? If he had Rácz's youth, nothing would keep him here! In the city money is lying on the streets, you just have to pick it up. Why not go there and make some money? Eržika will wait for him if she really loves him. Kišš will take care of Rácz's animals and land in the meantime. After all, he is like his own son to him. But he shouldn't hang about; he should set out for the city right away. No point wasting time.

Rácz wants to see Eržika before he left, but Kišš sees no sense in it. Why? He knows what she looks like! He pours the last shot of moonshine for them. Then he sees the suitors out.

Rácz sadly gallops away on his plough-horse, his head bowed. Out of the corner of his eye he sees a curtain twitch in Eržika's window. The same day he drives the pig, the cow and the horse off to Kišš's stable. He swears that he will return as soon as he gets a chance.

At daybreak Rácz sets off to catch the train.

"I heard you were leaving," says proud Feri with a fake smile on his face. Feri Bartaloš, his biggest enemy since they were at school, is one of Eržika's suitors. It was to impress Rácz that he galloped in the dark to the railway station on a sweaty horse with a mighty behind, and now he's prancing on it up and down the platform. He smiles wildly, his white teeth glistening in the sun rising over the wasteland. Rácz, dressed in an ill-fitting suit he first wore at confirmation, is sitting on a cast-iron bench with his suitcase at his feet.

"Hey, are you really moving to the city?" Feri shouts, since Rácz ignores him. The horse turns under his weight and neighs. "Off you go, then!"

Rácz stops watching the fingernails of his right hand and calmly lifts his head. When he returns, he says unemotionally, if he finds out something, and Bartaloš knows what he means, he'll beat him up, maybe kill him. Eržika is going to have Rácz's children. Bartaloš can get that into his head!

"Ho-ho-ho!" laughs proud Feri Bartaloš, as if he'd been told a good joke. He wildly digs his heels into the giant, clumsy horse and makes it gallop. Soon all that is left after him on the platform is a pile of steaming horse dung.

* * *

All of Rácz's possessions fit into a suitcase that he puts on a floor covered in spittle, spilled beer, cigarette butts, and dirt. Tired after a journey of several hours he orders a beer and a shot of rum. He takes a look at himself in the mirror wall behind the bar. He is small and thin, but so bony and square-cut that he gives the impression of being quite stocky. His ill-fitting suit is wrinkled and the seat and thighs are shiny. His swarthy face, close-cropped head and large transparent ears make him look like an amnestied prisoner.

Rácz considers his next step. There's plenty of work in the city, he can choose any career. He could work in a factory, in city services, or on the railway. The main thing is to make as much money as possible. Only then can he soon go back and marry Eržika Kišš. Rácz won't fail. The city is huge, and there are plenty of openings.

Rácz takes out a newspaper and begins to study the classifieds. He marks the most interesting offers with his fingernail.

"Are you looking for a job?" an old man asks Rácz affably: he's wearing dirty overalls and his toothless mouth has been chewing hard on two bread sticks and a dried-up rissole saturated with cigarette smoke.

Rácz is sullen and dislikes talking to strangers. "Yeah," he finally responds unwillingly, lifting the rum to his mouth.

The old man laughs, showing his toothless gums, and lifts a mug of beer to his mouth, suggesting "Cheers!". "Just arrived in the city?" he asks.

"Just now," Rácz responds gloomily. He hates questions. He puts the empty glass of rum on the high table and queues at the counter. He buys a bread stick, a rissole and another beer.

"Hungry?" the old man inquires and smiles amiably.

Rácz nods and chews. What's it to the old fool, whether Rácz is hungry or not?

"Fuck you, I'm Donáth," says the smiling old man, offering his huge hand covered in calluses and ingrained dirt.

"I'm not," Rácz felt like saying, and would have said, had he been at home, in the village pub. But he's in a strange city, a strange world. "Rácz," he says without enthusiasm, and reluctantly shakes the offered hand.

"You have hands that could kill an ox," the old man praises Rácz.

Rácz just shrugs and returns to his rissole.

"I know of a good job," says the old man after a while.

"Do you?" Rácz asks as if bored, but pricks up his ears.

"You'd get two salaries," Donáth continues, "and it's easy work."

Rácz coughs, as a crumb of rissole goes down the wrong way. He runs his tongue round the inside of his lips, and then slowly lifts the beer mug and washes the food down. "What sort of work?" he begins to ask.

Donáth heads for the bar with a mysterious smile on his face, leaving Rácz without an answer.

"What sort of job is it?" Rácz repeats, when the old man comes back with two mugs of beer.

"Boiler-room stoker in a hotel," says Donáth.

Rácz is not sure about it. Are there any exams he'd have to take? He pointedly ignores the beer the old man obviously brought for him.

"What exams? Why exams?" the old man sniggers. If it's OK by Donáth, they'll take on Rácz with no exams. Just consider, it's the most de-luxe hotel in town. A hundred years old! Unfortunately, so is the boiler-room. Donáth's mood darkens, but he soon cheers up. "Do you have a trade?" he asks Rácz.

"I did two years' agricultural college," Rácz says, not without pride.

"That should be enough," Donáth nods.

"And what sort of job is it?" Rácz inquires.

"It's good easy work. But it's very responsible. You have to take care of the whole boiler-room by yourself, day in and day out. You get two salaries and all the bonuses and awards. If you came here to make a pile of money, you won't find a better job. You won't fill your pockets so quickly anywhere else. And you won't wear yourself out. You just have to be there all the time. In five years you'll save half a million crowns and say good-bye." Donáth downs his beer.

Rácz is excited by what he hears and accepts the beer. After all, he came here for the money and nothing else interests him. It wouldn't bother him in the least if he had to spend all his time in the boiler-room. At least he wouldn't spend much money.

"I've been slaving there for fifty years," Donáth admits, "but I'd like a break. I'm coming up to seventy now." Donáth wouldn't like to leave just like that, slamming the door behind him and saying good-bye. Not like that. He'd promised to find a replacement.

"And how do you know I'm the right man?" Rácz asks.

"You've got a wide, honest face. You don't look like a layabout or con man. The big city lights won't tempt you." The old man empties the rest of the beer into his toothless mouth and then spits on the foul floor.

Through the murky and dusty windows of the bar you can see the trams come and go. The morning cold has gone and the sun begins to radiate heat. Rácz feels as warm as in a greenhouse.

"Another beer?" Donáth asks.

Rácz shakes his head. "Is it far to the boiler-room?"

"No," answers the old man, "ten minutes' walk. Want to have a look?"

"I wouldn't mind," admits Rácz. "But I'm not promising anything."

The old man quickly nods. "You'll like it, you'll see. Let me get you another shot of rum," he says and queues at the bar.

Rácz won't say no. He can drink like a horse. They clink glasses. "I want to get married and move out of here," Donáth says proudly. "An old man needs a bit of love too. A young man needs money. That's life." Donáth philosophizes. The rum has cheered him up.

* * *

It is a sunny, humid morning. Some woman had a nervous breakdown in the middle of the busy street in front of the Hotel Ambassador. She was waiting at the tram stop. She just flipped, as they say, and began to strip in front of all the passers-by on the tram stop island.

The crowd consists of people all as exhausted, nervous and unhappy as she. Their psychology, however, can cope better with the morning heat. The woman stripping at the tram stop doesn't escape the attention of the passers-by. They all stop, surround the island and feel a collective need to get involved in the affairs of the unfortunate half-naked woman. At the sight of the madwoman, men's pulses race, blood rushes to their heads, and the skin on their faces tautens. Whistles, sarcasms and disparaging comments are heard. But the woman pays no attention; her face reveals total concentration on herself. One of the gypsies who always hang around the Hotel Ambassador snatches the shopping bag, which the woman threw down when she started her macabre strip-tease, and nonchalantly wanders off. No one notices, as the sight of a woman undressing in the street blots out all other events.

Video Urban is also watching and he too is also more or less excited by the sight of the wretched woman's white body. But he is disgusted by the heartless mob of joking people and so he rings the emergency services on 158 from the telephone in the entrance of the Hotel Ambassador: "SOMEONE IS STRIPPING IN FRONT OF THE HOTEL AMBASSADOR," he says and hangs up. He has no desire to meet the cops. He needs that like a hole in the head. He has in his pocket a thousand-deutschmark bank note and he needs to hustle up a few more hundred marks, by changing money illegally for tourists, to get enough for a camera that Mr. Hurensson from Sweden promised to bring him. Then Video Urban will really start to live it up! The camera guarantees him a happy future. Urban has great plans for it. He'll film weddings and family celebrations. You can make good money that way. Everybody wants a souvenir of some milestone and will gladly pay for it.

"She's got guts to show herself naked with those tits," says the parking attendant, nicknamed Piggybank for good reason, as a comment on the performance. Urban is silent. He watches a yellow and white car with flashing lights, and two cops with a grey blanket as they throw themselves on the naked woman and drag her violently into the car. The madwoman resists, bites, and jerks her head, kicking wildly, while, at the same time, revealing the most intimate parts of her body, something that Piggybank finds very amusing.

"Have you seen Hurensson today, by any chance?" asks Video Urban.

"Who?" The attendant is nonplussed.

"My friend, the Swede," says Urban impatiently.

"The Swede," Piggybank muses. "Well, the Swede hasn't shown up today."

The passengers at the tram stop stay excited long after the police car leaves. The extraordinary situation has brought them together, just as a calamity to be overcome brings people together. But the trams keep coming and each takes a few of the crowd and then adds new faces to it. The latest people have no idea what's just happened. For them the woman's high-heel shoe discarded near the rubbish bin has a different symbolic value. The plot's been lost.

"What'll they do to her?" Piggybank asks Video Urban. Piggybank's face is pink, reflecting his happiness and good mood. He hasn't been working here long and he radiates the servile happiness of a person whose salary of two thousand crowns has increased several times over. Piggybank got the job through his connections and now he wants to be in everybody's good books.

"Perhaps she'll cool down when a couple of cops screw her real good," he says breathlessly. Urban watches Piggybank take money from an incoming driver, put the ticket behind the windscreen wiper and point to a vacant space. Disgusting, slimy, stinking swine, he thinks. "You really should finally get laid," he says to him coldly, looking with disgust into the fat man's watery eyes, overcoming the temptation to hit his red money-bag and tip it up so that the coins scatter all over the parking lot.

"Beg your pardon?" Piggybank pretends not to understand.

"I said you should get laid," says Video Urban. "I can tell by your eyes that all you've ever done is wank."

"Come off it!" The attendant smiles.

He won't even take offence, Urban thinks, he's so pleased with himself. "Since you save so much, you should invest in some woman who'll fuck your brains out."

"I've never had to pay for it," Piggybank counters, and blushes.

"I can see that," Urban agrees, "you've never had it. Look over there." He points two girls out to Piggybank: they are getting out of a large Mercedes with a West German licence plate. "They could help you. They only work as a duo; it's their speciality. They're medical students, so you'd seem a bit stupid to them, but if you keep your mouth shut, they might not notice. They'd only want to know how much you'd pay, anyway. I'd say three hundred marks," Urban estimates. "That'd do it." He laughs. "And if you tell them that at your age you're still a virgin, they might even do it for you for free. What do you say?" he asks the stunned fat man. "Shall I arrange it for you?"

"Are they friends of yours?" asks Piggybank.

"Sure," says Urban. "I'm friends with all of them. You didn't even know about the Hotel Ambassador when I was cabbing here a long time ago. I went into the money-changing business later, when cabbing stopped being so lucrative. Now there are so many moonlighting taxis that people are happy to make two or three hundred crowns a night. Well, do you want those medical students?"

"You mentioned that they might do it for free," remarked the red-faced Piggybank.

Video Urban can't keep it up and bursts out laughing. Piggybank looks offended.

"Sorry," says Urban, "I don't know those girls at all. I know a lot of people, but only a few hookers. I only know the ones that I used to drive occasionally." He saw Piggybank was embarrassed and added, "Don't shit yourself! Believe me, I have the same problem with women as you. It's even harder for me, as I'm a slave to my æsthetic standards."

Piggybank can't understand. He thinks æsthetic standards mean using a knife and fork. Luckily, the influx of cars keeps him so busy that he stops paying attention to Urban.

Urban is free to look for more business. Quite brusquely he goes up to an incoming Austrian Opel with the usual question. He does not feel good doing this, demeaning himself, but he needs at least another three hundred marks. Hurensson might come any day now with the camera of his dreams and he has to be paid. And then, it's good-bye money changing! Video Urban will become a businessman. He'll come to the Ambassador only occasionally for a nightcap and will never again submit to this degrading job for a few marks. To make a lot of money is no problem. The problem is how to make it and still preserve one's self-respect.

Urban reflects that he ought to show up for a bit of work again, in the department store opposite the hotel, where he works as a window dresser, but he shows up there only in an emergency. Now he notices a group of policemen charging from the parking lot and the pavement opposite the Hotel Ambassador. A raid, he realises. And he has twelve hundred marks on him! If they nab him, the camera is history. He presses against the wall and without being noticed, inches his way towards an entrance into the yard. Luckily, he hasn't been spotted. Keeping the policemen in sight as they search the gypsies and currency dealers and bundle them into a police van, he gropes his way along the wall. When he touches the corner, quick as lightning, he jumps into a dark underpass and runs into the yard. He's still not sure that he's got away unseen. Fear that his longed-for dream might not come true throws him into a panic. He opens the boiler-room metal door and leans against it from inside, breathing heavily. He's safe. He looks around. Wrought iron steps lead to the basement. He runs down them and decides to stay in the boiler-room. It is better to stay for a while, until things outside clear up. He sits down on a bench at the rough table and takes out his crisp, handsome banknotes. Their velvet touch and metallic colour calm him down. That must surely be enough, he thinks; he told Hurensson exactly which type to bring. It can't cost more than eleven hundred and fifty marks. All right, it could cost more in Sweden. Maybe he should buy another couple of hundred marks. When he has the camera, he will get his cash back within a year.

* * *

The summer is slowly reaching its peak and the leaves are beginning to take on autumnal tints. Everywhere there is noise, colour, people, and cars. Rácz walks hesitantly. He wonders how Donáth can find his way in this madhouse.

"Here is the Mototechna car parts shop," the old man points at a shop window full of stickers, motorcycle helmets, and tyre pumps. "Upstairs is a chemist's," Donáth continues, "and here in the Tatra Mall is the leather shop, and the household goods shop. We heat all of them," he stresses. "And around the corner is the Ambassador."

The hotel truly looks impressive. It is all of six storeys high. With its weathered and unkempt look it has evidently seen better times. In front of the hotel is an attended car park. Cars with foreign licence plates are parked in two opposite rows. In the basement is a bar and cabaret. Donáth tells all this to Rácz, who stares at the liveried porter standing under a canvas awning, looking stern and keeping his hands behind his back. The hotel entrance gleams with mahogany and smoked glass. Rácz has come into a world of completely new phenomena. He is looking at most of the things around him for the first time in his life.

"The girls who dance in there are almost completely naked," Donáth continues, winking at Rácz.

"And have you been down there?" Rácz asks.

"Not as a guest," Donáth admits, "it's for foreigners only. But in winter I sometimes go there to bleed the radiators, and so on. I go there in the morning, when they rehearse. They dance on stage and wear next to nothing. They're all hookers. After the show they go out with foreigners. And why shouldn't they? I say to myself. Let them make money while they're young. What do you think?"

Rácz is silent. Basically, he's not interested. All he wants to do is start making money. This world is of no interest to him; it's useful only to get him into his own world as soon as possible. He'll crawl into his boiler-room and crawl out when he's ready to travel back with his money. That's how he was on military service. Everyone was dying to get out on leave, but Rácz had no leave for two years. Instead, he locked himself in the gym and lifted barbells. What ingenuity he had to use to avoid the officers sending him on forced leave! His friends used to touch their foreheads meaningfully. But Rácz didn't mind being locked up in the barracks for two years. He familiarised himself with his world right from the start and then he felt at home in it. Excursions into an unknown terrain didn't tempt him. He often said how beautiful it would have been if he'd been drafted to serve in a submarine. It would submerge and two years later would surface again. When they let Rácz go home from service, he gave them back his leave uniform almost unused. With the exception of a few film shows during basic training, the service oath, and the trip to his parents' funeral, he never used it.

The boiler-room would be his submarine, Rácz decided. He'd keep only minimal contact with the outside world. He'd be interested in nothing except how much money he could bring home.

"This way," says Donáth. Rácz nods. He bends down and picks up a little plastic bag. He takes a look and sees it's got foreign banknotes inside. "Where are you?" Donáth shouts impatiently. Rácz puts the little bag in his pocket and follows Donáth through the dark passage into the yard. "Up there is the kitchen," Donáth points to a grey annexe, obviously a later addition. "And down here is the laundry room. Buy them a coffee occasionally and they'll wash your things."

Rácz wonders: who could have lost the bag of foreign money? He can't get his head round it. It looked as if someone had deliberately hidden it in a big concrete plant tub with an ornamental shrub. As if that someone meant to retrieve it later. Rácz can't get his head round it, but he's not going to ask Donáth. Why bother the old man? Rácz will figure it out on his own.

"And here is the boiler-room," Donáth explains. He opens the metal door and they both run down the narrow stairs. "Put your suitcase over here," says Donáth, pointing to the rickety table. It takes Rácz some time to see where things are in the dark room. Rays of daylight penetrate through dirty little windows, filtered through bright particles of dust floating in the air. At the back are the boilers, now dead and cold. Only the one on the left is heated. Steam leaks from the pipes.

"It is an old boiler-room," says the old man and sits down. "Everyone uses gas and oil for heating now. If they wanted to redo this and modernise it they'd have to demolish half the hotel. They'd have to stop all operations and the hotel wouldn't meet its targets. The shops would have to close as well," says Donáth.

A door opens at the back and a long-haired young man enters. "What are you doing here?" Donáth says, laughing. "Are you on the run again?"

"Are the cops still up there, Mr. Donáth?" asks the young man.

Donáth shakes his head. "Not a soul. Has there been a raid or something?"

"A big one," the young man says emphatically, "I had to hide in your place."

"Well, the old man shrugs, "you know what you're up to. But I'll make you sorry if you land me in the shit! I don't want to know about your rackets, understand? It's all right," says Donáth, when he sees Urban taken aback by the sight of Rácz. "Well, boys, get to know each other," he suggests. "This is my replacement, Rácz."

"Urban," says Urban.

Rácz nods but doesn't get up.

"Stick close to this crook," Donáth advises. "He'll get hold of anything you need."

"I won't need anything," Rácz thinks, but decides to keep quiet.

"Well, I'd better go, if the coast is clear," says Video Urban. "See you."

"I really like crooks like him," says Donáth, when the metal door upstairs bangs shut. "He takes it easy all day long, doing nothing. But he's got lots of money. One of these days he won't take cover in time and he'll end up in Leopoldovo prison. You don't want to be one of his sort," Donáth warns Rácz. "Keep on the straight and narrow!"

Rácz sits down. Donáth starts to describe life in the boiler-room. For example, he won't have to worry about food at all. The stoker always goes to the kitchen to eat. They always have scraps in the kitchen. You have to keep on good terms with the cooks and kitchen staff. Let them have all the steam they want. When they're cooking dumplings, for example, they let Donáth know, and he increases the pressure. When the dough has to rise, the kitchen has to be as hot as an oven. Donáth will show him all the ropes.

Rácz nods. He quite likes it here. He walks around the boiler-room and looks with bafflement into the furnaces. Cold air blows from the open muzzles. The draught roars in the chimneys and pipes. From the ventilation shaft you can hear the street sounds, distorted by travelling down the long metal pipe.

The old man sits at the table, fiddling with his ashtray. He'd be glad if Rácz decided to stay. Donáth promised to find a new stoker. It's a matter of principle. He's old; he'd like to have a rest. He's got to take it easy.

He's been a stoker all his life. Never managed to do a thing. And now he's found a lady friend. She's the right age. She owns a house in Zahorie. A widow. They want to leave together. Donáth's spent forty years of his life here. Before, he worked as a crane operator in the Czech country. Worked on different sites, here and there; in Ostrava, Vitkovice, and Kladno, the steel heart of the republic, and so on. He liked looking down on the world from a high crane. And he had a Czech wife, from Česká Lipa. She started to screw around in the spa, Marienbad. They divorced. She took the children. Ever since then Donáth's worked here. But he doesn't want to croak and still be stoking boilers.

Suddenly the old man gets up. Yes, he's decided. He'll introduce Rácz to his lady friend! He doesn't wait for an answer, runs upstairs and slams the door behind him.

Rácz is alone. He looks over the black hall and sleeping boilers. He takes his find from the back pocket: *Deutsche Bundesbank*. There are five hundred-mark notes and four fifty-mark notes. Rácz has no idea what this money might be worth. Never mind, he'll find out. He carefully wraps the money and hides it in the lining of his suitcase. He climbs to the top of the boilers and takes a look at the coal room. It is empty, spacious. In the corners is what's left of last year's coal.

He's still up there, looking into the openings where the coal is stored, when he hears banging on the stairs. Donáth is climbing down and behind him comes a massive woman in a white coat, scarf and white rubber boots. "Well, Ilonka," Donáth smiles, "here's my replacement!" Rácz has to put up with another introduction.

"So you're our saviour," says Mrs. Tóthová coquettishly.

"What?" Rácz can't understand.

"Our Donáth wouldn't leave the boiler-room if he hadn't found you," explains the old woman. "He's been saying: 'I can't leave them in the lurch. I've spent fifty years with them. I promised to find a replacement and I'll keep my promise.' But no," the old woman stresses her words, "he didn't have to find replacement; it was his decision. He wanted to leave like an honest man. And now —" here Mrs. Tóthová looks lovingly at the beaming Donáth "— his dream is going to come true. Do you want a cigarette?" she asks him, taking a pack of *Spartas* from her bosom. "No, I don't smoke," replies Rácz. "I used not to smoke," nods the old woman, but you get used to it among those girls in the kitchen. It's the only way to kill time. You'll have to kill time, too. But it's good you don't smoke."

"He will, don't worry," Donáth laughs dryly.

"Never!" insists Rácz. His blood freezes in his veins imagining going up to Kišš to ask for Eržika's hand and suddenly getting a fit of coughing, trying in vain to keep a blood-spotted handkerchief out of sight. Everyone would be horrified if Kišš said: "No, I won't give my daughter to this consumptive!" He tried smoking in the army. If you didn't smoke, you weren't a man. But he never liked the taste of cigarettes. And when his comrades gave him, as the dunce of the squad, a specially doctored cigarette that gave you the squits as well as making you throw up, he went off smoking and took up body-building and boxing.

"Well, what do you think?" Donáth asks. "Have you decided? Will you stay?"

"Only if I make as much money as you promised," says Rácz.

"Do you want to see my pay slips?" The old man pretends to be angry. "Do you?"

"No need to," Rácz shrugs.

"Well, what do you say," Mrs. Tóthová asks, "Will you shake on it?"

"I don't mind," says Rácz. He shakes Donáth's hand.

"We have to drink to this," exclaims the beaming old man, and he fishes out from somewhere a bottle of cheap brandy and three glasses. He pours the brandy and lifts his glass. "Good luck to you here!"

Donáth can't take too much. After two or three glasses, his eyes start to shine. Longingly, he paws old Mrs. Tóthová.

* * *

Silvia dances in the Cabaret show at the Ambassador, although she had wanted to be somewhere: La Scala, the Metropolitan Opera, doing *Swan Lake*, or something. This was what she was led to hope for during her six years at the conservatoire. Today, Silvia dances in a night show called *Secrets of the Night*. It's basically a strip show livened up with a few dramatic interludes. It is art, but cabaret art. And men are crazy about her. It is clear to Silvia why. But she will only go with men she finds interesting. The man has to be rich, successful and, of course, likeable: a foreigner, of course.

Edita would not have even dreamt of becoming a professional dancer. She used to work the spools in a textile factory and in the evenings she danced in a folk group. It was a hobby to keep her sane. It was the hotel lawyer who got her the job. He usually promises something to every girl, but Edita wouldn't go to bed with him until he got her the job. She likes it here. She loves it when everyone admires her slender body when she moves in a bewitching rhythm.

Like almost all the girls from the Ambassador bar, both Silvia and Edita hope to meet a millionaire from Texas, or an Arab oil sheikh who'll fall in love with them, marry them, and take them to a distant country.

They're both sitting in the dressing room, changing after the morning rehearsal. "How soft your hair is," says Edita, touching Silvia's head, "how blonde!" She is amazed. Edita is a blonde, too, but her roots are showing. If she didn't use peroxide to bleach her hair, everyone would notice she had gypsy blood.

Silvia was born a blonde. And if she hadn't been, she'd have had to dye her hair blonde. But she doesn't have to. Arabs, negroes, Italians are all crazy for blondes. *Swan Lake* is history, but Silvia has accepted that. She'll work for a few years. Then she'll marry a westerner. The higher one's expectations are, the smaller the choice. She'll come here only for visits. And anyway: whom would she visit? She stops dressing for a moment and thinks about it with her tights in her hand.

"Wow, how long your legs are," Edita wonders, putting her hand on Silvia's knee.

Silvia takes no notice. Well, she'll visit somebody at any rate. She'll find someone ready to envy her at any time, day or night, she thinks. A car with an American or a Kuwaiti licence plate will park in the parking lot. She will laugh at the long queues. Even if she doesn't buy anything! Let all those suckers die of envy.

Edita has now moved her hand some way up. Silvia, herself apathetic, lets her increasingly aroused colleague try to excite her. She stretches on her chair and looks in the mirror. Wrinkles are forming under her eyes. Maybe she needs a good night's sleep. On her life, she can't remember if the door of the dressing room is locked. She starts to caress with both hands Edita's head which has now got between her legs. She places one hand on Edita's mouth to muffle the latter's noisy moans. With the other she jerks Edita's hair, as if trying to push her away from her crotch. But it's too late. A sharp wave traverses her body and she utters a series of stifled moans. Then she remains seated, as if bereft of all power, like a rag doll.

Edita smiles. "Well, what do you think about that?" she asks victoriously.

Silvia, as though awoken from a deep sleep, gives Edita an uncomprehending, apathetic look. "Why did you do that?" she asks in a grave voice. "Don't do it again. I'm not a lesbian."

"Neither am I," says Edita. "I learned in prison. It was the only fun we had."

"But I don't *like* you doing it to me," Silvia says angrily. Instead of an answer, Edita gently and protractedly kisses her on the lower lip. "But I'm not a lesbian," Silvia repeats helplessly.

"Well, neither am I," Edita laughs. "But only a woman can be really nice to another woman, right?"

Silvia, unresponsive, wrenches herself out of the embrace and goes to the washroom. Edita follows her.

"Let's take a shower together, shall we?" she says. They both get in the shower. "Why don't you try to be a little bit nice to me, too?" asks Edita. "Relax, it's no big thing. Don't tell me this isn't better than when some fat old Kraut does it to you."

Silvia nods. There's oblivion in an embrace. There's truth in a cuddle. All the world's males remained locked outside the shower.

* * *

When Mrs. Tóthová goes back to the kitchen, Donáth pours another drink of schnapps. "Now take it easy after your journey; this afternoon we'll get the paperwork done in the personnel department and you'll get your work clothes and protective gear," he tells Rácz. "Tomorrow we start training in earnest. There's enough time, but not too much. Soon August will be over, and then things get worse. Winter's not far off."

He takes him to the back, to his cubbyhole. It is dark, stuffy, and smelly. There is a dirty bunk and a wardrobe. There's a magazine on the chair, which serves as a bedside table. "At the back, at the end of the hall, are the bathroom and the toilet," says Donáth. "You can sleep here. There should be an air mattress somewhere," he mumbles, half-hidden in the wardrobe. "Ah, here it is. Blow it up and take a rest. I'll call you when it's time for dinner. Then I'll come with you for the paperwork." He throws him the folded mattress and leaves his hideout.

Rácz blows the mattress up and lies down on it, but he can't get to sleep. It's hard to fall asleep in this new environment. The air is saturated with all sorts of smells and sounds. Who knows what's in store for him here? It's an alien world, designed by other people for people not like him. But basically it's begun well. He's not been here a day, but he has already got a job, a roof over his head, and, what's more, seven hundred German marks. Soon he'll be given dinner. He didn't expect things to move so fast.

* * *

Early the next day, the hotel manager himself comes to inspect the pair of them. The hotel chauffeur and sidekick Ďula flings open the metal door and reverentially announces: *"The manager is coming!"* and steps aside. The manager enters with mincing steps and stops on the landing, looking distinguished and kind. He adopts a vainglorious pose, like a portrait of Louis XIV with his stylized absent-minded irony. Clearly, the manager has a lot of admiration and affection for himself. The manager's expansively raised right eyebrow and his moustache enhance this impression.

Finally he speaks: "I'm glad that you've found a replacement, Donáth. Make sure you train him well, so that nothing goes wrong and we have heating this winter. Not like last year. That must not happen again!"

"That wasn't my fault!" Donáth defends himself. "I do what I can. The boiler-room is out of date. What can you do with circulating pumps a hundred years old?"

"Well exactly," the manager cuts him short. "They've been working for a hundred years and suddenly they don't? I find this a bit strange. I'll have to take a closer look at you, Donáth!" The manager turns to Rácz. "Adjust your clothing, man," the manager nervously blurts out. "Do you go about dressed like that?"

Rácz buttons his newly issued dungarees up to his neck.

"My people, the Hotel Ambassador staff, are well dressed," the manager adds huffily.

"We don't have any degreaser," Donáth approaches the manager, "and soon we'll be doing the, you know, preventive check-up. All the pumps will have to be taken apart and there's no degreaser."

"You dare to bother the manager himself with this, you dolt?" Ďula shouts at Donáth from the landing. Donáth keeps quiet.

"I have to see effort first," says the manager, "and results. Then I can be generous! Then you'll get degreaser and other things!" With these words he climbs the iron steps and leaves the boiler-room. Ďula turns to Donáth and Rácz, shakes his fist at them and runs after the manager.

"The manager's stupid, but strict," says Donáth, when the coast is clear. "But the hotel lawyer is the biggest swine. Keep away from him, if you can." Donáth shrugs it off, and shoulders his tool-bag. "Come," he orders Rácz, "we're going to change some valves. They were leaking last winter, but I didn't have any spares. You won't get bored here, my boy. But the time flies by. Before we even notice, winter will be upon us."

They spend the whole day in the hardware shop, in the stores office, in the storage room, in the sales girls' changing room. Many of the valves are rusty, blocked, or leaky. The whole heating system is obsolete. Fortunately, the radiators are cast iron and can take a lot. But all the bends are blocked with rust. You often have to isolate a whole section of the pipe and run a wire or high-pressure water through it. The men work hard, concentrating, and they get dirty. The basement is damp and smells of mould.

"It's all buggered up," Donáth concludes, "we'll have to shut it off and drain it down."

They stand watching the foul water from the heating system go down the drain.

"Well, when are you getting married?" asks Donáth.

Rácz is silent; the black, muddy whirlpool seems to hypnotize him.

"What?" he asks. But Donáth doesn't ask again. The most obscene swear words bubble up from his drawn lips. The drain can't cope with so much water. Soon, the stokers are up to their knees in water that stinks of anti-rust solution.

"The best way to catch a cold and kick the bucket," Donáth rails. "There's no bloody way I'll survive to see my little house in the country with all this piss!"

Finally, the water is all drained, Donáth takes the valve apart and inserts a long steel wire. "Look at the sediment," he says irritably. Rácz hands him the tools and carefully watches his hands. He realises that soon he'll be doing this on his own. At last the blockage is cleared.

"Refit the valve!" Donáth orders Rácz, and wipes his hand on a cleaning rag. The shop manageress and the sales girls look at Rácz with interest.

"Bleed the radiator in my office, Mr. Donáth," asks the manageress.

"Not today. Today I'm up to my neck in work," says Donáth. "That can wait. It's only the end of August."

"And what about the pipes?" asks the manageress. "Will they be all right? Are we going to freeze like last winter?"

"We'll see when we fire the boilers up," says Donáth.

The manageress slips a pack of ground coffee into Donáth's pocket with a discreet but meaningful gesture. "That's for your trouble," she says.

"People are shit-scared of winter," Donáth tells Rácz when they're in the street. "They're more afraid of cold than of death! Better remember that, it might come handy. That's why we get free restaurant food and drink proper coffee. Sometimes we even get good cigarettes. Even American ones."

They return to the boiler-room. Their trousers are wet, their work boots squelching with water. "I don't feel like doing any more today," says Donáth. "We'll make some coffee and get dry. Tomorrow we visit more shops. There's plenty of time!"

Rácz isn't bored. When he is free of work, he lies down on the bench, with his hands under his head and listens to the radio. Or he closes his eyes and remembers his childhood. He thinks above all of Eržika. How beautiful, sensible and hard-working she is!

From time to time Donáth stokes the furnace heating the water. It's dark in the boiler-room. Flashes from the fire paint fantastic pictures on the scruffy walls. Watching the flames is calming and hypnotic. Rácz falls asleep, but soon wakes up.

Donáth reads the paper and a fit of rage and hatred comes over him. He presses both hands to his head, and his eyes pop out of their sockets. The afternoon passes. Soon it's dark.

"I'm going to the kitchen to see what they're cooking," says Donáth, who is hungry by now. Rácz goes off for a pee. If you watch flames all the time, you pee more often. Then Rácz shoves a wheelbarrow-load of coal into the furnace, on a whim, so that he can watch the fire seize its quarry. A little later, he lies down on the bench and looks at the fire.

* * *

The next day they visit the chemist's and the leather shop. It's raining. The street is glistening. The parking attendant feels the chill, as he huddles under an umbrella. They dine in the kitchen, in the dishwashing room. One of the staff brings them soup, stew and potatoes straight from the pot. Donáth takes a knife and cuts a piece of meat in half. "Tastes all right?" he asks with his mouth full.

"Tastes good." Rácz nods.

They gobble their food — it's already getting cold and doesn't burn their tongues or gums. They glance at the girls washing the dishes. Rácz is about to wash the plates, but Donáth stops him. "No need," he says. "The girls will wash up for us. We give them heating, don't we?"

In the afternoon they check the heating in the Ambassador bar and cabaret. "You still can't be a hundred-per-cent sure it will work," Donáth says on the way there, "until you've tried it out for two or three days." As they're going through the service entrance, they meet one of the dancers. Donáth points her out. She's just stepped out of an Opel with Austrian licence plates. She blows a kiss to the driver and walks towards the stairs. The stokers let her go first. She deliberately ignores them as she passes. She's as slim as a racehorse. A smell of perfume follows her like a comet's tail and wafts over them.

"Nice bit of skirt, isn't she?" the old man remarks, when the dancer vanishes from sight.

"Too thin," Rácz puts in like a man of the world. In fact, he's upset at a woman ignoring him so pointedly. Ignoring him, a man who, when he was a soldier, was paid by a Czech whore! She paid him, not him paying her! "Oh God, I'd teach you a thing or two," Rácz reflects. But then he thinks of Eržika. He imagines her pure, virginal face and becomes sentimental. What could Rácz find interesting in a whore of Babylon when a girl like Eržika is waiting for him at home!

"A thin pig has the best meat," Donáth remarks. "Her name's Silvia. Pretty well anyone rides her. She's a fucking slut."

The Ambassador Cabaret is quite small. A stage with maybe twenty tables around it, a long bar with ten stools, a dance floor and a band stand in the corner with drums, an organ, and speakers. The dancers sit around the pianist in their sweaters and gym gear, laughing at some joke. Donáth shows Rácz into a corridor. "Here are the changing rooms," he tells him. "Bleed the radiators. I'll go down to the basement to check the distributor pipes." Rácz takes the tool kit and enters the first changing room. The room is about sixteen feet long. The mirrors, chairs, and make-up tables are on one side. On the chairs hang items of women's clothing. Shoes are kicked under the tables. On the right yawns a row of wide-open cupboards. All sorts of silver costumes, peacock feathers, and leather harnesses are revealed for all to see. The radiator seems to be OK. Rácz opens the bleed valve on the side of the radiator and puts an empty can under it. When the air blows out and the can fills with black water, Rácz shuts the valve. He takes another breath of the smell of female sweat, powders and perfumes, and then goes out into the hall and opens the door to the next dressing room. The thin dancer they saw in the front entrance is changing her clothes. When she notices Rácz, she gives him a hostile look. "Can't you knock on the door before you enter?"

"I didn't know you were in," says Rácz, and laughs.

"But now you do," the dancer says firmly.

"Yeah, now I do," Rácz agrees and enters the dressing room. "I'm just doing my job," he says, when he sees her lips pursed in contempt, and the angry shake of her blonde head doesn't escape him either. Disgusting slut, he thinks, night after night she shows it off on stage to the whole bar and now she's shy? He squats at the radiator and tries the valve. The dancer takes no more notice of him. She pulls off her bra, and then her panties. She's sitting on her chair wearing only a gold bracelet and earrings. The valve is stuck, maybe corroded. With every pore of his primitive sensual organism, Rácz senses the ethereal signals given off by her naked body, which is charged with energy. The dancer puts on a knitted white gym suit. Rácz works on the radiator, but glances at her out of the corner of his eye. Silvia is in no hurry to get dressed, the presence of a strange man doesn't seem to bother her.

"Can you do up the zip on my neck?" she asks.

Rácz jumps up from the radiator, wipes his hands on his overalls. The dancer turns her back to him. Rácz struggles with the little zip, his hands are trembling. The woman radiates warmth and a dark musky smell.

"Thanks," says Silvia. She doesn't even look at him. She sits back and between her fingers appear a thin long cigarette and a miniature gold lighter. Rácz kneels at his radiator and gathers his thoughts: they're scattered all over the place like an egg smashed against a wall. What was it he wanted to do? Oh yes, he was going to turn the valve. He takes an extension wrench, places it round the valve shaft and gently tugs it. It was only limescale. A bit of pressure and the valve turns. He turns it a few times back and forth, and then he puts the washer on and screws in the cotter pin. By now the dancer has put on her trainers and disappeared from the room. Rácz is sitting on the floor and carefully sniffs both his hands. They still smell of warm female skin. Eržika is so far away at this moment. "I'll get you one day," Rácz promises himself stubbornly. "I'll get you and I'll teach you some manners!"

* * *

In the army Rácz learned to use every free moment for sleep. He was young; he needed a lot of sleep. He managed to sleep no matter how much noise or light, in any position. Even five minutes' sleep refreshed him. Once, during manoeuvres, somebody stole his sleeping bag. It was winter and he faced two weeks of rough conditions in the exercise area. The other artillery crew members were freezing; at night they shook with cold and were going crazy, marooned by snow. Rácz just laughed. He wrapped himself in his coat, put his hands in the pockets and slept.

Donáth hardly sleeps at all. "I take a snooze for an hour or two," he says. "The rest of the time I just sit there, smoke and think about things." After working all day they lie down on the bench and smoke. Rácz has now acquired a taste for cigarettes. They don't talk; they're both quiet and thoughtful. Once in a while one of them feeds the furnace and checks the steam pressure. Outside autumn has begun. The days are still sunny, but wild winds howl at night. The hot-water boiler is small and quiet. Rácz occasionally wakes up in the night and listens to the wind moaning in the cold chimneys. Then he falls asleep again. "Just get a good night's sleep," the old man, looking into the fire with a cigarette in his mouth, tells him. "When I was young, I used to sleep, too. The older you get, the less you sleep." Donáth loads a wheelbarrow with coal and shovels it into the fire. Rácz isn't bothered by the noise. He can fall asleep any time, even in the day. Sometimes he thinks of Eržika. Maybe he shouldn't have left for the city, it occurs to him. He should have run off with her. That might have softened old Kišš. On the other hand, he's not so sure. He could have just ruined his chances. Who knows what she's like in bed? That matters a lot. What if she's frigid? And what if she has a fanny as tight as a sheep's? Rácz is suddenly scared. Then he wouldn't even be able to get into her. He's had some experience of this. A soldier's whore nicknamed "the graduate" once told him that when the good Lord was handing out sexual organs, Rácz must have got a double portion. She used to follow the soldiers back to the barracks. He once screwed her in the quartermaster's stores, when he was the assistant quartermaster. The "graduate's" moans woke up the whole regiment. "Those were the days!" Rácz recalls. After the army he serviced a pretty widow, his neighbour, in a barn a few times and then he fell in love with Eržika Kišš and that was the end of it. He couldn't imagine doing it with anyone but her. In fact, he couldn't even imagine doing it with her.

Rácz is not the kind of man a woman would fall madly in love with. He's taciturn, sullen-looking, and moves clumsily. Only a very experienced or even depraved woman could recognize at first sight that he'd make a passionate, wild lover with relentless endurance and monstrous physical endowment. But Rácz isn't bothered. A wild lover still sleeps inside him; he has not yet woken up. He is in fact reserved. He's not yet felt in life that burning, all-consuming passion that could derange him. Even his feelings for Eržika, however intense and genuine, stem from his need to organize his life at any given time according to certain rules.

The blonde dancer from the Ambassador cabaret has now injected poison into his veins. He's met her a few times. She often arrives for rehearsal when Rácz is emptying the barrel of ashes. Rácz has caught himself rushing outside just so that he can see her yet again. True, he can walk into the cabaret any time and pretend to fix the radiators. But he's too proud and shy for that. All he can do is to steal a glance that goes right through her whenever they meet. Silvia has from the start pretended to be unaware of him, but recently she's been giving him restrained smiles. She's amused by the stocky young man's serious, steely, anthracite eyes, and passionate facial expression.

* * *

"We've got to go to the car parts shop, too," says Donáth one morning. "And then we have to check the heating in the hotel itself. I really love that," he says ironically. "If I never had to go there, I'd be the happiest man in the world."

"Why?" Rácz asks.

"You'll see for yourself," Donáth says. "Nothing but hassle. Everyone gives you a hard time, from the manager to the receptionist, and even the messenger boy."

They have breakfast in the boiler-room. Donáth has brought in a loaf of bread, a chunk of butter and some ham left over from the foreign-currency guests' breakfasts. The big teapot is steaming. Donáth, lost in thought, presses a lemon into it. "After that we'll have covered it all. From then on you have to stand on your own two feet." After a minute he adds, with emotion: "I'll be gone in two weeks."

Rácz spreads butter on the bread and puts slices of dried-up ham on it. On the one hand, he is happy that he will be getting all the money which induced him to come here: two salaries and all the bonuses. On the other hand, he is apprehensive.

"When are we going to the parts shop?" he asks matter-of-factly and takes a bite of bread.

"Right after breakfast," says Donáth.

They eat in silence. Donáth is greedy and occasionally his food goes down the wrong way. His shoulders jerk and he chokes. He reaches with a trembling hand for his tea, takes a drink, closes his eyes for a while and then goes on stuffing himself.

It's foul weather outside. Yellow leaves are falling off the trees. Muddy water rushes loudly down the drain. Water is leaking in a corner of the boiler-room. "The downpipe from the gutter is cracked," Donáth says, watching the damp patch spread. Drops form on the blackened ceiling. Black drops begin to drop onto the dust.

The men drop in at the parts shop. They check the state of the radiators and the manager invites them for a drink. Donáth gives Rácz a meaningful wink.

"I've heard you're leaving, Mr. Donáth," the manager says after they've drunk each other's health. "Yes, I am," nods Donáth. "This young man will be taking over from me." – "Well," says the manager, "it can't be helped." The manager looks at Rácz. "You won't let us freeze, will you now?"

"See how shit-scared they all are?" Donáth laughs when they turn the corner. "They'd sell their own mother for a bit of heat!"

Donáth has a lot of ill-suppressed contempt for anyone who depends on his boiler-room in winter. It's like the feeling doctors have, however humane and good they are to their patients, for the faceless mass wailing and spluttering in their waiting room and grabbing them by their white sleeves every time they stick their noses out of their surgery. Donáth judges people by the way he imagines he'd have to produce heat for them. He goes out to buy beer and looks at a man standing in front of him with a shopping basket. He'd want me to heat a lot, Donáth thinks, and he'd always complain he was cold. That one over there — he looks at the woman at the till — would want adjustments all day long. At night she kicks off her blanket and sleeps naked, for sure, just like a tape-worm. And so on.

* * *

A prostitute hails a taxi. Inside her the sperm of Zdravko G., unemployed, residing in Vienna, Austria, is still dying *en masse*. The prostitute is tall, blonde, well dressed. She puts on lady-like airs.

Urban loathes this woman and doesn't hide his feelings from Rácz. They're standing on the pavement in front of the passage to the yard. Urban is waiting for Hurensson to show up: the Swede is bringing him the video camera he promised. Rácz is carrying a carton of cigarettes and a bagful of bottles of beer. He listens to Urban and watches him with his unblinking gaze. Women like these remind Urban of a gutter. They remind him of a public lavatory. Anyone with foreign currency can jerk off in her. No, he hasn't been to the cabaret yet. He's not interested. He prefers listening to Charlie Parker on a tape recorder at home.

Rácz looks the prostitute up and down with eyes wet with desire.

"I drove her home once," Urban says. "She was putting on her lady-like act." He didn't fall for this act. He let her know, without being vulgar, that he considered her nothing more than a dirty scrubber. This was done so subtly, in fact, that she didn't even get it. He asked her where she wanted to go. She opened her mouth to tell him the name of the street. Even half an hour later the car stank of the decaying semen of some dirty Yugo or Kraut.

Rácz silently looks straight ahead. Not a muscle moves on his face. It was Silvia. He clenches his fists inside the pocket of his overalls until the bones of his hand crack.

"But then she paid," Video Urban adds. "She gave me five hundred, afraid that I'd grass her up." Suddenly, Video Urban has to leave. He has to check out the other car parks, to see if Hurensson has shown up yet. It's possible that he's avoiding Urban, that's he's just shat on Urban and not brought the camera, and is avoiding him. That's not fair. Urban still thinks that all the trouble he went to for Hurensson in June, when the Swede showed up for the first time, was a kind of down payment for the promised camera. Hurensson didn't spend a penny on taxis, as Urban drove him everywhere. In any case, Hurensson is behaving like an arse-hole, like a shitty, unreliable hippy. Urban has to look for him all over the city. Maybe he's left already. Anyway, you obviously can't have a normal conversation with Rácz today.

Rácz has a stony look on his face. He is still clenching his fists when he gets to the boiler-room. He keeps them in his pocket like a hand-grenade with the pin pulled out. He puts down his shopping and looks around. He looks for a suitable object. "Whore, for fuck's sake!" he shouts and hits the nearest boiler with his fist, making a dent the size of a wash-basin. "I'll get that whore one day, anyway." She'll suck him too. And he'll beat her. He has to punish her for cheating on him for so long with other men. "Just you wait," he tells himself. He lies down on the bench. He closes his eyes in anticipation of future delights to be provided by her supple little abrasive tongue.

Donáth crawls sleepily out of his cubbyhole. Why is Rácz smashing things, why is he making so much noise? Donáth has only just got to sleep. Yes, he managed to get to sleep. That has to be respected. Rácz mustn't bang about here. He's not the boss here yet. And anyway, where's he been for so long? There couldn't be such a big queue at the grocer's. Donáth nervously paces the boiler-room, pointing with his long finger. Where was Rácz hanging about all that time?

"Outside," says Rácz through clenched teeth, and, perturbed, Donáth opens his eyes.

"With Urban, I'll bet?" asks Donáth.

"Yes," agrees Rácz. "Urban has tons of money. And he's only a moonlighting taxi driver. Sometimes he does deals. Just imagine the kind of money the real racketeers must make!" Urban told him. Millions!

Donáth finds that funny and laughs. "You can't believe everyone," he says. "Let me give you some advice. Urban's no friend for you. He's a crook. You've got to be honest, you understand? Take this rag over there, and the solvent and go clean the boilers. I'll take a snooze. Millions? Rubbish!"

Donáth leaves. Rácz sighs and gets down to work. In the evening he'll watch the hotel entrance and parking lot opposite through a narrow little window in the coal store. Maybe he'll see Silvia. He'll wait hours for her.

* * *

At this very moment in Austria, Zdravko G. is in a bouncing van, happily travelling home from the job centre. Again, he's struck lucky. He's found a job, cash in hand, of course. Zdravko G. doesn't want to lose his unemployment benefit. The owner of a historic mill in the Viennese Woods has decided to demolish and remove a two-hundred-year-old outdoor privy. Zdravko is made for this kind of work. He'll get five thousand schillings for it. The work will take him a couple of days to finish. He can go back again for a weekend in Bratislava. He'll look up the tall whore.

"Shit stinks," Zdravko G. says to himself as he carries bucketfuls of it up and down, "but life is beautiful." If he'd stayed back home, in Kosovo, he'd still be herding donkeys.

* * *

Silvia is happy, too. Zdravko, the swarthy Yugoslavian doctor, who works in Vienna, left her a thousand schillings. If she sells them at just three crowns each, she'll have three thousand crowns. To this she has to add a hundred marks from the German whom she satisfied in his car, in the parking lot in front of the hotel. A hundred marks at twenty-five crowns each, together with the schillings make five and a half thousand crowns. Of this, five hundred go to the taxi driver and a thousand to the receptionist in the Ambassador. That leaves four thousand crowns clear profit.

Before two in the morning. She even got a good night's sleep. Alone. Edita comes to see her less often now. The season is ending and everyone does their best to get as big a piece of the action as possible. But four thousand crowns is not bad at all. For an amateur.

Silvia is no professional. She has her own profession. She's a cabaret artist. After the show she does a couple of punters. Nobody can take that away from her. It is like a hobby, just moonlighting. One day she'll get married and will stop screwing in cars and hotel rooms.

Her landlady thinks Silvia is a student. Any doubts can be smoothed over with money. The landlady isn't bothered. If the money runs out, she will be. That's life. Silvia also keeps to an unwritten and unspoken rule: she never brings anyone home. No men.

"You're such a good girl," her landlady says. "You shouldn't exhaust yourself studying. Let your friend study on her own so late at night. Or she can come over to your place once in a while. She hasn't slept here for a long time. And anyway, you should take a break. Relax. Have some fun. Do you have a boyfriend yet? No? That's good. You've plenty of time left for that."

Silvia opens a metal casket and puts the money in it. She has to make all the money she can while her breasts are firm and her vulva is pink and tight. Whatever's left over will be good enough for a future husband. Silvia knows almost everything about him already. He'll be tall, greying, West German, Austrian, American, rich Arab, whatever. He'll own at least a Mercedes. He is a widower, an old bachelor, something like that. He has to have Good Samaritan tendencies combined with acquisitiveness. Only a man like that can take a whore out of circulation and make her his wife without reminding her about it during every little quarrel. But so long as this silver panther is still hiding somewhere abroad, Silvia makes do with Zdravko G.

* * *

Rácz is polishing brass parts. The boilers are ancient. Every boiler is marked with a faded plate saying: HANS-KOKESCH-WERKE IN WIEN 1895. "Don't spare the polish," Donáth tells him, after he finally gets up. "But don't overdo it. Use something in between. Then we'll go and eat," he says emphatically. "We'll have a good meal." Rácz says nothing.

"You bought the beer," says Donáth, "but I thought of us, too. Take this," he addresses Rácz in a conciliatory tone. "Take a swig!" A long bottle glistens in his black hands. "You know, when you've worked in the boiler-room for fifty years, you'll get bees in your bonnet, too. But Urban's a layabout, a loser. Have a drink!"

Rácz won't say no. The home-distilled schnapps is weak, but it does warm you up on a cold morning. Work gets easier straight away. But all Donáth's attempts to start a conversation get only a yes or a no out of Rácz. Just so the old man knows Rácz is no doormat. Donáth has to realise that Rácz may like a drink, but can't be bought.

After dinner Donáth decides to do what he'd been putting off for a long time — testing the heating controls for the actual Ambassador Hotel. Meanwhile the coal is delivered.

"Right," says Donáth, "this is where our real work begins. This is your coal and you have to unload it. Get a move on, or the gypsies will bring their buckets and there'll be nothing left. Best to do it today. I'll check the hotel controls myself. Then I'll sit and knock a few drinks back. It's been fifty years, after all."

The coal depot lorry makes ten trips. Long into the night Rácz keeps hurling coal down into the cellar by lamp-light. Now and then he runs downstairs to shovel the pile away from under the window chute, so that there's room for all the coal. From the bar and cabaret ventilation openings comes the muffled sound of music. It's raining heavily, but Rácz works bare-chested. Steam rises from his back and neck. The rain washes away the sweat. Rácz spits on his palms and keeps working, without a break, mechanically, monotonously.

Only towards dawn does he knock off. Exhausted, he goes down and drops onto his bench. He puts the rolled coat under his head and sleeps like a log. His arms throb.

The next morning is overcast and wet. Rácz looks with distaste at what's left of the coal glistening in the rain. In the dark the heap looked smaller.

"At the end of the week we'll fire the boilers," says Donáth after breakfast, looking at the thermometer. It really had got cold.

Rácz unloads the rest of the coal by dinner-time. He waits to see if Silvia will appear, but he's out of luck.

For the last few days and nights it's been cold in the boiler-room. One boiler can't heat the boiler-room any longer. The men have nothing to do and sit huddled in their coats, sipping tea with rum. At night Rácz often wakes up and listens to the coal heap settling down behind the wall. It makes a dark, greasy sound.

"Good coal," remarks Donáth and crushes a little piece in his hand. "You won't have to stoke too much, it will burn for a long time."

Every day the old man explains to Rácz something about the boiler-room equipment. Rácz's notebook is full of drawings, diagrams and tables. Rácz is no genius, he's rather simple-minded, but he can learn quickly, like a chimpanzee. He draws diagrams of the distribution pipes system running snakelike along the walls. And the steam distribution pumps are soon no mystery to him.

"The circulation system is the Stanford-Schroeter type," Donáth tells Rácz proudly. "You fire the boiler. When the steam in the generator reaches the right pressure, you open the valve to the pump. When the steam begins to blow through this small safety valve, you turn the circulation wheel a few turns. You can do it easily by hand. The pump will start by itself. Then you add more steam and the revolutions speed up. Then you open the circulation system. Understand? Right away the water temperature will drop, since the pump brings cold water from the heating system back to the boiler. In a nutshell, the steam pressure, the pump revolutions and the water temperature are the three things that have to be carefully matched. But I'll teach you all this when we fire it up."

Rácz writes everything down. He wants to learn as much as possible.

In the evening, Rácz goes out in the yard to get some fresh air. It's cold now. You can't see the stars; only the moon occasionally emerges from behind the ragged clouds. Hungry stray dogs fight in the dark for the kitchen waste. Their greedy black muzzles glisten. They snarl in the air and at each other. The strongest one grabs a huge boiled bone from the skip and drags it out of the yard. Rácz turns on the light. The dogs take fright and instantly run away. Rácz can hear the sound of the bone being dragged over the cobblestones by the hungry dog.

"They're not so bold yet," says Donáth. He's heard the noise and the barking and followed Rácz upstairs. "You have to watch them in the winter," he warns Rácz. "They can attack a man, too. I used to have a small-calibre gun and shoot them. They're like wolves. Once I shot a drunken guest and the hotel lawyer smashed my gun. At least he managed to straighten it out without getting the cops involved…"

Donáth coughs and spits in the yard. Moaning, he urinates into a pile of ashes. Steam rises from the puddle. The dogs are fighting in the next street now. From the distance, one can hear their terrified barking.

* * *

The manager came in the morning. "You have to start heating!" he ordered in a strict voice and wiped his nose. His chauffeur, Ďula, stood next to him and looked menacingly at the stokers.

"That's what we were going to do," says Donáth and gets up from his breakfast. "The lad will back me up. Just yesterday I told him: tomorrow we fire the furnaces."

"That's right," nods Rácz.

"Shut your face, dolt," Ďula shouts at no one in particular.

The manager gives Donáth a long hard look. "You have to start heating."

Donáth nods. "Yes, we will, why not?" he says philosophically.

"It was cold last night," says the manager. "The French millionaire from number eighteen, and that pair of American businessmen from the red suite complained. It was embarrassing. Do I, the manager, personally have to stoke the boilers?"

Donáth nods wisely. "Yes, that's a problem. But it's easily solved. Tell them," he begins solemnly, but the manager has already gone.

"Shut your face, dolt!" Ďula the chauffeur barks harshly and viciously. "You should be grateful that the manager has come down here to talk to you, but you answer back. Do you think that the manager has nothing else to do but deliver messages to you? Heat the place this very moment or else we'll make your life hell!"

Ďula leaves and bangs the metal door behind him. Rácz throws a wrench at the wheelbarrow and makes a loud din. He's upset: "If he'd said another word, I'd have…"

"You'd better be careful with that man," Donáth says. "He creeps all round the hotel spying and then he reports to the manager. He sets people up. He tells on the manager to the lawyer, and on the lawyer to the manager."

Donáth takes the matches from the table. He shakes them to make sure the box is full. "Let's do it," he tells Rácz. "Now watch me. Next year you'll have to do it all by yourself…"

He doesn't finish his meal. He breaks up some firewood, brings some paper and spreads a little in each furnace. Rácz goes back to his meal but watches the old man and tries to remember everything. The paper lights with a clear flame, Then the wood starts to crackle. The stack of firewood settles and the sparks fly. Donáth adds a shovelful of coal to each boiler. It gets noticeably warmer in the boiler-room. The old man takes his padded jacket off and sits down at the table. "Now we have to wait a bit until the steam pressure goes up," he says, and starts to eat. "Then you can get the pumps going, I'll explain everything, don't worry."

A few wheelbarrows of coal later and the boilers start to hum like the wind at the tram terminus. The metal grid door slowly gets red-hot. The pumps, newly oiled, gather speed with a quiet hiss. The large circulation wheels turn faster and faster, as Donáth steps up the steam. The piston runs to and fro.

Donáth takes Rácz to the back wall, which is interlaced with serpentine pipes and a forest of red valves.

"This is the heart of the whole boiler-room," he tells him. "From here you regulate the temperature in the hotel rooms, the stores, and so on. This is the uptake pipe that heats the offices and guests' rooms in the left wing. This one heats the right wing. The brass plates say exactly where everything is, but a lot of pipes have been re-routed and they're no longer reliable," he warns him. He taps his crooked finger on a big valve. "This connects both halves of the hotel and you can then heat them with one boiler. If you close all of these valves, all the people who rely on you will freeze. Make sure that everything is properly set."

Rácz nods, closes one of the valves as an experiment and then opens it again. It's heavy going. Steam escapes from the loose connections, the rubber belts on the circulation wheels of the pumps whistle quietly, the fires burn under the boilers. The boiler-room looks as if it has come to life, submerged in a flashing reddish glow reflected on the dirty walls.

"Now you'll learn more than during the whole time you've been here," laughs Donáth. He's happy; he'll soon be gone.

* * *

In the meantime, it's begun to freeze. In the morning Rácz runs to the supermarket for beer, and his boots slip on the suddenly frozen puddles. There's not a lot of work. Everything is running smoothly. In the morning Donáth is fidgety. He's leaving tomorrow and can't believe it. He looks into the furnace and grabs his head. He suddenly jumps up and breathes in so as to say what's on the tip of his tongue. At the last moment he stops and instead of the expected liberating word, the boiler-room echoes with only a well-worn curse. Rácz can understand. He drinks beer and smokes. He nods. Donáth doesn't know what to do first. He runs up the stairs so fast that he slips. He bangs the door. Rácz can hear him from his cubbyhole arguing with the laundry room gypsies.

Then the yard grows quiet. Soon Donáth is back with a litre bottle of gin. "Make the tea," he shouts with authority, "I've got company."

"Company" means Mrs. Tóthová and one of the gypsy women who wash the dishes. She is wearing an apron and her hands are red from the hot soapy water. The women drink like fish. Donáth does not need much. He drinks a few shots and is already giggling and pawing both women. Rácz watches and drinks. He can take as much as a bull. The old man brings the radio from his cubbyhole and tunes it to some raucous station. Like anyone who is, for any reason, forced to listen to the radio at work, Donáth knows all the theme tunes and can sometimes sing along in his tuneless voice for whole sections, comically distorting the lyrics, of course. Emboldened by the gin, he pulls Mrs. Tóthová off her bench to the space in front of the boiler as it were a dance floor. The old woman laughs, tipsy on the cheap liquor.

"What's your name?" the drunken gypsy woman asks Rácz.

"Rácz," he answers.

"And first name?" asks the gypsy.

"None," says Rácz. "Just Rácz."

The gypsy is ugly and skinny. Her withered breasts dangle under her chintz full-length apron. Her hands are bleached from washing dishes. "My name's Ribana," she says proudly.

"Ribana?" asks Rácz with ill-disguised indifference.

"Ribana Salay," confirms the gypsy. "My brother's called Vinetú Salay," she adds proudly.

"Never heard of that name," says Rácz unwillingly.

"You see," says the gypsy with satisfaction, as if Rácz's comment were a confession which gave her an advantage or an extra point in a contest. She pours another drink for herself and Rácz. She touches his glass with hers and then offers him her lips. Rácz doesn't feel like kissing the gypsy, on the other hand he is tempted. He's never had a woman of a different race. He kisses her. The gypsy grabs him as if he were a piece of soap she'd dropped in the bath.

Donáth and Mrs. Tóthová drunkenly dance in front of the boilers, the radio plays, barely audible or comprehensible.

"Are we going to do it?" asks Ribana.

"Do what?" Rácz doesn't understand.

"Do you feel like *doing* it to me," repeats the gypsy.

"You mean like…" Rácz finally gets it.

The gypsy nods with her tongue between her lips. They jump up and head for the cubbyhole. The gypsy lies down on the dirty bed, lifts her dress and spreads her legs. Rácz's brain has stopped working, he drops his dungarees to the knees and gets on top of her. The gypsy uses her hand to help him and then just passively holds him.

"What a huge one you've got," she tells him after a while and gasps for breath. "I can feel him all the way to my kidneys." Rácz writhes wildly. Suddenly his face freezes and he lets a suppressed exhalation escape from his mouth. Then he turns onto his side and, still lying, he pulls his dungarees back over his bare body.

"Good, wasn't it?" Ribana asks. "You can do it to me any time you like. Just come and get me from the dishwashing room."

Rácz nods.

The women have gone somewhere. It's getting dark behind the cellar windows. Donáth has collapsed onto the table. The bottle is empty. Someone grabbed the radio and smashed it against the wall. The boilers hum, the pumps silently puff. The wheels whistle. It's hot in the boiler-room. Rácz sleeps half-naked on the bench, his jacket under his head.

When Rácz wakes up in the morning, Donáth is standing over him, dressed in his Sunday best and trying to say good-bye. Mrs. Tóthová is there as well. They both look somewhat embarrassed. "So, we're off," says Donáth. They sit down for a while before they set out on their journey. They are silent. "We had a ball last night, didn't we?" Donáth suddenly shouts with a forced cheerfulness. "I've still got a headache!" Mrs. Tóthová smiles. Rácz nods and gathers his dulled facial muscles into a smile. "Our train leaves at seven," says Donáth. His tears flow. He blows his nose on a dirty handkerchief. "Come and visit us when you're in the neighbourhood," he suggests. Rácz nods. They both know it will never happen. "That's how it is with us…" Donáth waxes philosophical after a moment of embarrassing silence. They get up and part. Rácz accompanies them to the yard. They shake hands.

Rácz returns to the boiler-room. He takes off his boots and lies on the bench to finish his sleep. He is the boss here now.

* * *

The next day Ďula comes. He behaves arrogantly, talks down to Rácz and is rude. The leaking radiator in the manager's office has to be fixed. Right away. Ďula doesn't hang about and leaves haughtily.

Rácz gets his tools ready. He realises that he hasn't been in the actual hotel building yet. When Donáth had to fix something, Rácz was busy unloading the coal. "Well, I'll find it somehow. If the worst comes to the worst, I'll ask someone how to get to the manager's office." Rácz takes the tool-bag and sets off.

It's wet outside. The fat parking attendant is shivering under his umbrella, and his wet fingers are raking through the red bag he carries. Video Urban is hanging around the entrance to the bistro, discussing something with three gypsies.

"Still not shown up?" Rácz asks him in sympathy. He admires Urban though he'd never admit it. He admires Urban's smooth style, his comfortable way of life, his articulate speech, his city attitudes and city problems, such as his waiting for a Swede. Isn't that enough? Someone supposed to come all the way from Sweden just to see Video Urban! And Rácz has never even spoken to someone from Sweden. Once, when he was on his way to buy some beer, an elderly couple addressed him in some weird language, probably wanting him to show them the way. Rácz was so scared that he ran away in confusion and hid in a passage leading to the yard. He was afraid to go to the supermarket all that day, thinking the couple might be waiting for him and wanting something from him. Rácz hates foreigners, but at the same time, he's irresistibly drawn to them. And Urban? He can talk to them just like that in any language (Rácz has seen for himself), he jokes with them, laughs with them. He even does deals with them, the same way he would with Rácz, and then he gets mad when the foreigner doesn't keep his side of the bargain. Urban comes to work only occasionally, so he can be seen as someone who is there, but has just stepped outside. It's a different kind of work — no dungarees, no dirt, no noise. Rácz catches himself envying Video Urban. If someone asked him how he'd like to live, Rácz would have answered without hesitation: like Urban.

Rácz then made a decision: he'd return home, marry Eržika, as planned, but he'd persuade her to adopt Urban's cool city attitudes. Rácz will change the whole village. It's easy. The world is not just full of work and suffering, the real world is comfortable.

"So he hasn't come yet?" Rácz repeats the question, since Urban didn't hear the first time.

"Oh, hello…" says Urban absent-mindedly, and gives the leather-clad gypsies an embarrassed look. It's hard to tell if he's ashamed to be seen with Rácz by the gypsies, or vice versa. Rácz generously assumes the latter.

"So he still hasn't come?" Rácz asks in a friendly manner, to let the gypsies know that he's linked to Video Urban by a secret they share. Urban shakes his head. "No, Hurensson hasn't come yet."

"Come and see me in the boiler-room," Rácz asks him, "I've got something to show you."

"What?" Urban wants to know. Rácz won't tell him, and hurries off to the hotel to avoid getting wet. By the time he's run into the hotel entrance, he is all wet.

"Where do you think you're going?" The liveried doorman stops him.

"I'm from the boiler-room," says Rácz. "They asked me to…"

The doorman looks him up and down with obvious distaste, as if he were something that a dog had brought in off the street. "Who cares?" he says arrogantly. "You don't plan to walk into reception like this, do you?"

"Let me in," says Rácz, "I'm going to fix the manager's radiator."

The doorman yells at him. "Get lost, you wretch, I don't ever want to see you again! Who wants to see you? You only spoil the view from entrance!" He looks around to see that no western hotel guest is going to come out and see him in the compromising company of the stoker.

"Let me in!" Rácz yells and makes a feint to the left only to sneak in on the right past the clumsy doorman, and goes through the revolving door. The doorman blinks his piggish eyes and runs cursing after him.

All black, in greasy boots, Rácz enters the reception hall. A soft runner-carpet muffles his clumping steps. "You can't loiter here!" the receptionist calls to him from behind his counter. "Do you hear me? You have to go through the service entrance!" Rácz looks him over briefly, but pays no attention to him. A huge crystal chandelier hanging from the ceiling has caught his attention. With his bag on his shoulder he gawps at this amazing object. He taps the runner on the floor with his foot, and runs his finger along the marble top of the reception counter. With his rough hand he feels the quality of the tapestries decorating the wall. He bangs his fist on the mahogany panelling of the restaurant door.

"God!" he says. "Great God! What a place!"

The doorman is standing behind him, not knowing what to do. Rácz's entrance has created a stir. In the fashionable cosmopolitan atmosphere of an international hotel his dirty dungarees and shaved skull look like a gob of phlegm in a champagne glass. The assistant manager enters. He looks over the hall and in an instant works out what's happened. He nods to his underlings. The doorman and the receptionist grab Rácz and drag him to the exit. Rácz is so overwhelmed by the hotel's luxurious appointments that for a moment he obediently lets them lead him out. Then he notices the stir that he has caused by his entrance and becomes unsure. Why are all these foreigners watching him? He angrily shakes both underlings off. The doorman pounces on him determined to tackle him with a double Nelson. Rácz disdainfully knocks him down with a blow of his fist. The receptionist tries to grab him from behind, but Rácz hits him with his bag full of steel tools. They lie on the floor, not uttering a sound. Rácz is on guard, with his huge black fists ready. The assistant manager gives him a cowardly sidelong glance and backs off towards the stairs. Rácz uses the confusion to leave the hall, retreating through the revolving door.

He runs across the wet street and returns to the boiler-room. He hurls the tool bag into the corner and sits down at the table. He knows that something is wrong, but his psychology is too simple to be overcome by panic. Instead, he clenches his fist and hits the table with all his might. Donáth's ashtray and beer bottles jump and a crack runs the length of the table top.

Ďula turns up. He can't hide his broad malicious smile. The manager has sent him. Rácz is going to be carpeted right away. They'll fuck him over, ha ha!

Rácz leaps up, his shoulders tensed and ready for a fight. "Let's go then," he says.

Ďula is amazed by such boldness, but says nothing. He leads him across the yard, then by the back entrance up the tradesmen's stairs to the upholstered door of the manager's office. "Wait here," he tells him sternly and he enters the office, bent double in a servile bow. "Well, come in, get a move on," he barks after a while at Rácz from the doorway.

The manager is sitting at his desk and is purple and roaring with rage. He stuffs some pills down his throat. He sips water in an unprepossessing manner; his hair hangs over his forehead. Rácz enters and stops in the middle of the office. He looks around. The manager watches him for a long time with revulsion, while his fingers drum on the desk. "What have you done?" he shouts at Rácz out of the blue. "I ask you again, what have you done?" Rácz is silent; he shrugs in embarrassment and shakes his shorn head. "For heaven's sake!" The manager is livid. "The hotel is full of westerners and he shows up in dirty dungarees and filthy boots! Do you think they've come to our beautiful country to look at some shitty stoker? Well?"

"Appalling!" The chauffeur Ďula, standing behind Rácz, agrees obsequiously.

"I didn't ask you to speak," yells the manager. "Get lost!"

"OK, I'm going," Ďula obeys zealously, and darts like lightning out of the office. For a second his rat-like face reappears by the upholstered door. "If you need me, boss, I'll be with the lawyer."

Rácz says nothing, he just looks ahead. The manager falls silent. He swallows a pill, washes it down with water and inspects his tongue and palate in a little mirror. Then he continues in a milder tone: "I'm going to punish you. You are new here and you have to be taught a lesson. I never liked you from the start, but I want to be a just leader to my people. No, you won't be sacked, even if that's what you wanted. Why are you looking like that? As a stoker, you can only be seen in employees' areas. If you have to work in guests' areas, you cannot be dressed the way you were today. You need a decent grey suit, a pastel-coloured tie, and a shirt that's not too loud. Your tools will be concealed in a neutral-looking bag. I shall punish you with a fine equal to a month's salary. Your next salary will be forfeited in favour of the Hotel Ambassador."

Rácz fights for breath. Blood rushes to his face. He won't see any money for a whole month! His return home will be put off by a month! "But I…" he objects and raises his arms.

"Hold your tongue!" The manager peremptorily shuts him up, and bangs a fist on his desk. "And don't wave your arms about! There's nothing I hate more than my employees waving their arms about."

Rácz feels like silencing the manager with a punch in the head, but the manager catches him off guard. "And now fix the radiator quickly. The hotel manager is not going to freeze."

Rácz is gasping with humiliation and anger. He runs out of the office in fury, lest he kill someone.

* * *

Only in the boiler-room does mad rage overwhelm him. He feels the veins in his head are at the point of bursting, as the blood roars in his ears. He grits his teeth until his gums go numb. He grabs a steel rod and angrily bangs it against the distributor pipes. He throws the bent piece of steel on the coal heap. Then he grabs a chair and hits the wall for so long that only a few splinters remain in his hand. "*A kurva hétszentségét,* Fucking hell," he curses in Hungarian, blinded by hatred.

To rob him like that! Rácz still can't believe it. He stands in the middle of the boiler-room and, like a bull a slaughterer has failed to stun, shakes his head, looking this way and that. A translucent film covers his eyes and his clenched fists are a deadly threat. Anyone who came into the boiler-room now would be a dead man. After standing around a while, Rácz resolutely steps towards the distributor and all its valves. He calmly reads the markings on the valves, moving his fingers over the worn out labels. Then with mighty gestures he closes the valve feeding hot water to the administrative section radiators. He imagines the manager's face full of self-satisfied disdain.

"You'll freeze," he shouts, "you'll all freeze!" He thinks of Ďula, the doorman, the receptionist, and the hotel lawyer. "Enjoy your cold!" he says, closing one valve after another on the distributor.

The pipes gradually go cold and creak as they contract. Rácz slows down the circulation pumps. He imagines the manager jumping to it when he's swamped by complaints about the cold from all sides. He's bound to send Ďula down to the boiler-room. But Rácz will throw him out and, if he makes a fuss, Rácz will punch his face. Nobody will try to boss Rácz about. Here, in the boiler-room, Rácz is the boss. Nobody will order him around. Donáth was an old fool and he let those cripples bother him. "Get lost," Rácz will tell a shattered Ďula. "I want to talk to the manager." That's how things are going to be.

Feverish with thoughts of revenge, Rácz collapses onto the bench, adjusts his padded jacket and puts it under his head. He closes his eyes and tries to imagine everything getting cold and a penetrating chill invading the rooms, everyone in the household goods and other shops rushing to call the manager, trying to find out what's happened.

And finally, Rácz imagines the manager willy-nilly coming down to the boiler-room, with a cowardly sidelong look and a nervous twitch of the head. Rácz won't take any excuses. He'll tie that nice manager to the pipes and heat the poker red-hot... Oh, Rácz's revenge will be really horrific.

Violent indignation sends Rácz to asleep, though only briefly. Soon the noise of shoes on the stairs wakes him up. Rácz is startled. The car parts shop manager is coming down the stairs.

"So, how are things?" the manager begins and takes a seat. "Don't you miss Mr. Donáth?"

Rácz just shrugs. "Can't be helped," he says, faltering.

"It was easier when there were two of you, wasn't it?" says the shop manager. Neither speaks for a while; they watch each other. Then the manager after some humming and hawing comes to the point. "The heating's broken down, chief," he says jovially. Rácz is pleased by the title; he gets up and nods. "We've had nothing but cold for the last hour in the shop," the shop manager goes on. "We're working in our coats. The customers are complaining. What's happened, chief?"

Rácz jerks into action. He quickly babbles whatever comes to him. "Maybe the vertical pipe is blocked." He goes red. "You see?" he says emphatically. "The boiler-room is old," he continues, when the car parts manager nods. The pipes rust from the inside. The water pressure moves the rust as far as the bends and it sticks there. Rácz describes a bend with his hands. "You see? When the flow decreases, the bend clogs up. One day the pipes get blocked, and that's it." Rácz is intoxicated by his own ingenuity. After a short silence he goes on. "We'll have to open the pipe and take all the filthy muck out."

"OK, I see," says the manager sadly and gets up.

On the stairs more footsteps can be heard. "Are you there, chief?" a woman's voice asks. The household goods shop manageress comes down. "Chief, it's cold," she says to Rácz. "The girls are shivering, poor souls. Can't something be done about it?"

"Why come to me about it?" Rácz ask with ill-disguised joy at his new title of chief. "Tell the manager. Why me? I'm just a stoker."

The car parts manager throws his head back in a gesture of contempt. "The manager! When Mr. Donáth was here, we always came here, if something went wrong." Rácz is confused. He did not foresee things turning out this way. Now there is no going back. He explains the situation to the woman in a few brief sentences. He'd like to help. Of course, he can't be blamed for the mess Donáth left. It seems to him that stupid old Donáth timed things so that after his departure they'd all start to break down. Anyway, he assures his visitors, it is not that cold yet. What are they going to do when it really starts to freeze? The visitors are dumbfounded. Rácz gets up. He is stocky, a head smaller than either of his visitors, but now he seems like a father to them. Rácz is wondering. Maybe communal services should be called in. They're equipped to handle this. But they won't come earlier than a month or two. The visitors are even more hunched with despair. Communal services work all round the city, Rácz stresses. And here, there is a lot of work to do. Everything has to be closed off, the water has to be drained, and so on.

"What was all that talk that everything would be in working order?" the car parts manager complained.

"Well, I didn't make any promises," says Rácz, "and Donáth didn't give a toss. He could promise anything."

"Right," says the household goods manageress. "But couldn't you help us? Maybe you'd only have to poke the pipes clear." Rácz shrugs.

"It might work. But it's a terrible job draining the water and then pushing the wire through the muck. There's no guarantee."

"That's all right," she says quickly. "Just give it a try! We'll have gone crazy from cold by the time those communal services come."

Rácz clears his throats. "I'm a bit limited in what I can do," he declares, scrutinizing his visitors' faces. "Besides it's not in my job description. It's an extra."

The car parts manager makes the first move. Yesterday he had a delivery of several Škoda windscreens, he admits shyly. If the chief is willing, he could bring him a couple. They're very sought-after and the chief could easily sell them profitably, even if he himself doesn't have a Škoda himself. Rácz shrugs again. He's not bothered. The manager quickly leaves to get them, as long as he gets the heating back. He runs up the stairs and bangs the door. Rácz has nothing against the idea. He sits down at the table and massages his sleepy face. Then he looks at the table and sighs. He fixes his gaze on a piece of cheese. He takes a slice and puts it in his mouth. While he chews, he looks at the household goods manageress and tries to imagine her naked.

"It's quite hot in here," she remarks when they are alone. "Could you give me a glass of soda?" Rácz jumps up while chewing, but realises he has an erection and sits down again. His mouth full, he lifts his eyebrows and waves his penknife about. "What, you don't have a soda bottle?" She is astonished. "But that can be sorted, chief. We happen to have put some aside for good friends, the glass ones, of course. They're so hard to get nowadays. I'll bring you one, and some gas cartridges. You'll be able to make your own soda water in this heat, as much as you want. You'll see how easy it is to work." Rácz doesn't drink soda, he never has. He drinks beer, but he shrugs nevertheless. While he swallows the cheese, she runs off, as if kicked up the backside.

Rácz is alone again. The manager does not show up. Instead, Video Urban comes down. Without further ado he sits at the table. "Anything interesting?" he asks Rácz. Rácz nods with his mouth full, swallowing a huge piece with his eyes wide open and the knife lifted high. When he finished, he wipes the knife on his dungarees, closes it and puts it into his pocket. Then he gets up, goes to his cubbyhole, running his tongue round his mouth for remnants of cheese. He pulls down the suitcase and from behind the lining takes out the seven hundred marks that he had found.

"Seven hundred marks," says Urban when Rácz puts it on the table, which is covered with newspaper.

"How much might that be worth?" Rácz asks.

"Where did you get it?"

"I found it," Rácz admits.

"Where?" Urban is amazed.

"It was in front of the hotel; in one of the big flower tubs."

"When?" Urban inquires.

"The day I arrived."

"Was it the day they raided the currency dealers?"

"How would I know?" Rácz laughs.

"Obviously," Urban nods, "the raid. I ran downstairs, too. That money belongs to some currency dealer. He hid it in the flower tub so they wouldn't find it on him. He meant to come back later for it. That's clear."

"So?" says Rácz. "Finders keepers. It's mine now."

"I wouldn't be so sure," Video Urban warns him. "When the dealers find out the money is here, they'll skin you alive. Seven hundred marks is no joke, it's a nice little stash."

"How much," Rácz tries to pin him down.

Urban tries to back down. "Well, it's not that much, you know, but still…"

"How much?" Rácz insists.

Urban stalls. "I don't know. I'd give you seven thousand. You want it? Right here and now, cash in hand."

"Seven thousand?" Rácz sits down in amazement. "That's not bad," he thinks. "I'd make up the money I've lost because of the manager's fine." On the other hand, he's noticed Urban's nervousness and a flash of greed in his eyes. Peasant wisdom demands that he wait. "I'll think about it," he promises Urban.

"I'll give you ten thousand!" Urban bids and as proof, shows him a huge wallet stuffed with banknotes.

Now Rácz is quite sure. This city slicker has been trying to fleece him. So he tells him evasively: "Forget it, I'll think about it. It's not that simple."

"As you wish," Video Urban says and puts his wallet away. "But when the dealers find out who's got their money, you're screwed."

"And who's going to tell them?" asks Rácz.

"Not me," Urban stresses, but they have their own people every-where. "They're a mafia."

"I look forward to meeting them," says Rácz.

"So you're not selling?" Urban doesn't give up.

"I told you I'd think about it," declares Rácz. "If you're right, I'm screwed anyway, so it's all the same to me. When I'm ready to sell, I'll tell you," he assures him.

"As you wish," Urban gives up. "I hope you don't regret it."

"We'll see who gets screwed," Rácz thinks when he's alone again in the boiler-room.

But he's not alone for long. Soon the household goods manageress is back. She has a big grin on her face. "You'd never get hold of these, they're so hard to find." She puts two crates of soda bottles on the table.

The car parts manager arrives very promptly with his two windscreens. Out of breath with the effort, he looks for somewhere to put down his load. "You'll make a fifty-per-cent profit on this easily, chief," he assures Rácz. They both stand there, waiting. Hope shines in their panting faces.

To calm them down, Rácz gets up and lazily gets his tools together.

* * *

Zdravko G. has driven to rainy Bratislava early in the morning in an old orange Opel borrowed from a friend, another Yugoslav in the hostel. The car was in a bad shape, but all the unemployed Yugoslavs in the hostel would borrow it for their trips to visit Slovak whores. To gain the whores' devoted admiration, they would show off and drive out of the car park doing sporty handbrake turns, making the tortured engine roar, the tyres shriek, and raising stinking clouds of burning rubber. The old car, meant by the manufacturer for quiet family driving on well-kept West European roads, protested at the racing-driver tricks of dynamic young men originally destined to herd donkeys on the rocky hills of Kosovo. Now the gearbox is hopelessly buggered. Luckily, while the car is still in the car park in front of the hotel.

Zdravko's last job was cleaning the ditch of a slaughterhouse owner in a Vienna suburb. The five thousand schillings he'd saved would last him a week. By then someone would surely fix his gearbox. Zdravko has big plans. He's going to buy Slovak Marlboro cigarettes, a lot of them, at least twenty cartons. They sell well in Vienna. Zdravko will make a profit, not a big one, but a decent one. But that can wait till tomorrow. Piggybank approaches, breathing hard, his bag hanging round his neck. "I'll pay you later," he tells the sweaty parking attendant, leaving him standing there with a long face.

"Four crowns for half an hour and, ten crowns for three hours and any extra hour or part of an hour ten crowns.."

"Why are you telling me this?" Zdravko wonders, looking with curiosity at the unprepossessing extortionist.

"So you don't park here for three days," Piggybank explains. "That would cost you six hundred crowns. You won't get away by giving me a hundred this time!"

"OK, OK," Zdravko tells him, "we'll do a deal."

"Now, up front!" The attendant is adamant.

"Here, take this for the time being," says Zdravko G. contemptuously and sticks a crumpled hundred-schilling bill into his red bag.

"Thanks a lot, boss," Piggybank mumbles and starts bowing. He accompanies Zdravko G. to the pavement, ignoring the cars pushing into the crowded car park.

On the pavement at the entrance to the hotel, Video Urban waits for Zdravko G. After a brief talk, banknotes change owners. Schillings go into Urban's wallet, Zdravko packs a fat bundle of thousand-crown notes into his pocket. "How are you?" he asks out of habit. "Did Hurensson show up?"

"No, he didn't." Urban shakes his head. "He didn't give a shit."

Zdravko shrugs. Actually, it's not his problem. He nods to Urban and goes into reception. The receptionist knows him as an old friend. "Could I have room thirteen?" Zdravko asks. It's his lucky number.

"Yes," says the receptionist, "room thirteen is free. Do you have any luggage?" he asks when he sees the seventy-three-year-old Torontál moving from the lift with a face like a hungry vulture.

Zdravko shakes his head. "No, my luggage is still in the car."

Torontál does not hide his spite and frustration. Even the receptionist can hear his cries of outrage. His stressed face shows disappointment, and his shaking hands open and close like crab's claws, in frustrated expectation of the warm handles of suitcases, bags, and above all the highly desirable tips. Zdravko G. did once entrust his suitcase to the senile porter, a long time ago, the first time he came. It took a quarter of an hour for the suitcase to reach the lift. The shaky old man walked carefully, with minute steps, nodding his birdlike head on its thin, wrinkled turtle neck. Breathing heavily, like someone under torture, he almost collapsed under the weight of the luggage, so that Zdravko G. was forced not only to take the suitcase, but also to give support to Torontál who, without hesitation, sank his spidery fingers into his shoulder. When they came to the lift, they found that it was stuck. From the shaft came the faint whine of foreign guests stuck in the cabin. Nobody paid attention to them. The hotel personnel passed by the lift unconcerned. They were used to it. By the time Zdravko G. had dragged the suitcase and Mr. Torontál to the second floor, sweat stains showed on his elegant jacket. The old man looked fragile, but was as heavy as an ox. Zdravko G., breathing heavily, fell into his armchair in room number thirteen. Porter Torontál came up to him with eager anticipation and the joyful expression of a job well done. It took Zdravko G. a moment to realise that the greedy old man expected a tip. So he picked out a ten-crown note. A crestfallen Torontál took it and tottered downstairs to greet new customers.

Zdravko G. has learned his lesson. Straight away, at reception, he offers the old man a ten-crown note and is left in peace.

* * *

First, Rácz crawls into the basement under the car parts shop. He bangs his wrench on the pipes to make people think he is working. He takes vaseline from the valve and smears it on his face. He sprays water from bleed valve onto his trousers. Then he sits down for a while, but soon feels cold. He climbs out of the basement. "It'll warm up soon," he says in a weary voice. He had had to clean the whole system. There was so much muck in those pipes that it turned his stomach. But Rácz had done his best for them.

They all follow him with grateful eyes. The manager pushes a red-faced salesgirl towards him with a bunch of flowers. Rácz accepts the flowers and, equally embarrassed, kisses the girl's cheek. The salesgirl giggles as she runs off.

Humble and grateful stares follow him out, they're glued to him, as, with a purposeful and preoccupied expression, he walks through the passage only to be greeted by other humble looks that welcome him into the household goods shop.

When Rácz gets back to the boiler-room to open the valves he'd closed, the manageress of the chemist's is already there, waiting impatiently for him, trembling with cold. Rácz invites her downstairs. She can't stop her teeth chattering from cold. They agree on a carton of apple-scented soap. When the manageress notices the soda bottles, she can't resist asking him for one. She's not on speaking terms with the household goods shop manageress. That woman's a real bitch, the chemist's manageress stresses. She writes anonymous letters denouncing the chemist's manageress and bringing in the government inspectors! The chemist's manageress would rather die than beg for a bloody soda bottle. Yet she needs one so badly. Rácz will let her have one in exchange for a carton of soap. This time a mandarin-scented one. Then he picks his tools up and follows the manageress. From the window of the laundry room that faces the courtyard Ribana smiles at him, luring him by rhythmically clapping her right palm on her clenched left-hand thumb and index finger. But Rácz pretends he can't see her. He's not Donáth and doesn't have to sleep with gypsies or whatever's on offer.

No sooner has Rácz finished his act in the basement of the chemist's, than the leather goods manager shows up. "Fix my heating, and when the leather jackets come in, I'll put one aside for you," he offers Rácz.

Rácz shrugs. Why not? A cheap leather jacket can always come handy. "Cheap, but good," he stresses, looking the manager in the eye.

Rácz stops working at dinner-time. He hungrily gulps down some soup and an under-cooked piece of meat that he fished out of the pot. The chef eyes him hesitantly, but doesn't dare object.

Rácz returns to the boiler-room. A good meal has pleasantly warmed his belly. He tends the fire and then stretches out on the bench. The manager could come down now, it occurs to him. Rácz would snap him in two. Indeed, nobody from the hotel has shown up to whine about the heating. But God help them if they send Ďula. The manager can come down himself. Rácz will cut him to pieces and flush him down the lavatory, if he doesn't cancel the fine.

Still sated with food and lulled by thoughts of revenge, Rácz falls asleep.

* * *

Rácz seldom dreams. He sleeps like a log — with his mouth half-open. His toes twitch. At home he used to dream occasionally, but his dreams were mostly sober, realistic — about work, about Eržika, about Mr. Kišš. What he dreamed about could easily have happened to him in real life. When he woke up, he often wondered if it had happened, or if it was only a dream.

He doesn't have dreams in the boiler-room.

Half asleep, he takes his boots off and hangs his socks to dry on the back of the chair. Then he stretches out, relaxed, without waking up. He begins to have his first dream since arriving in the city.

He is returning home, to his native village. He walks along the muddy road from the little station. Suddenly proud Feri Bartaloš gallops past him. He sprays Rácz head to toe with mud and dirt. Rácz takes no notice, but walks straight to Kišš's house, his throat gripped by tension. His pockets are stuffed with thousand-crown notes that won't fit in his rucksack. He resolutely enters the Kišš house. The Kišš family are all dressed in their Sunday best, sitting stiffly round the table. "Take this!" he roars at them and empties the contents of his rucksack right in the middle of the table. Mr. Kišš raises his eyebrows incredulously. Mrs. Kišš yelps. Eržika starts to sob and buries her face in her mother's shoulder. Rácz keeps pulling crumpled banknotes from the pockets, adding them to the heap. "I made all this," he says. "I'm a rich man. Now give me Eržika, as you promised!" The butcher buries his fingers in the banknotes, reluctant to pull them out. He looks disconcerted. "Son," he finally says in a weak voice, "I can't give you Eržika now. I married her off a month ago!" – "Who to, mister?" Rácz yells. His fingers clutching the banknotes freeze in their gripping movement. "Who to... Who to..." Kišš mumbles, pulling his fingers out of the heap of money on the table. "Well, to Feri Bartaloš. We thought you weren't coming back. Thought that was the last we'd see of you. You wouldn't be the first one... Not many people feel like coming back from the city..." – "But not someone who has a girl waiting for him..." says Rácz and collapses on a chair. Demonic rage builds up inside him. He's about to bang his fist on the table, but he controls himself. From the courtyard comes the clop of horse's hooves. The rider jumps off his horse and enters the kitchen. He is ruddy-faced, well built, smelling strongly of tobacco, leather, and horse sweat. Eržika jumps up from her chair and throws herself into his arms for protection. "Why have you come?" Feri Bartaloš asks Rácz menacingly. Rácz says nothing and makes a half-turn away. His hands are still clutching the crumpled banknotes. He gets up and begins to stuff them back into his rucksack. "I'm asking why you've come!" Feri Bartaloš proudly repeats, bringing his whip down on the table into the banknotes. "Eržika was mine," Rácz says stubbornly. The Kišš couple sits crestfallen at the table. "I'll squash you like a maggot!" Rácz declares. His eyes fill with tears, but suddenly somebody puts a cold hand on his face. "Leave me alone!" he barks at the owner of the hand, whoever it may be, and lets his fist fly. He suddenly tumbles into an abyss. The kitchen full of startled people disappears.

He wakes up on the cement floor with his tail bone hurting badly. "Wake up," says a female voice above him.

"I'm not asleep," mumbles Rácz and comes to properly. He is lying under the bench and bending over him is — it can't be — Silvia. Silvia, the dancer from the Ambassador Cabaret Bar.

Astonished, Rácz sits up sharply. His head is heavy and the place where the girl touched him burns like fire. Rácz touches his cheek. He really had been crying. He furtively wipes his tears.

"You were asleep," says the dancer.

"OK, I was asleep," mumbles Rácz, "I must have been." He gets over his surprise and puts on his act again. He's very busy. He doesn't know what to tackle first. The pipes are clogging up. Everyone wants him to fix those pipes. Is that what Rácz is here for? He doesn't even have the tools for that. Lucky he was trained as a tractor-driver and mechanic.

"Is it possible?" he asks himself. She's here, alive, in all her beauty. The blood pulses in her and Rácz can sense close up the energy radiating from her healthy supple body. He had that sensation once before, when she asked him to do up her zip. It must be damned cold in the cabaret bar by now.

"I just dozed off," says Rácz. "I've been on my feet since morning." He's working flat out. He's doing his best.

"We're terribly cold, too," says Silvia. "We can't rehearse. Can't anything be done? We have to rehearse a new number. You must have heard it; it's playing everywhere: *Pampa Jam*. That's the name."

Rácz shakes his head. No, he doesn't know it. He knows other songs, old ones, like *Rivers of Babylon*. But she probably doesn't know those.

"No, I don't know that one," says Silvia. "Can't something be done about the radiators?"

"It's not easy," says Rácz. He gazes into her bright light-blue eyes. The equipment is in a hopeless state, and suddenly everyone expects him to perform miracles. He pauses. He'd love to grab that slut, drag her into his cubbyhole and screw her on the bed. He gets up, but realises he's got a hard-on. He sits down again. "There is something we can try," he says. "What wouldn't I do for you?" he adds and his face goes red. The anger she aroused all the time he was watching her has evaporated.

Silvia knows that she can twist him round her little finger. He's going to eat out of her hand, she tells herself. In her face there is a remnant of that cold brazenness of girls who once wore their straw-blonde hair tied in two pigtails, played with boys and tortured frogs or beetles. Rácz senses her closeness on a primitive level. No, he can't say that he likes her. After all, she's not his type, as they say. Rácz prefers Eržika: dark, strong, with a big behind, breasts and reddish thighs. Silvia strikes him as a bit sickly.

Despite that, or perhaps because of that, he fancies her. He's never desired another woman like that before. Not even in the army. The fragrance of Silvia's perfume is alien in the boiler-room, which permanently smells of hot ashes doused with water. Rácz summons all his civilized self-control to overcome a sudden desire to grab her by the thigh. He rubs his hands in confusion.

The prostitute sits next to him on the bench. The square-cut, sweaty, swarthy village lad has roused her dulled senses. After all that she's gone through in life, only a powerful stimulus could excite her. A disturbing aroma wafts from Rácz's half-unbuttoned flannel shirt, which reveals his broad hairy chest. She'd love to touch it and run her hand under his shirt, touch his muscular belly and his narrow loins. She runs a finger over her lips. She feels how hot they are. Something stirs inside her. "How well-built you are!" she says and puts a hand on his shoulder.

Rácz flushes bright red again. "That's because of work." He's strong, all right.

The dancer says ambiguously: "Strength isn't everything..."

Rácz nods absent-mindedly, thinking now about something else. "I used to do weight-lifting," he confesses after hesitating for a moment whether to say so. I was the strongest kid in our school. I once hanged Feri Bartaloš — that's a lad from our village, he's a bit stuck up — on a hook. You know what I mean? Like this, look!"

He gets up and approaches the valves. His confidence has returned. Full of pulsating excitement at Silvia's presence, he grabs a steel rod with two bolts welded to it, used to tighten the valves. He bends it like a piece of plastic. He lets out a proud yell. Then he grabs a shovel and breaks it on his knee. He punches a dent in the metal door to the hall. He bends a piece of railing and winds a poker around his forearm. He roars from a surfeit of strength seething in his mighty body.

Silvia watches him, amused, but more and more aroused. She gets up and approaches him. They stand facing each other. Breathing heavily and sweating from the performance, he keeps rubbing his scraped fist, while she is excited by his animal strength. She has got so close to him that she can see his muscles pulsating on his sharply outlined jaw. "Could you grab me like that too?" she asks him. "Why not?" Rácz laughs and burrows his fingers into her shoulders and arms.

Silvia gasps in pain. "More, more," she whispers. She pushes him to the bench and sits astride his knees, facing him. Rácz does as she asks and leaves big bruises on her shoulders. The dancer begins to moan. She rips the stoker's chequered flannel shirt open. Buttons fly everywhere. Her hungry hands encircle his chest. The tips of her fingers can feel his thick black chest hair, dewy with sweat. Rácz presses her thighs. She sucks his mouth like a leech. Soon it is full of her hot, slippery and flexible tongue.

"It's hot in here," the prostitute says after a while. "Don't you have somewhere we could crash?"

Shivers run down Rácz's spine. His stomach contracts with nervousness. "Here we go," he tells himself. The more often he imagines something, the more hurdles he has to overcome when he wants to make it come true. But now there's no going back. He gets up and takes her to his cubbyhole behind the boiler-room.

Unembarrassed, the slut takes her clothes off, settles back on the rumpled bed and looks up at Rácz. "Well, what are we waiting for?" she asks. It takes Rácz a while to get going. Still upright, he hastily undresses, and stands there in his socks and boots. Then he hurls himself hungrily at Silvia. He runs his mouth all over her. He's never had such a sophisticated woman before. He rams himself between her legs. They wriggle about a while to find a comfortable position.

* * *

Not long after, Rácz is lying on the bed and the dancer is wiping herself with a crumpled towel hanging on the bedstead. "Have you got a cigarette?" she asks.

"I've some *Mars* cigarettes in the boiler-room," says Rácz, a bit upset that the dancer has recovered before he has.

"Oh no, you smoke *Mars*?" Silvia reacts, disgusted and astonished. "Where can I take a shower?" she asks him.

"Open that door," says Rácz, and go to the end of the hall, last door on the right. You want some soap?"

"I could use some," Silvia says. Rácz tears open a carton of the mandarin soap and gives her a bar. When she notices the brand name, the slut nods in approval. "You surprise me!" she says and disappears down the hall.

"So that's that," Silvia says offhandedly when she returns and starts to get dressed. "Try to do something about the heating."

"When are you coming back?" Rácz asks her, now that he is overcome by sadness.

"I'll come when the heating in the bar breaks down again," Silvia jokes.

"It'll break down again tomorrow!" Rácz declares.

"Just so we understand each other," says the prostitute holding a shoe in one hand, looking up at Rácz. "I was serious. Now you try to be serious and YOU show me what you can do. Don't think I'll put out every day. Do you have any idea how much other men think I'm worth?"

Rácz sits down on the bed. He doesn't like the idea of Silvia going with anyone but him. What's she after? Money? Big deal! Rácz has money.

Silvia can't help bursting out with contempt. A few crumpled hundred-crown bills? Silvia's not interested in those.

"What?" Rácz reacts, jumping up. A few crumpled hundred-crown notes? He opens the cupboard and puts his suitcase on the bed. He takes out a stack of *deutschmarks*. He holds them in his fist so that the stack looks bigger. "How much do you want?" he shouts. "A hundred? Two hundred? Here you go!" He peels off two hundred-mark bills and throws them in her lap. "When are you coming?" he asks.

Silvia takes the money, checks them against the light. She rubs them against each other, and listens to the sound of the paper. They're real. "Today was for free," she says. "But I'll take these." She'd come the day after tomorrow. "Deal?"

"You're a bit pricy," Rácz's peasant mind hesitates. "For two hundred you come tomorrow."

"Tomorrow I can't," Silvia shakes her head.

"Then give me back a hundred!" Rácz orders her. He takes the banknotes and carefully wraps them. Then he hides them in the suitcase and puts it in the cupboard. "They'll all be yours one day," he says, "if you're nice to me, really nice."

"Same time the day after tomorrow," the slut promises. She combs her hair in front of a fragment of mirror and touches up the lipstick on her sensuous lips.

When her steps die down on the stairs and the outer metal door bangs shut, Rácz gets up and looks for his trousers. He's satisfied.

* * *

"Mind if I phone the bar?" Zdravko G., speaking more in Serbian than Slovak, asks the waiter in the coffee shop. The waiter silently points to the phone. Silvia is back. The radiators in the bar are working. Her colleagues praise her, but gossip behind her back. "She's screwed the stoker! How vulgar!" But Silvia couldn't care less. The heat is back on and she'll gradually get those *deutschmarks* out of him. She's glad to hear Zdravko

G.'s voice on the phone. Everything is working out for her today. The darkly handsome doctor practising in Vienna is sure to have brought her some sort of present. He's not stingy. There's no rehearsal today, anyway. While she was working on the stoker, some of the girls were killing time drinking rum and coke. Now they are wobbly on their chairs and keep giggling stupidly. That's unprofessional, Silvia realises. The drunken Edita puts her hand up Silvia's legs, trying to get her into the dressing room. Silvia picks up her bag and coat and goes up to see Zdravko G.

"How are you doing," he greets her, when she joins him in the day bar.

Silvia smiles. "Fine."

"Have you missed me?" Zdravko G. wants to hear her say yes.

"You've been away a long time," says Silvia.

"I had a lot of operations to do, you know." Zdravko G. explains. "I've had to work a lot. It's a private hospital. Not enough doctors. Too many patients. I'm the best doctor and all the patients want me to operate on them." Zdravko G. lifts his glass and drinks. Silvia understands, nods. Zdravko G. has a beautiful profession. Zdravko G. agrees. "Most certainly!"

"What are you doing tonight?" Zdravko G. asks her.

"Nothing," Silvia says. She doesn't feel like doing anything today. She'll take the day off.

"Do you want to eat?" Zdravko G. suggests.

"No. I'm not hungry," Silvia declines. Who'd want to be banged on a full stomach?

Zdravko G. pays and takes Silvia to his room. There they take off their clothes and have sex. Zdravko G. can't wait; he's really randy. He only has sex in Bratislava with Slovak whores. In Austria Zdravko G. has to be celibate. Austrian whores are expensive, Slovak whores are cheap. Besides, even if he found one willing, there's nowhere to take her. His hostel, with twenty other Yugoslavs and Turks in his room, wouldn't do. They'd all gawk at him as he screws her. Maybe one of them would want her as well. In Vienna Zdravko is a beggar, just rubbish. A few miles east and Zdravko G. is a somebody and all around him are beggars.

He slowly undresses Silvia who is sitting in the armchair. He's upset when a naked Silvia forces a condom on him.

"Put this on," she says.

"What for?" Zdravko G. wonders aloud.

"I don't want to end up like the last time when you pumped it all into me!" Silvia says.

"I don't like rubber!" Zdravko G. resists. "I promise I'll watch out today! *Aufpassen!*"

"That's not the point, whether you watch out or not," Silvia insists. "I'm on the pill anyway. But nowadays you don't know what you might catch from somebody. It's for your own good, too."

"But Silvia!" Zdravko G. finds it funny and laughs. "We only live once. *Nur einmal*. We're here today and gone tomorrow. I don't want us to fuck in rubber."

"Now you don't sound like a doctor at all!" Silvia frowns. "If you want to get into me, you have to put it on. Either with a rubber, or just with your hand!"

Muttering and grumbling, the Balkan stallion finally gives in to Silvia and she opens her long legs to let him into her embrace.

Zdravko's long abstinence from the Hotel Ambassador is soon demonstrated by a gigantic, superhuman load of sperm that inflates his condom to the size of a baby's head. Zdravko G. gets up and flushes it down the lavatory.

"Why is it so cold here?" He is shivering when he gets back. He feels the radiator. "It's cold!" he says angrily and slips into bed, trembling with cold.

* * *

The heating is on everywhere, even in the cabaret bar. Only in the actual hotel is it cold. And the manager is cold. He sits in his overcoat at a desk covered with condensation, straining his ears. He listens to the heating system. He doesn't miss even the slightest noise from the radiator. Steam rises from his mouth. Occasionally he gets up and eagerly feels the radiators. His plump hands try to detect the faintest sign of warmth. Nothing. It's cold. From a distance he hears furious grumbling in German, English, and other languages. Someone knocks on the door.

"Come in, for God's sake!" The manager shouts and wraps himself in his coat. A French industrialist, here for a convention, enters. Behind him is the face of the Englishman from number twenty-eight and a number of other faces peeking into the manager's office. The manager huddles up. He's quite small now. He nervously rubs his hands. The guests assault him in various languages. The manager can't speak any except his own. It's easy to guess what's bothering them all. The Englishman points to his wet handkerchief, the journalist from Mozambique monotonously intones: "*Bal-lá! Bal-lá!*" The French industrialist takes off his jacket and his shirt and discreetly shows the manager his war wounds from Algeria. A stocky German with a walrus moustache and blond hair stridently pushes through to the manager, showing him photographs of his wife, children, and parents. He lets them circulate. As his trump card, he shows them a picture of his mistress. He has an annoying, pushy smile on his face. "*Ja, ja gut!*" the manager mumbles in confusion, trying to get them all out of his office. If the lawyer were here, he'd explain it all to them. But the pen-pusher is out — somewhere in the city, doing his own deals.

An Arab comes to the doorway. His face is purple; he is desperately shaking with cold. His wild eyes are bloodshot. "*Ya kalb!*" he says. "*Ya mikassah!*"

"*Ja, ja,*" the manager assures him. He pushes all the guests out of the office and locks the door. A plaintive "*Bal-lá! Bal-lá!*" echoes through the hall. The manager sits down in exhaustion and goes on freezing. The frozen guests pace nervously and disturbingly in front of his office. The black Mozambican has fallen silent. Everyone is waiting. The manager can hear their footsteps and foreign, hostile voices. They're planning something. The manager puts his ear to the upholstered door, but can't understand a word. Soon someone knocks on the door and peeks through the keyhole. The manager moves away from the door, and presses his body against the wall. He's afraid. He wants to urinate, but is afraid to leave his office. He decides to urinate on his potted palm. Then he places his armchair so that he can't be seen through the keyhole and dozes off. Soon someone bangs at the door. The cowardly manager jumps up and lets out a frightened scream in a high voice.

"Open up, boss, it's me, Ďula!" says the voice behind the door.

"Is it really you?" the manager asks, after listening at the door for a while.

"It's me all right; let me in!"

"It's cold everywhere, comrade manager!" Ďula shouts in dismay when he enters.

"What are you saying, you dolt," the manager is aghast, and quickly locks up after Ďula. He sits at his desk and stares dully ahead. "It's that stoker, the new one!" he tells Ďula. He'd bet that the stoker is behind it all. That man was suspect from the very start. Maybe he wants to take revenge on the manager for the heavy fine. "Go," he orders, "and tell him that I order him to heat the entire hotel. And he has to fix my radiator too." Then, lost in thought, he starts to fidget with bits of string that he picked up on his way to work. His eyes glaze over, as usual when he is busy with anything especially important. He pays no more attention to Ďula.

* * *

"And what do I care about the manager?" a recumbent Rácz laughs, as he hears what Ďula has to say. "You can fuck with Rácz only once." If the manager needs something, he can come down himself to see Rácz.

Ďula sits down in bewilderment. He's been the manager's flunkey for a long time, but he has never in his life met anyone with the courage to stand up against him. Even the hotel lawyer and assistant managers, however much they loathe the manager or make fun of him behind his back, still show respect and do their best to carry out even his frequently insane orders. And even if they didn't carry them out, they still pretended that they had. Rácz must have someone behind him, if he's so fearless. Ďula has a good nose for that. He always senses a bit earlier than the others which way the wind blows. He has had this weather vane since childhood. He always knows whom to serve and when to switch his allegiance to a new master, without seeming to be treacherous. Rácz has risen in his estimation.

"The manager won't come to see you," says Ďula.

"And why not?" Rácz wants to know.

"He's afraid of you... chief," says Ďula.

"So he's afraid of me?" Rácz mulls over Ďula's admission.

"But I'll have to tell him something... sir," Ďula insists, when he sees that Rácz has closed his eyes again.

"The pipes are blocked," mumbles the stoker, half asleep. "It'll have to wait," he adds. He pays no more attention to the driver.

"Good, I'll pass on the message," says Ďula and runs up the stairs.

Rácz sleeps in peace. A little later he sits up, startled, as he senses that he's not alone in the boiler-room. Ďula is gone, and in his place some foreigner stands there awkwardly. "What do you want?" Rácz barks at him from his bench and, annoyed, searches for his socks. The Englishman from number twenty-eight stares at the sleepy bully uncertainly. His fingers are blue with cold. He tries in vain to explain why he's come to the boiler-room. "I don't understand," Rácz stubbornly repeats and shakes his head furiously. He listens carefully to sentences in an unknown language, but when the Englishman falls silent, ending with a question mark and a plea in his eyes, Rácz helplessly spreads his arms. "Who the hell can understand you?" he says. "Why haven't you learnt to talk like us?"

The foreigner can't believe that someone could be so slow on the uptake. He is beginning to suspect that the stocky stoker is pretending. He hands him a carton of Benson & Hedges. Now Rácz can understand. He puts the cigarettes on the battered table and ambles off to find his shoes. The Englishman gestures that he's cold. Something has to be done. Rácz lights up a Benson & Hedges and, with a cigarette in his mouth, the smoke making him screw up his eyes, he puts on his shoes. He understands. It's all clear to him now. He's enjoying the cigarette. He scans the cigarette name on the box. Ben-son et he-gyesh. Fine, yet strong. Just right. These are the cigarettes that Rácz will smoke from now on. The Englishman runs off, but is soon back. He brings the moustached German and his pictures, the angry Arab, and the African monotonously repeating *Bal-lá! Bal-lá!* They all look uncomfortable. They are embarrassed. Rácz feels sorry for them. He gives in to greed. After all, they can't be blamed, he concludes in a conciliatory mood. If they give him presents, then, fine! Let them have heating! It's the manager who has to be punished. Rácz won't hesitate, he won't give in to empty, cowardly pity. But these people are not to blame.

The foreigners admire the boiler-room equipment for a while. Rácz shows them with signs and gestures where the problem lies. The visitors nod. Then they take gifts out of their pockets. There is a hundred-mark note from the German, with a carton of cigarettes. By some miracle he has found out Rácz's favourite brand. The Arab wants to show his appreciation with some strange thick-rolled cigarettes with an unusual green tobacco and a fifty-dollar bill. His gestures stress that he is freezing. The African gives him nothing; he is stingy and, anyway, has nothing to give. He draws attention to his situation by whining, and begs for help. Rácz can't take his eyes off him. He's never seen a black man in his life.

After focussing his thoughts for a while, he sets off for the hotel. Just the way he is, in his dirty dungarees. No one gets in his way, no one tries to throw him out. The freezing employees see him as their Messiah. "Can you do anything about it?" The receptionist's teeth are chattering. Rácz is silent for a long time. He downs a shot of vodka brought to him on a salver, and turns the empty glass around in contemplation. "Ah," he says and then gives the receptionist a long hard gaze.

From the staff room and the changing room of the reception area comes the porter Torontál's heavy cough. He has caught pneumonia from eagerly hanging around the cold reception area. The liftboy and two waiters from the day bar had to pry his greedy fingers from the mahogany reception desk by force. They carried him to the staff room, like a piece of luggage, to die. The staff room serves as a smoking room for the receptionist, his assistants and lift boys. The men sit in the corner, smoke, and talk in hushed voices. Occasionally they take a look at Torontál. The old man is lying on the floor with his big nose pointing up and his eyes glazed over. His throat rattles and hisses. The men check their watches, quickly put out their cigarettes, button up their jackets and tie their loosened bow-ties. They go back to work. The old man is left on his own. Nobody likes him; they're all waiting for him to expire.

The doorman smiles nervously at Rácz. The assistant manager offers him a cigarette. "I've got my own," says the stoker dryly and takes out a Benson & Hedges given him by the Englishman. A collective unsynchronized clicking of lighters, with gas hissing in various tones, and also a belated hysterical, panicky, hopeless striking of match against matchbox, descends like a tornado on the tip of the long cigarette casually hanging from his mouth. Rácz takes a mighty draw. "Well, let's do it," he decides.

The assistant manager himself summons the lift, as if he wanted to cancel the injustice committed at the scene.

Rácz walks through the rooms, pretending to fix radiators. He bangs on them, listens to their sound. He shakes his head, seemingly worried. They can all see that he is doing his best. He lies down close to the radiators and performs thousands of unnecessary actions. In each room he gets something. The German couple gives him a picture of the Pope; a grey-haired Canadian takes a five-hundred-crown note from his wallet. A young Italian furtively hands him a pornographic magazine showing four men quartering a live schoolgirl. A dishevelled long-nosed American violinist gives him a hundred-dollar bill. It all depends how badly they are shivering and freezing.

Most of the rooms are empty. The guests are keeping away from the building. Rácz has taken a liking to playing the saviour. "I don't think," he tells the assistant manager while putting the hundred-dollar bill into his wallet, "that the heating will be back on today. Tell them all I'll have to come back tomorrow. I'm doing this in my free time. I'm not getting paid for this. Tell them what I said. It is up to them if they want to have heating or not."

The assistant manager lowers his eyes. He nods.

"I'm relying on you," Rácz adds. "If you don't let me down, you'll have all the heating you could dream of. But if you let me down me, then I can't guarantee anything…"

Rácz enjoys looking at the gifts from the freezing guests. They forced Rácz to take these things. He hasn't asked for a thing. A giver is a fool, but a refuser is an even bigger fool. And, anyway, hasn't Rácz earned it? He's been working here almost four months without pay. Thankfully, he doesn't have to pay for his food. Who gives Rácz anything?

From the laundry room window Ribana grins at him. Rácz pretends he hasn't seen her. He takes a glass bowl and spoon from the table and approaches the soup pot. The chef gives him a ladle: "Bon appétit, boss," he tells him obsequiously.

"You don't give a shit about my appetite," says Rácz indifferently and stirs the thick, fragrant stock.

* * *

The next day by lunch time there is heating everywhere. Rácz carries off downstairs into his cubbyhole windcheaters, jeans, cartons of American cigarettes, pornographic magazines, chocolates, sports bags, French cosmetics, chewing gum, bundles of *deutschmarks*, francs, dollars, and pounds sterling. Every guest has given him something, or has left gifts for him on the bed in their room.

After a freezing night everyone considers Rácz a saviour. He is all over the hotel. You can meet him in the halls dragging iron rods or wires about. Or he needs a bucket, or somebody to hold a nut. Everybody takes a liking to him. The assistant manager follows him like a dog and wants to be on first name terms. Rácz ignores him. "Everyone should know their place," he finally declares. The assistant manager is puzzled as to what he means. The waiters serve Rácz hot tea and rum. When he's made a big enough impression on them, he crawls back to his boiler-room and finally opens the valves he closed. Soon everyone is cosy. The receptionist takes the coat off his shoulders. The guests smile. Torontál gets up from the couch and goes for a pee. Then he returns and wraps himself in a blanket. He feels better. He'll take another day or two and will be back at the reception. His hands are itching in anticipation of leather suitcase and bag handles. He wants to live and be useful a little bit longer.

Rácz is counting his foreign money and putting it at the bottom of his suitcase when Silvia enters. When she notices the colourful banknotes that the stoker has stowed away in the suitcase, her eyes begin to shine.

"Let's do it really quickly today, okay?" Silvia says. "We're rehearsing a new show. I won't undress, okay?" Rácz doesn't care. He gets up and unzips his fly. Silvia takes off her panties, lifts her skirt and, gripping the door jambs, offers her behind to Rácz. The stoker enters her and writhes for a while, holding her hips tightly. Soon his face stiffens and a mighty sigh escapes his lips.

They both adjust their clothing. "What are you going to do with the foreign currency?" Silvia asks with studied indifference.

Rácz doesn't answer. He doesn't know, anyway. "What should I do?" he asks after a pause. "Next time you come, I'll give you some. I don't care about money. Back in the village I often paid for everyone in the pub."

Silvia smiles. "Tell the receptionist when you need me. He'll get me even when I'm at home. Or call me. You want my number?"

"Why should I call you?" Rácz shrugs. "I'll tell the receptionist."

Rácz has never in his life used a phone. Not even when he was in the army. When he was on guard duty, he would walk around the ringing phone suspiciously, but he never answered it.

Silvia leaves. Rácz reaches into a heap of Western goods spread on the table in his cubbyhole and takes a bottle of alcohol. He reads the label following the letters on the black paper with his finger: Chivas Regal Scotch Whisky. Oh well, let's try this *Heevash Reygahl*, he decides. He looks for the tin coffee cup.

* * *

The weather is bitterly cold. Snow has been falling at night. There are snowdrifts three feet high. The hotel is packed with guests. The temperature has dropped. The thermometer often drops below minus thirty. When the wind blows through the empty night streets, it gathers terrific speed. It ravages the courtyard like a tornado and overturns the dustbins.

Rácz relishes his importance. Thoroughly grimy with coal and oil, he walks through the hotel. Willy-nilly, everyone praises him.

Only the manager's radiator still doesn't work. It's snowing outside. The manager is freezing in his office. His face is glued to the window as he watches the goings-on in the courtyard and in front of the boiler-room. The furniture in his office is all cracked. He has brought in an electric hob from home. He warms himself over it. There are blisters on his hands and his back is freezing. He runs around the hotel in a tracksuit and a fur hat tied under his chin. He moves with his back sliding along the walls, carefully looking around corners. He is afraid of the wild stoker. He had made a mistake. And he wanted to put it right. He set out several times to see Rácz to apologize and say that he was cancelling the punishment. But each time in front of the iron door to the boiler-room he was overcome by fear and went back to his office. He is always hanging about in the vestibule, getting warm. Torontál doesn't like it, fearing that the manager is after his job. The unhappy senile old man's angry shouts send the manager back to his freezing office. Everyone is pointing a finger at him.

In his office, the manager unzips a sleeping bag and sits in it at his desk with an expression of hopelessness on his face. Icicles hang down from the ceiling. The manager's fingers ache with cold; it has got under his nails. Even a triple layer of winter underwear is useless in this cold.

Rácz has become the star of the hotel. Everybody bows to him. Ďula calls him "chief". The hotel lawyer calls him "Mister Rácz." They know that Rácz hates the manager and so they all avoid the manager, or pretend they can't see him. Nobody wants to be compromised by being seen talking to a condemned man. Desperation has given the manager a tic round his mouth and face. He trembles and his teeth chatter even in the warmth of his home. He doesn't make sense when he talks. His wife is beginning to distance herself from him. She's decided to take a lover, and is trying to do something about it. The manager can't get it up any more.

Unlike the manager, the stoker has frequent hard-ons. And Silvia also sees him frequently. Ribana shouts at him, but he ignores her. He's aiming higher. He sits in his boiler-room and smokes American cigarettes. He uses lemon soap. For aftershave, he pats Cologne N° 1148 on his face. He chews gum. When he can't taste it any more, he spits it out and unwraps another piece.

Occasionally, he checks the guest book at the reception desk. Nobody minds, and people bow to him while he's looking at it. When Rácz sees that a guest has moved out, he enters the empty room and turns off the radiator. He'll turn it on only when the guest, informed by other guests or by the staff, pays a suitable sum, or offers a gift of appropriate value.

* * *

Urban tries to make a living any way he can. He has to live. He almost never comes to work. His salary is small, so what do they want from him? He works only as much as they pay him. From time to time he dresses a shop window, but not often. He works only when inspiration seizes him. He spends the mornings in a white coat in view of the watchful passers-by. He does not think of himself as an ordinary artist. He graduated from an applied arts college, but he is a life artist. He did not complete theory of culture at university. He lives in an artist's attic studio in the old town. In summer he hustles in the centre, buying and selling foreign currency.

You can live well doing this. Then the season ends. There's no business in winter, because few tourists show up. People who come on business need a receipt. They wouldn't change money with him. In winter, Urban lives modestly. But he's not destitute. He ekes a living moonlighting as a taxi driver. He criss-crosses the frozen snowbound city at night. Drunken freezing people coming out of the clubs often wait in vain for a licensed taxi. There aren't any. But Urban shows up and gladly takes them. He charges according to distance, the temperature outside and the alcohol content of the passenger's blood. If the passenger's very drunk, Video Urban lets him pay twice: at the beginning and at the end of his trip. The drunk is happy, so is Urban. He's not hurting anyone. He's simply pursuing his quarry.

Urban is in the middle of adjusting a neatly shaped fold on a roll of fabric when someone knocks on the shop window. Urban gets up and looks behind him. On the pavement he sees the stoker trying to tell him something. "What is it?" Urban asks.

"Come down and see me!" Rácz shouts. "When you're free!"

Urban nods. "When I finish this," he shouts through the window. "I've still got the Christmas decorations to hang." He realises that Rácz wants to unload his seven hundred marks. Oh well, Urban will buy them if the price is right. He can always make a profit on them. Urban feels quite pleased.

Rácz is waiting for him in the boiler-room with a pile of foreign currency on the table. "Will you have something? Whisky *Heevash Reygahl*? *Benson and Hegyesh* cigarette? The notes are here on the table." Rácz needs to sell them. "There's a list on this bit of paper." Next to the paper is an estimate of what they'd fetch according to the bank rate. Rácz is no fool. All you have to do is to buy the Friday newspaper. Rácz could insist on the bank rate, but he knows that Urban needs his cut, too. He'll be happy to get X crowns.

"How much?" Video Urban asks: he thinks he must have misheard. Rácz repeats the sum.

Urban is ready to do the deal immediately. He gets out his wallet and looks into it. Rácz drinks his whisky and puts the tin cup down on the table. Of course, Rácz is no idiot. Yes, Urban heard right. X crowns. Rácz knows it's a very good deal. Urban can count on him for more foreign currency in the future. Rácz is not interested how much Urban sells the money for or what he does with it. That's Urban's business. But Rácz needs a favour. Rácz is a stranger here. He needs Urban to tell him from time to time what people want, what everyone's after, what's in short supply. Rácz will get it and Urban will sell it. No, Rácz stresses, he's not talking about stolen goods. It's just that Rácz has no time to get information or tip-offs; he's too busy working.

Urban nods, he understands. It sounds like a good idea. But what are the currency dealers going to say? Not the small fry, like Urban. He's thinking of the big currency dealers: Harry, Fedor, Khunt, and mainly the Albanians.

"Albanians?" Rácz wants to know: "Who are they?"

Urban explains. "They're Yugoslav Albanians. The Ambassador is teeming with them. All the big foreign currency deals, cigarette smuggling and so on is done by them. You don't want to tread on their toes. And they're police grasses; otherwise they couldn't do their deals so calmly and boldly in broad daylight. They're trouble!" Urban stresses the last point.

Rácz thinks hard. Then he makes his decision. "Screw them," he says. "We'll do as we like and we won't worry about them. You can do a deal with anyone. First we'll try the nice way!" Rácz says and clenches his fist until his hair stands on end. "Well, what do you say?" he asks, pretending to lose patience. "Are you in or out?" Urban can't resist this tempting offer. He puts the cash Rácz asked for on the table. "Can I rely on you?" Rácz asks as he counts the money.

"Sure," says Urban, "I'll tell you the moment I know anything. What would you like to know?"

"Let me know, let's say," Rácz explains, "about car spares. Or when someone needs a leather jacket, or something. Understand?" Urban nods. Rácz gets up. The audience is over. He has to go to the hotel, and sort out a few things. They can't do anything without Rácz.

Silvia needs money. She has savings, but is still short. She wants to buy a used car, a white Fiat Uno. Rácz shakes his head. He doesn't lend money, he needs it himself. He wants to go into business. But he will give her advice. Be nice to Rácz, very nice, and she'll gradually save up the money. Anyway, Rácz thinks that Silvia should have saved more than she has. He's often watched her through the cellar window coming and going, he adds, with a hint of bitterness. "What about the gypsy?"

"He's not a gypsy!" Silvia counters. "He's a doctor from Vienna."

"I'd no idea the Viennese look like gypsies," Rácz says. "But he could easily help you buy a car if he's a doctor."

"We could go on trips to the country," Silvia tries to tempt the stoker.

"I don't go on trips!" Rácz gets worked up. "I get enough running round the boiler-room and hotel." Rácz does not travel anywhere. He hates travelling.

"What's the furthest you've travelled?" asks Silvia.

"All the way here," says the stoker, "to this effing city."

"But going by car is different," the prostitute objects.

"It's all the same, by car or plane," the stoker declares. Rácz never travels. He's too busy working. He's got duties. He came here to make money, so he will. Silvia would love to get money out of him, wouldn't she? Well, be nicer to Rácz and she'll get more money, too.

Anyway, Rácz feels he's spending too much, as it is. Every time warnings come from his inner voice, Rácz silences them: you only live once. Yes, perhaps the city lights have blinded him. Who wouldn't they blind? He's never known this sort of life. When he goes back home and marries Eržika, he'll have only memories left. Then he will work, bring up his children, and on Sundays go to church and a football game. On Friday nights he will go to the pub for a beer and a shot of spirits. Everyone will respect him. He knows all about the city and nightlife. Don't anyone try to tell him about them. After all, he's even had a strip-tease dancer! They'll all envy him. They've never in their lives experienced anything like that and never will. Rácz can't complain about Kišš. If it weren't for the butcher's stubbornness, Rácz would never have even seen the city. But still, he shouldn't spend so much. He hasn't saved up anything. And he could have. On the other hand, you can't say that he's wasted his time. He's made investments. After all, he had to get to know the sleazy scene at the Ambassador hotel, so as to find his way about.

Now Rácz no longer eats leftovers. Every day he eats breakfast, lunch and dinner right in the hotel restaurant. He enters with panache: in his work boots, a bag full of tools over his shoulder. He has his own place. It's reserved for him. The waiters rush to him. Rácz slurps and tears wildly at his meat. With greasy fingers he takes the cork out of a bottle of Chateau Valtice Reserve, he takes a brief look to see how much is in the bottle, and pours it down his mouth. He stomps his boots wildly on the floor. All the different cutlery round his plate drives him berserk. He never uses anything but a spoon. Waiters hover over him, passing him pepper, salads, meat, and ketchup. The entire staff surrounds his table. The guests are now used to it. They're happy to be kept waiting. The sight of Rácz at table is not easily forgotten. Only new, inexperienced guests nervously murmur and click their fingers for service. Others try to stop them. Including the terrified personnel. They all look at Rácz with fear, as he wrestles with boar's head in rosehip sauce. If the impatient diners aren't stopped in time, Rácz will be disturbed and, from a table littered with spilled sauce, wine, and broken glass, turn to fix the newcomers with a look that they are unlikely ever to forget. He has only to say a word to the headwaiter and that guest will not be served. He might as well clear off, wherever he pleases. If anyone angers Rácz, everybody suffers. If they don't want to freeze, they'll have to pay again.

* * *

The mall between the Ambassador restaurant and the shops serves as the gypsies' headquarters. They stand and sit there from morning till night, surrounded by their womenfolk and screeching children. They have a good life. Their organisms, genetically designed for roaming free over the wide steppes, for quick travel and modest nourishment with periods of famine, have adapted badly to a sudden change in lifestyle, and they have become fat, monstrously so. All the male and female gypsies doing business in front of the Ambassador are terribly obese. Like shapeless whales, gasping for breath, eyes popping, they move clumsily to and fro. They're on the lookout for a tourist sufficiently stingy and foolish enough to do a deal with them. They'll offer him more than other currency dealers. Except they pay in Polish zloty, not Czechoslovak crowns. Probably, the foreigner will notice his mistake only later, usually in his car in the car park, bragging to his wife about the wonderful deal he got. Sometimes, however, the mistake is not discovered until he tries to pay in a restaurant or shop.

The furious foreigner will run back into the mall. The almond-eyed gypsies will give him a sympathetic look. No, it wasn't one of them, they're good gypsies. They would have known! They won't stand for people like that, they're good gypsies. It must have been one of the bad gypsies. What did he look like?

The foreigner hesitates. They all look so similar that they can't be told apart. Like eggs. Each one is fat, with a moustache, dressed in an expensive leather jacket and a green hat with a boar-bristle tassel. All the gypsy women are huge, noisy, with loudly painted faces and dyed hair. They don't know each other that well. The foreigner should give them his address. When they find out who that cheat was, the good gypsies will force him to give it all back. They'll send it to the foreigner. But why is the foreigner yelling at them, they're good gypsies? He wouldn't want the good gypsies to call for police protection? They've met racists like him before! They're good gypsies and only want to help. But they can see the foreigner hates their race. So he'd better go away. They won't have anything to do with him.

The gypsy children scurry about under their feet. When they grow up a bit, they get bored with the mall, which is illuminated only by light from the shops and by blinding neon tubes, only half of which work. They need to run around, to get fresh air. While they ask for directions to some imaginary point from any passer-by they encounter, they inconspicuously relieve him of his wallet, watch, rings and chains. The passer-by will never cease to be amazed by the incident.

When a foreigner in a car or a bus enters the car park, gypsy women race off from the mall. They run at breakneck speed, some even lose their shoes in the effort and have to go back for them. Sometimes they fight among themselves, tear each other's hair out, and bite each other. The children gawk at them and scream in shrill voices. The gypsy men stand around, dignified in their obesity. In the summer they wear Hawaiian shirts outside their trousers, in winter they prefer expensive fine leather jackets. Fur coats are now out of fashion. (They made them look like bears going into hibernation.) They holler at each other in Romany. Sometimes they scream so loudly that their eyes seem to pop from their olive faces. When they argue about money, customers in the shops have to speak louder to be heard. Sometimes the gypsies fight. Often they use knives. The cops are in with them. The gypsies pay them off and inform on non-gypsy currency dealers.

Freddy Piggybank licks the gypsies' arses. He's afraid of them. When they park their beaten up Russian Ladas in his car park, he doesn't charge them. Piggybank just smiles and waves them in, though he keeps quietly plotting. His visions are full of crematoria, forced-labour camps, and sterilizing adult gypsies using a couple of bricks. He spends whole days in the parking lot, often putting in sixteen-hour days. He's a stingy capitalist. Greedy. He has no use for free time. What for? He has no girlfriend; he's fat and stupid. Besides, he's balding and has bad breath. When he explains something to somebody, he stands very close. He lives in a dirty white camping trailer on the parking lot. He has a chair, a table, and a narrow bunk there. Electricity comes via a cable from the hotel. There's a TV antenna on the trailer roof. Piggybank also has a double hotplate. He rarely feels like going home to his even stingier parents, who always ask him for money; he prefers to stay in the lot. He has to be there in the morning anyway. He needs the money. It's hard to see what for; he either walks everywhere or takes a tram, he wears cheap clothes from a shop for the bigger man and habitually stuffs himself with the cheapest tins of sausages and beans.

On Friday nights Yugoslav *Gastarbeiter* from Vienna come to let off steam. Sometimes even Austrians take the opportunity for fun with cheap Slovak whores. In the nightclub Cabaret they perform an erotic show *Secrets of the Night*, while in the day bar there's a disco dance. Piggybank stays in the car park all night. Yawning and sleepy, he gets money for his nocturnal vigil. He warms up his sausages and beans, and quenches his hunger while watching television. Around midnight, his eyes begin to close behind his thick prescription lenses. He locks himself in the trailer, turns the light off and lies down on his narrow bed. Nothing will disturb his deep sleep. He only wakes up about six when the empty streets begin to reverberate with rumbling trams.

Occasionally, mostly in the summer, after seeing a lot of prostitutes and other women in tight miniskirts, Piggybank pulls down the blind, reaches for some well used pornographic magazines hidden in the trailer and masturbates. That's the sum total of his love life. He hasn't been himself ever since Video Urban showed him an Italian magazine, borrowed from the stoker, depicting an underage girl being tortured. He'd like to have bought the magazine on the spot, but was too embarrassed to suggest it. He doesn't know the stoker that well, though they say hello to each other. Piggybank wouldn't want him to think that he was a sadist. He wouldn't want him to think that the magazine was all that important. Piggybank is thirty and is still single. He has a blond moustache on his lip. He's never had a woman in his life. Who'd want him? And he's quite fussy: he wouldn't go out with just anyone. He wants a perfect woman. He doesn't realise that perfect women are all taken, either by perfect men, or because they've become whores. A whore would go out with him, but he'd have to pay for it. But he wouldn't pay for it. One day he's sure to get a free roll in the hay! He often fantasizes in his free time: a whore arrives in a car. Preferably the tall, blonde one, but it could be her friend, Edita, the dyed gypsy. They both dance in the cabaret and have good bodies, so it doesn't matter which. The whore will pay for two hours' parking. That makes four crowns. For three hours it is ten crowns. Still more for each additional hour. But the blonde comes late at night. Piggybank will wait for her behind the window. Then he'll get his bag and leave the trailer. "Lady," he will address her, "you paid up till eleven in the morning and now it is one o'clock after midnight." "Yes," the whore will say, "I am a bit late. How much do I owe you?" "Well, the difference is one hundred and thirty-six crowns," Piggybank will say." –

"That much?" the whore will sigh. "Yes," Piggybank will confirm victoriously, reciting the parking fees. "But can't we come to some arrangement?" the whore will ask, pretending to be naïve. Piggybank will point silently to the trailer. The blonde will smile coquettishly, get out of her car and walk, swinging her hips, her extra long legs in front of Piggybank. They'll lock themselves in the trailer and have wild sex. Piggybank will do anything he wants with her. The prostitute will leave the trailer early in the morning. On all fours. Her whole body will ache. Above all, she'll fall madly in love with the parking attendant. A love affair will begin.

Piggybank is dreaming. Yes, that would be lovely. Except no prostitute will ever park in his car park. They all use taxis. And Piggybank knows that, even if it came to this, a prostitute would rather pay. What's a hundred and thirty-six crowns to a prostitute? Even he would rather take the money. Long legs or not, thighs or no thighs, he can always slap the bishop, though nobody pays him for it.

The gypsies in the mall found out in the summer how much the fat parking attendant makes. The car park was always full and Piggybank never let anyone leave without paying a fine for over-staying. And so, one hot day, they paid him a visit. After a few introductory phrases, Berki came to the point. "You stay here overnight quite often, don't you?" Other gypsies were hanging around nearby in the shade of a sycamore, fanning themselves with newspapers.

"I do," Piggybank said.

"And are you guarding or sleeping?" Berki inquired.

"Guarding," Piggybank declared confidently.

Berki nodded as if that was a fact that he already knew and didn't doubt, but just wanted confirmed for the other gypsies.

"So you take money even at night?"

"Of course," Piggybank said and unwittingly stroked the red money bag hanging on his belly.

"No, you don't guard at night!" Berki laughed victoriously and all the other gypsies joined in the laughter. Even Piggybank laughed, as he had no idea what the gypsies were getting at. "Just the other day we took a look at you," Berki continued, "at night. You were snoozing."

"I do doze off sometimes," admitted Piggybank.

"And what if you had something stolen?" Berki pounced.

"That can't happen," said Piggybank. "I sleep so lightly that..."

"No, you don't," Berki contradicted him. He nodded to a young gypsy who took from under the colourful folds of his Hawaiian shirt a couple of windscreen wipers. "Look," Berki said, "this is what we took from you last night. We're giving them back. We're good gypsies. When the Yugo from Vienna shows up, the one in the orange Opel, give them back to him. We just wanted to test you."

Piggybank stared at them in shock. It was lucky that Zdravko G. hadn't noticed! The gypsies were enjoying the attendant's embarrassment.

"And just you think," Berki went on, "what if somebody worked the parked cars over on Friday night, and took antennas, windshield wipers, hub caps. What would you do?" Piggybank was speechless with shock. "Fortunately," Berki stressed, "we're good gypsies here. We'll guard the lot for you at night. Of course, you'll have to share the parking fees with us. We know how much you take." Berki named the approximate amount and while Piggybank got over his shock at the precision of the gypsy's guess, Berki continued: "Let's say you give us a third. Fair, isn't it?"

"What?" the attendant exclaimed, horrified. "You want a third of my money?" He couldn't believe his ears.

"You've got it wrong," said Berki, and the other gypsies under the sycamore murmured in approval, nodding their heads and fanning themselves with newspapers. "We only want our money, the share we'll earn honestly guarding your car park. We could even save your life. What if a bad gypsy comes in the night? You can't tell what he might decide to do. He might bring petrol, matches, and burn you alive in your trailer. If you share the takings with us, we'll protect you. We're good gypsies. You can rely on us."

Piggybank wouldn't listen to them any more. He angrily told them to go to hell. Piggybank could keep watch by himself. He didn't need anyone.

The gypsies watched him calmly, almost pitifully. Very well, then: they, the good gypsies, had tried to be helpful, but he shouldn't be surprised if something happened.

That night Piggybank brewed some strong coffee and decided to stay up. He was on the lookout. But around midnight his head slumped and he nodded off, still sitting in his chair. By morning the bad gypsies had stolen the wipers, antennas and hubcaps from all the parked vehicles. Piggybank was aghast. The good gypsies were right! Luckily, none of the customers, buoyed up by their memories of cheap Slovak whores, noticed anything missing. Piggybank sighed with relief. If anyone shows up with a claim, he'll send them packing. Late claims cannot be accepted! Imagine Piggybank paying for damage that might have occurred somewhere else: in the street, in another parking lot, and so on.

This easy resolution of a seemingly desperate situation gave Piggy-bank confidence. When Berki showed up again, Piggybank, surprised by his own courage, threw him out. Fear for his money triumphed over fear of the gypsies.

The next weekend night the guard was again sound asleep after even less of an effort to keep awake. He slept soundly, after taking his trousers off and stretching out on his narrow bunk. That was why he heard no engine noise and saw no lights in the car park. Somebody was walking around the trailer. Hushed voices were talking. Then there was a metallic sound and the trailer shook. Piggybank did not wake up even when an unknown car gathered speed. Piggybank slept soundly even when the trailer bumped over the city's potholes and when it passed the last of the city street lights and sped southwards. On the contrary, the monotonous noise of the engine and the rocking kept him asleep, so he plunged ever deeper into a world of dreams.

He woke up suddenly at about six. His eyes closed, he was wondering why he couldn't hear the morning trams rumble as they rolled round the Hotel Ambassador. No cars were speeding down the main street either, and there were no voices of pedestrians to be heard through the thin fibreboard wall of the trailer. Piggybank leapt out of his bunk. He flung the trailer door open and was stupefied. The trailer was all on its own in the middle of a field of yellow rape. The only sound to be heard was a lark's malicious trill of joy in the blue sky. This was soon accompanied by Piggybank's howls, expressing wild hatred of this disagreeable surprise and fear of an unknown environment.

It took a good week for the trailer to be got back to its place in front of the Hotel Ambassador. When Berki came to ask the attendant, who had lost weight, what those bad gypsies had done, he got his first payment right away.

"I knew that you couldn't manage without us," said Berki, putting the thousand-crown bills in his wallet. "We're good gypsies, we'll protect you. The bad gypsies are afraid of us."

And so Freddy Piggybank and the good gypsies became friends through thick or thin.

* * *

Rácz also needs money, a lot of it. He counts his cash every night. He enjoys this ritual. All day he looks forward to it. Sometimes he counts his money twice, just for the fun of it. Marriage to Eržika has now become a rather vague misty goal in a distant future; he doesn't think about it. He now saves for her just out of habit. His thoughts are now occupied by another woman: Silvia. She has got right under his skin. He is jealous of her and he hates her. He knows she's a whore, and that torments him. Every time she comes to him, he feels like sniffing her for traces of other men. Sometimes he can't hold back and gives her a slap. Or even two. Silvia gets her own back. She's mean and snide. She demands more and more. On the other hand, the fact that you can't talk to Rácz about anything, except business deals and money, gets on her nerves. He has no hobbies. He never goes into town. He feels good in the boiler-room and in the hotel, in his overalls and work boots, staying within an area that he knows inside out and where there are almost no surprises. But the money makes it bearable, Silvia tells herself all the time. If only he weren't so wild and rough. A lad who used to be modest and not very bright has turned into a tyrant. There's always an arrogant and bossy smile on his face. Everybody bows down to him. He likes it. Recently he's started to refer to himself in the third person: Rácz doesn't want that, Rácz never lends money, Rácz this, Rácz that. He takes Silvia without the slightest feeling or tenderness. This roughness upsets Silvia the most. But she's used to far worse treatment. Rácz acts without any refinement or charm. He takes her as if he were at home in the village, saddling or harnessing a mare. Sometimes he bites her. Sometimes he punches her. When he comes, he rolls over and lights up. When the stoker does that, he gets on her nerves more than anyone. So he can pay for it!

Rácz can't give her up. Eržika has receded into the background. He can't even remember what she looks like any more. She's become a colourless faded photograph with a name, but no face. She exists for him only in the remote past and vague future. Rácz knows that Silvia dislikes him. That irritates him. He takes it out on her. He pinches her viciously. She is, after all, his property. He owns her, just as he owns a carton of American cigarettes lying on the rickety battered table. He knows very well that she puts up with constant humiliation from him only for the money. Nevertheless, when he hits her, he feels pangs of remorse. He doesn't hesitate to hand out money in compensation. Silvia does not flinch at his blows. She knows that the more he hurts her, the more emotional he gets and the more he dishes out afterwards. When Rácz wants her to shout, she shouts. When he wants her to shut up, she is quiet.

The stoker is jealous. He doesn't want her to go with other men. He yells: "Doesn't Rácz give you enough money?" He appeals to her femininity: "Doesn't Rácz satisfy you?" Silvia can only laugh at that.

She's never had an orgasm with him. Not even the very first time. That's something it doesn't even occur to her to think about. After all, that's not the aim of the exercise.

Silvia has to break off all her previous relationships. She has even had to give up her steady customers. Rácz keeps watch on her for days on end. Silvia is afraid of what he'll say when Zdravko G. shows up. But fortunately Zdravko isn't coming any more. Sometimes Silvia feels that all this will drive her mad. Again and again, she assures herself that she'll get as much money out of Rácz as she can, and when she has enough, she'll drop him. When she gets enough money, or when she finds the stoker too revolting to bear. Silvia knows that Rácz's money is hard-earned. But she hasn't had enough yet. Rácz pays well. Silvia's lifestyle has been turned upside down. All that remains of her former life are morning rehearsals and night performances. The room she rents on the other side of town is empty most of the week. She spends her time with Rácz; she lets him have sex with her, listens to his speeches and angry outbursts. As a passive spectator, she takes part in his business deals.

Suddenly she can no longer bear it. She doesn't go out anywhere. She spends entire days lying at home, staring at the ceiling. Or sitting by the window, watching children playing in the sandpit. Occasionally, Edita comes around to tell her what's new. Zdravko G. showed up. He asked after Silvia. When he heard she was away on holiday, he took up with Wanda the Trucker and spent the whole weekend with her. There was a big raid two days ago. They picked up a lot of blokes. Apparently, the gypsies ratted on them. But Berki said that was all lies. Silvia only pretends to listen. When Edita begins to get too pushy, she gets up and locks the door so that the landlady won't burst in. She meekly lets herself be undressed and put to bed. Her eyes closed, she submits to her friend's caresses. After a while she comes to life. She changes position and repeats Edita's pleasuring. It's not too long before they both come together.

Sometimes Silvia lies in bed, wondering how to get away from Rácz. She knows that the stoker would never come and fetch her. She is not afraid that one day he might kick the door in, grab her by the arm and drag her back to his place in the Hotel Ambassador. Silvia is afraid of herself. She knows that she will never be able to resist money. Money is what she prizes most: it's never let her down. That's how it is and always has been, ever since as a schoolgirl she let older boys touch her for five crowns, so as to top up the modest pocket money her parents gave her. There wasn't much to touch then, but the boys were excited just by the idea of being allowed to touch her. And today she has made it all the way here. *Swan Lake* isn't going to happen. Rácz really doesn't have to come looking for her. Rácz will calmly and coolly wait for her to come of her own accord. Rácz will wait with a smile.

* * *

One night Rácz wakes up on his bench. He can hear a quiet rustling. He lies for a while, listening, and then he gets up, grabs a poker and goes after the noise. Ever since he's kept money and goods in his cubbyhole, he's been careful. He's had bars put in everywhere; Ďula found a welder. When he enters the dark corridor, two unknown fat men rush him. The fight doesn't last long. The panting intruders stand no chance against the fast-moving, square-cut stoker who fights viciously and mercilessly in defence of his property. He punches both fat men to the ground. They are stretched out on the floor with their eyes closed. He ties them up tightly with telephone wire and with an enormous effort drags them to the boiler-room. There he gets a better look at them. He knows their faces: they're gypsies from the mall. He slaps them harshly to bring them back to life. They stop pretending to be dead and look at him out of the corner of their eyes. The stoker begins with an interrogation. He menaces them with a white-hot poker. What were they looking for here?

One of the gypsies licks his lips. They're good gypsies, they were coming back from the Ambassador bar and lost their way. They got lost.

Yes, they somehow got confused, the other gypsy joins in. Where are they anyway?

Rácz pulls the poker from the furnace and casually runs it over the gypsy's leather jacket. The leather scorches and smokes.

"Ouch, what are you doing?" the gypsy shouts. A smell of burning fills the boiler-room.

"It won't hurt the jacket," says Rácz. "But it'll hurt you."

Yes, they came to steal, Berki admits. They'd heard that the stoker was hiding a lot of money, gold, jewellery, and other nice useful things. Berki had no idea what had got into them. But now that they'd confessed honestly, the stoker ought to let them go.

Who told them that Rácz had gold and foreign currency hidden away? Rácz is livid.

Unfortunately, they can't answer that question. Nobody told them. Everyone says so, though. Everybody respects Rácz. They all consider him a rich and powerful man. They're all for him. Berki can't understand how they, the gypsies, could ever have done such a thing.

Šípoš, the other gypsy, says that the only thing he can say in his defence is that he has a swinish character.

Both gypsies start to swear that they'll never steal again as long as they live. They'll even give up hustling. They'll both find work as soon as he lets them go and will start to live an honest life. Berki will even go to night school as well as work.

They fall silent under the threat of the poker. Rácz sadistically enjoys their fear. He is touchy about his property and the wealth that he has acquired with his brains and hands. He knows how to step up his activity and increase his wealth. The boiler-room is too small for him. He has to rise to the surface of the earth and penetrate the circles round the Hotel Ambassador. Stoking is now a hindrance to him. Rácz needs to find someone to do the work for him. By hook or by crook.

Both gypsies agree enthusiastically. What he says makes sense. When they find out that Rácz has chosen them to do his work, they panic. Šípoš has bad lungs and kidneys. He's not allowed to lift heavy objects. Berki has problems with his head and spine. He often has fits. Especially when working.

Rácz screams at them. He lifts his poker. The gypsies fall silent. They agree. Why doesn't kind sir let them go? They'll say goodbye to their wives and children, pack their things and come back in no time at all. Rácz snorts menacingly. Do the gypsies take Rácz for a fool? Could he wait? No! No tearful scenes, goodbyes, etcetera! They'll stay here from right now. They'll get a quick training course, and off to work. If they break anything, or forget anything, Rácz will torture them to death with a red-hot iron. For them he will invent tortures that nobody has ever thought of. They'd better not play games with him, or they'll take whole days to die. Their howls and groans of pain will be heard in the hotel!

The gypsies are afraid of pain. They're quiet now.

Rácz knows that none of their clansmen will look for them. They won't be missed by anyone. Everybody will think that they got homesick and took off eastwards, to see relatives in a gypsy camp, to guzzle wood alcohol and sit with their hats on at a table in the middle of a busy camp. Gypsies know all about that. Their clansmen in that camp won't help them; they'd never guess that Berki and Šípoš were being held prisoner less than a hundred yards from the mall.

Rácz promises them a little pocket money, if they obey. He unties them. The gypsies stand and rub their wrists. They're afraid of the explosive stoker; he can easily overcome them. They're clumsy and sluggish. They shouldn't have eaten so much. Rácz doesn't waste time.

He immediately starts training his slaves intensively. The valves must not be touched. They are only to stoke the furnaces. The pressure must not go over fifteen bars. "This far, look." Rácz will come every day to check on them. He'll bring them food in the morning. It will have to last till the next day. But the gypsies needn't worry, there will be enough, and it will taste good. The lavatory's at the end of the hall. Maybe they'll lose a bit of weight, which would be good for them. They'd better not try to escape. There are bars everywhere. The chimney is narrow.

Rácz shows them how to stoke and how to remove the ash. He's proud of his ingenuity. Rácz is smart: fixing things like this! Only now, when the stinking boiler-room is no longer hanging round his neck, only now can he show what he's made of. A whimsical mood comes over him. He shouts rebukes at the gypsies and the next instant smiles benevolently at them. He shakes his fist at them and the next minute offers them spirits. Scotch. There is only a drop left, the gypsies can keep it. He lets them know: if they obey Rácz, he'll treat them fairly. If they try to screw him, they'll never get out of here.

It's dawn. Rácz is no longer sleepy. He pulls his suitcase out and slowly packs items of everyday use. The gypsies mutter unhappily and fearfully. They find the shovels too heavy. The wheels of the wheelbarrow squeak unbearably.

* * *

Rácz moves into the hotel first thing in the morning. The receptionist gives him a suite with a river view. Rácz likes it there. The bed is soft and smells clean. Rácz lies down, but keeps his feet, still shod in work boots, on the carpet. After a moment's relaxation, he takes off his dungarees, which are covered in coal dust. He takes a shower. Then he puts on new clothes that he's brought from downstairs. He has a loose-fitting, fashionably loud orange and green tracksuit. The jacket has AMERICAN FOOTBALL printed on the back. The fabric is shiny and nice to touch. The leather-laced Adidas that reach halfway up his calves smell seductively new. They're a couple of sizes too big, but the Italian who gave them to him in exchange for heating told him it was fashionable to wear oversize shoes. That's fashion for you. Rácz gets up and goes to the mirror. The hair on his spherical head has grown a bit. His big ears have a disturbing effect. He presses them to his head with both hands. He listens to the sound of his blood for a moment. It occurs to him that just six months ago he was still driving a tractor over his native fields. Old Kišš should see Rácz now. For a moment he feels he hates the butcher, his daughter and all.

There's a knock at the door. It's the waiter. He's pushing a trolley. A bottle of *Moët et Chandon* lies on ice in a frosty silver bucket. "Compliments of the restaurant manager," says the waiter, lingering. Rácz figures he must be waiting for a tip. "Rácz hasn't unpacked yet," he tells the waiter. "He hasn't got anything yet. Next time. Clear off!" The waiter backs out respectfully. His face registers disappointment.

* * *

There's a snowstorm outside. Everything is covered in snow. It is pleasantly warm in the hotel, though. The gypsies are stoking the furnaces like crazy. The manager wanders down the corridors. He talks to himself. He is shivering with cold. He can't get warm now even when he clings to the red-hot electric hob.

Things are bad at home, too. His wife's lover has moved into his bed and wears his pyjamas. He combs his hair the way the manager does. He sits in the manager's favourite armchair. The manager has to sleep in the kitchen, on chairs in a row. With tears in his eyes he has to listen to his wife's moans and suppressed cries and his bed squeaking wildly. This often goes on late into the night. One day he comes home and finds the locks changed. He gets angry and bangs and kicks at the door. The door opens and his wife's lover appears. He punches the manager in the mouth and throws him downstairs. In a flash the manager notices that the lover is growing his, the manager's, moustache.

He moves into the hotel. The receptionist refuses to give him a room. "Those times are over," he says stubbornly. "Maybe you can stay in a broom-cupboard where they keep the buckets," he suggests. "There's one on every floor. The cleaning lady has the key." Let him wait for her. She could come any time. "And then again, she might not," he adds maliciously. Even if he can have a broom-cupboard, then the manager would have to sleep standing. "Like in a lift," the receptionist adds cheerfully, since he, too, had had his pay docked by the manager. He smiles. If the manager wanted to lie down, his legs would stick out of the cupboard. "That wouldn't do. Despite everything, this is still an international hotel," the receptionist stressed. "We can't afford such eccentricities. What would the foreign guests say?"

Anyway, the receptionist says impatiently, pointing a fly swatter at the manager to stop him gripping the reception counter so hard, for this would leave greasy fingerprints, the receptionist doesn't want to get into trouble. He's not interested in politics. He doesn't know what's gone wrong between Rácz and the manager. The stoker is now the boss, though. The receptionist has survived several bosses. He wants to survive them all. He has a wife and kids, and so on. Rácz has eyes everywhere. The receptionist must ask the manager to stop compromising him, and to clear off. He's still got his office, nobody's taken that away from him.

With the last of his money the manager buys a pyramidal mountain-climber's tent and pitches it in his office. It's a question of survival. He spends most of his time in the tent now.

The news that Rácz has moved into the hotel shakes him. He crawls out of his tent and looks fixedly out of the window. Ďula is crossing the yard with a lunch-box in one hand and a loaf of bread in the other. He stops at the locked door of the boiler-room, searching for the keys. The manager is now used to the constant cold. On his hotplate a pot of thick vegetable soup is boiling. The manager makes it out of green tops and vegetable peelings thrown out by the cooks. The soup is full of warmth and vitamins. The manager has been afraid to go down to the restaurant or to ask for food directly from the kitchen, ever since the head chef told him to go and eat elsewhere, adding that the hotel kitchen was not a Salvation Army soup kitchen. They've somehow forgotten to pay him his salary. He's penniless. He spent his last penny on the tent. Fortunately, the skips in the inner courtyard are a cornucopia. Last time he found a whole loaf of bread in there. It was quite good, just a bit dry. The manager believes that his situation is only temporary. At the very least, his wife and her lover might pardon him and he will be allowed to come back home.

He throws himself at the pot and hungrily slurps the thick liquid. The soup will warm him up a bit. The manager is carefully protecting himself from frostbite. Unfortunately, he can't light a fire in his office. The walls that he had panelled in mahogany in happier times would go up in flames right away. When he's finished his soup, the manager slinks along the wall, so as not to be seen, to wash his saucepan in the toilet. He walks carefully in his shapeless felt boots. His thick ski trousers make a swishing noise. The manager sings to himself to overcome his fear.

When he returns to his office, he drinks hot tea. He bursts out crying. His tears freeze instantly on his cheeks. He still feels like the manager of the hotel and so he goes out on an inspection. Like a big puffed-up snowman he trudges the corridors, singing sad songs. Nobody respects him any more. Nobody is interested in his advice, let alone his orders. Everyone is afraid to be seen in his company by Rácz, or by someone who might tell Rácz. Rácz has his people everywhere. Now he is the master here. When he left the boiler-room and moved into a suite, he made it quite clear what he was after.

The manager is merely tolerated now. The guests share this attitude. To the regulars, he is a pathetic wretch. To new guests he seems a weird, tragicomic figure to be met in a dark corridor any time by day or night.

* * *

Gunnar Hurensson sits in his Volvo and slowly drives from the border crossing, which is set deep in the fields, towards the ugly, snowbound and muddy city in the distance. The city reminds him of a monstrous tumour: each time he comes, it seems bigger and more monstrous than ever.

He's not been here for a while. He'd been nursing a venereal disease that he caught from a Slovak whore. The hospital subjected him to such thorough and painful treatment, that ever since then he has been able to see with each eye a different side of the world.

He's got a camera in his suitcase. He's promised it to a young man whom he met last summer. The boy is sure to be expecting it. He is slender, with a sad yet charming face. Hurensson likes boys like that. He likes girls, of course, but he likes boys, too. He has decided. If the young man is nice, really nice to him, he'll get the camera as a present. It will be a gift from an older friend from Sweden.

It is snowing heavily. As far as the bridge over the river Hurensson crawls along in a queue behind a snowplough. Two men on the back of the snowplough are generously shovelling coarse salt onto the road. In Sweden they'd be lynched for it, Hurensson thinks. But in this dim and depressed nation, nobody takes any notice. Dozens of Škoda cars have overtaken the plough without any trouble, so why should he get out and argue with them? He wouldn't be able to make himself understood, anyway. He's fluent in five languages and can get along anywhere, even Thailand. But that's not the slightest use to him here. In the Hotel Ambassador café Hurensson waits for a coffee. This small nation with its artificially hypertrophied and incomprehensible national pride is a nation of geniuses misunderstood and unrecognized by the rest of the world, he feels. They all believe that they're better than they seem at first sight. The young hustler and unlicensed taxi driver thinks he is an artist. The blonde whore never fails to stress that she was originally a ballet dancer. The stooped porter with spidery bony fingers who takes your bags turns out to have been at one time a lecturer at the evening university, now closed, of

Marxism-Leninism. He was a philosopher, or so he says. Whatever they do now is only temporary, done out of necessity. The café waitress is miserable; no doubt, she originally planned to be an actress. She finds it degrading to serve Hurensson coffee. As if Hurensson were partly to blame for her failure to become an actress. This is a nation of the underestimated, it occurs to Hurensson. They could have given the world some of the most brilliant artists, ballet dancers, and scientists — at least that's what they claim. Why didn't they — that's the question?

Hurensson found out about the existence of this nation only because of its ridiculously cheap prostitutes, willing to put up with anything that doesn't leave visible traces. Only then did he find out from the residents of this nation about the apparently famous artists, astronomers, and inventors whom he'd never heard of before. But so far Hurensson has only been able to meet cheap whores, black market hustlers, arrogant waiters and taxi drivers, lazy room-maids and venal policemen. However, Hurensson does not condemn anyone outright. He believes the milieu in which he circulates as a bisexual tourist has shaped his opinion. He has no doubt that this nation is composed not merely of parasites and fools, but also of honest and educated working people. The point is that Hurensson has never yet met such people, nor even found a trace of their existence. He needn't give a toss. He doesn't aim to do sociological research while deep among these people. He is a serious employee of a top Swedish furniture company; he is forty, and a follower of the great Marquis de Sade. He is a self-indulgent libertine. He doesn't mind spending a whole week's income coming over here to have fun with pretty Slovak prostitutes who have no taboos and who are stunningly cheap compared to their colleagues in Bangkok, where Hurensson used to go.

But this time Hurensson has come with a different aim. He's firmly decided to induce the handsome young man, whom he promised a video camera, that the Hurensson way of life is one of freedom and pleasure. As an older special friend he will gladly guide the young man through an unknown and perhaps thorny, but eventually dizzily sweet garden of enchanting passion.

During his involuntary stay at a clinic for sexually transmitted diseases in Uppsala he never stopped thinking of his cherubic Slovak, and seducing him became the first thing he'd do when he was cured. Hurensson considered the splendid camera a sufficient means of enticing the young man and guaranteeing them both a pleasurable weekend in a suite at the Hotel Ambassador.

Hurensson does not have to go looking for Urban, who's come of his own accord. He rushed out of the department store where Piggybank's panting phone call caught up with him.

"Hi, how are you doing?" Hurensson calls out in his Swede's English, getting up and giving Urban a friendly hug.

"Thanks," says Urban and adds reproachfully. "Long time no see."

"I ain't got time," says Hurensson.

"Have you got the camera?" Urban asks.

Hurensson smiles. "Of course," he says.

"The same type I wanted?" Urban wonders...

"Not exactly, but much better than this."

"Can I take a look?"

"Sure, in my hotel room," Hurensson suggests. "Here's an owner's manual, here you are."

"Thanks," Urban answers and leafs thoughtfully through the manual.

"Do you like the camera?" Hurensson asks impatiently.

"Oh, sure!" says Urban. "But it must have been very expensive. I wanted the other type because it was much cheaper than this one. How much do I owe to you now?"

"Don't talk of money," Hurensson suggests and grabs Urban's hand. "Let's talk about ourselves!"

Urban's face flushes red.

"Actually, I do not understand," he admits and frees his hand from the Swede's big, dry, fatherly hand.

Hurensson smiles patiently. "I mean that you can have this camera if you want," he explains to Urban. "You don't have to pay. It's up to you. C'mon, let's go to my hotel room. You should go with me if you want to see the camera. I think we can go much closer to each other, can't we?"

Urban knows only too well that he doesn't have enough money for this camera. It cost almost twice as much as the one he ordered. On the other hand, he can't tell the Swede that he doesn't want it because he wanted the cheaper model. The picture of the camera on the manual is seductive.

"Yeah, let's go upstairs," he sighs.

He's got to have that camera, no matter what.

* * *

At first the manager considered fixing the broken heating himself. But he's afraid Rácz might find out. He'd rather freeze.

Ďula sometimes stops by the manager's office, but not out of pity. He checks everything out and then informs Rácz.

"Tell me, Ďula," the manager asks him one day, "what would happen if I fixed the radiator myself?"

"I'd have to tell Rácz," says Ďula, looking straight at the manager's pale face.

"But why?" the manager asks full of bitter aggrieved emotion. "Did I pay you badly? Were we on bad terms? Aren't we friends any more?"

Ďula shakes his head. "You don't understand. You're very stupid. Rácz is a personality. At last, a strong personality in this hotel! And you? A few months ago you were the big boss here and where are you now? Just look at yourself! Your father-in-law won't help you; he's got enough worries of his own. Read the papers! I've got to go. I'll tell Rácz what we talked about."

A little while later Ďula drops in for a word. He stands in the doorway. "Rácz wants you to know," he tells the manager, "that if you try to screw him he will come up here and make your life hell. You see, everybody treats you like a piece of rubbish," he adds with contempt and malice. "You've got only one way out: beg him to forgive you."

The manager sits up with a jerk.

"Rácz wants you to come over to him in the lobby on your hands and knees and beg for his forgiveness in front of everyone."

"Never!" the manager says in anger. "Apologize politely, admit a mistake was made — yes. But that kind of a circus show…"

"But you're a circus act, anyway!" Ďula says angrily. "How do you think people see you?"

The manager angrily puts his fat fingers in his ears. He curls his upper lip.

Ďula leaves.

The manager is on the lookout in the doorway. When the lawyer passes by, he addresses him in a friendly manner. He believes the lawyer will help him. For years the manager has covered up the lawyer's deals. But the lawyer is fearful.

"Are you out of your mind?" he bursts out. "Do you think I want to end up like you? Kindly don't talk to me. After a while, when the air's clear, I may drop by. That's all I can do for you at the moment. We'll see what happens in the future." The lawyer looks around. "Well, clear off," he tells the manager impatiently. "We might be seen together and I'd have problems I don't need."

The lawyer hurries off. Yes, his prediction has come true. The manager's gone to pieces. In effect, the lawyer runs the hotel now. He should be made the real manager. That would be something! It would become the lawyer's gold mine. He knows so many tricks with the paperwork that he'd be a millionaire in a year. Yes, the lawyer realises, the time has come to organize an election for the manager's job. That would be the lawyer's great chance. Were it not for Rácz. The lawyer is apprehensive. What if Rácz has the same ambition? The lawyer calls for an election, and the staff elects Rácz instead! Or if not Rácz, someone else who'll run things on Rácz's behalf. No, Rácz will have to be rendered harmless, the lawyer decides. Rácz has gone too far.

The manager is sitting in the tent in his office and reflects. He can't fire Rácz. He can't do anything. The manager is lost. If his wife and her lover don't take pity on him, by spring he'll freeze to death — either freeze, or go mad. He can't last much longer.

* * *

Rácz sometimes comes to check on the gypsies locked up in the boiler-room. They have resigned themselves to their fate. They don't try to escape any more; it's impossible. The bars are solid. When they see Rácz, they work like mad. They're afraid of him. They are strong only in a mob. As individuals, they are against violence. They fear physical pain. The pump wheels turn round and round. Rácz checks to see that the bearings don't overheat. He checks the pressure and the temperature. If anything is out of order, the gypsies go without food for a day. After his inspection, Rácz calmly leaves. Ďula shuts the door and slowly turns all the complicated locks.

Rácz spends most of his day in the hotel. He often sits in an armchair in the lobby, pretending to sleep. That's an illusion: despite his almost closed eyelids, he keeps a watchful eye on his surroundings. Nothing escapes him. The new guests report to him. They agree a price on the spot. Rácz's calculation of the price depends on how a guest is dressed. The better they're dressed, the higher the price. If a guest refuses to pay, Rácz goes down to the boiler-room and turns off the heating. The non-payer pays up after the other guests, who've paid, force him to. The guests are dismayed, but they can't do anything about it. They know nothing about life in this country. They don't know if it's normal or not. But nobody complains. They fear Rácz's revenge.

Rácz spends his evenings in the Ambassador cabaret bar. He sits at the bar and drinks cocktails that he has taken a liking to, or, when in company, he takes a table close to the stage. In that case Silvia, Edita, and sometimes their friend, Wanda the Trucker, keep him company. Ďula, his sidekick, is always there, as he loves to drink and eat for free. His mouth full, he laughs with gratitude at Rácz's rough and clumsy attempts at jokes. Rácz sometimes forces him to do tricks; for example, he might ask him to drink a litre of cold water in one gulp, or to climb under the table with a schnitzel in his mouth. Ďula obediently does as he is told, and the stoker applauds by strumming his fingers on Ďula's ears, a sign of praise among senior conscripts in the army, or so Rácz solemnly says.

All of this time, Rácz never forgets his duties. In the middle of all the fun he gets up, takes Ďula along and they vanish somewhere for half an hour. Anyone who followed them through the dark passage into the boiler-room courtyard, would see them move barrels of ash and empty them onto a big heap. Rácz could never let the gypsies do this job. He'd be afraid that they'd make a run for it. So while this job is being done, both Berki and Šípoš are locked in the cubbyhole.

Rácz urinates onto the ashes and remembers times past. The gloomy courtyard and the scarcity of public toilets always tempted passers-by who were bursting to relieve themselves then and there. Donáth used to battle against them, he hated them. He divided them into two groups: The pissers and the shitters. For the old man the pissers were a socially less objectionable group than the shitters. The urine usually evaporated and only a pervasive smell remained. It couldn't be detected down in the boiler-room. The shitters left behind a tangible and often very substantial artefact, and that drove Donáth into a frenzy. Spying through the keyhole, Donáth and Rácz would often keep a lookout from the boiler-room metal door. They waited for the moment when the shitter dropped his trousers, about to do his business. The moment the artefact seemed to be ready, Rácz, armed with a pickaxe handle, would fly through the door, followed by Donáth. The offender would have to deposit the still warm artefact into a skip with his bare hands and then use his shirt or other piece of clothing to wipe where he'd deposited it. "No, we don't have any water," the old man would answer the inevitable question from offenders who'd been caught and taught a lesson.

Women, often decently dressed and of educated appearance, who usually entered the dark courtyard quietly, formed a quite distinct group. They would carefully look around and in a flash would get rid of a sanitary towel often right in front of the boiler-room. They'd often use the occasion to have a loud pee. "Madam! You've forgotten something!" Donáth would call out after a woman hurrying out of the courtyard, waving a sanitary towel skewered on a poker at her.

Donáth also had a trick he played on desperate lovers who couldn't wait and, misled by the remoteness and apparent peacefulness, decided to do it in the dark courtyard. When their audible moans betrayed them at the height of their passion, the old man would turn on all the lights and, coughing his dry cough, would come out into the courtyard lit by blinding neon lights. "Couldn't you screw somewhere else? Who's supposed to listen to this? People like to sleep here!"

Only the vomiters didn't bother him that much. After every night, but mostly on Fridays, in the area around the Hotel Ambassador, including the courtyard, a few sizeable dried up star-like objects, a mixture of alcohol, food, and gastric juices, appeared, but Donáth just shrugged. "Can't be helped," he used to say. "People throw up because they have to. It's no problem. A little bit of rain will wash it away."

Rácz finishes pissing and reminiscing. It's gone. It was a long time ago. He shakes his member and zips up his trousers. "Let's go," he tells Ďula. "Let's go down to the bar. It's cold here." Donáth was a nobody. Not like Rácz. Rácz lives life to the full. He doesn't ask for much, but he's fussy. He's successful. He's capable.

He sits down in the cabaret bar and everybody comes to see him. The small-time currency dealers want to unload their foreign currency. They buy at eighteen and sell at twenty crowns. Sometimes it's two hundred deutschmarks, sometimes five hundred. Westerners change at most two hundred. In any case they're not in the market to buy a wind surfer or a huge camping tent. The small timers let Rácz make two hundred crowns on a hundred deutschmarks. Rácz buys everything and piles it up. Then he sells at twenty-one. That's enough for him. Daily he turns over ten, maybe fifteen thousand deutschmarks. That's enough to live on. Add the money for turning the heating off and on. Rácz can't complain. The Albanians give him hostile looks, because he's infringing their monopoly. Rácz doesn't worry about them. They greet each other with a perfunctory nod. This implies: "I am aware of you." They more or less respect each other. Rácz unconsciously learns from them how to behave, dress, and walk like a black-market currency dealer — a preoccupied, fast mincing gait, with the toes of the shoes pointing outwards, the torso inclined forward a bit, and the head to one side. The Albanians try to make him out. They can't help seeing that he behaves as if he owns the entire hotel. They see the cabaret dancers blatantly toadying to him and foreign guests frantically buying him rounds. Ďula keeps watch like a bodyguard. They finally come to terms. They've decided that it's better to have Rácz on their side. Business takes off. The labour is distributed. The Albanians do deals outside the hotel; they're all mobile, they drive rickety used cars: old Mercedes, Fords, Opels and various battered cars with Austrian, German, and Dutch licence plates. Rácz doesn't go anywhere. He doesn't leave the hotel. He holds all the strings. At first he wants nothing to do with stolen goods, but when he does his sums at night in his suite and sees how much it would bring in, he agrees. For jobs outside the hotel he uses Ďula. He has the use of the hotel Renault minibus. He can do anything. They managed to move a wagon-load of stolen cement. It went in a day. Private builders almost fought to get at it. Rácz made three hundred thousand crowns and he never saw a bag of cement. He didn't have to lift a finger. He just did the deal and took the cash. Even Ďula got a share. He was so shattered that he kissed Rácz's hand. Rácz accepts with dignity, his lips clenched, as if this was natural. Then he adds a few thousand on top. It's good to have a faithful and reliable servant. Out of sheer joy, Ďula downs two litres of cold water without stopping and, with a schnitzel in his teeth, he crawls under all the tables in the cabaret. Then he painfully vomits for a long time in the toilet. But this doesn't spoil his joy.

Urban shows up as well. "Well, how is it going? Did you get your camera? Sit down, why stand?"

"Thanks, I'll stand," Urban mutters. He has the camera.

"And what are you going to do with it?" asks Rácz.

"All kinds of things," says Urban. "Make money on weddings, christenings, graduations. Do you realise how much money people are willing to spend to see their own boring mugs?"

Rácz shrugs. No, Rácz has never been interested in that sort of non-sense. Still, he'd like to know how much Urban spent on that toy. Why won't Urban sit down?

Urban sits down with an expression of pain on his face.

"I haven't seen you for a long time," says Rácz. "Must be a week, at least. How much did you fork out on that new toy?"

"A lot," says Urban. Here, Urban could easily sell it for fifty thousand. But in Germany you could buy it for a month's salary. Even less.

"And how much did you pay for it?" asks Rácz.

"Enough," Urban says evasively.

"Just asking." Rácz backs off; he's not really that interested. It's Urban's business. As long as it was worth it.

Urban has some Austrian schillings.

"How many?" asks Rácz.

"A thousand." "I'll give you twenty-eight hundred," Rácz offers. Urban agrees. "See how times change," Rácz laughs, counting the cash. "A month ago you'd have been buying from me. That's life. One day up, next day down," Rácz philosophizes. A sentimental mood comes over him. He grows sad. He summons the waiter and to cheer himself up orders Ďula a litre of cold water and a huge fried schnitzel.

Closing time is four in the morning. Rácz and Silvia take the lift upstairs to the stoker's suite. Sometimes, when Rácz is too busy, he asks Ďula in and, while taking his shoes off, tells him what to do the next day. Ďula has plenty of spare time. He's single and also lives in the hotel. He would even sleep with Rácz for that kind of money. Sometimes Rácz is tired and falls asleep the moment he hits the bed. Then Silvia undresses him and covers him up. This is not out of love; if Rácz got cold, he might catch pneumonia and die, and Silvia's source of income would dry up. Now things have gone so far that the whole economy around the Hotel Ambassador would crash. The foreign exchange rate would drop sharply, or rise vertiginously, the price of gold would change, and so on. That is why Silvia covers the exhausted Rácz. The experienced prostitute realises that when so much power is concentrated in a single person's hands, he becomes irreplaceable. And she doesn't want to screw in hotel rooms and parked cars any more. She's used to a comfortable and peaceful life now. She wallows in bed in the morning. Rácz has been up for a long time and Silvia can hear his imperious voice in the corridors when she opens her eyes. She has breakfast in bed. Sometimes she watches a video, and sometimes satellite TV. She prefers MTV, a pop music station. Rácz is allergic to MTV. If he happens to come into the suite when MTV is on, he angrily turns it off. He switches over to Eurosport. He can stand motionless, watching a rough wrestling match for hours. He knows all the fighters by name. His favourite is Hulk Hogan. Rácz sometimes grabs Ďula and tries out wrestling holds on him. Ďula often remains on the floor without moving, his eyes glazed over. Silvia has to revive him with a spray from the soda water bottle.

"Oh, you really let me have it this time, boss!" Ďula shouts with servile cheerfulness, feeling the back of his neck and getting off the floor. "You could easily go and join those guys on TV! You could have beaten them all! Ha, ha, ha! You're so strong!"

Rácz is proud of his strength. A life of luxury hasn't yet managed to soften his muscles steeled by years of hard work. Rácz could floor the lot of them! He demonstrates it: with one punch he knocks the stuffing out of the door and then punches through it. Silvia and Ďula applaud.

When Rácz and Ďula leave, Silvia reads magazines. Sometimes she gets bored and goes shopping. She even takes Edita along, so that she has someone to envy the money Rácz gives her. Sometimes she buys her a trifle and secretly enjoys it when Edita gets resentful. "You could have gone down to the boiler-room instead of me when we were freezing cold," Silvia teases her. She knows that this isn't true; the square-cut stoker had noticed her long before he got the idea of shutting the valves and began his dazzling career. When they get home from shopping, Edita stops sulking. Her nostrils flare in anticipation. Silvia lies down on the couch in the living room of the suite and lets Edita take her boots, fur coat, sweater, panties, everything off. Naked as a tapeworm and with a domineering look in her cold eyes, she lets herself be caressed and excited. Edita also undresses. She puts her lips, swollen with excitement, over Silvia's moist and open crotch.

"Ow!" Silvia hisses and, with her lips angrily clenched, she slaps Edita on the cheek. "Oh God, I'm so sorry," she says, frightened, then embraces her friend. With gentle caresses she tries to erase the red mark her five fingers have left on Edita's face.

* * *

"You should apologize to the boss, like I told you last time," Ďula advises the manager during one of his inspections of the icy office. "He might forgive you."

"Me apologize?" The manager leaps up and his ski trousers swish. "On my knees? Never!"

"I don't care," says Ďula calmly, chewing a piece of American gum. "It's too late now anyway. It'd do bugger-all for you. I just wanted to get you worked up. You're so funny when you get upset. It's all your own doing. Nobody else is to blame. You were acting the strong man, but you didn't have what it takes. Why bark, when you can't bite?" Ďula turns up the collar of his leather jacket and sits down next to the red-hot embers of a fire in the middle of the office. "Look at me," he tells the manager. "I managed to adapt. I want an easy good life. But you just won't take advice. You could have had peace and quiet by now. The boss would have let you keep your job. You could have had tons of money. The boss isn't mean."

"Boss! Boss! Boss!" The manager gets livid. "Not so long ago you were kissing my arse."

"You can't criticize me!" Ďula shoots back and gets up. "Look at yourself and look at me. I just want to live! And when I try to help you, you insult me!"

"I don't need help!" The manager shouts and bursts into tears. Ďula shrugs and leaves. The manager gets out of his tent and sits at his desk. He wonders if his former driver might possibly be right. But not on his knees! He desperately thinks what he can do to save himself. Maybe no one can help him now. Rácz is adamant, vengeful, and vicious.

The manager reaches for his accordion, picks it up and draws the air in. Ever since he flung it at the window, only the bass notes have been working. Deep plaintive notes are heard in the cold office. The manager plays a romantic melody and tears flow down his cheeks. His wife and her lover are probably sitting down to Sunday dinner now. The table is set and the kitchen smells of food: a schnitzel, potatoes and cucumber salad. Or beef in cream sauce. Yes, the manager's wife is a good cook. Her lover will lick his chops. The manager can't remember when he last ate, it's been so long. His stock of packet soups and tins has long run out. He's drunk all his tea. Someone must have taken the fuse out of the fuse box, as there's no power in the office. The toilet is locked. The door handle has been removed. Fortunately, the water is still running in his sink. Nobody has turned it off. The manager lets it drip a bit so that the pipes don't freeze. He can urinate in the sink. For anything more he has to wait until night. Then he goes to relieve himself furtively in the dark courtyard in front of the boiler-room. But for the last few days he's been spared that ordeal. He's not eating. He drinks boiled water and imagines it's tea. The used tea bags in the skip are no good, as the waiters use them three times in a row. They bring a guest a cup of tea with the teabag already in it. They throw them out when there's nothing at all left in them. The manager's stomach is now used to being empty. He can contentedly ponder various dishes and is not likely to go mad with hunger.

Suddenly, he jumps up from the embers. He's got it now! The manager now knows how to win the powerful stoker's favour and yet still keep his dignity. It's a fact: the way to a man's heart is through his stomach. The manager has heard that Rácz likes to eat, and eat a lot. He's decided: tonight the manager is going to cook dinner for Rácz. He already imagines the stoker consuming with pleasure the piquant delicacy he'll prepare, licking the plate and asking for seconds, and himself, the manager, then entering the dining room, bowing deeply, while Rácz applauds loudly and then shakes the manager's hand passionately and warmly.

There is amazement in the kitchen. The manager hasn't been seen there for a long time. Ever since the chef kicked him out.

"What do you want here?" The chef jumps at him, wielding a filleting knife.

The manager shakes his head. He pats the chef on his back trying to calm him down with a pleasant smile. He's come to lighten the chef's workload. He promises not to leave any mess behind him. Everything will be cleaned up and the dishes will be washed. He'll cook for Rácz all by himself. "It's vital," he adds.

The cooks exchange glances of dismay. In the end, they agree. The daily menu is ready. And they were about to cook the special orders, and of course one for Rácz. Lately he's been asking for special meals. He prefers simple dishes, the ones he was used to at home. Bean soup, bread with pork lard and raw onion, potatoes with butter and sour cream, and so on. He's lost his appetite for the delicacies that the kitchen used to cook for him in an effort to win his favour.

Finally, they shrug. They're as lazy as cats and welcome any opportunity to skive. The manager gets to work. He puts a white apron over his tracksuit. He quivers with impatience. The cooks go out for a smoke.

Soon the manager's special dish wafts its seductive aromas all over the place. The apprentice chefs reluctantly fetch him spices, mustard, soy sauce, Cumberland and Worcestershire sauce. Choice larded morsels of meat braise under bouncing lids. The manager is chopping onions. He rids his eyes of tears by blinking frequently.

The chef enters the kitchen, a cigarette in his hand. "You think that'll do you any good?" he asks, ironically screwing up his eyes.

The manager deliberately ignores the comment. He starts to sing ostentatiously. The chef spits angrily and leaves. He lacks the courage to kick the manager out. The cooks play cards in the changing room.

"Has he come?" the manager asks a pop-eyed waiter.

"Who?" asks the waiter, baffled.

"The stoker," says the manager.

"No," the waiter shakes his head, "the boss isn't here yet."

Finally, the manager is ready. He wipes his hands on his apron. Then he takes it off and throws it on the table. The waiters watch him with astonishment through the serving window. The apprentice chefs are jolting each other and playing catch on the slippery floor. The manager keeps an eye on them, while occasionally checking the bouncing pot-lids.

Soon the moment has come. The waiters whistle. Rácz is sitting in the dining room, banging the table impatiently with his fist. His stomach is rumbling. An old blue-rinsed American lady turns around in panic. When she finds out that the source of the strange stomach noises is the stoker himself, she gives him an ingratiating grin. She knows what an unheated hotel room is like.

"What are you staring at, you stupid cow?" Rácz mutters; he is calm, alert, and in a good mood. Silvia and Edita went shopping in the morning and haven't come back yet. Rácz can eat any way he wants, he doesn't have to suppress the noisy lip-smacking or banging the spoon against the crockery, as he has to do when his girlfriend and her friend are there. His business is also running like clockwork and that's another reason to be content.

"Well, what have you got for me that's good?" The stoker jovially asks the headwaiter approaching him with dignity from the left.

"We have a few specialities for you, boss," says the headwaiter with servility. "They've been cooked by…"

"Just put it on the table and don't blather, damn it!" Rácz bangs his fist on the table and his brow is furled capriciously and, seemingly, angrily. The headwaiter silently bows and motions to a waiter bringing the soup. While the waiter ladles the delicious soup for Rácz, the headwaiter nervously looks for the musician, who immediately enters, catching his breath, with a violin under his arm. Stojka, the fat gypsy from the cabaret band has to play every day at dinner for Rácz's pleasure. Rácz often puts aside his cutlery and is moved to join in, singing the refrain of a popular tune before continuing his meal.

"The boss has finished the soup already," the incoming waiter tells the manager who is nervously hiding behind the curtain dividing the dining room from the kitchen.

Rácz has slurped his soup and waits impatiently for the second course. The manager clumsily arranges a plate of veal medallions and accompanies the waiter to the curtain. One can hear Rácz singing to the accompaniment of the violin. Then comes the sound of the guests' insincere, embarrassed applause. No one dares to eat while Rácz sings. Everybody pretends to listen to him. They wait for the song in an unfamiliar language to end before they resume dining.

"He's started on the veal," the waiter reports. "He's tried the potatoes! He doesn't like the sauce! It's sour!" All this is reported in a panicky voice to the kitchen where all movement has stopped.

"He's smashed the salad bowl with his fist," the waiter following the action in the dining room cries in desperation.

"To hell with the salad," the manager says to himself. "That doesn't mean a thing. How about the meat?" he asks the waiter. "Does he like it?"

"He's taking it out and putting it on the side of the plate," the waiter tells the manager and leaves to get a drink. He's been on his feet since morning.

The manager is pale. He gets even paler, when he hears the sound of smashing china. Stojka's violin falls silent.

"Quick! Get him the next course!" shouts the headwaiter, running into the kitchen, his face and hair covered in sauce. Everyone starts to run around in panic, but nobody knows what to do.

"I'd really like to know what miracle you've cooked for the next course," the chef tells the manager. He's just come in from the changing room, a cigarette in his hand. Through the open door, the cooks could be seen drinking rum originally meant for the flambé.

"Give me goulash, Szegedi style!" shouts the headwaiter. "I expect it was too hot," cries a trainee waiter, holding his cheek, which bears the mark of five fingers.

"Ice! Give me ice!" somebody shouts hysterically.

All work in the restaurant has stopped. All the kitchen staff are clinging to the curtain. They dare not let Rácz see them. They all realise that the situation is unsustainable and cannot go on much longer. Sooner or later a waiter or cook has to enter the abandoned dining room from which come guests' muffled voices and Rácz's terrible silence.

"You ought to go in," the frightened headwaiter suggests to the chef.

"Send in an apprentice," a cook suggests. The trainee waiter with the mark of the stoker's hand on his cheek starts to cry.

"Don't you have any apprentices?" the headwaiter addresses the cooks. "Who screwed up, anyway? You, the cooks!"

"Us?" The chef gets furious, and throws his cigarette butt away. Before he can suggest anything, there's another proposal: send in the prettiest waitress topless. Maybe that will appease the stoker. There are two waitresses behind the curtain; at a vigorous nod from the headwaiter, they take off their blouses and bras. The staff assess them. They shake their heads; both waitresses are flat-chested. They're as tall and thin as bean-poles. Offended, they put their clothes back on.

"I might as well go in there with my top off," the chef mumbles. "Well, go," the headwaiter says, watching through a hole in the curtain.

The noise in the dining room has stepped up. Nervousness reigns behind the curtain. "Let the man responsible for the cock-up go," a waiter suggests. All eyes are on the manager.

"Yes, that's right," the headwaiter agrees. The manager makes an evasive manœuvre, but two waiters firmly grab him by his shoulders.

"*Scheisse!*" says the chef. In emergencies he relieves his stress with foreign words. "*Scheisse!*" he repeats. "That would be even worse," he counters. "Rácz hates the manager and if he sees him, he'll destroy us. No, not that," he shakes his head. "I suppose we'll have to send in a woman, a waitress. But not a topless one, a bottomless one! Get it? Bottomless!"

They all agree, except the waitresses. They resist desperately. "This isn't what we agreed!" they repeat in unison, but illogically. Finally, they are forced to take off their skirts. Now it's clear why they resisted so hard: they are naked under their skirts. In chagrin, they explain that it is hot in the restaurant, and wearing knickers would make them sweat.

The men in the kitchen like it. (They also like lace-edged black tights.) Tension subsides. It is clear to all that they're out of the danger. Even Rácz won't be able to resist. Everyone wants to grope them. The waitresses squeal. Only the headwaiter keeps a worried eye on what's happening in the dining room, which has been left unsupervised. And when the bottomless waitresses, one with a tray of the manager's speciality, and the other with a bottle of red wine, (both red with embarrassment), are ready to enter the room, the headwaiter shouts: "He's throwing up! Throwing up! I told you this would happen!"

Chaos reigns behind the scenes. The waitresses run away and quickly dress, as if they have until then been acting under hypnosis, and have only just woken up. The waiters and cooks run around in confusion and yell with penetrating, surprisingly screechy voices. The headwaiter is about to hang himself. He makes broad, very graphic gestures, as if hoping that someone will try to stop him.

Only the chef has not given in to panic. He is all red from drinking rum. "See, what you've done?" he turns on the manager. The latter has in the meantime profited from the chaos to stuff his jacket with tins, vegetables, meat, and bottles of wine, together with biscuits and sweets. Do you see? "Now you want me to go to the boss and fix it? I don't think even a case of Havana Club will be enough to calm him down. Lucky we economized by using the local hooch instead of real rum for the flambé!"

The manager fearfully peeks into the dining room. Rácz is sitting at the table. His head is bent down and a shock of hair hangs down in resignation. His orange-green jacket and fashionable tracksuit bottoms are covered in vomit. In the silence that now reigns he smashes his fist into the table. He stubbornly tries to get up, but he doubles up with a spasm of vomiting and helplessly sinks into his chair. The terrified guests watch him. Everybody is afraid to make a move. "Uuuppp!" comes out of the stoker and a new stream shoots out of his mouth. "Uuuppp!"

"What are you hanging around for, you dolt?" the chef says to the manager, and lights up. "Haven't you done enough to mess us up? Get lost! I don't want to see you here ever again!"

Sadly, the manager goes away. The chef catches up with him on the ramp. The manager had better give back everything he's stolen from the kitchen during the chaos! On the double! The chef has no time for jokes. He has to cook goulash and sauerkraut for the boss. "Move it!"

The manager unbuttons his jacket and unwillingly takes out his loot: a frozen chicken, five potatoes, a bottle of soup stock, a bottle of red wine, two raw pork steaks, a side of bacon, a bunch of onions, three carrots, a lemon, a can of mushrooms in brine and a jar of mustard. "And now get lost!" The chef orders him out, after feeling the manager's jacket to check he hasn't got away with anything.

The manager runs to his office. Then he impatiently sits down to the cold fire in the middle of the room and from his ski trousers he takes out his loot, his prize — a jar of caviar. Here's a reason for celebration! He looks for his accordion and soon the office resounds with the bass notes and the manager's booming voice.

The jar of caviar is soon finished. The manager is thirsty. The water has stopped running. Strange sounds come from the water pipe and soon they stop, too. Luckily, there are snowdrifts all around the hotel. The manager takes a bucket, fills it with snow from the yard and warms it up over the fire in his office. The water is a bit sour and salty, but it quenches thirst and warms him.

* * *

Freddy Piggybank does the rounds of the snowbound car park among the cars, which are covered in snow. He is dressed warmly; his cheeks are red with frost. Sausages and beans warm his stomach. His hands in knitted gloves rest on his red collecting bag filled with change. He is making vindictive plans involving shootings, mass executions, and torture. Today the gypsies came for their money. Berki was not among them, nor was Šípoš. Young Čonka was the spokesman. He told the parking attendant that it was getting harder for them to talk the bad gypsies out of attacking his trailer. That's why the good gypsies have to ask Piggybank for an increased contribution. Otherwise they can't answer for anyone or anything. Piggybank burst into tears, but ended up paying what Čonka asked. As soon as the overjoyed gypsies left, a bitch from the town council showed up and announced to Piggybank that the rental contract for the car park would be void for the next two weeks: tomorrow the car park will be fenced, booths and tanks full of carp will be brought in, and a Christmas market will open up in front of the Hotel Ambassador. Piggybank exploded. He didn't dare to protest to the gypsies, but now he gave free rein to his emotions. The bitch from the town council was not impressed; she waved a document at the furious miser, and all was calm. The fat attendant tried to appeal to her better nature, but it got him nowhere. "You're free from tomorrow until Christmas," said the bitch maliciously and left, wriggling her behind.

Cars come and go. Piggybank is strict, almost cruel; he carefully checks the parking tickets and pedantically collects the fees. If a customer is just five minutes late, the attendant charges him an additional hour. Gnashing of teeth does not help the customer.

The lot is full of big Austrian cars. The Austrians are feverishly doing their Christmas shopping. The department store and the city are full of them. In this foul weather, gigantic, garish painted buses, bringing more and more customers, force their way into queues of slow-moving cars. These are happy times for the currency dealers. They all bravely hang around the parking lot and the entrance to the Hotel Ambassador. They freeze and wait for new punters.

"I'm in the shit," Piggybank tells Urban. "In the shit," he repeats, when Urban fails to react as he expected. Then he continues anyway: Freddy is the victim of incredible ingratitude. The gypsies are swine. He's always known that. The time will come when they'll beg him on their knees for mercy and to let them give him back the money they stole. He'll torture them one by one. He'll start with their children. The parents will have to watch. To stop them closing their eyes, Freddy will cut off their eyelids. "Just wait, you pigs, your turn will come," he'll tell them. "You'll envy your filthy kids' easy death!" He'll spend a week devising the tortures he'll inflict on Berki. Then there's the bitch from town council, Piggybank remembers. For her, too, Piggybank has thought up tortures. Finally, at the very end, after two or three days, Freddy will sharpen the end of a pole this thick! And he'll slowly impale her — or what's left of her — on that pole! "Selling carp? I'll show you carp! Two weeks, that means a total…" Freddy takes out his calculator and works out how much money he'll have lost in two weeks. "Bugger," he says with resignation. He still can't and won't believe that today is his last day here. He finally collects himself and with a martyr's expression on his face throws his red money-bag into the corner of his trailer. "Let's go and have a drink," he says to Video Urban. "Drinks are on me."

Urban can't believe his ears. He thinks he's misheard. Freddy Piggybank paying for a round? But the attendant locks up his trailer and makes a beeline for the entrance to the Ambassador's bar. Urban follows. "I have to get rat-arsed," says the miser when they sit down at the table. "I'm so pissed off. Know how much money I'll lose? Business is bad. The Germans come by bus. They do their shopping and go back to Austria by bus." Buses can't get into Freddy's car park. What he earns by changing money is from car drivers. Not a lot. It's less than he'd get from one bus. But what can he do when the buses can't park in the lot? The buses come around nine and by that time his lot is full. He can't afford to block spaces until nine because of the buses. The car drivers would tear him to pieces. People are swine; they don't understand that you have to make a living. Freddy Piggybank hates them.

Urban agrees. He understands. But he doesn't think Freddy Piggybank should make a tragedy out of it. He will lose some money, true, but he'll get a break, too. It'll soon be Christmas. After the holidays, the car park will reopen and he'll make up his losses.

Like hell he will! Freddy Piggybank gets livid and downs a shot of gin. He coughs and farts. It's the sausages and beans. Freddy works and saves. He spends nothing on himself. And what does he get for his effort? A carp sale! A painted floozy from the town council! He'll never catch up, because nobody will pay for his losses. But don't let them think that Freddy Piggybank will pay taxes for those two weeks. He doesn't spend money on himself. He only saves. And now this? To him? Shit!

Urban has his drink and quickly reaches for a coke. He hates the local gin. The attendant ordered it because it was the cheapest drink. Urban suggests that Freddy should look after himself, indulge himself, find a girlfriend, get some decent clothes, eat better. There's more to life than making money: life's for living. Women and fun. Why, for example, can't Freddy Piggybank get a car? He wouldn't have to fucking walk to work or take a tram.

The attendant downs another gin and orders expensive cigarettes. He bangs capriciously on the table. "The menu! Steak and eggs! One more coke and two more gins! No? All right. Just one gin and one Becherovka liqueur for this gentleman!" Freddy Piggybank doesn't give a damn today. They've destroyed him. Beggared him! What a fucking life! What's he going to do for the next two weeks? Why doesn't he have a car? Because he doesn't have a licence. He couldn't get one either. Freddy Piggybank hasn't even done army service. He lowers his voice to a conspiratorial whisper. He's got an exemption certificate from military service. He's a head case. Nerves. But not a word to anyone.

Urban sighs. This isn't fun any more. The fat attendant is pissed. His breath stinks. His eyes shine madly. He attacks his steak wildly. Urban coughs politely. He has to go now. He's got things to sort out. But Freddy needn't worry. Urban hopes he has fun, and thanks him for the drinks.

Video Urban goes out into the cold. He grins. The attendant's complaints have given him an idea. He stands by the entrance and is happy. The idea is simple and ingenious. Starting tomorrow, he'll put it into action. He's already done the Christmas decorations; nobody can complain. Every minute a loudly sign-painted mammoth bus stops at the pavement and spews out a new batch of shopping-besotted Austrian tourists. Albanians with professional smiles on their swarthy faces are waiting with fistfuls of banknotes, ready for the onslaught. Urban's ears are freezing, but he laughs as he anticipates outwitting them all. And the funniest thing is that this magnificent idea was inspired by stupid and stingy Freddy Piggybank.

* * *

The next day Urban gets into his car and drives across the river, deep into the fields, towards the border crossing. He slams the car door shut, feels the weight of his full wallet in the inside pocket of his windcheater and then sits down in the espresso bar, drinking coffee, waiting for the first bus from the Austrian side. Soon the punters arrive. Urban calls the waitress, pays, goes out into the cold and joins the Austrians. Furtively, sotto voce, in a muted monotone, he repeats his pitch. The Austrians smile. They take out their wallets. Urban does the same. Money-changing starts. The buyers are happy. They prefer accepting this well dressed and polite young man's offer to supporting the economy of a foreign state, an insatiable Moloch that devours without trace money and other valuables. It is a usurious state that takes, at a disgracefully extortionate rate, real money backed by real assets in exchange for worthless socialist pieces of paper. They all crowd around Urban and push their banknotes at him.

"Gut! Gut!" says Urban politely in primitive German. "I've enough for everybody. No worries."

It's snowing again. All around the fields shine with whiteness. The sky is grey-black. The road is covered in a murky brown slush. Urban feels the coarse salt corroding his expensive fine leather boots. He goes to the car and puts on a bright baseball hat. When the next bus arrives, he daringly gets into it. He's welcomed by pleasant warmth and a pleasant aroma of perfume. He says a few words to the driver, who is also the owner of the bus. The latter announces Urban's offer through the microphone. Urban slowly moves down the aisle and with ill-disguised impatience reaches for the proffered banknotes. These are *deutschmarks*. It's a German bus. The Germans are well dressed, their bags smell of leather and they all wear thin-framed glasses. An elderly gentleman is smoking a cigar and offers one to Urban. He politely accepts. He leaves the bus with a wallet filled with western currency and a Havana in his mouth. He feels like having a juice or a coke, but decides not to waste time. He gets in the car and speeds off to the Hotel Ambassador. Water is splashing into wooden vats in the parking lot. Men are setting up wooden booths. Urban parks on the pavement and, taking no notice, puffs on his cigar as he passes through reception.

The stoker is in the living room of his suite and, bored, is watching a video. On the screen a very nice-looking madman has decided to tear a young girl in two by chaining her arms and legs to two lorries. The stoker nods at Urban. Urban obediently sits down. Rácz's feet are on the coffee table.

"How are you?" Urban asks jovially.

"Rácz is always fine," is the answer.

"Need any currency?" Urban asks.

"I don't need anything," says Rácz. "But if you have any, I'll take it." The hero of the video sits down with the madman and spends a long time persuading him there's no need to rip the girl in two. Rácz takes his eyes off the screen. "What've you got?" he asks, pretending to be uninterested.

"All sorts," says Video Urban. "Schillings and marks."

"How much do you want for them?" asks the stoker.

"What'll you pay?" retorts Urban.

"The usual," says Rácz.

"Look at today's paper," Urban argues.

"I never read it," Rácz states with pride. The blond madman is toying with the accelerator, smiling demonically. The girl tied to the bumper is groaning. "This is a film for Freddy!" Rácz roars with laughter: his eyes are not laughing, but watchful.

"The schilling and *deutschmark* are both up," says Urban.

Rácz just waves his wrist, which is adorned with a thick golden bracelet. "Want a drink?"

"Do you have any juice?" asks Urban.

"In the fridge," says Rácz, pointing.

By the time Urban comes back with a frosty can of pineapple juice, the girl has been torn in half.

"Fine," says Rácz, after a short pause. "I'll give you five cents more for a schilling and twenty-five cents more for a *deutschmark*."

Urban shakes his head. "Fifteen and fifty," he says.

Rácz turns the video off and puts the remote control on the table. He looks at Urban. "OK, he agrees, "ten and thirty."

Urban takes his wallet out, removes the money, counts it and puts it on the table. "Sixty-eight thousand schillings and eight thousand *deutschmarks*. Is that OK?"

Rácz is so astonished that he forgets to close his mouth, but he quickly gets a hold on himself. He stands up, leaves and soon comes back with a little metal safe. He takes his time counting the money. "You swine," he tells Urban, piling a stack of one-thousand-crown banknotes on the table. "If you make just thirty cents on a schilling and one and a half crowns on a *deutschmark*, you'll take about thirty thousand off me. That's almost my daily take!" Rácz shakes his head, pretending to be upset.

Urban smiles. He stuffs the money into his wallet and gets up. He hasn't got much time.

"Leaving already?" asks Rácz.

"Yes," says Urban. "I've more work to do." He can't afford to take it easy. Would Rácz be interested if he brought more marks and so on?

Rácz lifts his eyebrows. "Just bring it," he says. "I'll take it all." He pours a shot of Chivas Regal. "You've stunk the place out. What crap are you smoking?"

"Crap?" Urban, offended, takes the cigar out of his mouth. He reads the name on the ring and pronounces: "Davidoff."

"Throw it away!" Rácz insists and reaches into a wooden humidor on the table. "Here, take this one, he says, giving Urban a cigar. "Cohiba. It comes all the way from Cuba."

Urban stubs out his cigar in the ashtray and lights up a Cohiba. Through the cloud of smoke, he looks at a haughty Rácz. So, may Urban bring him more schillings and marks?

Rácz sees no need to answer. He spreads his arms in a gesture signifying "whatever you like, whenever you like."

"I hope you'll have enough pocket money left," says Urban ironically.

But Rácz can't take a joke against himself. "Rácz has enough money," he declares, almost offended.

In the doorway Video Urban almost bumps into Ďula, who has been eavesdropping behind the door. Urban can't be bothered waiting for the lift and runs down the stairs. He stops in the lobby: the glass entrance to the bar has been smashed. Long jagged pieces of glass, as sharp as swords, hang from the door-frame. "Closed owing to technical problems," Urban reads on a paper notice. "What happened?" Urban asks the receptionist.

"Yesterday a drunken customer wrecked the whole bar: even four waiters couldn't calm him down," said the receptionist. "They had to call the cops. It was the fat bloke from the car park." The receptionist can't recall his name.

"I know," says Urban. "I know the guy."

"When the cops arrived he was going to hang himself," the receptionist continues. "Another moment and it would have been too late."

Urban arrives at the border crossing just on time. The customs officers had just cleared a huge orange monster with smoked glass and a sign reading LISCHKA REISEN. The travellers welcome Urban with satisfied expressions. The hands clutching banknotes have a liberating effect. He reaches for them greedily, with a crooked smile.

This time Rácz does not hide his astonishment. Looking at the piles of hundred-*deutschmark* and five-hundred- or thousand-schilling banknotes, he sits behind his desk with a stupefied expression. Not raising an eyebrow, however, he takes out his small safe, opens it, and wets the thumb and index finger of his right hand.

"Have you robbed a bank in Austria?" he asks, putting on the table the sum Urban names. Ďula stands near the radiator at the window. He bursts out laughing with amusement. "Shut your face, you fool," Rácz turns on him. "Clear off! Don't you have work to do?"

"Yes, boss," mumbles the driver, "I'm going." He reluctantly leaves the window.

"You can tell me, no problem," Rácz urges Urban, after Ďula closes the door behind him and presses his ear to the other side of the door.

"Tell you?" Video Urban asks cheerfully, as he stuffs money into his wallet. He meant to ask the stoker to give him hundred-crown notes. It's stupid when a tourist wants to change two hundred *deutschmarks* and all you have is thousand-crown notes, and the tourist has no change. But then Urban decides to change them at the department store. The cashiers will do whatever he asks.

"You can tell me where you get the currency," Rácz tells him. "I'm not going to use the information. You know I'm too busy to run around." The stoker takes out a cigarette case and offers Urban a Players. Rácz is not a gossipy old woman. He'll keep the information to himself. He's not stupid, he knows it's not easy to exchange that much money at one go. When a Kraut or Austrian shows up, he needs at most maybe two or three thousand crowns. Rácz can see that Urban must be doing whole busloads of them. But where is it happening? Certainly not in front of the hotel: Rácz has already asked the Albanians. So where?

Urban smiles, even though he doesn't feel like it. Luckily, the door opens and in walks Silvia and her friend Edita, both weighed down with shopping bags and rosy from the cold air. Urban takes his opportunity and says goodbye.

"Will you bring me more today?" Rácz asks, as Urban heads for the door.

"I don't know yet," says Urban a bit annoyed: the stoker's high-handed manners have been getting on his nerves lately.

"Going already?" The stoker sounds almost disappointed.

"I've got things to do," Urban says evasively.

When he starts the engine and bumps off the pavement, he notices a movement in his rear view mirror. Round the corner appears the hotel's Renault minibus, driven by Ďula. He hangs back, but is obviously following Urban. "Aha!" Video Urban concludes: Rácz has told Ďula to follow him. Instead of being happy to get a steady supply of currency, he's jealous of Urban. It clearly annoys him that Urban is making just as much money as him on the deals. The stoker wants to trace the source of Urban's currency and tap into it himself. Then he'd make not just what he gets already, but Urban's cut, too. Urban thinks back to when he first met Rácz: the uncouth gestures, the ill-fitting suit, the pudding-bowl hair cut. He can't help grimacing at the steering-wheel when he recalls having to explain to the sullen peasant what a *deutschmark* was, and what use it was. The stocky young man was silent and listened to Urban attentively with an inscrutable expression in his dark metallic eyes. "Bugger," Urban relieves the tension with a curse. He jumps a red light at a crossroads and hears minibus's brakes shriek. He takes a sharp turn to the right, and then another one. His mood improves. It would be odd if he, an experienced unlicensed taxi driver, couldn't shake off an inept, stupid pursuer in the streets of his native city! Rácz has to be taught that Urban is not some moron who can be followed as in an American video. Urban takes another right turn and then one more. Soon he arrives at the crossroads where he got rid of that idiot Ďula. Now he calmly waits for a green light. There's no sign of the minibus. He races the engine and takes off when the light turns yellow. He rushes to the border crossing. He's wasted a lot of time as it is.

In the evening Urban has good reason to celebrate. He's made almost a hundred thousand crowns' clear profit in a day! Why didn't he work it out sooner? He decides to take Lenka out that evening: she's one of the girls that he cultivates, whom he phones from time to time, and who sometimes let him take her out to dinner. Naturally, he won't take her to the Ambassador. He can't risk meeting someone who might say something untoward.

Lenka is certain that Urban's high standard of living comes from his job as a shop window dresser and video artist. To her, Urban is basically one of life's losers, but a nice and entertaining loser. For a college girl like Lenka, anyone who fails second-year theory of culture can't be anything but a loser. She's not impressed by money; she grew up in a rich home. Lenka is a language student. English and Arabic. She may sleep with Urban one day, but not yet. Who knows if she ever will? She likes leading him on. Sometimes she even lets him kiss her. She's a big, slim, silent, walking promise. Urban has the right phrase for this type of girl: "dry whore". But it's still fun going out with her. One day she'll stop being faithful to her future boyfriends. Meanwhile, Urban can screw married women. There are plenty of them in a department store. It's nice and warm in the shopfitters' room and both he and the married woman are paid for their efforts. Life is beautiful, Urban concludes. He decides to get up early the next day and set out for the border crossing once again. It's a gold mine. All that money for the taking.

Lenka has seductive eyes. The champagne foams. Urban puts his hand on hers. A slant-eyed waiter hovers noiselessly. "A dry whore," Urban tells himself silently. He is a slave to his own æsthetics.

* * *

Rácz is having supper, too. He is drinking because he's angry. He kicked the incompetent Ďula in the testicles when he got back to the suite with a long face and threw up his hands in a tragic manner. He'd have kicked him to death, if Silvia hadn't stopped him. She paid for that. A slap. Two slaps. Then it was the shopping bags' turn. He tore up all her parcels. Both women were in tears, trying to save the clothes they'd bought. They fought Rácz for the shopping, like chicks fighting a rooster for a juicy worm they'd caught. "How could you let him get away?" Rácz went on raging at Ďula.

After a long while spent dithering and moaning, Ďula got off the floor. Silvia had to spray a whole bottle of soda water on him.

"You certainly know how to kick a man, boss," said Ďula humbly, his face drawn with pain, his hands between his legs.

By now Rácz is standing in front of a mirror with his right hand solemnly raised. Rácz won't rest until he finds out where that city slicker, that hustler Urban gets all his currency. Nobody, but nobody will make a hundred thousand a day out of Rácz! Who ever heard of such a thing?

Rácz only calms down and cheers up in the cabaret bar. He requests his favourite song and then orders a bottle of cherry brandy. "What would you like to have," he asks his company, Silvia, Edita, and Ďula. "Order anything you like. My treat! You want to eat? Eat! Musicians, play my tunes one more time!" Rácz shouts and bangs his fist on the table. Ďula quickly gets high and starts to laugh stupidly. The drunken women move their bodies in rhythm with the music. "That's it! That's it! That's it!" the stoker shouts and, with a bottle of cherry brandy in his hand, he jumps up and dances around the table. His eyes are hazy, as if covered by a cloud. The musicians sweat so hard that their temples are shine. They smile a forced smile. Their faces are sleazy professional masks, grimacing with insolence, conspiracy and connivance. They meekly follow the drunken stoker on his way of the cross through the Ambassador's cabaret bar.

* * *

The snow is shining; it creaks under the runners of the dog-sledge. The hunters run over the ice, shouting. The sea, covered by cracking ice floes, is close. Its cool, salty breath can be sensed from far away. A vicious wind whistles in their ears. "Walrus! Walrus!" the oldest Inuit shouts, pointing at the crack. The manager weighs his harpoon in his hand and hurls it at the herd of snarling walruses. Then he wakes up in the dark, in his office. He yells with fear for a while, but then he collects himself. He unzips the tent flap and emerges completely frozen. It's dark in the office. The manager looks at his watch. It's nearly midnight. A snowstorm rages outside. Icicles hang from the ceiling. Lately, the manager has spent most of his time asleep. His teeth are loose in his gums. He is troubled by nightmares about the Inuit. It takes him a long time to wake up and recognize his surroundings. He's got to keep moving, he tells himself and starts to pace the office up and down. Standing still means certain death for a hunter: keep on moving, constantly do something! The manager quickly splits some firewood and starts a fire in the middle of the office. His fear of freezing overcame fear of burning down the hotel a long time ago. There's nothing flammable left in the office, anyway. The parquet floor, furniture, and mahogany panelling are all gone. There's no danger of a conflagration. Now he roams the building at night, stealing a chair or armchair where he can. He once managed to get a settee from the lobby; he stole it right from under the nose of the dozing receptionist. It burned for a long time. The manager got warm burning it, singing a happy song. At the same time he roasted a small dog he'd caught near the skips in the courtyard. Crouching motionless in the dark, he waited hours for that dog.

That was before he'd hunted out the hotel's immediate surroundings. Now he has to get his prey further away from the hotel. He ended up finding a relatively rich hunting ground across the street, in the courtyard of the cancer clinic. But he caught almost nothing but cats there. That was one drawback. Secondly, the manager had to get into the courtyard furtively, since the lodge porter at the rear entrance kept a careful lookout. In his thick anorak and ski trousers, carrying arrows and a long bamboo bow made from a foot-scraper, wearing baggy felt boots, the manager had a hard time climbing the fence of the cancer clinic. It was even worse on the way back with his prey: a cat, dog, or small rodent. Happy moments of careless feasting only took place when the manager made it safely back into the hotel building, hugging the walls, keeping to the shadows until he was in his office. Such moments were rare. More often the manager starved and froze until he was so weak that he could barely lie in his tent, motionless and staring vacantly.

The fire does not warm the whole office. A few feet away it's still cold. The manager has to sit very close to the fire. He can light a bonfire only at night. Then the smoke coming out from the half-open office window can't be seen.

The manager has somehow come to terms with his fiasco in the kitchen. For some time he has even been considering *not* sucking up to Rácz. However, as winter goes on, he desperately realises that only making peace with the stoker will enable him to survive. Nobody else will help him. So the manager decides to make one more attempt to win the stoker's favour and pardon. Then the heating in his office will be turned on again and the manager can take off his baggy ski trousers and peacefully get his position back. Then the manager's salary will no longer vanish somewhere in the hotel corridors. He could buy food, even raspberry soda. The manager's wife and her lover would take him back. In time he would then push the lover out and once again sleep in his managerial bed.

But first, the manager has to regain Rácz's favour. Fortunately, he knows how. This time he really does. A sudden revelation came to him one evening when he was putting on the fire the last leg of a chair he'd looted in the lift. This epiphany was so powerful and intense that it made the manager jump up as if he'd been bitten. He walked up and down his icy office for a long time, issuing various shrieks of astonishment, stumbling into the stretched skins of various small rodents he was drying, drumming his chest with his fists in blissful triumph and hope for a speedy solution to his problems When he was worn out, the manager sat down by his fire again and shook his head until he was giddy, as if baffled at someone like him having such a brilliant idea.

Music is the way to a man's heart — that's irrefutable. The manager has vivid memories of that from happier days, before Rácz arrived on the scene. Those were the days when the manager, together with the hotel lawyer and his faithful sidekick Ďula, held interviews with prospective waitresses, room maids, and dancers. Then all you needed was a drop of cheap brandy served from an empty Martell bottle, soft lighting, and sweet muted music. Each new female employee soon relaxed and readily gave of her best. Of course, the manager was happy just to let the naked girls ride him like a horse and then whip him with bamboo canes. He would go back to his wife happy and content, while the lawyer and Ďula went on interviewing. No, the manager cannot believe that the stoker could be immune to the magical effect of music.

After the cabaret bar closes, Rácz and Silvia always go to the stoker's suite. Once there, according to their mood, they screw, or watch a horror film. That much the manager knows for sure: he's spent many moments in the dark corridor, his ear pressed to the door of Rácz's suite, trembling with fear of being discovered and grabbed, but at the same time racked by a chilling, unnatural pleasure in his loins and gut. Oh, the manager knows very well the effect melodious music has on lovers, when played in their ears. And that's what he'll do. The moment the stoker and his girlfriend disappear into their suite, the manager will be there, in the corridor, playing melancholy, sentimental, romantic tunes. Of course, he'll be cunningly disguised. And when Rácz, stirred by tears of emotion, comes out into the corridor, too moved to speak, and embraces the unknown troubadour, then the manager will take off his false beard and dark glasses and let himself be recognized. There'll be no going back: the stoker will have to shake the manager's friendly hand.

The manager has already practised a few simple songs, soulfully sung to the accompaniment of an accordion or the wistful melodic line of a mouth organ. All he has to do now is to get a big drum with shoulder straps, bells to put round his calves, a car horn, and children's cymbals. He is content; things are going to plan. He plays his whole repertoire one last time. Soon it's four in the morning. The bar closes. The manager begins to attach the drum, the accordion, and the mouth organ holder. He glues on a long black beard and puts on some dark glasses. A glance at a shard of mirror assures him that his appearance is changed out of all recognition. He carefully opens the office door and looks outside. There's no one about. He tiptoes into the hall and goes up the service stairs to the top floor. There he hides behind a corner, waiting for Rácz to arrive. He makes sure he isn't given away by the untimely ring of a little bell or an unwanted bang on the drum.

Soon the lift stops on the top floor. The stoker and his girlfriend come out and vanish into their suite. The manager hugs the wall and almost stops breathing. He creeps up to the door and listens. He can hear the noise of the shower and their voices. Then the shower stops and he hears the muffled but energetic creaking of the bed. "They're screwing," the manager thinks. This is his moment! He attaches the drum strap to his shoe, extends the accordion bellows, silently counts the beat, breathes in and begins:

> *I used to love a girl*
> *A beautiful dark-haired girl*
> *And now I am waiting*
> *To hear what God will say.*
> *I loved my dark-haired girl,*
> *My beautiful dark-haired girl*
> *And all I got for my love*
> *Was an axe stuck in my back.*

The manager pauses, then stops playing. He is listening to the noises from the suite. The copulatory creaking stops for a while. He hears muffled talking. Then the creaking resumes, much more energetically and faster. The manager sings:

> *My love was true*
> *My love was good*

And for that love of mine
I now lie in my grave.
I did not know that today
Is not like yesterday,
And this mistake of mine
Has sent me to my grave

The other rooms are quiet. The hotel guests think that this is another of the stoker's quirks. Nobody wants to confront him, so they prefer to lie awake and quietly wait for it to end. His hands trembling, the manager draws air into his accordion with a mixture of stage fright and excitement; he wets his lips and goes on singing:

Mother, dear Mother,
Do not cry so much.
I have suffered in the world,
In the grave I'll rest.

The door of the suite opens violently and Rácz himself appears on the threshold. The manager grows ten inches smaller.

"Who dares to do this?" the stoker shouts and raises his clenched fist like an anti-tank grenade. "Who's so mad they dare to disturb Rácz?" he asks, but instead of an answer, the manager produces only a monotonous, muffled whimper that seems to come from outside the building. "Who is laughing at Rácz? Who's trying to take the piss?" And silently deliberating for a moment, the stoker punches the wall. The hotel shakes down to its foundations and the corridor lights flicker. The manager shrinks four more inches. Rácz approaches him and with his steel fingers grabs him by the neck like a rabbit. The manager lets himself be taken silently to the stairwell. Here the stoker stops and pushes him down head first. Instantly, the manager finds himself a floor lower. The stairs down are littered with broken pieces of his instruments. "Once more!" Rácz warns him, "ONCE MORE!" He doesn't seem to have recognized the manager in disguise. Rácz turns around, enters his suite and slams the door behind him.

The manager stops pretending to be unconscious. He struggles to his feet and feels his arms and legs. He takes the broken and bent drum off his back. He gasps for breath out of sheer mortification and humiliation.

"What's the meaning of this mess?" A cleaner attacks him. She's just arrived at work by the first bus and looks down at the manager. "That's what men would like: make a pigsty everywhere they go! Then women have to come and clean it up, put up with it! Do women exist just for cleaning? Don't women have any rights? Women want a life, too!

Women aren't work robots! Well, women know about cleaning, of course. But if someone deliberately makes a filthy mess, then he can clean up after himself. Right now, at the double!"

The manager feels his chin and finds that his false beard has come off. He lost his dark glasses when he fell.

"Ah, the manager," the cleaner notes with joy. "Here's a broom! At the double! Then you'll get a bucket and mop. The stairs have to shine!"

Through the windows a chilly and sharp winter sun shines faintly. The rubbish men are banging about in the yard. Rácz peacefully snorts in his sleep, which is always deep a couple of hours before he wakes. In the yellow snow in front of the kitchen are grey boxes of bread and pastries, stacked on top of each other. In the parking lot are barrels of water where the fish are kept. Here and there, a silver fish back surfaces just for a second and vanishes with a powerful splash in the freezing water. The porter Torontál is at his post near the receptionist's desk and loyally waits for suitcase handles to grab. The receptionist has made his last coffee. He rubs his sleepy eyes, and waits for the morning shift to relieve him. The hotel rooms are dead to the world. Everyone is asleep. The manager is still cleaning up. The remnants of the accordion and the drum had to be taken out to the skip. He's swept the stairs and corridor, washed them, and now he's waxing them.

The cleaner is having a coffee in her broom cupboard. Now and then she checks up on him.

"A little bit harder on this spot," she tells him strictly. "Can't the manager see that dirt?"

The guests have woken up. Phones ring in the kitchen. Everybody wants breakfast in bed. The waiters have a last puff of their cigarettes, drink up their coffee, adjust their bow ties and grab their trays or trolleys. Nobody uses the lifts now. They all take the stairs on purpose. As soon as the manager has polished the stairs to the cleaner's satisfaction, stiff-necked waiters walk on them with their dirty shoes. The manager has to clean them all over again. He is embarrassed and puts his false beard and dark glasses back on so that they won't recognize him. The cleaner has finished her coffee, morning cigarette and newspaper; she now stands over the manager, watching his every move. She tells everyone walking up or down: "This is the manager! I caught him making a mess on the stairs. Women are not here to clean all the time. Men can do something, as well. Women need peace and quiet, too. Carry on walking, he can polish them again!"

The manager waxes the stairs again. He forces his tears out by squeezing his eyes shut. When he's finished, he stands by the window and lets people pass, so that he can continue his work with the facial expression of Christ scourged. The cleaner has left long ago, but the manager still goes on working. It is only around noon that he is struck by the sudden silence in the hall. He furtively approaches the door of the cleaner's cupboard, and finds it locked. Then the manager gathers up the courage and runs to his office like a hunted animal. He clambers into the tent and instantly falls asleep.

* * *

Video Urban has gone right off money-changing. He's had his fingers burned. Morning after morning he'd been driving to the fields across the river, to the border crossing and waiting for the orange, toxic green, and loud red buses, getting into them and relieving shopping-crazed westerners of their *deutschmark*, schillings, and dollars. Rácz gave up hope of finding the source of Urban's sudden wealth. He went on buying Urban's currency without further comment; after all, he made money out of it too. Wealthy peasants who longed to buy a used car, TV, video etc in Austria came running to Rácz, ready to pay outrageous prices for currency.

Disaster struck Urban one chilly, but rare sunny day, when everything seemed to be going like clockwork. A huge bus full of Austrian tourists stopped in a lay-by after customs, and in stepped Urban in a cheerful festive mood. He was making his way towards the back of the bus, taking schillings left and right from outstretched hands, counting and handing back one-thousand and five-hundred crown bills from a fat wad fastened with a red elastic when, at the end of the bus, he came face to face with two plain-clothes police ID cards held out by two shyly smiling slender youths. Dressed in windcheaters and jeans, they looked ordinary.

"No hysterics, please," one of them said politely and got up with a sigh. "Let's go," he said, gently pushing Urban towards the exit.

"No funny business, OK?" said the other one, shouting hysterically, and, jumping up, he grabbed Urban by the collar and thrust him down on the floor. He kneeled over him and checked him for weapons. He found Urban's wallet and put it in his pocket. "He hasn't got a gun," he shouted. "Go, go!" He pushed Urban out.

Urban got off the bus with his hands up.

"Make him keep his hands behind his head!" the undercover police-man was shouting, when suddenly a huge hand-gun appeared in his hand out of nowhere.

Video Urban noticed hundreds of eyes watching him indifferently through the misted windows of buses, trucks, and cars.

"Where's your car?" the polite one asked.

Urban's lower jaw began to shake; he couldn't speak. "So that's it," he thought, accepting the possibility in the far recesses of his soul, but he couldn't believe it was real. He dropped his right hand to scratch his cheek.

"Hands behind your head!" yelled the angry one, jabbing him in the ribs with the gun.

Urban had encountered this situation many times in his nightmares. But when he wanted to wake up he always did. This time he couldn't. He felt for his car keys and the polite one took them from his hand, unlocked the car door and said, "Get in, please."

"Move it, move it," the angry one yelled and motioned with a gun that was at least two sizes too big.

Urban sat at the steering wheel with the polite one next to him and the angry one behind him. Urban was afraid to look in the rear-view mirror, but he sensed that the angry one was pointing the gun at him. Everyone kept quiet for a while.

"Can I see your ID again?" Urban asked, because he couldn't think of anything better to say.

"Yes, of course," said the polite one and shoved his ID card in front of Urban's nose.

"May I put my hands down?" asked Urban. His bowels urgently needed to be relieved, but he managed to master them. He took the ID card and studied it for a while. Then he gave it back.

After a moment's silence, the polite one asked him casually, "Have you ever been in prison?"

Urban shook his head and swallowed. His mouth was dry.

"Well, let's have a look," said the polite one cheerfully.

The angry one took out Urban's wallet and they both began counting. When they'd finished, both were visibly impressed by the size of the total.

"Well," the polite one said, "this money is now confiscated." To show he meant it, he stuffed a bunch of banknotes under his belt. He put the empty wallet, Urban's ID and address book into the glove compartment.

"Now the question is whether you want to be locked up or not," said the polite one, looking out of the window. "You're young; you've got your whole life ahead of you."

Urban couldn't help smiling: the undercover policemen did not look any older than him.

The polite one continued, "They'd tear your arse to pieces your first night in the cells."

Urban remembered Hurensson and the camera that he'd put away, as soon as he'd unwrapped it, in the cupboard, where it had stayed ever since. If he'd stuck to the video business, as he originally planned, this would have never happened to him.

"But it all depends on you," the polite one concluded.

"What do you mean?" Urban put the question in a hurry, as he felt instinctively that at the end of this dark tunnel of fear and horror flickered a small light of hope.

"Are you that stupid?" the angry one yelled, pushing the barrel of the gun into the back of his head.

The polite one smiled patiently. "Look," he said, "this money," and he patted his now bulging windcheater, "this money is officially confiscated. You won't get any of it back. No way. We'll give you now a receipt to say that we've confiscated it. As well as giving you a receipt, we'll handcuff you and take you in. You'll be on remand because we'll hand your case to the prosecutor. He'll prepare the case. In a nutshell, you won't get out of this. You're looking at a good five to eight years, the way I see it." The polite one paused for dramatic effect and then turned away from the misted window. "That's one option," he added dryly.

Video Urban swallowed hard and took a breath to ask a question.

The polite one beat him to it. "The second option? Well, the second option is that you don't ask for a receipt for the money we've confiscated, and we don't handcuff you." He smiled like someone used to doing favours and making people happy. "You'll drive us into town and let us out, say, at the Stefanka Café. Then we'll say goodbye and everyone goes their own way. You choose." The polite one put his hand in his pocket. He asked, "May I smoke in here?"

"Yes, of course," said Urban, startled, as he had been imagining miles and miles of barbed wire, cold mornings in a prison yard, and black, dark, gloomy buildings.

The polite one took out a package of *Mars* cigarettes. "Want one?" He offered them to Video Urban.

"Only then did Urban snap out of his numbed state and reach for a package of Marlboros. "Have one," he offered.

"With pleasure," the polite one said happily. He took the Marlboro, let Urban light it and smoked, piously holding the cigarette between thumb and index finger.

"I don't smoke," said the angry one when Urban offered him the pack. "So what have you decided?" he yelled at Video Urban.

"Why would I want a receipt?" asked Urban.

"Just what I think," the polite one chimed in. "You can always make more money, but nobody will give you back your freedom. So, start the car and take us into town."

Urban started the car and moved off. He looked at a red light on the dashboard. He had meant to fill up.

"Listen, gentlemen," he turned to the undercover policemen.

"What is it?" the angry one reacted menacingly.

Urban explained the situation briefly. The tank was empty. They were running just on the fumes left in it. They absolutely had to stop at a petrol station if they wanted to get back to town.

"So?" asked the polite one "Let's stop. What's the problem?"

"Well, I don't have any money for petrol," said Urban.

"Oh, I see," the polite one smiled. "I understand." He grabbed the bunch of notes from under his belt, peeled off two hundred crowns and gave them to Urban with a magnanimous gesture. "You'll have enough left over for a coffee and a shot of liquor. You're going to need it, right?"

The young men got off at the café they'd mentioned. "Well, good luck," the polite one said.

"Same to you," mumbled Urban, and headed for the Hotel Ambassador. He didn't know whether to be happy or angry. He'd lost almost all his money, but, on the other hand, he was as free as a bird.

* * *

Video Urban never ever wants to do currency changing again. His losses have almost driven him mad. He hasn't been able to sleep for a couple of nights. He doesn't even phone that "dry whore" Lenka any more. He can't get the money out of his mind. But she wouldn't let him screw her, anyway. Now Urban is quite sure: fast money is no good. It's better to make money slowly. If he hadn't been so greedy, he'd have had more by now. Nobody could have robbed him of his profit and his capital. He should've gone into business with his camera, as he originally intended.

He would pay taxes and have peace of mind. Urban was not meant to be a currency dealer: he's an artist.

He's sitting at the Ambassador bar, drinking whisky. He's not completely broke yet, not at all. But he's still upset. He shouldn't have hustled so much. He brought this all on himself because of insatiable greed. From now on, he'll stop racing like a greyhound after an artificial hare. He had always been lucky, until he started hustling. Yes, Urban will go back to his old nonchalant ways. He won't be a millionaire this year. So what? What does he actually need to live on, to be happy? Just enough to eat, and not to feel the cold. And a car. It doesn't have to be a Mercedes or a BMW; no need for those. A nice Škoda Favorit will do. And he's got one. That's all you need around here. Why make people envious? What else does he need? Petrol money; he's used to driving everywhere and has forgotten what the inside of a tram or a trolleybus looks like. He needs money for entertainment. To have fun at a bar, to invite a bird out to dinner, to buy a videocassette, a CD, or a cassette tape to play his favourite music. Basically, he wants a relaxed worry-free life.

He explains all this to Wanda the Trucker who's sitting next to him at the bar. Wanda agrees. She cheerfully nods her head and smiles with her giant painted mouth. Urban lifts his hand and snaps his finger at the waiter. Soon two glasses of whisky appear. Urban knows that this is a blend of the cheapest Scotch, Grant's, with local spirits, but pretends not to notice. He pretends that he's drinking what he ordered. This is a game played by customer and waiter. Most customers don't know they're playing it; Urban plays it, because he does not feel like quibbling. His motto is not to spoil somebody's racket as long as that person does it decently. Everybody has to survive somehow. Video Urban downs the blend and focuses on Wanda's extra-long indigo-black thighs, showing from the narrowest of miniskirts.

He asks her. "Aren't you cold?"

"I've got a long coat," replies Wanda the Trucker.

Urban is shivering with cold. "Another one," he calls to the waiter. "Make it two," he corrects himself, after exchanging glances with Wanda. He asks her, "Why are you called the Trucker?"

"Because I started with long-distance lorry-drivers at the petrol station," says Wanda.

"And I thought it was because you're so tall." He stirs his coffee and drinks it.

Wanda's real name isn't Wanda, but Anča. She was married to a man called Polgár. He used to work in the Water Department. Anča used to bring him lunch and then sat and watched him eat. Polgár would sometimes tie her to the pipes in the basement of the pumping station and took his pleasure that way. She liked it until the day Polgár had to run up to answer a ringing phone and forgot about her. Then the foreman came and found Anča all blue with cold, crucified on the pipes. Polgár ended up in a crew as a waterworks digger on a salary of just one thousand crowns. He started to beat Anča, blaming her for his misfortune. She divorced him, kicked him out of the flat she'd inherited from her father, changed her name to Wanda and began frequenting the petrol station on the main road, screwing lorry drivers. Polgár was later killed when a shaft he was digging caved in. They had no children.

"Why don't you work as a model?" Urban asks admiringly. "They're desperate for girls over five foot eight. How tall are you, actually?"

"I'm six foot two," Wanda the Trucker says proudly and downs her drink.

"You know," says Urban, "I feel depressed. Nothing is coming right for me. I had a huge stack of money" — he gestures — "that close. Start with a gold mine and end up with a heap of shit. They stole it from me."

"Who stole it?" asked Wanda the Trucker.

"Oh, forget it!" Urban dismisses it. "Let's talk about something else. Why don't you do modelling?"

"You think I've got what it takes?" asks Wanda happily.

"Definitely!" Urban decides and orders two more whiskies. "I can still pay for a couple of whiskies. But you're not drinking," he says.

"I'm not used to drinking," says Wanda the Trucker and lifts the glass to her lips.

"What!" Urban says dismissively. "Everybody drinks here. It's a local tradition."

"Who took your money?" asks Wanda.

"Forget about it," says Urban and orders two whiskies. "You don't drink at all. You should be a model. You've got what it takes."

"I'm pissed off, too," Wanda the Trucker admits. "Zdravko was supposed to come today. You know, the Viennese doctor. And do you think he came? No, he didn't!"

Wanda the Trucker drinks up.

"That's all right," Urban says. "He'll come tomorrow."

"He can fuck himself tomorrow. Fuck him." Wanda gets upset and bangs the counter with her fist. "I made sure I had nothing doing. He's a very demanding client. He keeps you busy all day, sometimes two days. There's dinner, champagne, and then it starts: oral, anal, pissing, from the back, from the front, and again, without stopping. But he doesn't care about money. I didn't make any plans, because I was waiting for him. And he was fucking me about. He didn't come at all."

Wanda pulls out a cigarette and lets Urban light it.

"OK, OK," says Video Urban to calm her down and shoves the lighter back in his pocket. It's not that late. You can turn a few tricks. He looks round the room. "There are plenty of Krauts here," he adds.

Wanda lifts her head and from her great height scans the room and the westerners sitting at the bar with their bulging trousers and worldly expressions on their fleshy faces. "Screw them!" she explodes, but immediately becomes despondent. "I really don't feel like doing anything," she admits. "I have this strange feeling inside me. Maybe I'm getting my period. That's when I don't feel like doing anything. But that won't interest you." She drops her head to the glass and her giant mane falls on her face.

"Why do you think it doesn't interest me?" Urban says, although actually it doesn't interest him. "So what do you want to do?"

"Just sit here and stare into space," says the prostitute, throwing her hair back. That delightful gesture makes up Urban's mind for him. "You know what? Let's go to my place," he suggests. "It's warmer, quieter and nicer there. I'll put on some music. I've got the latest Michael Franks. That's the sort of music for us. Come on!"

Wanda the Trucker shrugs. She doesn't seem too interested.

"What's wrong? We know each other, don't we?" Urban insists. "You've spent lots of time with me, haven't you?"

Actually, Wanda has never been to Urban's. They did spend a night together in his car. Urban was an unlicensed taxi driver, he was driving passengers all over the city, and Wanda was depressed, so she went along with him.

"There's nobody at your place?" asks Wanda the Trucker.

"No," said Urban. "I live alone."

"I don't really feel like going anywhere," says the prostitute indecisively. "I don't feel like doing anything."

"Don't be silly, come on," says Urban and pulls her by the hand, almost by force. He pays the bill and gets off the bar stool.

"All right," Wanda the Trucker agrees, as if to spite him, gets off her stool and lets herself be led towards the cloakroom.

The westerners comment with unhappy mutters on the departure of the best-looking, tallest, and most striking prostitute in the bar.

Outside they're met by cold, flickering street lamps and a snowstorm that hurls fine crystals into their faces.

"Shall we take a taxi?" asks Wanda.

"I've got a car," says Urban.

"But you've been drinking," Wanda protests.

"Nothing worse can happen to me," says Urban.

"Right, I feel the same," the prostitute agrees.

"You've got the longest legs I've ever seen on a woman," says Urban, when he has to help Wanda push back the car seat.

"Really?" Wanda is happy.

Video Urban scrapes the snow off the windscreen and they drive off.

When Urban shows Wanda his flat, built on the roof of a pre-war apartment building, the prostitute nods in admiration. "This is something!" she says when she looks at the furnishings.

"I like living somewhere comfortable and pleasant," says Urban as if apologizing. "After all, I'm a professional. Make yourself comfortable. No need to take your shoes off."

They don't end up listening to music after all, not for long, anyway. Wanda spots a huge black television set and video player in the corner of the room. "Let's watch something," she asks. Urban puts on music videos. "You have a camera, too, right?" says the prostitute.

"Yes," Urban replies reluctantly, realizing that Hurensson must have been with Wanda, too, and could have blurted out anything to her.

"How do you know?" he asks.

"Rácz mentioned it," says Wanda the Trucker. "Have you made any videos?"

"Not yet," says Urban.

"Then make one of me," asks Wanda the Trucker.

"Why?" Urban asks.

"Because," the prostitute shrugs, "I've never seen myself on a TV screen."

Urban sighs, but fetches his camera. He puts in a cassette, a battery and starts to shoot Wanda. The prostitute gets out of the armchair. She slowly takes off her sweater. She sways in rhythm to the music. She unbuttons her blouse, takes it off and drops it onto the floor. She begins to pull down her narrow skirt. Urban circles her with his camera. Wanda kicks off her shoes, then down come the black seamed stockings, suspender belt, bra, and finally her panties.

"Super," says Urban, but the show's not over yet. Wanda sits on the couch and spreads her long thighs wide apart. Her fingers part her crotch's pink butterfly wings. Then she does various things that excite Urban so much that he puts down the camera, takes off his clothes and follows her onto the couch.

"Let's film ourselves," suggests Wanda. Urban gets up, his member erect, takes the camera stand out of the cupboard, sets it up, and aims the camera where he expects to copulate with Wanda.

"What's wrong?" Wanda asks, when she sees Video Urban hesitate for a moment.

"Will you give me a rubber?" Urban asks using his hand to get a full erection. "I don't have anything here. I live like a monk."

"Just come as you are, don't be afraid," says Wanda. "Punters have to use condoms. You don't. I want to feel you in me. I want to feel when you come. We could even kiss, if you like."

"You know how dangerous it is now?" Video Urban asks, as he lowers himself onto her.

"And what isn't dangerous?" the prostitute says philosophically, as she takes a position in range of the camera. Urban kneels between her spread out knees, embraces her and slowly opens her vulva with his tongue.

An hour later, they drink, smoke, and, amused, watch the recording. Urban slows down the interesting moments with the remote control, which he holds.

"We're good, aren't we?" says Wanda. "We could easily make a living with this. But now wipe it, OK?"

"That'd be a pity, wouldn't it?"

"No," says Wanda. "Who knows who you might show this video to?"

"I swear I won't show it to anyone," says Urban. "I'll keep it for personal use only."

"I've heard that before," says Wanda. "What if I marry some rich bloke in the future and you blackmail me?"

"Blackmail you?" Urban ponders. "I'll sell it to the tabloids. I'll get more money that way."

"Please, wipe it, OK?" says the prostitute, as she turns over on her side and falls asleep.

Video Urban is an honourable man, not a crook. He watches the video once more from the beginning and then he erases it, although his heart bleeds as he does so. He sits at the table naked, with a shrivelled, drooping penis. He gets up and makes himself a nightcap. The prostitute, fully contented, breathes out loudly, her hand tucked like a child's under her head. Urban gets up from the chair and, his drink in his hand, goes over to his desk. He takes out a flyer with the text of an advertisement that he meant to insert ages ago: "VIDEO URBAN IS HERE FOR YOU! I WILL MAKE THE SIGNIFICANT MOMENTS IN YOUR LIFE AND THE HAPPY SMILES OF YOUR CHILDREN LAST FOREVER." He crumples up the flyer and throws it into the wastebasket. What stupidity! Who cares about their children's happy smiles! There are so many people in this business and they steal each other's jobs. No, he won't make any money this way. He takes the pen and writes on another piece of paper: "VIDEO URBAN WILL CAPTURE AND IMMORTALISE YOUR MOMENTS OF PLEASURE WITH YOUR PARTNER IN YOUR HOME, OR IN THE HOME-LIKE ENVIRONMENT OF THE STUDIO. DISCRETION ASSURED." He looks at the text for a while and then inserts the word "ABSOLUTE" before "DISCRETION". Yes, that's it. The "absolute" inspires confidence. Video Urban is content. He realises that it's the idea, not the work, that pays. The first comer takes everything.

He finishes his drink, washes his member and brushes his teeth. He turns off the light and calmly lies down next to Wanda the Trucker's long body with the feeling that, despite everything, he's completed a useful bit of work today.

* * *

The hotel lawyer no longer visits the manager. He's avoided him ever since he realised that contact with the manager might endanger him. He's working out how to become the new manager. The current one will soon go mad and hang himself. Or freeze to death. Or die of starvation. The lawyer considers the hotel a lucrative place to be. His tactics are to feign loyalty to the stoker and to try to be inconspicuous. He is succeeding; Rácz is not in the least interested in him, since he never sees him. There's a simple explanation: usually the lawyer comes to the hotel early in the morning and soon drives off to do his deals. These are dirty deals, but not like Rácz's deals. The lawyer is not interested in currency deals or trading gold or smuggled goods. He specializes in complex transactions involving accounting documents, phony acquisitions of antique furniture, expensive carpets, electronics, and even food for the hotel. It is all fake. Non-existent furniture and installations are sold off at a residual value. The lawyer pockets the difference between purchase and sale price. The Renault minibus is parked in the hotel garage. But there were originally supposed to be three minibuses there. After a while, the two non-existent ones were sold at a write-off price. The lawyer keeps tight control over everything; even the commercial assistant manager only exists on paper. He does not exist in reality. He simply doesn't exist. His name would be Haluška, a forty-year-old divorced business studies graduate on a good salary. No such person exists in reality. The entire administrative section of the hotel is empty. The lawyer, the personnel manager and, for the time being, the manager are the only actual living staff. The others live only on paper and in the lawyer's imagination. But they do get paid. That is why the lawyer couldn't even think of officially accounting for the stoker. He'd have to account for himself as well. Attracting too much attention is harmful. Rácz can only be intimidated. But the lawyer is not altogether certain if anything would intimidate this savage who is now king of the hotel. Everybody is afraid of Rácz, but he's afraid of no one. Yes, the lawyer knows that the stoker could only be tamed if a couple of undercover policemen came to investigate his dealings. But that would result in a disaster for the lawyer, too. They're both in the same boat.

That is why the lawyer comes in to work on his paper frauds, to share the salaries of the non-existent hotel employees with the assistant manager, and tries to keep a low profile. He knows that one day his time will come.

* * *

Mozoň (alias Silent) is content and in a good mood. His booming voice resounds through the rooms of the villa, which is a safe house. When he sees the amount of money Šolik (alias Livid) and Tupý (alias Bear) have brought him, he is completely stupefied for a minute. He's never seen so much money in his life. This money will enable them to live in the safe house for several more months. And by then things will be sorted out, the abolition of State Security will be annulled and Mozoň (alias Silent) and his underlings will be back on active duty.

"Where did you get all this money?" he asks Tupý (Bear).

Tupý (Bear) stops counting the pile of banknotes on the table. "Your idea to use the police warrant cards was brilliant."

Mozoň (Silent) contentedly preens himself. "I told you," he says. "And this is just the start!" He waves his fist menacingly at the window, which is covered, for secrecy, by a heavy curtain. "They haven't heard the last of us! We're going not just to make money, but get recognition for all we've done! When this democracy is laid to rest, we, the working people, will be in power again!"

"The labouring classes!" adds Tupý.

"Workers and peasants!" Šolik joins in. A celebratory mood fills the room. All three men have sparkling eyes.

The day the three men were sacked, it seemed like the end of the world. They all had very conventional wives who had no idea that their husbands worked for State Security. So they could not be told that State Security had been abolished. In a rare flash of intelligence, in the short period when something could still be saved, Mozoň got into the archives, found a file with a list of safe houses, flats and villas, and tore out a page. If he'd destroyed the whole file, that would soon have aroused suspicions and the new men in power would have discovered the list of apartments and houses some other way. Like this, nobody noticed anything. One villa more, or less... So Mozoň (Silent) kept for himself and his subordinates a safe place to hole up and plot their future. Every day Mozoň got up, had breakfast, got dressed and, briefcase in hand, after adjusting his tie in the mirror, unlocked the door of his apartment. He kissed his wife, who knew him as Ščepán, and left for work. His wife thought that Mozoň (Silent) alias Ščepán worked as a bank clerk. Mozoň then took a trolleybus to the safe house in a prestigious part of the town high above the city. It was so prestigious that nobody paid any attention to anyone. And you didn't have to worry about the neighbours poking their nose in. The neighbours also valued discretion and nobody was out to rock the boat. "We haven't done so badly," Mozoň reflected, as he observed the old, bent, former communist bigwigs as they slowly and carefully shovelled snow away from the entrances to their manor-houses. He felt they were kindred spirits; it seemed to him that what linked them was common membership of a sort of secret fraternity or sect. "We'll see," he would say at such moments, shaking his fist.

Mozoň, Tupý, and Šolik spent the whole morning and most of the afternoon in the villa overlooking the city. They were bored, but it was pleasant boredom. Mozoň spent ages looking out of the window, or he locked himself in the bathroom and looked at pornographic magazines. Šolik slept on the couch with a newspaper over his face. Tupý drew up lists of people he would visit after this interlude ended. He noted in brackets following the names the tortures that he would inflict on them after arrest. He spent entire days on this and often loudly expressed his disenchantment with, and hatred of, those who'd destroyed his existence. At three thirty all three packed up, locked the villa, and went to their homes, as if returning from work. The first days and weeks were tolerable. They were all certain that in a week or two the situation would resolve itself, the guilty parties would be punished and everything would go back to normal. A month passed by slowly, and nothing happened. There was no money. Pay-day came round, but there was no pay. They realised they might have to wait longer. They'd have to think of some solution, so as not to come clean to their wives. After all, that was unthinkable, purely from an official point of view.

Mozoň came up with the idea of police warrant cards. They'd had to surrender their State Security cards when they were sacked. But all of them had still their police cards. "Look, there's something here," Šolik told them one day, tapping his finger impatiently on a newspaper, "about a black market flourishing around the Hotel Ambassador. Suppose we started dealing on the black market, chief?"

"What do you use for money, you idiot?" Mozoň turned on him. "We've got nothing. We don't even have money." Mozoň remembered that his wife had been asking suspiciously when his salary would be paid. He explained his plan to Šolik and Tupý. He had to tell them twice before they understood.

"It's a brilliant idea, chief!" Tupý smiled.

Both subordinates were shaking and yawning with impatience.

It only took a few hours of hanging around the Hotel Ambassador, standing under the plane trees and drinking coffee in the hotel bar and keeping their trained secret-police ears alert to work out what was worrying the Albanians, the gypsies, and the Slovak currency dealers. All the hustlers were angry with an unknown smart-alick who'd neatly jumped the queue and grabbed the foreign currency right from under their noses. Šolik and Tupý conveyed this information to their chief in the conspiratorial villa. When Mozoň found out that his subordinates hadn't brought any money with them, he got really angry. Šolik and Tupý had to explain everything in detail.

"Well then, let's squeeze that bloke! The one buying all the currency. That'd be a great catch!"

"Yes, chief," Šolik nodded and sighed. "But how do we find him? He doesn't operate near the hotel. If he did, he'd have been lynched a long time ago."

"Do I have to think of everything?" Mozoň complained and got up from his chair. He began pacing the room with long strides. He stopped by the window and looked onto the street. "I've got it," he said after a while. "We've got to find out where the mystery man does his dirty deals. We've got to find the point where he comes into contact with foreigners and buys their money. That's where we've got to catch him. All clear to you now?"

"Yes," agreed Tupý uncertainly.

"No," confessed Šolik.

"You fools," said Mozoň, and laughed. "How are we going to find the location? Simply by covering the itinerary a western tourist covers when he comes here. From customs to the hotel. Somewhere along this route our mystery man appears. You catch him and squeeze him hard. I mean, hard! And then, when you show him that there is a way he can get himself out of it, he'll kiss both your hands. Now go! Go to the border crossing and elbow your way onto a bus. The customs officers will let you in when you show them the warrant cards. And if you don't succeed on the first bus, get out and get on the next one. Repeat from the beginning. And don't even think of coming back without money! Dismissed!"

That was a few days ago, and there's still plenty of money left. Joy reigns in the safe house. There's fine food and champagne from morning till knocking-off time. Waiting for the good old days to come back is much more pleasant now. Mozoň's booming voice cheerfully reverberates through the rooms of the safe house.

"Only don't let's cock it all up, or blow money on stupid things," Mozoň says firmly, but kindly when he spots Tupý bringing in a Lego set costing thirteen hundred crowns. However, at heart, Mozoň does not grudge his subordinates their naïve extravagance. Times are hard. Political change can't be expected soon. Mozoň believes that shopping sprees help his subordinates keep up their ideology and morale, so he lets them shop. He's reintroduced the ten-minute morale-boosters that he used to give his men when they first came to the safe house, and which he'd neglected when they suddenly became rich.

"Where did you get all this money?" Mozoň asks, expecting a familiar, often heard answer.

"It was a brilliant idea," says Tupý.

"A brilliant idea to use those police warrant cards," says Šolik.

"Really? Brilliant?" asks Mozoň. "And what do you two propose to do?" he rebukes them. His subordinates are taken aback. However, Mozoň continues to show his disappointment, saying that he does what he can. And if it weren't for him, they'd have to go begging. Who'd employ them? They've got a dubious past. What's more, they're totally unskilled. Mozoň doesn't mind admitting this about himself. He's never done anything in his life. He was kicked out of Law Faculty after a couple of semesters. Then for three years he worked as a barman. Then he joined the Secret Police, State Security. But nobody can deny he did those two semesters. At least he'd been a student. And that is why he, Mozoň, is the chief and not Šolik, or heaven help us, Tupý! And as their superior officer, he orders them to go and do something.

"Like what?" Tupý asks.

"There are a lot of possibilities," says Mozoň. They could go into the streets and find out the popular mood, listen to what people talk about, what they like and what they don't like. Or get back to that hotel and try to squeeze some other hustler. Does Mozoň have to come up with all the ideas? Couldn't they think of something, too? Does he have to lead them by the hand all the time? They're on enemy territory and they must never forget it! They should act accordingly. They're at war. It's a war without trenches or shooting. It's a battle of wits. Mozoň touches his forehead meaningfully. Šolik and Tupý are both puffed with pride. They've never looked at their pathetic existence from that angle. "Victory is assured," said Mozoň, "but everyone has to contribute." Above all, they have to think for themselves, so that he doesn't have to do all the thinking and plotting by himself! Where would Šolik and Tupý be without him? Yes, up shit creek!

* * *

Another early morning, and Rácz has put in a lot of useful work. First, the cops dealing with the Ambassador Hotel area showed up. A big raid on currency dealers was planned in two days' time. Rácz should take care and warn his people about the threat. When it happens, the local cops won't be able to help: special police from Prague will be carrying out the raid. The fat cop throws up his hands helplessly. Rácz is quiet and reflects. Certainly, he has to warn his own people. He doesn't know if he should alert that bastard, Video Urban. He's still furious with him for not revealing where he'd got currency for a whole week. But that's not the point: over the last few days things have gone back to normal. Buses come to the hotel with currency not yet changed and the Albanians are busy again. Urban has disappeared somewhere. Rácz will think about letting Urban know of the risk, or fall into the hands of the Prague cops.

The fat cop seemed a bit ruffled, as if he had more to say.

"Well, what is it," asks Rácz.

"You know, boss," says the policeman, "how can I put it? Time is passing. It's the twentieth of the month already."

"So?" asks Rácz.

The policeman clears his throat. "You promised to keep us in mind. Christmas is coming… the bonus… the Christmas bonus."

"Rácz doesn't forget," says Rácz. "If he makes a promise, he keeps it. He doesn't need some pavement plodder to remind him of his promises!"

The policeman flushes red and lifts both arms in apology. Rácz reaches into his pocket and takes out an envelope. "Here you are," he says, "a little bit extra. Share it out."

Then Rácz goes and takes his seat at the bar. He orders vodka and waits for Khunt, the money dealer. Rácz gives Khunt the key to the hotel's Renault minibus: in it are boxes of poor quality imitation Omega, Breitling and other watches. Fools and people who don't know any better will fall for them. They have to be sold.

"I want X crowns," says Rácz. Anything over that sum is Khunt's. He can sell for as much as he wants. But that's not all. Rácz takes out a list. He's also got Denon and Sony cassettes. Obvious fakes. Cheap fakes from Hong Kong. Rácz doesn't know much about them. He only knows the price. He knows how much he wants for them. If Khunt is interested, they have a deal.

Khunt agrees. He won't say no. But he has to think a bit about it. For the time being, he wants to see the watches. If he likes them, he'll buy the lot. He grabs the minibus key and gets up. He goes off to have a look.

Rácz finishes his vodka and orders another. Khunt is back in no time. He'll take them. He takes his wallet out and counts the money. Soon, both men are sitting contentedly. If Khunt is interested, Rácz can get an unlimited quantity of those cassettes. Here are the brands and prices. As usual, Rácz will consider a discount.

Khunt nods in agreement. They always come to terms. Khunt likes to deal only with reliable people. And you can certainly rely on Rácz.

Rácz doesn't twitch an eyebrow, of course. He lacks any capacity for genuine emotion and has no idea how to react. He won't be humble and refuse to accept praise, since he is certain that Khunt is right. He doesn't even nod; he just coughs and orders another vodka in an unusually muted voice.

After Khunt's departure, the small-time currency dealers show up with their daily take of marks and schillings. They sit down in turn and hand Rácz their modest loot. Rácz pays them off on the spot. The Albanians come, too. They want to do a deal, too. Rácz is friendly, but does not suck up to them. When he can, he'll meet them halfway, but he warns them he doesn't want their dirty snouts hanging about the hotel. On the pavement is OK, but they mustn't dare come in! He's the boss inside. The Albanians put on an air of cool defiance, but they obey. They know that

Rácz is powerful. The cops are in his pocket, and the hotel staff do as he says. The Albanians wouldn't stand a chance.

"How's it going?" Video Urban calls to him. Wearing a new leather jacket, he stands at Rácz's table, deciding whether to join him or not. Rácz silently points to a free chair. Urban sits down.

"I haven't seen you for ages," says Rácz. "I suppose that friend of yours, the Swede, showed up, did he?"

"What do you mean?" says Urban, taken aback and beginning to regret joining the stoker.

"Nothing," says Rácz, "just asking what's kept you, as I haven't seen you for a long time. You haven't brought me any marks or schillings lately."

"I'm not doing it any more," says Urban. "I've finished with that."

"Really?" The stoker is incredulous. "Found something better? Are you working with that camera of yours, like you meant to?"

Urban nods.

Rácz shrugs. "I don't know," he says. "Who'd want to piss about, going to weddings and baptisms? Not me, I tell you."

Video Urban shakes his head. Urban doesn't piss about anywhere. He works at home, mostly. People come to him.

Rácz finds that strange. "How come?" Does the whole wedding come to Urban's place?

"No," says Urban. He doesn't do weddings. Hasn't Rácz read his ad in the free-ad paper?

Rácz shakes his head: Rácz does not read the papers. He doesn't read anything.

If he did, Urban thinks, he'd have realised.

Rácz is fed up exchanging banter with this brat of a currency dealer. Everyone does as they think best, he believes. If Urban thinks this will make him more money, fine! Rácz couldn't care less. But now that it doesn't matter, would Urban tell him how he managed to clean those buses out of currency?

Urban smiles, even though the memory is unpleasant one. It's very painful, in fact. "Well, I did it all at customs."

"Customs!" Rácz repeats.

"Yes, customs," says Video Urban. "But I wouldn't recommend it."

"Why not?" Rácz is curious.

"Too risky. It's full of strange cops."

"That wouldn't interest me," says the stoker indifferently. Rácz only works here in the hotel. Anything outside is of no interest to him. But he does know one thing. A big raid on the currency dealers is set for the day after tomorrow, and the cops are coming all the way from Prague. Urban should watch out. Rácz tells him just in case, even though he knows Urban has left the racket and so is in no danger.

"You're right," says Urban. Urban doesn't do money-changing any more. If he shows up, it is just to have a coffee and a shot of Becherovka. Money isn't everything.

Rácz throws up his hands: that is, after all, just Urban's personal opinion. Rácz doesn't agree. What are you without money? Shit. An absolute nobody.

Video Urban takes a sip of Becherovka and says nothing. "That's true of you," he thinks. "Even a dog wouldn't bark at you, if you didn't have money." But he doesn't say it. Urban is an artist. He doesn't have to be a hustler.

Rácz has his opinion of Urban, too. Lately Urban has been getting too big for his boots. As if he were somehow better than others. As if his shit didn't smell. He wants to make money, but he wants to stay clean, too. But that won't work. You're either as poor as a church mouse, or you get your hands in shit. Rácz unwittingly raises his hands to his eyes. They'd never been so clean and well kept. If he wants, he'll get a manicure today. "Either I have the money for it, or I don't," the stoker tells himself.

* * *

As Christmas approaches, the stoker can't resist an urgent flying visit. He arranges it all in one day. He leaves two days' dry rations for the gypsies in the boiler-room and orders Ďula to wax the hotel minibus. They find the way to Rácz's native village on the road atlas. Meanwhile, Rácz gets some presents together: French perfume for Eržika, a bottle of Cognac, Martell. He thinks of his Uncle Endre: another, cheaper bottle of Cognac. Rácz gets in the minibus and Ďula drives off.

On the way there Rácz is quiet. He smokes cigarettes and takes swigs of rum from the bottle. When they reach the village, first they drive up and down, so that everyone can see the car Rácz is returning home in. Pity they don't bump into proud Feri Bartaloš; Rácz would love to pay him back for splashing mud all over him. This spoils the stoker's mood a bit.

They park in front of the Kišš house. Ďula carries the presents. "Is that you?" Kišš is surprised as he noisily gets off his chair. Mrs. Kišš runs in from somewhere, dragging a blushing Eržika by the hand. Rácz looks at her with different eyes now. He no longer feels the torments of love;

the tremors are over, so are the butterflies in his stomach and the embarrassment. He is an experienced man of the world and Eržika is not such a great beauty.

Rácz hands out the presents.

"I can see you're doing well," says Kišš. "What do you do?"

"I'm a stoker," says Rácz evasively.

"And do they pay well?" Kišš asks, touching the sleeve of Rácz's new Italian-styled jacket. He winks at Mrs. Kišš and shows her Rácz's sleeve. She touches it, too. They murmur their approval. Kišš grabs Eržika's hand and forces her to feel the quality of the suit. Blushing, she pulls her hand away.

"They pay well," says Rácz. And he makes a bit on the side, as well.

"What do you mean, on the side?" Kišš doesn't understand.

"Just — on the side," says Rácz. He sorts things out, this and that, and he gets his share.

"So it must be him, then!" Kišš yells, and bangs the table for joy. "It's him! It is him, after all!"

Rácz is puzzled, but doesn't show it. He says nothing and waits. Kišš stops laughing and has a bad coughing fit, gesticulating with his arms and legs. Kišš's brother is a butcher in the next village, as Rácz well knows. Recently he imported a Mercedes from Austria. He had to buy hard currency in the city. They sent him to some hotel to see a Mr. Rácz. He was a rich powerful man. He doled out the money, which he kept in an enormous box. Kišš's brother had never seen so much money in his life. And he's a village butcher. Then he told Kišš all about it. "Suppose it's your Rácz, the one you sent off to the city?" Kišš's brother asked him. "Go on with you!" Kišš had laughed then. The age was right, so was the way this Rácz looked. Kišš had one more thing to wonder about. He woke up many a night, wondering: "What if it is him?"

"Yes," says Rácz, "it was me. I didn't recognize your brother, Mr. Kišš. If I had, I'd have given him a discount."

Kišš still can't believe it. Ďula has to confirm that his boss, Rácz, is the most powerful man around the Hotel Ambassador. Everybody has to do what he says. Even when Kišš finally believes him, he still incredulously shakes his head. He carefully puts the cognac in his bureau. He'll drink it later. He won't let anyone else have a single drop. He puts a half-empty bottle of pear brandy on the table and pours drinks. They drink. Rácz, used to cognac and fine Scotch, starts to cough.

"You must be wondering how your pig, cow, and horse are doing," Kišš remarks.

Rácz is not in the least interested: he's forgotten that he'd given the butcher his animals to look after. He finally gets up and follows the old man into the barn and the pig pen.

"They get good fodder," says Kišš. "They're warm here, too." They didn't have it so good at Rácz's old place. The horse does best of all. The butcher regularly puts on riding breeches and boots and gallops like the wind over the fields. Riding is healthy, and it looks good. "The gentry used to ride," explains Kišš. Kišš belongs to the local gentry. He knows that a riding horse would be more appropriate, but it couldn't take his bloated body.

Rácz's horse is a giant draught gelding: it can carry Kišš. Finally, Kišš concedes, Rácz is now one of the family, too. He too belongs to the local gentry. Kišš has heard a lot about Rácz from his brother. None of them had ever done so well. Rácz will come back to the village and will sit at the gentry's table. Kišš will be proud of him, his future son-in-law. They'll go everywhere together and Kišš will introduce him to everyone. "This is Rácz, my son-in-law."

Rácz is now utterly bored with this. He lets the fat butcher blether on in the dark humid pigsty. He goes into the yard and hungrily breathes in fresh air. When old Kišš joins him outside, he tells him: "Well, big deal: if it makes you happy, keep the horse." Kišš trembles with joy. "And as for the pig," Rácz adds, "we have to butcher it."

"When," asks Kišš.

"Why not now?" says Rácz. "We'll invite all the family and friends for the evening. Let everyone see I'm here."

"Good idea," says Kišš. "Right away. I'll just call in some people to help. You can go to the house. Keep Eržika happy. We'll manage all right. Off you go."

The news of Rácz's arrival spreads through the village. Soon Uncle Endre shows up.

"Why didn't you drop by?" he asks Rácz. "You know where I live."

Rácz says nothing. He shrugs. Kišš saves the situation.

"No need to get so worked up," says the butcher. "We kept him here, as a matter of fact. The boy wanted to go, but I said, 'Don't, he'll come here anyway.' Don't take offence, Endre, now we're as good as family."

They drink pear brandy. Endre softens.

"I just wanted…" he mumbles.

"Will you help us?" Kišš asks, pointing to the pig that had been let out to get the blood circulating. The pig grunts and digs its snout into the frozen ground. It can sense that something is not quite right.

* * *

Rácz sits in the living room, looking at his hands. Eržika sits in a chair opposite him, blushing and looking at the carpet. In a corner at the back of the room Mrs. Kišš sits in an armchair, smiling slyly, knitting. The window looks out onto the courtyard. The glass is covered with hoarfrost. Kišš, Endre and a couple of neighbours can be seen vainly trying to catch the pig.

"So, tell us," Mrs. Kišš addresses Rácz, "what's city life like?"

Rácz shrugs, and looks at Eržika. "Fine," he says.

"They say everyone does as you say," she remarks.

"They do," he agrees.

Silence reigns again, interrupted only by the clicking of Mrs Kišš's knitting needles and the shouting from the yard.

"Bugger," Ďula curses, when the pig bites him.

"And how about the city girls?" Mrs. Kišš asks. "Are they beautiful?" Eržika blushes. Rácz shrugs.

"I don't know." Rácz doesn't get time to look at girls.

Mrs. Kišš nods with satisfaction and goes on clicking her needles.

The living room is filled with the desperate squealing of the captured pig. The men, frozen stiff, are yelling.

"And what about you, Eržika?" Mrs. Kišš turns to her daughter. "Don't you want to ask him about anything? Aren't you interested?" Eržika blushes deep red. "And where do you live?" Mrs. Kišš asks. "Is there a dormitory?"

Rácz coughs and fidgets. Rácz lives right in the hotel.

"Isn't that expensive?" Mrs. Kišš asks.

"No," Rácz shakes his head. "It's free."

"So it's like a dormitory," says Mrs. Kišš.

"Sort of," Rácz concedes after momentary consideration.

Rácz's pig darts under the window, cheerfully dragging the rope tied round its neck.

"Up the Virgin Mary's cunt!" Kišš curses in Hungarian, running and stumbling in the snow.

"And who do you live with?" Mrs. Kišš asks. "Do you have a roommate?"

Rácz shakes his head. No, Rácz lives alone.

"Good heavens!" Mrs. Kišš says when the clock strikes half past ten. "They'll be repeating yesterday's soap opera. Eržika, turn on the television!"

Rácz's pig decides to sell its life dearly. It escapes to the other side of the yard and crawls under a tool-shed. When the men try to push it out with bean-poles, it squeals and runs away, taking the tool-shed with it for a few metres. The moving tool-shed gets Rácz so interested in the action that he presses his face to the window.

The soap opera shows a scene in a kitchen. A man explains to a woman that he can't marry her. The actress cries hysterically.

"Did you miss me?" Rácz asks Eržika barely audibly.

Eržika shrugs. She doesn't know. She's watching the soap opera. Mrs. Kišš's needles click. The pig squeals desperately. The men, tired and cold, curse. The frantic actress whimpers.

* * *

In the evening, the Kišš house is crowded with people. It's packed and noisy. Kišš drags in a demijohn of pear brandy. Everybody has to drink it. Rácz gets boisterous. They seat Eržika next to him. Everyone looks them over with amiable smiles and insinuating insolence mirrored in their faces. The rough, badly distilled spirits tighten Rácz's mouth into a grimace. He gets up.

"Where's my driver?" he asks.

They all fall silent, overawed. Ďula, covered in muck, runs in from the kitchen, with a chunk of meat stuck on his fork.

"Have you been drinking?" Rácz asks him.

Everybody turns and looks at Ďula.

"No," says Ďula. People look at Rácz.

"Are you sure?" Rácz responds in a stern voice.

"Honest to God!" Ďula affirms.

"Then you'll go to the tavern and buy supplies." The stoker orders three boxes of sparkling wine, three cases of red and three cases of white wine. "And get a couple of cases of Coke. And three cartons of Marl-boros. Got it?"

Ďula nods and starts to looks for the minibus keys. Kišš protests with insulted dignity. Kišš can afford to treat his guests himself. Rácz, his future son-in-law, need not spend his money.

Rácz dismisses the objection. Rácz is richer and it's his celebration. It's his *party*, as they say in the city. He's come back home after a long absence. He's come back a success. Rácz will treat his kith and kin. "And that's settled."

"And where's the tavern?" Ďula interrupts, embarrassed.

"Never mind," says Rácz, "I'm coming with you."

They drive through the dark village. Rácz says nothing. They reach the tavern and get out. Rácz just gives the orders. Ďula carries the cases and provisions. Then Rácz pays from his giant wallet. The men in the tavern watch in silent admiration.

On the way back, along the unlit, slippery road, they can see in the far distance the silhouette of a warmly dressed man on horseback.

"That's Feri Bartaloš!" Rácz says. "Step on it!" he orders Ďula and impatiently leans forward. Ďula obeys. Soon they catch up with the rider. Bartaloš's mighty horse rides at a gentle canter, taking proud Feri home. Feri Bartaloš is so well wrapped up that he doesn't notice anything around him. "Let's push him off the road!" Rácz suggests vindictively.

"But, boss..." Ďula tries to object.

"What do you mean 'but'?" Rácz asks instantly with menacing animation. "Don't give me 'but'!" He clenches his fist as always when someone tries to resist him.

Ďula shrugs uncertainly, as a sign of capitulation. He won't take responsibility, but he changes gear and veers to the side of the road, pushing the rider into a ditch. Then something hits the metal side of the minibus: both rider and horse vanish in a cloud of snow. Rácz looks round. The sight of Feri Bartaloš lying motionless with four huge hooves helplessly sticking up in the air fills Rácz with triumph. He can't take his eye off the scene. He turns his head forward and looks at the road surface only when his neck starts to hurt.

The windows of the Kišš house light up the night. Curious onlookers from the village stare through the windows and step on each other's toes. They draw back respectfully as the minibus drives up. Kišš brings a small barrel of pear brandy out onto the porch for them.

Inside, the corks from the sparkling wine soon start hitting the ceiling. Others sip mulled wine. The tables are filled with plates of steaming pork-belly soup and meat.

"Try the champagne, Eržika," says Rácz, lighting up a Marlboro. "It'll refresh you," he adds. He himself has drunk plenty, as he had to celebrate his victory over proud Feri Bartaloš and so, quickly, he's downed a few glasses of champagne in quick succession. Now he finds Eržika desirable. She is young, well built, with a round face. In her place Rácz imagines Silvia, made-up, bleached, and overdressed, smelling of cigarette smoke with breasts the size of a five-crown coin and with a crotch the width of a hand between her lanky, skinny legs. He suddenly sees things clearly. He controls a sudden urge to grab her full thigh, visible under her full-length apron. Compared to Eržika, Silvia looks like a spider in a privy, Rácz concludes. The same goes for the other scrawny bitches in the Ambassador Cabaret bar: Edita, Wanda the Trucker, Anča-Jožo, and even Dripsy Eve. Disgusting! Only now, at home, among his own people can Rácz breathe freely!

"And you, Ďula," he turns to his driver. "Why aren't you having fun?" Ďula is sitting drinking mineral water. Rácz gets up and gives orders. Rácz orders Ďula to drink. They're not driving anywhere today. Tomorrow. Later. Afterwards. Rácz is celebrating his engagement. Yes, engagement. He's going to be engaged. Ďula meekly agrees to a glass of champagne and downs it. Eržika, too, finishes her glass. Rácz immediately refills it.

"Tell me, how's life?" Rácz asks Eržika. He likes her. He's fallen in love with her and fancies her.

"Well, mixed," answers Eržika, her speech blurred, and laughs. "Nothing but work," she adds. Her father makes her work all the time. The old women in the butcher's shop are always getting at her, nothing is good enough for them. She'd rather go to the city and work in a meat-processing factory. She'd live in a dormitory. She'd come home for weekends. "It's better in the city. There's entertainment, discos, shops. What's here? Nothing."

Rácz disagrees. Rácz is a city man, you could say. He's been living quite some time, in fact, right in the city centre. He knows very well that there's nothing there like what Eržika dreams of. If he could, Rácz would come straight back to his native village. Life is good here. In the city there's no life! But Rácz has to stay there for now. Business. A lot of people depend on Rácz.

"And do you like me a bit?" Rácz asks Eržika.

"Me?" Eržika asks. Why not? None of her friends have boyfriends like him, with a car and a driver. Eržika is proud of him.

Rácz smiles, contented and proud. He pours another glass of champagne and downs it. A driver? That's not just a driver; he's a servant, too! To prove it, Rácz orders Ďula to do his trick: to drink a litre of water non-stop and then crawl under the table with a pork chop between his teeth.

They all laugh and clap. Rácz can't take his eyes off Eržika. How shy, young and fresh she is!

By now the guests are drunk. Some at table begin to sing mournful, drawn-out songs.

Rácz puts an arm round Eržika. He pours her another drink. He swallows a few times. His ears are buzzing. The blood has gone to his head. He's excited. "If you really like me," he says half-choked, "you'll come to the barn with me right now." Rácz takes fright: he has a feeling that everyone around has heard what he said. But they're noisily having fun. Someone has vomited on the table.

"Why the barn?" Eržika asks, "and then what?"

Rácz's broad, simple face has changed. His eyes are popping with passion and his nostrils flare like a bull's. His jaw shakes. He trembles all over. He's sure he's never felt this way before. Not even Silvia could unleash such a hurricane of feelings in him. He expects it's because he's never had much time for champagne before. But that doesn't matter. Rácz knows that this is it! The other affair meant nothing. He loves Eržika. It's all coming back to him. After all, he went to the city for the sake of Kišš's daughter!

"Why the barn?" Eržika asks.

Rácz gesticulates. "You'll show me there how much you like me," he says. "That's how it's done in the city. If a girl loves someone, she has to prove it to him first." Rácz is getting the feeling that she loves him only for his money. Yes, Rácz has got money. Why shouldn't he? But first of all, he's a man. And what does a man need? He needs proof of love! Rácz drinks a glass of champagne and forces Eržika to do the same. He fills their glasses and proposes a toast: "To us!"

At the other end of the table, Kišš clinks his glass and gets up. He starts a speech. Kišš is, you can say, loaded. A butcher can make good money, people will eat anything. Young Rácz would like to marry his daughter, his only daughter. Rácz is a smart boy. He's proved that he inherited all the good qualities of his parents who passed away so tragically. He left for the city and became rich amazingly quickly. But you have to admit that if it weren't for Kišš, Rácz would not be where he is today! This morning Rácz gave him his horse. Now Kišš will give him his daughter. Yes, first thing tomorrow, they'll go to the priest to arrange the marriage banns.

Kišš, all red in the face, finishes and sits down. Now they all expect Rácz to say something. But Rácz just sits there obstinately mute; he's not a talker. He'd rather go and hide somewhere.

Uncle Endre saves the situation. He gets up and makes a speech. He assures Kišš that Rácz will be an obedient son-in-law. At home, he got slapped for the slightest thing. His parents choked to death on money. Endre had his share when the inheritance was divided up, while Rácz was on the way to the funeral. There wasn't that much left. It was just a smidgen compared to what Rácz now has at his disposal. Such is justice: they all helped themselves to money that was not theirs and which — and Endre has to admit frankly — they robbed young Rácz of. They shared out someone else's inheritance. What a shameful act! However, on the other hand, would Rácz have been able to get so far if he'd inherited the money? Never! He'd have been an averagely well-off peasant, and Kišš would have given him Eržika in marriage there and then, and they'd all have lived happily ever after. A sort of justice arranged things in such a way that a shameful act eventually turned out to be a good deed, even a favour. Otherwise, Rácz would have never become such a wealthy man, a nabob, a tycoon. Uncle Endre now paused for a while. And therefore, he went on, looking Rácz in the face, he asks in the name of Rácz's aunts and uncles for forgiveness for making him… such a rich man. At the same time, he proposes a toast to the health of the young couple.

The drink has gone to Rácz's head. He can't make sense of Uncle Endre's speech. Something about money, and an inheritance. A few pennies! He's not interested in that. The point is not to save as much as one can, but to make as much as one can. So Rácz forgives Uncle Endre and his other relatives.

Now Kišš gets up. He'd like to say something else, as this company is all gathered here. In the future someone might spread gossip and slander him, try to damage him. No, Kišš does not want to say that this is inevitable, but it's quite possible that Rácz might find out from someone that his daughter was for some time, after Rácz left for the city, engaged to Feri Bartaloš. "Well," Kišš pauses, while Rácz is stunned. "Actually," Kišš continues, "it's true and it isn't." Kišš did consider it prudent to betroth Eržika, to protect her from the young men of the village. "After all," Kišš turns to his guests, "a girl is safer when everybody knows that she has a fiancé." They all murmur in agreement. "But on the other hand," continues Kišš, "he has to ask: 'What sort of a fiancé is Feri Bartaloš?'" Yes, Kišš will swear to Rácz that this was only a protective manœuvre. It was the obvious thing to do to get peace for Eržika, so she could wait for Rácz. Rácz needn't worry. Nothing happened, Kišš made sure of that. And that is why Kišš asks his future son-in-law Rácz: will Rácz pardon him for being so concerned for the safety of his daughter and her future happiness with Rácz? After all, she's always loved Rácz. Kišš hadn't meant to tell Rácz, but now he realises that it's better if he told him, and not some evil-tongued gossiping old woman. Kišš's conscience is clear.

Kišš stops talking. With a question in his eyes, he watches Rácz. Rácz's eyes focus on Eržika's blushing face. "If that's how it is, I forgive you, Mr. Kišš," says Rácz after a few moments.

Everyone starts clapping. The toasts are over and the wild party resumes.

"Well, how about it?" Rácz persists.

"About what?" Eržika fails to understand.

"Will you go to the barn with me?"

Eržika shrugs. "I don't know."

Rácz sees his opening in her answer. He grabs her thigh. Under the table. Nobody sees a thing. Eržika is afraid to shriek, she doesn't want to attract attention.

"Let's go then," he insists in a muffled monotone.

Eržika gets up with a sigh. Rácz follows her.

Nobody has noticed a thing.

It's dark outside. The windows illuminate the yard. The curious onlookers have drunk the barrel of pear brandy Kišš brought out for them and are lying motionless, scattered in various positions in the snow. The farm buildings at the back loom up in the dark. The twinkling stars freeze high in the blackness. Rácz grabs Eržika's hand and drags her to the barn. The champagne sparkles in his head. He feels all tense and stiff.

"I see," Eržika says, "there are rings round the moon."

But Rácz couldn't care less about rings round the moon. He burps and opens the barn door. A shaft of light from the yard falls on a pile of hay. Rats are chasing each other up in the rafters. Their eyes are phosphorescent red.

Fearfully, Eržika clings to Rácz's excitement. "Brrr, it's cold," she says, her speech blurred. "It's cold in here!"

But Rácz isn't listening to her now. He pushes her down into the hay and hungrily hurls himself on her.

"No! No!" Eržika tries to fight him off and keeps her knees together with all her strength.

Rácz puts his hand under her dress. In one powerful move he rips off her antediluvian drawers and throws them behind him. Then he forces her legs apart. He puts his weight on one of her knees and tries to pry away the other one with his hand. His muscles creak with the effort. He shoves his own thigh into the gap. Then he unzips his damp fly and takes out his member. When he lays it on Eržika's bare thigh, the girl shrieks with fear.

"Shut your mouth, stupid!" Rácz hisses. He pushes his whole body up higher. Eržika shrieks once more. Outside, the dogs start to bark. Rácz slaps her face.

"Rácz isn't used to anyone resisting him," he says hoarsely.

He forces himself into Eržika's limp body and sighs with relief. Eržika's teeth chatter with cold. "Does it hurt?" Rácz barks impatiently. Eržika nods. She lies motionless, biting her tongue. Rácz begins to move. He speeds up. Eržika lies like a corpse. When Rácz is about to come, he frees himself from between his fiancée's thighs. He uses his hand to ejaculate powerfully at precise intervals. "Ah, ah, ah," he comes violently and regularly. Then he falls into the hay.

Eržika sits up heavily and takes a handful of hay to wipe the still hot sperm from her breasts, face, and hair. Rácz wipes himself on her dress. His mind is now working normally. His last powerful shot of semen seems to have cleansed his blood of all desire and excitement. It's all clear to him now. His relatives stole his inheritance and, worse, then claimed they were doing him a favour; Kišš offered his daughter to proud Feri Bartaloš the moment Rácz was out of the village and then claimed he was doing him a favour. Eržika is a stupid village goose. And she's fat. Rácz has very different women in the city. They may be old hags, in their forties, even fifties, but when they put on make-up and dress up, any man gets a hard-on like a candle. And Eržika? Not even twenty. When she's thirty, she'll be twice as fat as now. She'll bear him three children and then lose her looks. Until the day she dies, she'll wear two sets of clothes: white butcher's shop-assistant overalls and a flowery dress at home. And she'll never stop chewing sunflower seeds, like her mother, until Rácz itches to slap her. No, Rácz has a brighter future ahead of him! No, he doesn't have scrubbers like Silvia in mind. One day he'll kick her out on her arse, too. When he's fed up with her. No, he doesn't mean her. Rácz will find himself a city girl, a young girl who likes him. Is it really so hard to like a man like Rácz?

Eržika wants to be kissed. She offers him her half-open mouth and closes her eyes. Rácz pushes her away.

Eržika opens her eyes. "So that's what you are!"

"What am I?" Rácz clenches his fists threateningly.

"Was that what you wanted?" Eržika bursts out crying. "You swine!" Her round face distorts itself into a grimace like a Chinese idol's. Rácz has never seen a Chinese idol, but he still feels an elemental revulsion for Eržika. He moves further away from his fiancée to avoid being polluted by her tears and snivelling.

"You weren't even a virgin!" Rácz says in disgust. "No hymen. No blood. Whore! Who knows who you've slept with while Rácz slaved for you in the city. The whole village? Half the village? Or Feri Bartaloš? Yes, of course, him!" Rácz jumps up and theatrically beats his brow. How could he not have seen it! Feri Bartaloš was her supposed fiancé, after all. Well then, Rácz can see what "supposed" means! Rácz's future wife has to be a virgin! He really wants to give her a slap. But he has to watch out. When he hits someone, it shows. He doesn't want to end up in gaol. As it is, he is a laughing stock. "Shit!" Rácz wildly kicks the barn door open and quickly strides towards the house.

"Took a fancy to my money, did you, Mr. Kišš?" Rácz shouts into Kišš's ear. Kišš is vomiting by the gate. The butcher's watery eyes turn to him and he says a few blurred words. He's drunk; he can't take anything in. Kišš's house is brightly lit. Rácz bursts in. "Ďula," he shouts in a wild, alien voice. "ĎULA!" Rácz repeats when he gets no reply.

"What is it, boss?" Ďula appears in the door to the kitchen, a glass of champagne in his hand. His shirt is pulled out of his trousers; he's dishevelled and dirty. He staggers, and smiles stupidly.

Rácz is enraged. He knocks the glass out of Ďula's hand. The glass smashes. "We're leaving!" Rácz orders.

"Where to?" Ďula asks, not comprehending.

"Home! To the hotel, you fool!" Rácz says.

"But I've been drinking," says Ďula.

"I don't care," says Rácz. "Get going! Out!"

Ďula looks around helplessly, but everybody is drunk, singing songs. Nobody pays attention to Rácz and Ďula. "You'll sober up on the way," Rácz declares. "Let's just get out of here!" Ďula watches him helplessly. "Move it, come on, move it!" Rácz yells at him and pushes him towards the door.

The Renault minibus, its lights off, starts jerkily and rushes across Kišš's front yard. It jumps ahead and then backs until it faces the gate, which no one has opened. Ďula puts it in second and steps on the gas. He turns on the lights. In the light is Eržika, her arms spread out, running toward the minibus, as if she wanted to stop Rácz.

"Out of the way, you snake!" Rácz screams at her through the side window. "Put your foot down!" he orders.

However, Ďula veers to avoid Eržika; the vehicle knocks down the gate and a section of the fence and gets onto the dark street. Ďula changes gear. The van roars through the sleeping village, occasionally hitting a fence at speed, or slipping into the ditch.

Rácz says nothing. He lights a cigarette. A few times he imagines he can see the silhouette of a man on horseback, but when they get nearer, it turns out to be a grotesquely shaped roadside bush, or sometimes nothing at all.

* * *

"Babylon!" A demented man on the pavement shouts, lifting his gaunt arms above his head. "The whore of Babylon!" he repeats in a stern voice.

Wanda the Trucker, clinging to an elderly Austrian, aims her long legs towards his white Mercedes, parked at the pavement in front of the hotel. Nobody pays attention to the grimy demented hermit flailing his arms, shouting, "Hosanna, I say unto you, the end is near! There is still time to repent!"

The passers-by look at him, but nobody sees that this demented preacher was once the placid, corpulent Freddy Piggybank. Gaunt, hairy, and covered in the filth of many weeks, Freddy has changed so much that he is unrecognizable. After his car park was turned into a Christmas market, Piggybank got drunk and wrecked the Ambassador Bar. Then every day he came to the hotel entrance, watching with stupefied silent reproval the goings-on in what had been his place of work. He greedily and angrily calculated how much money he'd lost. The fishmongers selling carp, the greengrocers, and the bartenders in their jerry-built wooden booths liked it near the hotel. Even after their lease expired they stayed put in the parking lot, and the long queues of customers supported their cause. They offered the town council much more rent than Freddy could afford. There were no two ways about it: Piggybank was out on the street. This personal tragedy took Freddy's breath away and for some time he was on the verge of apoplexy. Freddy Piggybank had paid his rent and taxes like an honest man. He'd never harmed anyone. And what did he get in return? For a while he tried to raise money by charging drivers to park at the hotel pavement, but the cops put a stop to that. They threatened him with gaol, if he went on collecting money illegally. "Well then, give me back my car park," the distressed pavement attendant retorted. The cops grabbed their truncheons and pointed them at Freddy, their necks straining and their eyebrows raised, as a sign of lively interest in his arguments. Instead of standing up for himself, the dismayed cowardly attendant avoided their gaze and left the scene in ill-concealed haste.

He could be seen spending his money on drink, pouring wine down his gullet at one of the jerry-built booths on his former parking lot. He wasn't allowed into the Ambassador Bar. Besides, it was too expensive for Piggybank's purse. It cost a lot at the wooden booth as well, but not so much. When Freddy got drunk, he cried. He grabbed chance listeners by their coat buttons and told them to their faces of his pain, of his heavy cross. Freddy Piggybank used to be an honest car park attendant. This here used to be a car park in the past, his only joy. He spent all and every day here. He was happy. Then came the bitch from the town council. She said the market would stay until Christmas. He said, "fine". So they built these booths and now they won't pull them down. Soon it'll be New Year. And then? The booths will still be here. Apparently for good. And so Freddy Piggybank is broke.

As the last sentence comes out, he always cries. He has no money left. Just a few crowns. All his savings went on paying for the damage done to the bar. Included in the bill was everything that had broken in the last five years. He's afraid to go home now. His parents demand money. They need it for food and electricity. But he doesn't have any. He eats what customers leave on their paper plates. It's not much; customers are mean and eat everything. They wipe the plate dry with their last piece of bread. Freddy Piggybank can't believe that this is what he demonstrated against the communists in freezing weather for.

But people soon tired of listening to Freddy. They chased him away, wherever he was. He stank. He didn't wash. His clothes were falling apart. His trailer had its electricity supply cut. He wasn't paying for anything. He had nothing to pay with. For nights on end he shivered with cold. He would sit, or lie and think. Then he disappeared for days. The sellers and servers in the market booths thought he might be lying dead in his trailer. But nobody went to check. First of all, they hated the idea of entering his stinking home. Secondly, nobody wanted to go to the police station and sign statements.

"If he's alive, screw him," said the manager of the drinks stall. "If he's dead, same thing! He won't rot fast in this cold. If he starts to stink, we'll have to do something. But he doesn't stink yet. So, what do we care? He's not one of us."

What a surprise when, after three days, the door of the trailer opened and Freddy Piggybank appeared! Between his moustache and beard appeared a scornful grimace, and his bulging eyes burned with spiritual ecstasy. "Pray, sinners!" he cried in a stentorian voice, lifting his arms. "Punishment is near," he added stepping between the shocked servers and drunks.

This was the beginning of a new life for Freddy. It consisted of imprecations, gesticulations, and a daily list of the most horrendous punishments which would fall on the heads of everyone around him. He lived on snow from the yellowish snowdrifts, leftover food, and rage. He became a demented hermit and, for the people from the Hotel Ambassador and its surroundings, just as well-known a character as when he ran around the parking lot with the red money bag and his fat face glistened with resolute self-importance.

"I say unto you," shrieked Freddy, "the Lord will be awesome in his anger. He will sweep away the sinners."

The elderly Austrian dithers. He looks back. The demented man is dressed in a baggy jacket made from a potato sack. His feet are bandaged in burlap tied with coarse hemp string. His bare knees are blue with cold. He patrols the salty pavement at a waddling run.

"You too, you Whore of Babylon," he yells at Wanda the Trucker, and a thin string of saliva dribbles from his mouth and instantly freezes. "You, too, will be punished! Your white sinful body will fry in the fire and the torments will never end."

"*Was ist das?*" Wanda's punter asks in alarm.

"*Nix, gor nix. Ein Trotl.* It's nothing; he's an idiot," she assures him.

The punter laughs knowingly. "*Ja, ich verstehe schon,*" he says in heavy Austrian dialect, "A madman, yes?"

They both get to the car and leave, spraying the immobilised hermit from head to toe in dirty salty slush. The hermit retreats into himself. He closes his eyes and feels the water running down the snowflakes on his moustache and beard. Yes, he deserved that! Even a man of God must suffer and expiate his sins. Yes, suffering is sweet! In his imagination he sees Wanda the Trucker's long white body writhing in the fire. "As she gave herself to her lovers, so she shall give herself to burning torment," says Freddy. He represses the shiver of joy that this thought gives him. The prostitute must suffer to pay for her moral laxity. Freddy focuses his wide-open, bloodshot eyes on the wooden stalls that have sprouted on what was his car parking. A few freezing, but obstinate customers gather at a counter, sipping mulled wine. The hermit stares at them impatiently with bloodshot eyes. He comes to a decision: they, too, will get their deserts. He hurries to the stand.

"How are you doing, Freddy?" the bartender addresses him. "Sleep well? They took the car park off him, and he lost his marbles," he whispers to the fellows at the counter.

The hermit approaches. "Throw away your money," he yells with pathos, lifting his arms over his head. "Throw those dirty little bits of paper away, for the end is near! Yes, I say unto you, the waters of Babylon have swollen greatly and they smell of sin! God will come to punish Sodom."

The customers listen and wink at each other in amusement. "And now, Freddy," the bartender suggests, "tell us something about the whores." He winks conspiratorially at the others, as if to say, "Just wait; you'll see something now!"

Freddy Piggybank warms up. He is a holy man and has been called to warn them all. "As for women who sell their bodies, there is no salvation for them." The man of God knows exactly what torments await them for selling their bodies. "They will be impaled on poles, quartered, gutted alive, boiled, and fried. Nothing will help them, even if they become models of piety. They deserve it!" Freddy was out of breath, and paused.

"And what about you?" one of the drunks asked. "Are you a Jehovah's Witness, or a Franciscan?" He asked just to show his friends that he knew all about the subject.

"I am from God," Freddy interrupts him. "The Lord appeared unto me and commanded me to tell everyone that the end is here."

"Take this," the bartender tells him, winking at the others, "have a drink! It's good, with cinnamon and cloves. Won't you?"

"There's no helping you either!" the hermit shouts. "You will end in torment in the fiery furnace!" He waves his arm wildly and knocks the glasses of mulled wine into the snow.

The men are enraged. "Not that," a drunk in dungarees and quilted jacket yells. He grabs the hermit by the beard and throws him into the snowdrift.

Freddy digs himself out of the dirty snow. He gets up and lifts his arms above his head in fury. A man of God had come to warn them. But he who will not be warned can't be helped. The holy man is leaving now. He has to proclaim the news of the approaching end! The hermit leaves with dignity, stomping his burlap shoes in the snow.

"And we get this all the time," the bartender sighs and takes a sip of mulled wine. "Sometimes it's funny, sometimes it's not."

* * *

Absolute discretion is not just a matter of refraining from stupid questions. It also means behaving always and under any circumstances as if nothing was happening, as if everything was quite normal and natural. Video Urban decided to mortify his natural human instincts. After all, it was a matter of money; you mustn't ogle, show surprise or disgust. In his advertisement Urban guaranteed absolute discretion: he has to offer it.

They call him out sometimes, but luckily not too often. Who would want to bother to piss about and go to some suburb like Petrzalka with a video-camera and all the equipment? Most clients can be persuaded on the phone to come to him, to Video Urban. It is not only more convenient for Urban, but also improves the quality of the shoot. Urban has given up his bedroom and turned it into a film studio. In the middle of the room is a big double bed. The camera is on a stand; there are studio lamps and umbrella-shaped light diffusers. Just like Hollywood.

People are not alike and they have different quirks. More often than not, Video Urban's clients are married couples or lovers who want to be immortalised having sex. Sometimes it doesn't work, when one of the partners, usually the woman, changes her mind in front of the camera. Sometimes the very opposite happens; the presence of a strange man turns many women into excited and voluptuous beasts and, compared to them, their partners seem like shrivelled horse droppings. Urban has seen some extraordinary things.

Sometimes queers show up, too. Urban thinks of Hurensson. It makes him sick, but he doesn't let on. After all, he is a pro and the clients pay well. Some of them take no notice of him; he is just as inanimate to them as the camera stand, or the painting over the bed.

It is not rare for him to be visited by women who ask him to film them masturbating. They often bring their own sex aids. One of them confessed that her husband had gone to build roads in Libya and asked her to send him a videocassette. This way she could hope that he wouldn't run after whores over there, the young woman says as she gets dressed, pays, and puts the thirty-minute cassette in her bag.

Then there was the time when a female customer, an ethereal being, showed up at the appointed time with an Irish setter on a leash. Urban did not raise an eyebrow when he heard her request. At least it's not boring, he thought. People differ, and so do their interests.

It's cold. The sky is overcast and it will soon snow. Urban looks through his window. Four floors down, on the pavement, people walk stiff with cold, sloshing through the snow. Urban represses a desire to spit on their heads, moves inside to the warmth, and closes the window. For some time now he has been feeling disgusted by his own flat. It is as if each customer leaves a drop of dirt inside. It means nothing to him that they pay him royally. It means nothing to him that everything that he eats and drinks, everything that he buys for his own enjoyment, or burns in the cylinders of his car, is paid for by them. Disgust is disgust. Urban would feel better if he'd chosen silly weddings, stupid anniversary celebrations and children's idiotic smiles. Or maybe he should have got a taxi licence. Even money-changing did not leave him feeling so disgusted. What was missing in his life? He had made all the money he could, and if he didn't feel like going on, he always had two thousand crowns a month from the department store, where he was among people who liked him. The people who've been coming to his place since he started his video business make him uncomfortable. They always seem to be perverts, male or females or some other kind of weirdos. Urban has even started dreaming about them. The good thing at least is that they're anonymous, quiet, and keep their distance; they don't try to involve Urban in their lives. When he films them, Urban feels like a doctor. He doesn't get excited.

Ever since his ad has appeared regularly in the free-ads weekly, he has to stay in, by the phone. The answering machine is no good; appointments with anonymous customers have to be booked personally. Sometimes he is the victim of a prank: an appointment is booked and nobody shows up. Sometimes he's abused on the phone. Urban realises that this is all part of the business. Nevertheless, it doesn't make him feel good. At least he has money, but there were times when he was making more. The advantage is that now no policeman can take his money away. He pays his taxes, so what can they do?

Urban reaches for the phone. He hesitates for a second and then dials the number of that dry whore Lenka. "What are you doing?" he asks her.

"Is that you?" Lenka asks and she seems quite happy. "You haven't called me for quite some time," says Lenka. "What's happened to you?"

"Nothing," Urban says. "I've been busy. I've started my own business."

She does not react as he imagines she should, so he asks her, "And what are you doing?"

"I'm on holiday," says Lenka.

"How I envy you!" says Urban.

Lenka laughs.

"You shouldn't have got kicked out of university," she says.

"Here we go again," Urban says. "Let's go out," he suggests.

"Where to?" asks Lenka.

"I'll take you to the pictures," says Urban. "Then we'll go and have dinner. Would you like to?" He quickly moves the paper closer and leafs through it with his left hand. "The Slavia's showing *La Dolce Vita*."

"Fellini?" Lenka asks. She's seen it already.

"*La Dolce Vita* is the ultimate film," Urban believes. "You have to see it several times. It's Fellini at his best."

The dry whore Lenka is playing hard to get. Apparently, she's got a lot of work on. Only after more persuasion does she let herself be talked into going. Urban puts down the phone, jumps up and starts to look for something nice to wear. Life has meaning, at least this evening. "I'm going to screw you one day, anyway," says Urban, knotting his tie. "We know about these virgins. It is all a question of the right circumstances." He knows all about it.

"By the way, are you doing anything on New Year's Eve?" Urban asks her after the film, as they sit in a Chinese restaurant, waiting for the food to be brought.

"That's what I wanted to ask you," says Lenka, taking the wind out of Urban's sails. "You want to invite me out somewhere," continues Lenka, noticing Urban's shock. "I've got an invitation to a classmate's party."

Urban feels sad. He nervously looks at the waiter, and drums his right hand on the table. Then he looks at Lenka. He likes her, naturally. Maybe he's in love with her. He is sometimes, certainly.

"I hope you don't think that's silly," she says.

"No, no," Urban assures her, shaking his head decisively.

"I hope you don't think it's silly, Lenka repeats, "but I wanted to ask you if you'd like to go to the party with me." Urban sits there, not smiling. "You know," Lenka says, "I want to make it look as if we're an item. Do you understand?"

"Yes," says Urban. "Actually, I don't."

Lenka is embarrassed. "I want to be sure that no one tries anything on. You know what I mean? I want them to think I have a boyfriend," she adds after a while.

It takes Urban time before he can speak. Of course, he'll find it pleasant, even fun to oblige. He meant to invite her to the Ambassador cabaret bar. Lenka surely knows her classmates inside out; they have no surprises left. Urban is certain no one would dare try anything on, even if Urban weren't her pretend-boyfriend: they're all impotent bookworms, anyway.

"You're wrong!" Lenka protests. "You don't know Krnáč and Taragel."

Urban nods in agreement. He must admit that he doesn't know them. But he wants to show her something she doesn't know: the hidden face of the city. Urban pauses, stirred by pride that he put it so nicely. The hidden face of the city. But the hidden face of the city doesn't impress Lenka.

"I'm sure you want to introduce me to those idiot friends of yours, the money-changing morons," she says accusingly.

The slant-eyed waiter brings hot stoneware dish-warmers and then the food. While he serves them, Urban and Lenka are silent. The food has a pleasant aroma.

"Bring me a knife and fork, please," says Urban, putting the chop-sticks aside.

The waiter bows. He leaves and soon returns with cutlery on a tray. A condescending smile plays on his immobile Asian face.

"It only takes a minute or two to learn to use chopsticks," says Lenka, when the waiter leaves. "I can't imagine eating Chinese food with a knife and fork."

She adroitly picks up the chopsticks and taps them together like a claw.

"Look, see? I'll teach you."

"I don't want to learn," says Urban. "I have a knife and fork."

"Shall I ask for chopsticks?" asks Lenka.

Urban shakes his head.

"I asked him to take them away," he says. "What's done, is done. They'll think I'm an idiot."

"Does it matter what the waiter thinks of you?" Lenka asks and taps her chopstick-claw menacingly. "Isn't it more important what I think of you?"

"Listen, we'll do a deal," Urban starts. "I'll go with you to the party and act as your boyfriend. But when it gets boring, we'll go to the Ambassador."

Urban smiles. Urban has an invitation, too. And not just anybody's: Rácz himself has invited him.

"Who is Rácz?"

"It's pointless trying to explain," says Urban, "or to describe it. You've got to see and experience it. Urban is certain that this would be a completely different sort of experience from Lenka's blasé and impotent classmates with their endless blethering about existence, truth, experience, background, values, epistemology, and all that crap.

"You're just jealous of them," says Lenka.

"Of them?" Urban is astounded. "And just what is there to be jealous of, if I may ask?"

"You could have been studying, if you hadn't been so stupid," Lenka said. "and next year you'd be graduating."

"And then I'd live with my dear parents until I'm thirty, making twelve hundred crowns gross a month," says Urban. "Not if I can help it."

"I bet your parents must be really proud of you now!" Lenka says.

Urban gets angry. He makes more in a day than his father makes in a month. Is that nothing?

"Who is Rácz, anyway?" Lenka asks after chewing for a while.

Urban pauses to reflect. "He's a natural calamity," he says. "A money-making machine."

"So he's just another money dealer?" Lenka asks, disappointed.

Urban nods in agreement. He thinks. "Rácz is the stupidest and the most limited person I've ever met," he finally says. He has less intelligence than Urban's left shoe. But he is incredibly adaptive. And predatory. Urban knows what Rácz wants. He wants everything. Rácz is a natural catastrophe. Urban looks at Lenka. Rácz would show her who's boss, he thinks, imagining Lenka's fragile white body in the stoker's paws. "She deserves it," he muses.

* * *

The stupidest and the most limited man Urban had ever met is sitting in his suite, silently watching the television screen. It's morning. An overcast sky can be seen through the window. On the screen a giant muscle man is brandishing a five-foot sword that emits sparks.

Ďula knocks and enters. "I've come, as you ordered. Here's that list of yours," he says, handing Rácz a piece of paper. "I've retyped it, like you told me."

Rácz takes the paper and looks it over, muttering approval. "You can see straight away it's better," he says with mild reproach. "And you have to add the lawyer," he decides.

"I don't know anything about him. I don't know what he's like and what we can expect of him. He doesn't let on. He keeps himself to himself."

Rácz looks at Ďula. "We'll invite him, too," he says. "Do it. Clear?"

"I don't know if he'll come," Ďula allows himself a doubt. Their joint foray to the stoker's village has strengthened, in Ďula's mind, his ties to the powerful stoker. "I mean if he doesn't have other plans," adds Ďula wisely.

"If he comes, he comes," says the stoker. "If he doesn't, he doesn't. So let's go through the list one more time." First Rácz and Silvia; her friend Edita; Ďula; Wanda the Trucker; Video Urban and companion; Khunt, who bought the watches from Rácz, and companion; two Albanian representatives: Bekim Bahmuci and Ahmet Sočila and their companions; a few scrubbers from the cabaret: Anča-Jožo, Dripsy Eve, and the others; a few important hotel guests. In other words, people who consider it an honour to sit at the same table as Rácz.

"A big honour, a big honour!" Ďula nods enthusiastically.

Rácz gets up. "Now go," he orders him, "and get me the restaurant manager!"

Meanwhile Silvia gets back from shopping. She takes off her fur coat and reveals a mini-skirt. She's wearing boots that reach above her knees, a Christmas present from Rácz. He bought them for her, but she doesn't like them. They look like fishermen's waders. But they're in fashion. Every whore at the Ambassador has them. Silvia puts down her bags.

"Where've you been?" asks Rácz.

"In Tuzex, the foreign-currency store," says Silvia.

"And what did you get there?"

"I bought a nice spring coat," she says.

"What do you need a spring coat for in winter?" Rácz asks.

"Spring comes next," Silvia announces stubbornly.

"Did you go with Edita?" Rácz asks her.

"I did," Silvia answers. "Why do you ask?"

"Just asking," says Rácz. He thinks the two women spend too much time together. It seems a bit strange to Rácz. He's heard about women who are such good friends that they end up screwing together. Rácz isn't sure what to think about that.

Somebody knocks at the door. "Come in!" Rácz roars. It's the restaurant manager. Rácz offers him a chair and briefly lets him know about his plans for New Year's Eve, which he proposes to celebrate with a circle of friends. He will need the separate lounge.

The restaurant manager says timidly that they'd be happy to welcome the boss and his much-respected companions, but unfortunately, the lounge is already reserved.

"Reserved?" asks Rácz. "Then cancel!" he orders severely, "I can't see the problem."

The restaurant manager politely clears his throat to gain time. He says, "It's not that simple. Dr. Renceš reserved the lounge at the beginning of December."

"And who's he?" asks Rácz.

"The boss doesn't know Dr. Renceš?" The restaurant manager is astounded.

"No," says Rácz. "Rácz has never been sick."

The restaurant manager chokes back his horror. "Dr. Renceš is the mayor of our city," he says in a trembling voice. Rácz doesn't lift an eyebrow. It's made no impression on him.

"You must understand now," said the restaurant manager, "that, with all the respect due to you, it's absolutely impossible to cancel the mayor's reservation."

"No, I don't understand," says Rácz. "Why is it impossible?" The restaurant manager just throws up his hands helplessly. Rácz loses patience. "Look," he says and gets up. "Either you cancel that reservation, or tell the mayor to dress very warmly for New Year's Eve. And his companions, too."

The restaurant manager turns pale. He is stumped, and falls back into his armchair in despair. "You can't do this to us," he murmurs, giving the triumphant stoker a look of entreaty.

"I can," Rácz says. "Why shouldn't I?"

"But you'll destroy us all," the restaurant manager moans.

"I've told you what I want," Rácz ends the interview, goes to the door and opens it. "Rácz never says anything twice," he adds. The restaurant manager sits in the armchair staring in disbelief. "Well, yes or no?" asks Rácz from the doorway. "I can count on the lounge?!"

"Tell me what to do," the restaurant manager whimpers in despair, "or how to do it." He reflects. He gets up and finally declares, "No. It's impossible. It's out of the question." Something inside him snaps. He falls on his knees and puts his hands together. "I beg you on my knees, don't ruin me!"

Rácz proudly sticks his chest out. "What do you mean 'Don't ruin me!' If Rácz wants to," he says menacingly, "he can ruin people, too. Now, out!" Rácz has said all he needs to. It all depends on the restaurant manager now.

The restaurant manager, a broken man, gets up and leaves. Rácz closes the door behind him. Silvia comes out of the bedroom dressed in black lace lingerie. She comes to Rácz, puts her arms round him and snuggles up.

"What do you say?" she whispers.

"About what?" reacts Rácz, still thinking about the restaurant manager.

"About my outfit," says Silvia.

"Well, it looks good," decides Rácz, and gives her buttocks a firm squeeze.

"Do you fancy me?" Silvia asks, inserting her hand under his sweater.

"Yes," says Rácz, feeling his blood pressure rising.

"And how do you fancy me?" asks Silvia. She lets Rácz slowly push her back into the bedroom.

"I fancy you a lot," says Rácz. He grabs her below the breasts. Silvia moans with pleasure. Rácz picks her up into his arms and carries her towards the bed.

"Watch out," Silvia reminds him, laughing, "you'll tear my stockings. You know how much they cost?"

"How much?" Rácz asks.

"Don't ask," Silvia says.

"But I am asking!" Rácz says and stops dead with Silvia in his arms half-way to the bed. Silvia tells him. Rácz freezes.

"That many crowns?" Rácz is astonished.

"No, five times as much, since it's in foreign currency vouchers."

Rácz opens his mouth. His excitement has ebbed away. The immobilised stoker clenches his fists. Silvia drops from his embrace. She falls on the floor. She hurts her tail bone badly, and groans.

"You bully," she cries.

Rácz stands above her, his eyes popping, all red in the face. Rácz has money, but not for stupid things! To spend so much on bloody stockings! He doesn't dare ask how much she paid for the lace panties she's wearing!

Silvia bursts into tears. She gets up and limps to the couch, pressing a hand to her tail bone. She moans disconsolately. And how much is her time with Rácz worth, she bawls. How much are her days and nights worth? For him she gave up the profession that she enjoyed so much! Has Rácz ever looked at himself in the mirror? And finally, for whose benefit, actually, did Silvia buy those trinkets? For herself? Or for the receptionist?

"Trinkets!" Rácz bellows. "Trinkets, you said?" He lifts a fist like an anti-tank grenade.

But there's no stopping Silvia. Rácz is a boring client. He's an oaf and ignoramus. As a lover, he's useless.

Rácz's eyes bulge out of their sockets. In his rage he puts his fist in his mouth so as not to kill the whore.

"Rácz might like to know," says Silvia, "maybe it doesn't happen in the country, but here, in the city, women usually expect when they make love to have something called an orgasm."

Rácz takes his fist out of his mouth. "What organism? What sort of organism?" He'll bash the bitch right away so hard she'll have a couple of organisms right away! Rácz keeps her and clothes her. Silvia gets anything she can think of! And Rácz asks nothing in exchange, except for her to be nice to him! She doesn't like him? Rácz isn't keeping her! He took her off the street and made her his mistress. Now, if she wants to walk the streets and kick her legs up in cabaret, she's welcome to it!

Silvia jumps off the couch. Rácz doesn't need to say it twice! Silvia opens the wardrobe and quickly begins to dress. She can't see for tears. Her bottom hurts. She gets dressed, puts on her shoes, takes her bag and slams the door with all her might.

Rácz races after her into the corridor. "Don't slam that door," he shouts, "or I'll slam you!"

By then Silvia is running downstairs. Her pattering feet sound like a bird's wings when it flees its cage.

"If you don't like it, fuck you!" the stoker bellows, and bangs the door so hard that the whole building shakes. He returns to his suite and sits down to a drink of whisky. "The gall!" Rácz reflects. "Who does she think he is? Rácz is no jerk off the street. Rácz is somebody. Somebody!"

There is a knock at the door and Ďula appears. "What's happened, boss?"

"Nothing," says Rácz. "Sit down and have a drink!"

"No, thanks, boss," Ďula declines. "I've got to drive today. I've got to get twenty new chairs from the furniture store. Chairs have been vanishing mysteriously recently."

"Just sit down and have a *Heevash Reygahl*!" Rácz orders. "Forget about the chairs. Let the guests sit on the floor, if there aren't enough chairs!"

Ďula reluctantly joins him and lets him pour the Chivas Regal.

"Your health," he says, and drinks.

"Your health," says Rácz, lost in reflection. "She'll be back!" he adds with certainty. "But cross her off the list!" Rácz orders Ďula after briefly mulling it over. "And cross Edita off, as well! I'll show them!" Rácz threatens them with his fist.

Soon the bottle is empty, most of it drunk by Rácz; Ďula was only sipping. Rácz can take as much as a horse. Alcohol seems to have no effect on him. He sits and watches. Occasionally, his lips mutter a Hungarian curse. But in the end, the bottle of Scotch has clearly calmed him down. He thinks about something else and even smiles. "Don't you worry, Ďula," he tells his driver, "we'll have a wild party. Oh, what a party we're going to have on New Year's Eve! We'll celebrate with Silvia or without her. Better without."

Ďula enthusiastically and obsequiously agrees. He greatly appreciates being allowed to sit next to the boss and being on close terms with Rácz, and drinks the Scotch, even though he doesn't like it. Rácz puts away his empty glass and gets up. So does Ďula.

"Have you got the keys to the boiler-room?" asks the stoker.

Ďula nods and shows the keys, with a query in his eyes. For quite some time Rácz hasn't shown any desire to see the boiler-room. It is Ďula who takes the food down to the gypsies. Sometimes he forgets, or can't be bothered: he's got no time. When Berki and Šípoš grumble, he threatens them that Rácz will come and torture them with a red-hot poker. Then the gypsies shut up. They're glad at least occasionally to get some food.

"And what are we doing there?" asks Ďula.

"You'll see," says Rácz. "There's something we have to sort out. Something very important."

This is a special occasion, Ďula realises. Rácz never smiles at other times. But then, why should he?

The gypsies are emaciated and watch them with big eyes. They hastily bow low to Rácz.

"Oh, boss," says Berki politely, "you've finally come to let me go and see my wife and children. Oh, what joy for a poor Roma!" Both gypsies are happy.

"Shut your trap, you filthy swine!" Ďula snaps at Berki. "If the boss wants to, he'll let you go. If he doesn't, you'll stay and rot here." Rácz remains silently on the stairs, deliberately ignoring the gypsies. He casts his eyes round the boiler-room. How long it's been since he worked and lived here! It doesn't seem true now.

Šípoš says, "Your Excellency, I am just an ordinary *romano chaneya*, a gypsy man. I have nothing, just a wife and a bunch of children— *chuprikane devlehureske*. It's him," he points at Berki, "who is the bad gypsy." He, Šípoš, is the good gypsy. There's no need for two men in the boiler-room. When His Excellency lets him go, Berki will easily manage on his own.

"You *baro kar*, big dick!" Berki shouts and clenches his fists. "*Haz yeg na mindzh*, I'll fucking knock you out!" He is about to throw himself at Šípoš.

"SHUT UP!" The stoker shouts. "Just tell me, if one of you can manage the work on his own. The other one can go. That way!" Rácz points to the noisy furnace. "Up the chimney you'll go!" he adds, sticking his index finger up. The gypsies fall silent. They tremble with fear. "Nobody asked you to come here," says Rácz. "You came by yourselves. You don't like it here now? Haven't you got everything? Are you cold? Hungry? Is the work too hard?"

"Gypsy swine find any work hard," says Ďula, and shakes his fist at them. "Now stand by the wall, over there, and keep your mouths shut," he orders. "We haven't come here to see you." He looks at Rácz.

Rácz points to the distribution valves. "Turn off that one, third from the left," he says.

Ďula snaps his fingers at the gypsies. "Did you hear?" he roars.

The intimidated cowardly gypsies run to the valves. Rags that once were precious leather jackets, Italian shirts and tailor-made fashionable trousers, flap on their shrivelled bodies.

"Turn off the third valve from the left!" Ďula orders.

The gypsies turn the valves as if it were a matter of life or death. When they're closed, Ďula approaches and tightens the valve firmly with a wrench.

"They talked too much," says Rácz about the gypsies. "They get no grub today."

"Right, boss," Ďula joyfully agrees. "That'll teach them to keep their mouths shut. May I ask, boss," says Ďula after they lock the metal door behind them and stride across the snow-covered yard, "may I ask what we were doing down there, actually?"

Dishwashers and cleaners look at them through the dishwashing room window. Ribana is there, too. The women shout at Rácz and Ďula.

"What do they want?" Rácz asks Ďula, as if he couldn't understand them.

"They want us to pay them a visit," says Ďula.

"Well then, let's go," says Rácz, who's in a sentimental mood.

"Do you mean it, boss?" Ďula wonders.

"Let's go," says the stoker and heads for the back entrance to the kitchen.

The kitchen welcomes him with its familiar and private aroma of cooking, disinfectant, and humidity. The chef almost faints when he sees the stoker himself striding among the cauldrons together with Ďula. He drops his cigarette butt and stands to attention. But Rácz ignores him. He peers under the pot lids, checks the electric fryers and ovens.

"Well, what'll we have?" he asks Ďula.

Ďula shrugs. Rácz picks up a serving fork and fishes out a big piece of boiled meat.

"A plate for the boss!" Ďula shouts.

Rácz decides to eat in the dishwashers' changing room. Ribana enters with a bottle of wine sent in by the chef. Rácz looks at the label on the bottle and then at Ribana. The gypsy woman is ugly and skinny. Her breasts droop under her colourful apron. Her hands are bleached from washing dishes, but there is enough to get Rácz's blood racing round with excitement.

"Are we going to *do it*?" the gypsy asks.

"What do you mean *do it*," says Rácz, putting the bottle on the table.

"Do you feel like *doing it*?" Ribana repeats.

"You mean…" the stoker finally gets it.

The gypsy nods with her tongue between her teeth. Rácz takes a bite of meat and gets up. Ribana puts her elbows on the table and sticks her bottom out. Rácz, still chewing, approaches her and lifts her apron. Underneath he finds the gypsy's bare bottom. He unbuttons his trousers. His member is sticking out and up. He weighs it in his hand and then enters the gypsy. They move wildly, but not for long. After a moment, Rácz stops chewing, his face freezes and a suppressed sigh escapes his mouth. He chokes. He has a coughing fit.

"Good, wasn't it?" Ribana asks. "You can do it with me any time you fancy," Ribana smiles, showing a mouth missing half its teeth. She knows that Rácz is a big boss now and has two women for every finger. But anyway, if need be, just ask for Ribana from the dishwashing room.

When they leave the kitchen and walk over crunchy snow in the yard, Ďula says, "Don't be cross, boss, but could you tell me what we were actually doing down in the boiler-room?"

Rácz stops and gives Ďula a look. "We've just begun celebrating New Year, you fool!" Ďula does not understand, but says nothing. "What do you think?" Rácz asks. "Why did we have dinner in the kitchen and not in the restaurant?"

"No idea," the driver admits.

"Well go and take a look," says Rácz, "I'll wait for you in the lobby."

Ďula is back almost at once, with a grin from ear to ear. "Boss, they've got an arctic night in there! The restaurant is empty. Any guest who comes turns round and leaves. The waiters are keeping warm in the kitchen. Did we do that with the valve down there, boss?" Ďula is amazed.

Rácz does not answer. He sits in an armchair by the reception desk, relishing his feeling of victory.

"And what now, boss?" Ďula asks.

"Nothing yet," says the stoker. "Now we wait for the restaurant manager to tell us that the lounge is available."

* * *

Mozoň (alias Silent), Šolik (alias Livid), and Tupý (alias Bear) are living it up. They've bought a video player and a computer for the safe house and aren't bored any more. They keep playing "Bomb Moscow" all day long. Mozoň does not need any more porno magazines; somebody always brings a new film on video. Their wives are happy. There's plenty of money. If they need some more, Šolik and Tupý take a walk around the Hotel Ambassador or some other hotel, spot a young novice currency dealer and shove their warrant card IDs in his face. The money changes ownership. There's always lots, though they'll never again get such a fat catch as their very first one. Lately, they've been getting tired of sitting in the villa overlooking the city. They meet in the morning, watch videos for a while and play a video game. Then they get bored. Mozoň looks out of the window, Šolik sleeps with a newspaper over his head. Tupý is now tired of drawing up lists of people he will personally arrest when things change: he now just sits there, looking vacantly ahead. Whenever saliva appears on his lower lip, he automatically wipes it off with the back of his hand.

"Why don't we go out for a coffee?" Mozoň suggests. His subordinates are startled. "Yes," says Mozoň. "We'll go out and have a coffee. Attention!" He gets up himself, as an example to the other two.

"And where to, chief?" asks Šolik.

"Where to?" Mozoň repeats ironically. "We'll go where we might get some money: we're going for a coffee, but we'll be, so to speak, on duty. To the Ambassador!"

Mozoň, Šolik, and Tupý don't have a car. They're glad they managed to save just the villa. They take a trolley bus into town. They don't need tickets. If an inspector gets on, they show him their police IDs.

The Ambassador lounge is not very busy. Mozoň, Šolik, and Tupý sit down and order coffee. They observe the room quietly and inconspicuously. The waiter moves noiselessly. In the corner sits a short, frowning man in an expensive, flashy leather jacket. Opposite him sits another very well dressed young man of Balkan origin, carefully counting out banknotes. Then he pushes them over to the frowning man. The latter just puts the banknotes into his pocket without counting them. The Balkan man says goodbye and quickly leaves the lounge. The frowning man stays for a while, then finishes his drink and moves towards to the exit, too.

Mozoň nods to Šolik and Tupý. "Go after him," he orders them in a muffled voice. "And don't come back without the money!"

Rácz comes out of the lavatory, buttoning up his fly, when he finds himself confronted with two police warrant cards.

"Well, so what's this all about?" he asks, puzzled by the two smiling men with ID cards in their outstretched hands.

"Come with us and no funny stuff!" Rácz is ordered quietly, but firmly by one of them.

"And why?" asks Rácz.

Both the very ordinary-looking young men ponder the stoker's question. "Show us your ID," the other one says.

Rácz takes out his ID card, but won't let them have it. "I work here," he declares.

"Really?" the second undercover policeman asks menacingly.

"And what do you do here?" the more polite one asks.

"I'm the stoker," Rácz says. "Here's the stamp: 'Hotel Ambassador', you see?" The ID card disappears into Rácz's inside pocket.

"Show us the contents of your pockets!" the less polite one orders him.

"Are you fucking nuts?" Rácz stares at him. "Don't I pay you enough not to cause trouble here? What department are you from? Are you new?"

"Will you empty your pockets, or not?" the angry one shouts at Rácz, winking at the polite one. In an instant the polite one grabs the stoker by the arms from behind. The angry one unzips the jacket and reaches for the pocket.

Rácz, red in the face, makes a jerking movement. His bulging eyes watch the cop as he slowly frees his hands. Like a vice, his right hand grabs the angry one's hand, pulls it out of his pocket and twists it back. Then he clenches his fist and punches the pushy undercover cop in the mouth. The blow is so violent that both cops fall to the ground. They lie on the floor and can't understand what is going on. This has never happened to them before. Worse, the angry one's mouth is full of blood and broken fillings and crowns. Rácz doesn't wait for the cops to come round.

He beats it fast to the exit. Tupý struggles to his feet. His head is swimming from the blow. He spits out blood, fillings, and crowns. A big hand-gun appears in his hand. Holding it with both hands, he wavers as he aims at the stoker's silhouette.

"No!" Šolik shouts from the floor. "Don't shoot!"

It's too late. The shot booms out and the hall fills with acrid smoke. The glass door through which the stoker has disappeared noisily smashes into shards. The bullet whistles into the lobby and buries itself in the wall above Torontál, who grabs the mahogany reception desk in fear. The old man wakes up from his apathy, realises what has happened, and faints. But his desire to be the centre of attention is frustrated. Nobody takes any notice of him; they all run to see what has happened in the lounge. They scream and retreat when a confused Tupý runs in, pointing at them a smoking gun that he holds in both hands. He runs out of the hotel and his partner follows him.

"Are you crazy?" Šolik yells at Tupý. "Let's get out of here!" Both cops run round the corner. Tupý puts the pistol in the holster and zips up his windcheater. They wait at the trolleybus stop, leaving their superior to his fate in the Ambassador lounge.

"I'll have hith gutth one day!" Tupý mutters, spitting blood and saliva into the snow. "I'll get him and put a hole in hith belly thith big!" Tupý uses his thumbs and index fingers to show the size of the hole.

Mozoň didn't get up after Tupý fired. In the general chaos that reigned afterwards he kept his cool.

"You were sitting with them," a waiter standing above him accused him sharply.

"Me?" Mozoň asked. "Yes, I was, but I don't know them." Mozoň was just sitting at their table. He doesn't know who they were.

The waiter eyes him suspiciously. "Wait here," he orders him. "Soon the assistant manager will come and decide what to do with you." He goes to the bar.

Mozoň is not afraid of anything. Just in case, he cocks the gas pistol in the pocket. One shot of tear gas will allow him to leave without hindrance. He finishes his coffee.

Through the smashed door enters the hotel lawyer. The phone call caught him at a rare moment when he was present in the building. Since the lawyer has been selling entitlements to five Škoda Favorit vehicles, he was in his office manning the phones. He couldn't wriggle out of it. The lawyer knows that the hotel works by itself, like a well-oiled machine. The department chiefs can handle everything. But extraordinary events, such as a shoot-out in the lounge, are different. If only because they have to be covered up. The lawyer can't afford any special attention to be paid to the Hotel Ambassador: even those unfortunate Škoda Favorit cars were ordered for the hotel.

"Yes, I'll take care of that," the lawyer tells the waiter after hearing a detailed report about an unidentified man who was drinking coffee. "First, the clean-up. Wash off the blood in the hall! Was it Rácz's?" he asks hopefully. "No," says the waiter. "The boss wasn't hit."

The lawyer goes up to Mozoň. The waiter listens eagerly.

"Good morning," says the lawyer.

"Good morning," Mozoň answers.

"Would you accompany me to my office?" the lawyer asks loudly, because the waiter is listening. "It's only a formality."

"No problem," says Mozoň and gets up.

The lawyer points, "This way, please."

In the lift Mozoň says, "Shit, how long is it since we last met?"

The lawyer reflects, "Ten years?"

"Could be," says Mozoň. "So you're the assistant manager?"

"Hotel lawyer, to be precise. But the manager is... indisposed, so I'm standing in for him. And what about you? If I'm not mistaken, after they kicked you out of law school, you went to police college. Still there?"

Mozoň's face takes on a confidential expression. He nods.

The lift stops at the second floor. They cross the corridor and the lawyer unlocks his office. They enter.

"Will you have a vodka?" the lawyer asks. Mozoň nods. "I'm so happy that we've met after all these years!" the lawyer says and pours the drinks. They clink glasses and the lawyer pours again.

"So how goes it?" the lawyer asks after the fifth vodka. "Are you here on duty?"

"What?" the drunken Mozoň just waves his hand. "It's all fucked up! Everything!" He'd served the people his entire life, if you please, and what did he get? The height of ingratitude! Nobody cares that Mozoň happens to be a family man. He never hurt anyone. Even if he had beaten people up, it was only because they were some kind of tramp: a dissident, student, or writer. "We won't let them destroy our republic!" And how did they repay him? They threw him, together with the others, out on the street.

"You're ex-State Security?" the lawyer asked almost jovially. All his worries had evaporated.

Mozoň is a lawyer, too. He studied law at cops' college. For two years he went to lectures every Wednesday, like an idiot. Mozoň has a doctorate, too. His classmate may pour him another drink. "Your health!"

Mozoň drinks his vodka. He's as good a doctor as any other policeman. But when they sacked him and he was looking for a job, he was told everywhere that his diploma was only good for wiping his arse. "So where's the justice?"

"So what do you live on?"

Mozoň's expression becomes confidential. Contradictory feelings do battle within him: on one hand, deeply inculcated service secrecy and confidentiality, on the other, the desire to show his old college mate that Mozoň, too, is somebody to reckon with.

"So what do you do? Private detective?" the lawyer keeps asking.

Mozoň shrugs. "Something like that. Come with me, and I'll show you something," he suggests.

"Is it far?" the lawyer asks.

"Let's take a taxi," Mozoň decides, stumbling into the lawyer's bureau.

The lawyer agrees. Even though he's had a lot to drink, a persistent instinct at the back of his cranium tells him that his old mate from law school could be useful to him.

"Shall we?" Mozoň asks, getting up with effort and moving towards the door.

"Let's go, then," says the lawyer. He takes the office keys off the desk and puts the bottle in his coat pocket.

A silent taxi driver drives them to the villa overlooking the city. The men start to sing. They cheerfully clap each other on the back. They imagine themselves always to have been the best of friends. Mozoň needs a friend, someone he could like and who'd like him in return. Comradeship is sacred.

"Women are cunts," he says to the lawyer sotto voce, as if afraid that the moment they get out of the car the taxi driver will go and tell his wife.

The lawyer nods. He's divorced; he's been through the mill. He pays crazy amounts of child support for three children. But the lawyer won't let himself be fleeced. His salary is small and they can't deduct much from it. What he makes, he makes on the side. His ex-wife, blast her, knows about that but can't do a thing about it. She'd love to have the shirt off his back.

The bottle travels from the lawyer to Mozoň and back. When it's empty, they throw it out of the taxi window onto the pavement. They soon reach their destination. The villa can be seen towering behind a sandstone wall. Mozoň pays the driver and keeps every penny of the change.

Standing to attention, with drawn faces, Šolik and Tupý endure a dressing-down from a drunken Mozoň. Mozoň had known he had the stupidest subordinates, but had no idea that they were that stupid. Their stupidity cries to high heaven. They couldn't sort out one bloody currency dealer. Go on like this and they'd soon be on the street scavenging from rubbish bins.

Mozoň relishes his anger. He'd like to impress his friend with his power. The lawyer is embarrassed at witnessing a scene he'd rather not see. But the two humiliated cops clearly don't mind. They peek at the lawyer with curiosity. They've never had a visitor before. They let Mozoň's pep-talk come in one ear and go out the other.

"They're the ones firing guns in the hotel!" Mozoň informs the lawyer. "These fools! As if they didn't know that if they were caught they couldn't have got out of it so easily. We're outside the law, you prats!" he reproaches Šolik and Tupý, "Outside the law!"

"He punched me in the fathe," Tupý says in self-defence. "Then he thtarted running. I tried to thtop him. To thtop him escaping."

Šolik hurriedly backs him up. "He wouldn't listen, chief. He wouldn't show us the contents of his pockets. He said that he worked in the hotel as a stoker. He reacted to a body search with violence."

The lawyer joins in, "Listen, men!" The lawyer has no idea what they're on about. And he's not interested. But he'd like to know what they'd charge to get back to the hotel and take the stoker out of circulation somehow. It doesn't have to be today or tomorrow. The lawyer just needs to know he can be certain about one thing: the stoker's days are numbered. Can that be arranged?

The three secret policemen, the humiliated and the humiliater, smile; their eyes soften as if they'd remembered a snatch of a long forgotten tune. Mozoň clears his throat. "Anything can be arranged," he says. But the lawyer should explain why he's interested in liquidating a petty currency dealer.

"A petty currency dealer?" The lawyer is beside himself. He explains briefly to the cops how dangerous a character Rácz is. He has the entire hotel and surroundings in his hand. Everybody is scared of him. The currency dealers do exactly as he says, he's their uncrowned king. The hotel lawyer has a lot of fine plans for the Hotel Ambassador. But he needs a free hand to realise them. The hotel employees would be sure to elect him manager, instead of the old one, who is completely incompetent, but everyone's afraid of the stoker. He's a blackmailer: he can close down the heating in the hotel at any time, and then people freeze. He's got tons of money. The lawyer is worried that, as things are, the employees would elect Rácz manager out of fear. The lawyer is offering his new friends a hundred thousand crowns to liquidate the stoker.

"A hundred thousand is good money," says Mozoň and sits down. But he thinks there's no need to kill the stoker. He just has to be taken out of circulation for a few months. When he gets back, he will be so screwed up by everything that will have been done to him that he'll choose to go back to his village. Mozoň has ways of doing that. There are some spacious cells in the basement of this safe house. They've never been used yet, but Mozoň believes it's time they were. The inconvenient stoker will be an involuntary boarder in one of them. He'll have ample time, living on bread and water, to reflect hard on the wisdom of leaving his village for the city. Mozoň thinks two to three months of solitary confinement will be enough for the stoker.

He gets up and motions to the lawyer. They go down to the cellar. Mozoň opens a door. Behind is darkness. Mozoň turns on the light and the lawyer can see a long corridor with a row of metal doors on each side. Each door has a small square hatch with a bolt.

"For keeping an eye on them," Mozoň tells the lawyer. The lawyer nods in admiration. "We'll chuck him in there," says Mozoň. "Don't worry; we'll put him off wanting to act the uncrowned king of the hotel. Want to have a look inside?" The lawyer shakes his head. He's shivering with cold. Mozoň turns off the light and closes the door. "A hundred thousand?" he asks the lawyer.

"A hundred thousand," says the lawyer firmly, "plus his keep in gaol." Mozoň nods.

"It'll be harder abducting him," says the lawyer, when they get back upstairs. "Rácz is never alone, not even for a second. There's always someone hanging around him. He has his sidekick, the hotel driver and buyer. He also has a mistress, a girl who used to dance in the cabaret. A hooker." The lawyer would suggest luring him out of the building under some pretext. "It'll be difficult, but I think it can be done." Mozoň and his subordinates can ambush him there. They can knock him out and take him away. That's how the lawyer envisages it.

Mozoň clears his throat. His head is still spinning, but a spate of applied thinking and the prospect of all that money has neutralised the vodka. "It's not that easy," he opines. Mozoň knows from experience. A well-done abduction needs extensive preliminary preparation. Reconnoitring the terrain. Nothing can be left to accident. It would be best for Mozoň to come to the hotel for a few days incognito. He could take a look at everything. He'd pretend to be a guest from the West and try to attract Rácz's attention. He'd make friends with him. It would all be easier that way. "See this?" Mozoň opens a steel cabinet, takes out a Bakelite box and opens it. It contains a needle with a transparent bulb at one end. "This is a powerful narcotic," he tells the lawyer. "If I can jab him in the arm and squeeze the bulb, he'll be out for an hour. That gives us time to transport him over here and lock him in a cell." Mozoň pauses and looks at his listeners. The lawyer likes the idea. Tupý and Šolik stare at their chief in admiration.

"What's more," adds Mozoň, after putting the box back, "we could get ransom money out of the stoker, beside the hundred thousand. That would gives us extra to tide us over the bad times. The situation will change very soon," Mozoň is sure. "Power will be restored to the working masses. Until then, we have to keep the faith," he says resolutely. "Victory is near. We mustn't let our guard down, comrades."

Tupý and Šolik clap enthusiastically. They are looking forward to the money they'll get out of the lawyer and the stoker. The lawyer is happy, too. What's a hundred thousand compared to the fortune he'll make out of the hotel when Rácz is out of his way?

"Time's up!" Šolik suddenly says, after a look at his watch. It's already three thirty-five. The secret policemen quickly change their clothes and pack their briefcases.

"Don't you worry, doctor of law," Mozoň tells the lawyer, as he locks up the safe house. "We won't leave you in the lurch! We'll help you."

It's slowly getting dark. The men amble to the bus stop.

* * *

Rácz's face is inscrutable and expressionless. Not a muscle moves on his dark face, where a bluish shadow appears a few hours after shaving. He does everything with his eyes. They bulge with anger, or are sternly immovable, and sometimes proud and half-closed with contentment. Somebody gave him dark sunglasses: since then he's never gone anywhere without them. His face seems cast in steel alloy. There are moments when he takes his glasses off and gives those around him a momentary look into his firm grey-blue eyes, only theatrically to hide them again behind the opaque black lenses. Few people can stand Rácz's direct gaze. The wrinkles fanning around his eyes on an otherwise stone-smooth face give him an almost intellectual expression.

The coal dust has long been washed out of the pores of Rácz's skin and the corns from his work boots have been massaged away by soft Italian moccasins, or crocodile or snake-skin cowboy boots. Rácz prefers to drape his angular body in Miami Vice-style loose-fitting jackets and trousers. Even his leather jackets — black, grey, brown, and burgundy — are a few sizes too big. He has prominent shoulders. His hair has grown longer and begun to curl. He had it cut, in the front and mostly on the sides, around his big ears. He has an Italian soccer player's hairstyle. Sometimes he combs his hair back with gel in a sleek, shiny style. He has an earring with a tiny diamond in his left ear. Silvia chose it. She pierced his ear with special pincers; it didn't hurt. In time Rácz found he liked it. It's not too striking, but it discreetly suggests his financial status.

To a practised eye Rácz looks a bit less well-groomed since Silvia ran away. Fortunately, he's hit on a few reliable combinations of clothes that he alternates and which can't spoil his style. For example, he'd never wear his black double-breasted suit with high lace-up Adidas boots.

* * *

The dog is small, thin and mangy. Its big ears listen for sounds. Any suspicious noise terrifies it. The night is clear. The snow in the yard of the Hotel Ambassador reflects the moonlight, but the manager stands motionless in the dark, holding his breath. The dog approaches the bait: a huge bone from the stockpot. A pointed muzzle (the dog's a spitz) sniffs it. The manager is even more motionless. Only his eyes shine in the dark. The dog greedily grabs the bone. In an instant it is writhing in the manager's noose. It wheezes and splutters as the rope strangles its neck. The manager darts out of his hiding place with the rope wrapped round his wrist. The dog realises that the more it fights the rope, the tighter the noose gets. It watches the approaching manager out of the corner of its eye.

The manager squats down. He reaches for his catch with a hand in a thick glove. The spitz sinks its teeth into the manager's fingers. That instant, the dog finds itself dangling. It is a few inches above the ground, helplessly paddling its legs. Only when it begins to lose consciousness and stops struggling, the manager lowers it. The dog begins to grovel. It recognizes a superior opponent. It had been only recently kicked out into the street. It still remembers how to deal with people. The manager offers it a bit of dried meat. The dog takes it; it's starving. The manager waits for the dog to swallow the meat and then firmly jerks the rope. The dog gets to its feet and trustingly follows its new master.

Getting to the Hotel Ambassador without alerting the receptionist, who is reading his paper behind the counter, is difficult, but not impossible. He noiselessly crosses the dark lobby with the dog, hugging the walls and taking cover in dark corners. Only when he's in his office in the administrative wing does the manager breathe a sigh of relief and relax. He's welcomed by the happy barking and whining of a pack of dogs. There are all sorts: big and small, pedigree, mongrel, various colours and sizes. There is a mastiff with a gigantic wise head, and a terrier, whining and scratching the floor with its thin legs because of the cold. The manager releases his newest catch into the pack. The dogs get to know each other, they yap and bare their teeth. The manager watches them for a while. He realises that he has to begin carrying out his brilliant plan: soon the dry meat will run out and the dogs will starve to death. He spends a moment by the embers in the centre of the office, feeding the fire with a chair leg. The hotel has recently taken a delivery of new chairs. They burn very well. The flames come to life and light up the whole room: the sitting manager and fascinated dogs.

The rest period does not last long. When the manager's head begins to droop, he is startled and gets up. He goes into the dark corridor and down the stairs. He gets out of the hotel unobserved and sets out on a long journey. It is a march through enemy territory, as the manager fully realises.

Only when the stars begin to pale and the sky turns light blue, will the manager get far beyond the city boundaries, to the foothills of the mountains whose snowy peaks shine on the horizon during his trek. Dawn breaks. The manager walks and observes the snow. He knows he is in the right place: the hills are marked by hundreds of ski and sledge trails. The manager is no amateur: during his hunting trips in the yards around the Ambassador, he has learned well to read footprints and trails. He has also learned to stay motionless in his hiding place, waiting patiently for hours, blending into the background. He watches the area from the bushes. Crows fly over an overcast sky. A sleepy village rests in the valley under the mountains. Acrid smoke comes out of the chimneys. Hours pass. Soon the cold air fills with children's voices distant, but getting nearer. The manager, invisible in the branches, stiffens.

The children are sledging and the manager, squatting in his hiding place, makes his choice. Yes, he decides: the girl in a yellow windcheater over there. She comes down on a long but lightweight sledge. The sledge flies down and the girl laughs. The children yell. The manager makes his decision. Now! He pushes the branches apart and comes out of the bushes. The children are scared. The manager is hairy, dirty, wearing a home-made fur coat. He hollers like a madman and the children are terrified. The manager with his arms spread wide begins to run towards the girl in the yellow windcheater: "ER-R-R!" he roars again. The children abandon their sledges. The strange sight of the manager and his roars panic and horrify the innocent little creatures. Crying and yelling, they run in all directions. The manager pursues them for a while, waving his arms wildly, hollering and grimacing. When the children vanish round a bend in the road leading down to the village, the manager stops. He goes back. He grabs his chosen sledge and runs off, pulling it behind him. He takes the road and for a while runs along the salty and slushy asphalt. When he hears a car in the distance, he jumps over the ditch and hides in the thin bushes on the other side. He runs toward a brook, steps into the shallow but shockingly freezing dirty water, fording it against the current for a few dozen yards with the sledge on his back. Then he gets out of the water. He climbs a tall tree, a spreading chestnut, pulling the sledge with him. There he squats on a thick branch and decides to wait until dark.

The manager spends the whole day sitting motionless in the tree, singing. He knows that he hasn't won yet. He puts a piece of dry meat in his mouth and sucks on it. After this breakfast he dozes off, stubbornly clinging to the branch. A tic distorts his face. He shouts something in his sleep, and that wakes him up. It is beginning to snow. The snow falls on the white fields producing a wet, feathery rustle.

A group of men and dogs passes the tree a few times: they are armed with guns and torches, but fail to notice him. The snow confuses the hunting dogs' sense of smell. They strain against their leashes and whimper. Then the wind starts to blow, carrying wet snowflakes from the fields. Soon it gets dark. The moon is hidden; the sky is as black as indigo paper. Thanks to the fresh snow, visibility is good. After a moment's hesitation, the manager lowers the captured sledge and then climbs down the tree. He stretches his limbs, heavy prolonged and tense immobility. Ahead of him is a night march through enemy territory. He sets out with determination, pulling his booty behind him.

* * *

Just before midnight, Urban and Lenka enter Hotel Ambassador lounge. The party is in full swing. Urban looks around the room. The guests have split into small groups, discussion circles. Urban knows most of them:

some are nodding acquaintances, others he knows personally. He knows the Albanians and hookers very well indeed. He does not feel a stranger here. Lenka, on the other hand, knows no one. She holds his hand, as he is her only support.

Rácz sits at the head of the table with a poker face, drinking. When he spots Urban, he gets up. "I knew you'd come," he says. "It's good you're here. There's plenty of everything," he adds, "Food and drink."

He notices Lenka and falls silent, as if struck by lightning.

Lenka, too, stands up and for a few seconds can't take her eyes off Rácz.

"I'll introduce you," says Urban. "Lenka, this is Rácz. Rácz, this is Lenka."

He steps aside. Rácz produces one of his smiles. He takes Lenka's hand and touches it with his lips. Lenka smiles in embarrassment. It seems so old-fashioned, yet it isn't unpleasant.

Urban is surprised at this, but doesn't stare. He'd never have expected such a gesture, however clumsily done, from Rácz.

Rácz accompanies his guests to the head of the table and seats them next to him.

"I'm glad, I'm glad you've... both... come. You've broken the spell. I had no one to talk to. They've all come here to stuff their faces and get sloshed."

Rácz waves a hand, smiles again and takes a good look at Lenka.

Lenka feels odd under the magnetic metallic stare of this strange, stocky, broad-shouldered man. His wide face radiates a kind of primordial energy. She is unsettled.

"Friends are precious nowadays," Rácz says, taking three champagne glasses from the tray.

This leaves Urban cold. Perhaps it's a new trick of the stoker's, he thinks. Rácz pours the champagne. He's skilled; he doesn't spill a drop. Lenka realises that Urban's strange friend probably drinks champagne far more often than once a year on New Year's Eve.

"To our friendship!" declares the stoker and raises his glass.

A sarcastic remark is on the tip of Urban's tongue, but he bites it back. "Why does Rácz want to talk about friendship?" he thinks. Urban still hasn't forgotten Rácz having him followed so as to find the source of Urban's foreign currency. And Rácz might well have set the two under-cover policemen onto him out of vindictiveness. Urban looks truculent.

Rácz downs his glass with relish and puts it back on the table forcefully. Perhaps too forcefully, Lenka thinks.

They are silent. From the restaurant they can hear muffled conversations, laughter and the bass notes of the band. At the other end of the table the Albanians are arguing in their incomprehensible language full of absurd sounding consonants. Ďula clinks glasses with a drunken Khunt. The whores have left their glasses half full and moved closer to the bar. They can't skive on a night like this.

"Urban let slip that you're the uncrowned king of the hotel," says Lenka with a smile.

Rácz nods. "Yes," he says. "It's true. They do as I say." There's no trace of self-consciousness in his voice. He responds like a man asked if he likes cheese scones.

Lenka says, "I can see you don't suffer from lack of self-esteem."

"No," agrees Rácz, "I don't. But you're not drinking," he remarks.

"I'm not used to drink," says Lenka.

"Are you Urban's girlfriend?" the stoker resumes after a pause.

Lenka shakes her head. No, they're just good friends. There's nothing between them. "Look at Urban: we're more like brother and sister, aren't we?" Urban absent-mindedly nods and looks at his watch. It's half past eleven.

"Are you married?" Lenka asks the stoker.

Rácz shakes his head. No, Rácz is single. Single, but unhappy in love. His girl left him. It was a blow, terribly painful. But he's got over it. Rácz can see now that she stayed with him only for his money. And because of his power. Rácz longs to meet a girl who'd like him for his own sake. Rácz knows that this is not impossible.

Lenka smiles. "Certainly," she says. She's sure that one day Rácz will find a girl like that. She takes the glass of champagne and drinks. She likes it. She doesn't object when Rácz tops up her glass, touching her shoulder.

Rácz's chat-up is beginning to make Urban want to throw up. Who is that oaf pretending to be? What sort of idiotic theatre act is this? Is the stoker getting back at Urban by seducing his girl? But Urban is convinced that sooner or later he will be rewarded for his helpfulness and patience and will have Lenka. Why else would he spend so much time with her? And what was she saying just now? Like brother and sister! The silly pseudo-intellectual goose! As if she hadn't noticed the way Urban looked at her, how eagerly his entire body reacted to every single accidental contact with hers.

"Would you like to dance?" he asks Lenka. Lenka takes her eyes off Rácz's face. "No," she says, "I don't feel like it. I'm fine sitting here." Urban pours himself champagne and downs it in one.

"Don't you have anything stronger?" he asks the stoker.

"Go to the bar and order anything you like. Tell them to put it on my tab," he adds.

Urban gets up. He can still pay for a couple of shorts. He turns round and heads for the door. Rácz intercepts him outside the lounge.

"What's wrong with you?" he asks, his arms spread wide. "You're my guest, so the drinks are on me. At least, don't insult me!" Rácz is smiling. "Are you angry because I'm chatting to her? She's not your girl-friend. If she was, I wouldn't even look at her. For Rácz, a friend's girl is off limits. Rácz doesn't need them." Rácz grabs Urban by the shoulder and with a broad gesture shows him the interior of the restaurant, the band and the dance floor in the middle of the room. "Look," he says, "there are plenty of women here. Pick one up and have fun. Eat, drink, and put it on Rácz's tab! I can afford it. Just don't act the insulted lover!" Rácz lets him go and pushes him back into the room. "She's not your girlfriend, or your sister," he says. "And I like her. She came with you, but she doesn't be-long to you."

Urban waves his hand dismissively. "All right," he says, and backs down. Wanda the Trucker grins at him from the bar. Her long indigo-black legs are crossed, and she sends him a signal that is hard to resist.

"Somebody over there's waving at you," Rácz tells him. "Go for her and have something nice." The stoker checks his watch. "Welcome in the New Year," he suggests. He invited her only for Urban's sake.

Rácz returns to the lounge. He pours Lenka and himself champagne. "Urban's a nice lad," he says. He smiles. "We've known each other quite some time. He's been a bit on edge lately. It's his work. Don't you know what he does?" The stoker is surprised. "How shall I put it?"

Lenka listens with growing horror and disgust.

"It would disgust me, too," Rácz adds finally. "You need to have a strong stomach for that." Rácz is a respectable businessman. Sometimes he bends the law, true, but only because the laws are still too strict. As soon as things change, Rácz will have no reason to get round the law. Where would we be if everyone observed idiotic laws and regulations? We'd still be climbing trees. Rácz looks at his watch: a few minutes to twelve. He looks at Lenka. "Lenka," he says. "May I call you Lenka?"

Lenka smiles. "Yes."

"Do you trust me?" Rácz asks.

"I don't understand," Lenka admits.

Rácz is embarrassed. It'll soon be midnight, New Year. Rácz would like to invite Lenka to see the fireworks high up, where the view is great, from the window of his suite. It's right on the top floor. He'd like to know if she'd come up with him, or does she think he's just like Video Urban?

Lenka shakes her head. No, she knows Rácz is different. She'd like to see the fireworks.

"Lift for the boss!" shouts the receptionist, when he sees the stoker and Lenka leave the restaurant and walk back towards the lifts. Rácz is carrying a bottle of chilled sparkling wine and two tall glasses. They get into the lift. They are quiet on the way up. Rácz assesses Lenka with his steely eyes.

"Well, this is where I live," says Rácz, opening the door to his suite and turning on the light. Lenka looks around the living room. Rácz draws the curtain. "I think we ought to turn the light off," he notes. "Do you mind, Lenka?"

Lenka says she doesn't. Soon it's midnight. Through the walls of the hotel come the thunderous roar of champagne corks popping and shouts from the restaurant and bar. Rácz with a practised move uncorks the bottle and fills both glasses with white champagne foam. They clink glasses. Rácz turns the light off. Across the river the fireworks start to explode. Bright points of light soar up into the black sky, are reflected on the surface of the river, and then go out.

"It's so beautiful," says Lenka.

"Do you like it?" asks Rácz.

"Yes," says Lenka.

"So this is where you live?" Lenka asks, when the fireworks end and the stoker turns on the light.

"Yes," says Rácz. "More champagne?" he asks.

"Yes, please," says Lenka, "but just a little."

Rácz thinks for a while whether to say it or not, but can't resist. "One day all this hotel will belong to me," he declares firmly, but a little shyly.

"Really?" Lenka asks.

"Yes," says Rácz. Lenka will soon see. Rácz will buy it — everything, lock, stock, and barrel!

"But a hotel like this costs a lot of money," remarks Lenka, feeling the champagne going to her head.

"Money's no problem," Rácz states. Rácz has plenty of money. He's no third-rate hustler like Video Urban.

"Shouldn't we go downstairs?" asks Lenka.

"Of course!" Rácz says, and collects himself. He stops fussing around looking for his wallet.

"I'd like to go home now," Lenka admits in the lobby. From the open doors of the restaurant comes a monotonous mix of music, conversation, yelling, and clinking of glasses.

"So soon?" asks the stoker. "We haven't even managed to have a good talk. I never showed you how everyone here does what I tell them." Rácz is clearly disappointed.

Lenka smiles wearily. "Thank you for a very pleasant evening," she says. "And thanks for the fireworks."

Rácz waves his arm. "It's nothing, my pleasure entirely. I'll call you a taxi," he offers.

Lenka demurs: no, it is not too far for her to walk home. She thanks him again.

Rácz won't take no for an answer. The streets are full of strange people. The taxi will take her right to where she lives, Rácz promises. There'll be no danger. Rácz orders the liveried porter, "A taxi for the lady! Right away!"

The stoker sees Lenka to the cloakroom and helps her with her coat. They both leave the hotel. The night is freezing cold. The taxi pulls up noiselessly and waits.

"Will we see each other again?" asks Rácz.

Lenka smiles. "I don't know."

"I'd be glad to see you," says Rácz. He loses heart.

Lenka takes a piece of paper and a Chinese fountain pen from her handbag. She writes a few digits. "This is my phone number," she tells him. "Call me some time. Maybe I'll have some free time." She gives him the piece of paper.

"Yes," says Rácz. He will certainly phone. He folds the paper several times and reverently puts it in his breast pocket.

Lenka suddenly realises that Rácz has been standing out there wearing only a light dinner jacket. "You'll catch cold," she says. "You ought to go inside."

"What? A cold?" The stoker laughs. He has experienced far colder weather. On military manoeuvres. In Boletice and Jince. Everyone was going mad, but Rácz was laughing. Rácz takes off his dinner jacket and unbuttons his shirt before Lenka can object. He shouts, "Look! Rácz can take it; he's a man! Cold doesn't bother Rácz! When he is out with a girl like Lenka, he doesn't even care if it is a hundred below! Rácz is all on fire anyway!"

Lenka bursts out laughing. "You're mad," she tells him, "but nice!" She lightly touches his shoulder and gets into the taxi. "And put your d.j. back on," she tells the stoker.

Rácz shouts at the taxi driver: "I'm paying. When you've taken the young lady home, come back and find me. You know who I am, right?"

The taxi driver nods. "Sure, boss! Who doesn't know you?"

Rácz murmurs with satisfaction. He steps back from the car window and waves. The taxi moves off.

Rácz adjusts his bow tie and puts the dinner jacket on. "I'll get you, my little dove," he tells himself, as he watches the taxi leave. By God he will! He'll get her and he'll teach her to dance to his tune.

When the stoker gets back to the restaurant, Urban blocks his way. Urban's face is red from drink.

"What is it?" Rácz asks.

"Have you sent her home?" asks Urban.

"Yeah, she went home to sleep," Rácz confirms.

"Did she go up to your room?" asks Urban.

"And what if she did?" Rácz wonders.

"Did you do anything to her?" Urban pulls himself to his full height.

Rácz smiles and pushes Urban out of his way.

"Get a grip on yourself, Rácz," says Urban. "Don't harm her! She's not one of the Ambassador scrubbers. She's not the right girl for you."

The stoker turns away.

And why should Rácz be restricted to the whores in the hotel? Who said that Rácz isn't allowed to fall in love with a decent girl? Who decided that Rácz has no right to love? Who decided that Rácz could only have gypsies and hookers? Urban can get off his back. Doesn't Urban realise that he means nothing to Lenka? She didn't even say good-bye to him. Isn't that proof enough for Urban? Rácz didn't even touch her. They went up only to see the fireworks. It was romantic. She gave him her telephone number, yes, him, Rácz! And why not? And anyway: Urban should stop behaving like a relative of hers. He's not. Urban is Rácz's guest. He should be having fun; he should be dancing. He can eat and drink his fill. He can screw Wanda: she's eager for it. But he'd better keep the fuck out of Rácz's business, or he'll be sorry. This isn't a threat, it's a friendly warning.

Rácz's steely eyes blaze with anger. His fists are clenched. He is sizing up Urban, whose hackles are up. Then he changes tone. He smiles. He comes up to Urban and slaps him on his shoulder like a friend. And anyway, he says, why would they argue? Aren't they friends? Haven't they done lots of deals together? Haven't they known each other for some time? So what's this all about? Over a woman? Maybe in the end she won't let either of them screw her.

The taxi driver turns up. Rácz pays him off. "Keep the change," he tells him. Rácz wants to know the girl's address.

"She didn't tell me," says the taxi driver. "After the bridge she told me to stop and she got out."

"Fine," says Rácz, and turns to Urban. "Give me her address," he says. "I'd like to send her flowers. The most expensive ones: a hundred orchids. Only, I don't know where she lives." Urban says nothing. Rácz grabs him round his shoulders and drags him off to the bar. "It doesn't have to be right now," he says amiably. "The flowers can wait. Let's drink. Two double *Heevash Reygahl* whiskies!" He forces Urban to down his drink in one. His strong teeth crunch the ice as if it were nothing. He orders another round. He signals to Wanda. "Show him a good time," he orders her. "Do anything he wants!" He pulls out two hundred-*deutschmark* notes and with two fingers sticks them down her cleavage. Rácz has money. He couldn't care less about a few hundred. Especially not today.

"Now we're going to drink!" Rácz shouts at Ďula and Khunt, who were getting sozzled in the lounge. "Bring us three bottles of champagne," he orders the waiter. "One each." Ďula and Khunt are as happy as schoolboys. They both habitually drink themselves senseless. They don't need any females for a booze-up. Rácz, on the other hand, can take his drink like a horse. He sits and drinks. His companions may still be sitting up, but their eyes are glazed over. They've already vomited. There are more and more empty bottles. When the waiter brings three more bottles of sparkling wine, Rácz just sweeps them off the table. The sound of broken glass wakes everyone up. "Enough of this gripe water!" Rácz yells at the waiter. "Bring us whisky! *Heevash Reygahl*!" Ďula only has to hear Rácz pronounce those words and he promptly vomits under the table. Khunt does not, because he can no longer take anything in. He sits there, his eyes open and his face frozen. Rácz spits point-blank into his face a couple of times, but the dealer does not react. "Shit!" The stoker is disappointed. Rácz is in a party mood tonight. He's extremely happy. No, there's no need to look too far ahead. But he's met the girl of his dreams. Not a whore, not a village goose. And Rácz doesn't leave her cold. She may even like him. He can't be quite sure, but he fancies he's in love. She's a city girl, educated. Rácz feels quite different in her company than he did with Silvia. Silvia is an ordinary whore. And Eržika? Only now can Rácz see that what he felt for Eržika wasn't love. He let them take him for a fool. He was the laughing stock of the whole village. And Silvia? Why, she was an ordinary dealers' hooker. She took a fancy to his money. But that's all water under the bridge. Rácz owes her nothing; he's paid for all the screwing he had with her! Is Ďula even listening to him? Rácz clenches his fist and punches the sleeping Ďula in the forehead. Ďula's eyes blink. Rácz can manage just as well without Silvia. But she'll have to give back the presents he gave her: the fur coat, boots, watch, gold, and so on. And Rácz will make sure she won't get her job back in the cabaret. He swears he will. And Edita will have to go, too. At least they'll have plenty of time for shopping. But not with Rácz's money! That's over! Is Ďula listening to him at all?

Ďula jerks to life. "Of course, boss," he says.

"Well, what was I saying?" the stoker asks grimly.

"That it's over," says Ďula.

"Right," Rácz agrees, "it's over!" Rácz is no longer a milch cow. He won't let that gang of hangers-on suck him dry. He'll make a fresh start here and now. Lenka is something quite different. Rácz has a drink of vodka. She doesn't see him just as a money-bag. Of course, Rácz's wealth and power impress her. But that is something different. Women will always be impressed by successful men, and Rácz is successful. Everything he's achieved and acquired has been done with these two hands and this head. How can somebody like Video Urban push in on him? "Spoiled city brat! Con man! Crook! Do these spoiled intellectual shits get the sexiest girls, and real men like Rácz make do with hookers like Silvia, or village geese, like Eržika? Not on your life!" decides the stoker.

Ďula has collapsed onto the table.

"Bring on the musicians!" Rácz roars and bangs his fist on the table. Rácz wants to party! "It's like a morgue in here, damn it," says Rácz.

Stojka's musicians run in, dripping sweat. Rácz gets up and walks from musician to musician, sticking thousand-crown banknotes to their foreheads. "And now play my tune!" he shouts at them sternly, raising his arms above his head. "Play *Rivers of Babylon*!" The gypsies exchange glances, count in the song in a regular csárdás beat and start playing with typical gypsy csárdás clarinet ornamentation. Their olive faces shine. Rácz dances, his arms above his head and his eyes closed. He doesn't sing; he's silent. He leaps to his table, takes the bottle of whisky and downs it straight from the bottle. Then he goes wild and smashes the bottle against the wall. The gypsies play another tune. Rácz dances, now on his haunches, now on his feet.

"Like that, like that!" he shouts to the rhythm. The world spins around him.

All the guests have left. The restaurant and the bar are empty. Empty bottles, plates of leftover food, colourful confetti, and overflowing ashtrays are scattered over the tables. The waiters hang around the bar, counting the takings. The musicians pack up their instruments and leave the room. Only from the lounge can you hear music and Rácz singing. Rácz dances and drinks on his own. He drinks and dances, because he's in love.

* * *

A few days into the New Year Mr. Mugambia Bwawenu takes a room in the Hotel Ambassador. He's as black as coal. The whites of his eyes shine. At reception he produces the passport of a citizen of the Republic of Mayoumbe. Then he wrestles for possession of his suitcase with the wild porter Torontál, but has to yield. The happy old man grabs the suitcase with his spidery claws and, breathing heavily with excitement, toddles quickly to the lift.

He puts the suitcase down in the room and waits, determined to get his tip. His dry palms open and close in anticipation. Mr. Bwawenu reaches into his pocket and pulls out a two-crown coin. He gives it to the greedy old man. Torontál's face grimaces with disappointment.

"I don't have any more," says the black man, "I haven't had a chance to go to the bank. Besides, I come from a developing country. There's nothing in our country except flies and sand. I speak Slovak," adds Mr. Bwawenu, noticing Torontál's surprise. "I was educated in your country. I'm black, but I'm a university graduate."

Torontál leaves, making disappointed noises. Mozoň collapses heavily into an armchair. He grabs his head. He feels like boxing his own ears. He hasn't even started and already he's made so many mistakes. He'll never find out anything this way. He's behaving like an amateur.

Mozoň looks at his hands. The black dye is coming off his face. Poor quality. Fortunately, he brought a whole bottle with him. Mozoň believes that he won't be kept here too long. He'll stay for one, at most two days. He'll find out what the stoker does all day, where he goes, and when he can be found on his own. Šolik and Tupý are on guard outside. As soon as he injects the stoker with the anæsthetic, he'll call them in. They'll all carry the body to the lawyer's office. There they'll decide what to do next, following Mozoň's plans. They'll either transport him to the safe house and imprison him there, or they'll just kill him, as the lawyer suggested.

The corpse can be taken out of the hotel in bits. Mozoň is against killing; he told the lawyer so. On the other hand, if they let Rácz go, they risk being given away by the vindictive stoker. But that's not certain, as the stoker also has a lot to hide and if he went to the police after being released from the basement cell and gave everyone away, he'd incriminate himself, too. Well, never mind, Mozoň reflected, he'd see what could be done.

The former secret policeman takes out the bottle of black dye, tears off a wad of cotton wool and starts covering his face and hands. Then he carefully closes the bottle and puts it back in his suitcase. Two days, he thinks. He can last two days easily. He's noticed that on everything he's touched he's left black fingerprints. What an idiotic idea, he thought, impersonating a black man. He had to tell his wife that he'd gone on a business trip, to accompany a very valuable bank shipment. Mozoň hates lying. Not out of morality or for other stupid reasons. He hates lying because a good liar has to have a perfect memory and remember what he said and to whom. And Mozoň doesn't have that good a memory. Yet his whole life is a big lie. Even his wife and children know him as Ščepán. That's his name in private life: Ščepán, the bank clerk. Those were his superiors' instructions. Now it's too late to change things. Mozoň can't imagine his wife's reaction if he were forced to tell her the truth. She's known him as Ščepán for years.

"Well, that's how it goes," Mozoň reflects. "Once you're at war, you've got to fight." He leaves his room and goes downstairs to the lobby. There are a lot of new guests at reception. Šolik and Tupý sit in comfortable leather armchairs, reading newspapers. Through holes cut into the papers they discreetly observe their surroundings. Bwawenu sits down nearby. He crosses his legs. "You pricks!" he whispers at them, not moving his facial muscles. His subordinates become uneasy. They put down their papers. They're both wearing dark glasses. Šolik has put on a giant false moustache and Tupý has covered his face with a long false beard. "I'm telling you that you look like idiots," Bwawenu addresses the wall.

"Why, chief?" Tupý asks in a hurt voice, observing movement around the reception desk.

Bwawenu sighs. He looks round the lobby. "Get out!" he orders quietly, but decisively.

Šolik (alias Livid) and Tupý (alias Bear) have settled into their armchairs. They don't want to go out. It's cold outside; inside it's pleasantly warm.

"Can't you hear me?" Bwawenu goes for them, still looking at the wall. "Get out and throw the false moustache and glasses away! You look as suspect as a sledge in summer." Bwawenu turns to his subordinates. "Did you hear me, or not?"

"But it's freezing out there, chief," Šolik objects.

"Then go to the snack bar in front of the hotel and get yourself some hot tea," Bwawenu commands. "But you've got to be outside. In an emergency I'll signal to you from the window. Out, you bloody idiots!"

Mozoň's subordinates reluctantly get out of the comfortable armchairs and slowly make for the exit, as if still hoping that their superior would call them back at the last moment. But Bwawenu takes no more notice of them. A stocky, broad-shouldered man in a leather jacket and an earring in his ear, who has just come out of the lift, claims his attention. Everyone greets him politely with a bow. "That's him," Bwawenu thinks, "it's Rácz!" That's Mozoň's target. Bwawenu gets up and inconspicuously follows the stoker.

* * *

An orgy is taking place at Urban's place. The music is blasting. Urban is embittered. Only after the event has he realised that he was in love with Lenka. Now it's too late. Rácz pestered him so long for Lenka's address that he finally let him have it. He couldn't refuse Rácz's offer. A thousand crowns is good money. Now he feels sorry. Rácz really has sent Lenka a hundred orchids.

Urban is copulating mechanically, with a sullen face. Wanda can't understand why he's in a bad mood.

"What's got into you?" she asks, lying under him with her thighs spread wide.

"Nothing," says Urban, interrupting the coitus and lighting a cigarette.

Wanda wipes herself on a towel and also gets up.

"Where are you going?" asks Dripsy Eva.

"To have a pee," says Wanda.

Hurensson sits naked in the armchair by a round table. His shrivelled penis dangles between his thighs. He's poured himself a whisky and is sipping it. He's back. He had some more money saved up, so he has to have some fun. The whores Urban has supplied are fine. They let you do anything you want. The sight of Urban having sex with Wanda wasn't too bad either.

"Put the music out," says Hurensson to Urban in his Swede's English. "I have a headache."

"What does he want?" asks Wanda, who has now come back.

"Says he has a headache," Urban translates. "We have to turn the music off." He goes to the stereo and turns it off.

"That's fine!" Hurensson smiles with relief. "I hate that kind of jazz you like," he admits to Urban.

"What does he want?" Wanda asks and bites into a sandwich.

"He doesn't like jazz," says Urban.

"I don't like jazz neither," agrees Dripsy Eva.

"I don't like jazz, either," Urban irritably corrects her.

"What about jazz?" Hurensson enquires. "They do not like jazz, too," says Urban in his English. "And so do I. You know, man, I mean the word 'jazz' in phonetical form. Like 'dzez', as is usual in our language, dig it?"

Hurensson reflects. "So you don't like your language?"

"Oh, God, no!" Urban shakes his head. "I only do not like the way they write the word 'jazz' Something like 'd-zhass'."

"But I don't like the jazz itself," says Hurensson. "And I don't give a fuck on the way other people call it."

"What's he saying?" asks Wanda.

"He says he doesn't like jazz," says Urban.

"That's what he said before," Wanda objects.

"Now he's said it again," Urban shrugs.

"Didn't he say anything about us?" asks Eva.

"No, he didn't." Urban shakes his head.

"What they speak about?" asks Hurensson.

"They think you are speaking about them," says Urban. "Will you have some wine?" he asks the prostitutes, reverting to Slovak. They both nod. Urban gets up and brings another bottle. He uncorks it and fills their glasses. "Gunnar?" he asks.

"Thanks," says Hurensson. "I'd rather stay by my whisky." He drinks and pours himself some more. "But the girls are really very fine," he remarks. "Very pretty, both. Especially that tall one. Somehow unusual. Almost exotic. Really fine. And both have great drive."

Urban smiles. "In our country people call it 'turbo'," he says "Do you understand? Turbo fucking."

The Swede bursts out laughing. "Yes, yes, turbo fucking. I like it! The girls are both 'turbo'," he adds gallantly.

"What's he saying?" asks Wanda, scratching between her legs with her long lacquered fingernails.

"He says you're both 'turbo'," Urban translates.

"Generally, I like your hookers," says Hurensson. "But they all make one great mistake. They are not professional enough, you know? They all just want to marry someone from Western countries. We call them 'Russian brides', you know? Who is such a fool to marry a prostitute from East?" Hurensson smiles. Yes, Slovak girls are very pretty. Hurensson likes coming here: this is his third time. He likes to have sex with Slovak hookers. Hurensson admits there are not many places where you can find so many beautiful women as here. The Slovaks are aware of it and so they're proud of it. Hurensson listens to the radio. He knows that there are various songs promoting Slovak girls. He can't understand the words, but he can imagine what the songs are about. He's learned a few Slovak words: *dievcha, soulozh, kurva, platit, nemame, zatvorene, buzerant* (a girl, sex, whore, to pay, we haven't got any, we're closed, a queer). Now a new word: turbo. *Turbo kurva.* (A turbo whore.) Pretty girls, that's one of the few things the Slovaks can be proud of. Although, on the other hand, Hurensson doesn't really get it: why be proud? It's something that Slovaks can't influence or prevent. If someone marries a pretty girl, then fine! Everybody will envy the man and imagine how good it would be to have sex with his wife. In reality, only her husband can. Hurensson believes that Slovaks' general pride in the beauty of their women has no basis. It's as if Arabs were proud of having the most sand in the world. Finns have more lakes than anyone, but Hurensson has yet to meet a Finn whose self-esteem is raised by this fact. Wouldn't it be ridiculous?

Urban does not know what to say. He is quiet. The hookers have discovered the video, turned it on, put in a cassette and are watching a Disney cartoon. They laugh and slap their thighs. Their breasts wobble.

Hurensson takes a sip of whisky. He likes sleeping with Slovak girls. But that's it. He would not want any of them as a wife. Does Urban want to know why? To marry her means to give her his name and make her the mother of his offspring. One organism couples with another and genes are replicated. But the women here, not just in Slovakia, but everywhere — in East Germany, Hungary, Poland, Russia (Hurensson has been to all these places and had sex with prostitutes) — have bodies polluted with all the junk the communists stuffed into them over the years. The stuff they gave them to eat, drink, and breathe. All that got into their skin when they washed or went for a walk. If Hurensson married one of these pretty local women, he would risk the lives of his offspring from deformed genes. And even if no deformed genes appear, how does he know that in a few years his pretty Slovak wife won't get sick? The effects of living in that environment will show up and he'll be left paying the cancer specialists. No thanks, says Hurensson. He'll gladly come and have sex with Slovak hookers, because they are firstly, exceptionally beautiful and secondly, ridiculously cheap. But marry a Slovak girl? Hurensson would rather marry an ugly Swedish woman with a healthy heart, no lead in her bones, no aluminium in her brain, no mercury in her intestines.

Urban says nothing. He's never looked at it this way. He ought to feel offended, but he doesn't. Everything passes him by. Urban is alone. He has no sense of 'us' with anyone. He may have lead in his bones and aluminium in his brain, too, but the Swede's theory strikes him as stupid. You only have to look at Urban or the two beautiful scrubbers and compare them to Hurensson's sickly physiognomy. One glance will tell you who is the more degenerate.

He tries to change the topic, but Wanda asks, "What is he blethering about?"

Urban waves his hand. "He's explaining why he doesn't want to marry either of you," he tells Wanda.

The prostitutes bursts out laughing. "What the fuck's wrong with him?" asks Dripsy Eva.

"What they say?" Hurensson would like to know.

"They say, that's very funny party," says Video Urban.

"It's just going to be a one!" says Hurensson, who puts aside his glass, gets up and picks up his jacket. He takes a foil sachet from the inside pocket. He unwraps it to reveal white powder. There's just a thimbleful.

"What is it?" asks Wanda.

"That's coke," says Hurensson, who's understood the question.

"What did he say?" the prostitute asks Urban.

"It's cocaine," says Urban.

"Cocaine?" asks Eva.

Hurensson pours a pinch of white powder onto the lacquered surface of the round table, takes a silver tube like a cigarette holder, sticks it in his nostril and puts a finger over the other nostril. He bends low over the table and breathes in the line of powder. His giant balls and his long, shrivelled penis swing comically as he sniffs the coke. He passes the silver tube to Dripsy Eva and prepares a line for her. The prostitute sniffs the drug, tears well up in her eyes, and she sneezes. Next is Wanda the Trucker, and finally, out of curiosity, Video Urban. They sit for a while quietly. Hurensson looks as if he is silently praying. The others watch him. They're afraid of breaking the silence that has suddenly fallen here.

Urban waits for any changes caused by the drug. He focuses, but nothing extraordinary is happening. Except that his penis is becoming tumescent. After a while it gets so hard that it is on the verge of painfulness. Urban gets a tremendous lust for Dripsy Eva. He pulls her by the hand. The hooker gets up, pulls away her suspender belt and her black-patterned stockings and, giving herself a helping hand, she mounts Urban's member. With her eyes closed she slowly begins to rock. Her face is ablaze. Wanda tries to revive Hurensson's manhood: after lengthy manipulation she succeeds. They hold hands and walk to the bed. Hurensson lies down and Wanda sits on him. They start to jerk wildly. Sweat appears on their faces.

Eva moves deliberately, as if in a slow motion film. Urban would gladly be rid of his painful erection; he grabs her by her hips and forces her to speed up. The prostitute opens her eyes. She looks as if Urban had woken her from a pleasant dream.

"What is it?" she asks.

"Nothing," says Urban. "Keep going." Eva closes her eyes and resumes her slow rhythmic movements.

Wanda shrieks. Then again. She tries to slide off Hurensson as fast as she can, but her hands slip on the Swede's chest, which is wet with sweat. She yells with fear. The Swede is lying motionless on his back. His eyes are closed.

Urban pushes Eva off and gets up. He approaches the bed. Hurensson is not breathing. He lies there, his passive face expressing calm dignity.

"Do something!" Wanda shouts at Urban. "Do something!"

Urban, not without squeamishness, puts his ear to Hurensson's chest. Wanda is quiet. Urban listens carefully, but can't hear anything. The sweat on the Swede's hairy chest is beginning to cool. Urban moves away with distaste. He gets up.

All three stand around the cooling body. The prostitutes in their sexy lingerie and Urban with his sinking erection. Hurensson's erection does not recede. It sticks up like a submarine periscope in the middle of an icy ocean. Wanda bursts into tears. She snivels and wipes her tears with the back of her hand.

"What happened, actually?" asks Urban.

"I don't know," says Wanda. She was riding him when his eyes suddenly popped, he gnashed his teeth, somehow rose up and then collapsed as if struck by lightning. She didn't kill him!

"I'm sure you didn't," Urban agrees. "It was a stroke."

"Let's call an ambulance, call an ambulance, call an ambulance," says Wanda, crying.

Urban shakes her. "Are you mad?" he shouts. "What are we going to tell them? That we had group sex and that he died on the job? Get a grip!"

Wanda weeps even more intensely. She licks away her tears with her long tongue.

"We've got to call an ambulance," opines Eva. "What if he still isn't dead yet?"

Urban looks at Eva, then at the Swede lying on the bed, his toes curled, his nose pointed. "We're not calling an ambulance," he declares in a firm voice. "They'll examine him and find out that he's taken drugs. Then we're screwed. He's as dead as a doornail, anyway."

The prostitutes pull themselves together. They go to the bathroom to make themselves presentable and to get dressed. They suddenly feel ashamed. Urban gets dressed, too. He pours himself a stiff drink, but he can't taste what he's drinking. He thinks. The prostitutes come out of the bathroom. Wanda is laughing now. She covers her mouth with her hand. That's Wanda for you. Her father also died at home. She was single then. Her maiden name was Prepichová (meaning 'penetration').

Eva bursts out laughing. "What?" she asks.

"None of that matters!" Urban says and gets up. "I've got a plan. First of all, we have to get him dressed. Understand? Dressed. Right then!" Urban loudly claps his hands. "Dress the body! Be quick about it!"

The prostitutes reluctantly get to work. Each one puts on a sock. Hurensson's face looks dreamy. Urban helps them. They put on the Swede's trousers, vest, shirt, and jacket. He wasn't wearing a tie. Only a cravat round his neck and tucked under his shirt. "Fuck that!" Urban orders when they fail to tie a proper knot round the Swede's neck.

"And what now?" Wanda asks.

Urban reflects. "We have to drag him away somewhere. Understand?" Urban has thought it all out: they'll take the body and dump it discreetly somewhere in the city. As if he'd had a stroke there. What do the girls say to that?

The prostitutes nod. They like the idea. But they don't like the thought of dragging a corpse right across town.

"The worst thing is that we'll have to walk," says Urban. "I've been drinking and doing drugs. If the cops catch us in the car, we're screwed."

"Walk?" The prostitutes repeat with disgust. They're wearing high-heeled shoes.

"Do you want to take him in a taxi?" Urban retorts.

"And why not?" Eva objects. "We'll hold him up like a drunk. We'll talk to him; I mean, you'll talk to him. The taxi driver won't notice a thing. He's paid not to notice things."

Finally Urban agrees. "But," he insists, "it mustn't be anyone we know."

The corpse lies fully dressed, looking bored.

"Hurry up, or he'll go stiff," Urban warns them. He goes to the phone and calls for taxi. He gives his address. "We need a taxi right away. A Mercedes, Sierra, or Fiat Mirafiori. Do you have anything like that? Thanks." He puts down the receiver. Now he's quite calm. There's no going back.

"Why does it have to be a Mercedes?" asks Eva. "Does it matter?"

Urban laughs. "Not to him, but it matters to us. None of the drivers I know has a Mercedes, Sierra, or Mirafiori. Get it?"

The prostitutes say no more. Urban reaches into the dead man's wallet. "We'll split this three ways," he suggests, when he finds a thick wad of banknotes. "There's enough for everyone. He won't need it any more."

"I don't want the dough!" says Wanda, feeling disgusted.

"Don't be stupid!" Eva shouts at her. "Who's going to give you anything these days? No one!"

Urban shakes the banknotes in her face. "We're all in the shit together, so take the money. We can all do with it. And no hysterics." Urban goes through the rest of the wallet's contents: passport, driver's licence, car registration. "Oh yes, there's the car. We can't leave it parked by the house. First we get this over, and then I call Khunt. It will have to be taken to a garage, resprayed, stamped with a new engine number: then we'll sell it," Urban decides. He'll keep the registration and the fine-leather wallet. Any other documents will be thrown in the rubbish bin.

"How much is a Volvo like that worth?" asks Eva.

"We'll ask three hundred thousand for it," says Urban. "We can't ask for more. It's basically a stolen car. Of course, we'll split it three ways. I'll deal with it, you just keep your mouths shut."

Now even Wanda agrees. She can't make that much money in a month. It wasn't such a bad fuck after all.

They put the corpse's shoes on. Wanda drops Hurensson's feet and the shoes bang on the wooden floor. That makes Wanda laugh and she lifts and drops the feet again.

"Stop messing about!" says Urban. He lifts the Swede off the bed. The girls wrap a scarf around the stiffened neck and put the corpse's elegant long winter coat on him. Urban puts a hat on the corpse's head. "Let's go!" he orders them. Wanda opens the door to the hall and Urban and Eva stumble out of the flat. The corpse won't stand. Its head swings from side to side. The hat keeps falling off. "Pick that hat up!" Urban whispers to Wanda. They have to stop again. The corpse is turning stiff; its knees no longer buckle. "Where are we going, anyway?" asks Eva.

"That's simple," says Urban. "Where's he staying? In the Ambassador. Right? We'll leave him lying outside the hotel."

The taxi is already waiting outside. The driver is a stranger, maybe he's new to the trade. He's smoking. Urban, Hurensson and Eva get into the back seat. Wanda sits next to the driver.

"I don't want him throwing up on my seat covers," says the taxi driver firmly, looking in his rear-view mirror. "Where did he get so rat-arsed?"

"A little party," says Urban as offhandedly as he can.

The taxi driver mutters something and engages first gear. "Where to?" he asks.

"To the Ambassador," says Wanda.

After a short night ride through the city, they stop at the Ambassador. Wanda the Trucker pays. Urban and Eva drag Hurensson out of the car and stop on the pavement to get their breath. The taxi drives off.

"Where do we leave him?" asks Wanda.

"In the old car park," says Urban. "Nobody will see us there. They'll find him in the morning and everyone will see: alcohol, heart attack, freezing cold. Let's go."

Now Wanda helps grab the body. Her court shoes slide in the snow. "Fuck," she says to relieve her tension. They make slow progress on the icy pavement. Wanda skids and falls on her behind. Urban can't hold Hurensson's weight and falls with him. "Ah!" says the Swede. Wanda and Eva take fright.

"He's alive!"

Urban is unsettled, too. He shakes Hurensson. It is cold, and rigor mortis is obviously setting in. "It was just air escaping from his lungs when he fell," he tells the prostitutes. "Help me with him. Let's get a move on!"

Piggybank's old car park is dark and unlit. It's fenced off by big cement flower tubs, to stop cars getting in. The wind gusts between the wooden booths. Waxed paper cups, plastic plates and paper litter the dirty snow. The wind blows them over the space round the hotel.

"This is where we leave him," decides Urban. Relieved, they drop the body down. Hurensson seems to stay on his feet for a moment and then falls, face down, into a snowdrift. His hat falls off his head and rolls under the tables. "*Arrivederci,*" says Urban.

"He wasn't so bad," says Eva.

"He was always generous," Wanda adds.

"Even more generous now he's dead," says Urban.

"Now where to?" Urban asks when they find themselves at the entrance to the Ambassador cabaret. Urban is going home. He's had it up to here. He points to his neck. The prostitutes can't make up their minds. "Oh, well, why don't we go back to my place? We'll make ourselves comfortable. You can watch the rest of the Disney film. Well?"

The whores agree. They'll take a taxi back. Urban will call the dealer Khunt.

Khunt is there in half an hour. He's brought a friend. "The other man will drive the car we came in," he explains, when he catches Urban's look. "I don't suppose you want me to park it in front of your place."

Urban nods. "Shall we take a look at the Volvo?"

Khunt shakes his head. "There's plenty of time for that tomorrow in the garage." Khunt gave it the once-over before they came up to see Urban. "You can relax and stay at home," he says knowingly, seeing two women's coats on the coat-stand. "Get nice and warm," he adds ironically. "And how much are you asking?" he says.

Urban ponders. "Considering that a new model is nine hundred to a million, then three hundred thousand is not too much."

Khunt smiles. "Three hundred thousand for a stolen vehicle is still too much," he says. "I'll give you two hundred."

"Two fifty," says Urban.

Khunt is silent for a while. "All right," he says in a tone that suggests he is doing Urban a favour. "Give me the keys and the registration."

Urban hands them over. "You're getting it for almost nothing," he tries to provoke Khunt, who does not react. Khunt nods at his companion standing motionless by the door, and they both go out onto the landing.

"When do I get the cash?" asks Urban.

"This week," says Khunt. "I don't know about the car's condition yet."

"You'll still sell it for six hundred, you piece of trash!" Urban thinks, when the men have gone and he locks the door. "Let's leave it at that! The money's come out of the blue. The hookers will have to make do with fifty thousand each," he decides.

The women are taking a shower together. The air in the bathroom is humid and hot. "Come and join us," says Wanda, lathering her crotch with a sponge. Her wet hair sticks to her face in long strands. Urban undresses and, laughing, joins them in the shower corner. There's not much room. All over his body he can feel slender female arms, legs, elastic breasts, and hot skin.

"Move in to my place!" Urban suggests unexpectedly. They live in different, bloody expensive rented rooms. In his place, they wouldn't have to pay for accommodation. And he wouldn't feel so lonely. They could live together. Urban would help them. He'd protect them, if anyone tried to harm them. People are swine. The girls need someone to take care of them, to help them. Urban knows they don't have anyone to do that. And he's just the right person for the job.

The prostitutes laugh. They lather their entire bodies.

"We'd have to think hard about that," says Wanda. It's true that she lives in an expensive private room rented from a money-grubbing landlady. She used to have her own flat, but when Polgár, her ex-husband, got killed, they threw her out. She wasn't an employee of the Water Supply Department. The manager of the Water Supply Department is a stupid dickhead. She told him so. A psychopath. A bureaucrat.

Urban gets excited. His member and its rolled foreskin stick out like a telescope. Eva massages it with smooth movements. The hot water forms a whirlpool over the drain. The shower streams down. Female voices mingling with the sound of falling water awaken strong desire in Urban. He thinks of the corpse freezing outside the Hotel Ambassador. He tightly embraces both young women at the same time, as if he needed proof that he and they, all three of them, were still dizzily alive.

* * *

Rácz lolls about in bed. It is morning and the trams rumble outside the window. Tonight he's going to the theatre with Lenka. To see an opera. He can't stand the squawking, but Lenka adores it. For Rácz this is a historic day in a way: for the first time he's going into town. There is a knock at the door and Ďula enters.

"Good morning, boss," he says. "You told me to wake you up at nine. The tailor is here. He's waiting in the living room."

Rácz jumps out of bed. He does exercises with powerful arm movements. Then he picks up his exercise springs and stretches and releases them a few times. He runs into the shower and turns on the cold and then the hot water. He cleans his teeth in the shower. Ďula is waiting with a towel ready. Rácz takes it and dries himself. He combs his hair back. "Rubber band," he tells Ďula. Ďula knows what Rácz wants. He takes an ordinary piece of red elastic off the marble shelf and hands it to Rácz. Rácz uses it to tie his hair at the back.

"Shall I get your shaving water, boss?" Ďula asks.

Rácz feels his face with satisfaction. Overnight, thick black stubble has sprouted, covering his face right up to the circles under his eyes. "No," the stoker decides, "from now on, I'm going to shave once every three days. We'll look like artists. After all, we are artists." He puts on a colourful bathrobe and enters the living room, opening the door energetically and firmly.

"I've brought your dinner jacket, professor," says a tiny old man with a bird's face, handing a dinner jacket on a coat hanger to the stoker. Rácz murmurs with approval. "If it needs more minor adjustments, we can easily do them by this evening. Please try it on. I want to see."

Rácz puts the dinner jacket on in the bedroom. It fits him like a glove. Even in the shoulders it's not too narrow. He returns to the tailor.

"Excellent!" says the old man. "It's a pleasure to work for the professor. He has a perfect figure."

Rácz looks at himself in a full-length mirror. The dinner jacket fits perfectly. He smiles.

"Wonderful work," he praises the tailor. "How much do I owe you?"

The old man promptly pulls out a piece of paper. "Here's the bill, sir."

Rácz looks at the bill. "Well," he says, "it's not cheap. But you don't have a dinner jacket made every day, to hell with it." He unlocks his desk and takes some money from a drawer. "Here you are," he tells the tailor. He throws the money on the desk. "The change is for your trouble," he adds.

The old man makes his exit from the Rácz's suite, bowing deeply.

A waiter enters, pushing a serving trolley with the stoker's breakfast. He stops and waits. Rácz throws him a coin. Then he looks at Ďula.

He decides: let's keep the list of things to do today short. Today Rácz is accompanying his fiancée, as he calls her, to the Opera. Then they'll go to the *Puszta*, a Hungarian restaurant, for a late supper. "There's no need to be stuck here in the hotel forever," he says with mock sagacity. He sits down to breakfast.

Ďula puts a finger to his mouth and tiptoes to the door. He opens it quickly. The corridor is empty. From round the corner comes the sound of a waiter's hurried footsteps.

"What is it," asks Rácz, shelling an egg.

"Nothing, boss," says Ďula. "I've been having this strange feeling lately."

"Screw feelings," the stoker advises. "Feelings are for old women."

"The cleaners were whispering about something on the stairs this morning, boss," Ďula reports.

Rácz eats. "Let them whisper," he says with a full mouth.

Ďula sits down at the table. When Ďula walked by, the cleaners shut up. But Ďula put pressure on them. There is a new guest in the hotel, an African, a black man. The cleaners find it strange that when they clean his room, everything is black; there are black fingerprints everywhere. Apparently even his pyjamas and the bed linen was black. The cleaners found it strange, and so does Ďula.

Rácz stuffs a piece of bread and jam into his mouth and chases it down with a mug of tea. "So what?" he says. "If he's black, he'll make everything black. Rácz is a businessman. He doesn't care who he deals with: black or white, they're all the same to him. The cleaners are paid to clean," says Rácz.

Ďula dares to persist. "If someone's black, it doesn't mean the colour comes off. A black man is black. The colour doesn't run."

Rácz finishes the hard-boiled egg and another piece of bread. He frowns. Ďula has to wait a moment until he's swallowed. "What do you think, Ďula?" the stoker addresses his driver. "Why do the blacks in Africa wear grass skirts? Why don't they have furniture? Why no bed linen? Can you answer that one?" Rácz pauses. He reaches into the basket and pulls another slice of bread from under the napkin. Ďula has no idea. He is silent. Rácz smiles with a feeling of superiority. "Why? So they don't get everything black." Rácz touches his forehead. "Couldn't that be the reason," he says, rebuking Ďula.

Ďula is embarrassed.

"Don't take it to heart, Ďula!" Rácz will have a look at the black man. You never know, that's for sure. It pays to be careful, but today he hasn't got time. He has to go to the Opera. Then he's having supper. There are a lot of other duties. Today Rácz wants to spend the whole day having fun.

When Ďula leaves to see to his duties, Rácz takes off his dinner jacket and puts on his red track suit. He turns the television on and tunes into Eurosport. For a while he watches the billiards championship. He gets quite engrossed. But before long somebody knocks at the door. "Enter!" Rácz shouts.

It's the restaurant manager. He enters, bowing fearfully. "Your secretary told me that you wished to speak to me, sir."

"Yes," says the stoker. "My secretary." He likes that title. Secretary. Rácz puts on a kindly expression. "So, how are things?" he asks the restaurant manager. "You seem to have survived New Year's Eve," he says. "I hope Dr. Renceš did, too. What excuse did you invent for him?" Rácz is interested.

"We told him that the lounge was flooded and out of use," says the restaurant manager.

"And then what? Did he have any objections? Was he unhappy about anything?" Rácz wondered.

"Not really." The restaurant manager shakes his head.

Rácz gets up and approaches the restaurant manager. "There you go," he says. "Things are never as bad as they seem." He moves to the window and watches the ice floes passing down the river. He put his hands behind his back. He is silent for a long time. As if he's forgotten about the restaurant manager. "That's not the reason I asked you to come," he says after a while, when the manager is beginning to think that they'll be standing there like that until lunch. "It's not about that," adds Rácz, almost to himself. He measures the room in long, energetic strides. He suddenly stops and jabs his index finger into the air in the direction of the restaurant manager. "What did you study?" he asks.

"Hotel management," says the restaurant manager.

"Why?" Rácz shakes his head and starts to walk up and down. Each time he stops by the window and knocks on the frame with his knuckles. "So you've got a doctorate," he states.

"No," says the restaurant manager, "I'm an engineer."

"Oh yes," says Rácz, as if he's remembered something. "An engineer." So it would not be too far from truth if he said that the restaurant manager knows all about those little trifles.

The restaurant manager throws up his hands. He's the restaurant manager of the Ambassador. He doesn't know what the boss is talking about.

"Oh, things like how to go upstairs with a lady," says the stoker, "how to go downstairs with a lady, what to do in the cloakroom; how to behave at table in a restaurant, how to use a knife and fork, how to say goodbye. That kind of little trifles." Rácz wishes to be taught all these things by the restaurant manager before lunch, if possible. After lunch, Rácz has things to attend to.

The restaurant manager is in a cold sweat. He'll be glad to teach the boss all these things, but he fears that not even a month will suffice.

"What do you mean by that?" Rácz asks and his face congeals into a stone mask.

The restaurant manager takes a deep breath. He has no doubts about the boss's abilities, absolutely none. But he would suggest that the rules of etiquette are a complex science. Take, for example, just table manners. Asking a lady for a dance, polite conversation...

Rácz shakes his head. "No dancing. No conservation. Some other time, perhaps. This evening, there will be going upstairs, sitting in a box, going downstairs, entering a restaurant and eating." Rácz is no idiot. He learns quickly. He's got a good memory. While the restaurant manager has been babbling about complex this and that, ten minutes' teaching time have been wasted, which could have been used to learn how to do it. "Here's a piece of paper and a pencil. Rácz is ready. No more talking!"

The stoker is a good pupil. He has a good memory. He is diligent. He writes everything down. Before evening Rácz will revise it a few times, he tells the restaurant manager. The latter explains everything: when to clap, when not to. Then comes lunch. Rácz phones downstairs and asks for the menu. He wants to choose. He will eat upstairs. He orders a meal for the restaurant manager, too. He wants him to teach Rácz how to use a knife and fork, how to pour wine and taste it and how to use a fish knife and dessert spoon. And to teach him how to summon the waiter; not by losing his temper and banging the table, or pulling the tablecloth and smashing all the china if the waiter is a bit slow. Not to make a toast with an apéritif, not to throw bones under the table, or drink from the bottle. The manager talks and talks. Rácz listens. He holds his knife and fork properly. He chews with his mouth closed. He eats without chomping sounds. He puts small portions of food into his mouth. His elbows are kept pressed to his sides. He knows this is the only way to win over Lenka. She is too young to be overwhelmed by Rácz's money and potential alone. She notices little trifles like these. But Rácz will master this, too. This evening Rácz will eat in the *Puszta* restaurant like a count.

* * *

This is the third day that Šolik and Tupý have been standing outside the hotel, freezing. The long-awaited signal from Mozoň doesn't come. They dare not enter the lobby; they're afraid of their superior. At the same time, with an agonizing feeling of resignation, they physically take in waves of heat, radiating from the revolving door of the hotel into the chilly street. Oh, if only they dared warm themselves up for just ten minutes!

From time to time the black face of Mr. Bwawenu-Mozoň appears, now in the lobby, now in the window of his hotel room. As if his strict expression were trying to remind them of their duties. They have no escape. In a snack bar in the old car park there is good mulled wine. The aroma of cloves, Jamaica pepper, cinnamon waft far and wide. The man in charge of the bar, a stocky moustached fellow in a white coat, can't complain. Everyone who walks by stops. Both ex-secret policemen are there, too. They have enough money; from time to time, they trap some country bumpkin who's seen a film about currency dealers and come to make his fortune in the city. They sip hot wine till their eyes water. They stamp their feet in the snow. They silently await the signal. In a snowdrift lies a drunkard, dozing, face down in the snow. Someone picked up his hat and put it on his head. The drunkard said nothing. The regulars treat him the same and ignore him. Šolik and Tupý don't complain. It's cold and their feet hurt before their day is over, but they know, too, that they could be standing outside the job centre. Nobody's keen to employ people like them. On the other hand, they have a safe house, money, and can still put the frighteners on somebody. And at three thirty they finish work.

Anyway, they realise that when they render Rácz harmless they'll get far more out of the lawyer than a shitty hundred thousand. They'll be able to squeeze him, blackmail him at any time. Whenever they need something, the lawyer will have to arrange it. And if not, then he can kiss his management job goodbye. They'll make things hard for him. That's their unwritten law. The lawyer should have realised that before he got into bed with them!

Šolik and Tupý drink their mulled wine. Time flies. Soon they knock off for the day. The drunkard sleeps like a log in the snowdrift. Pedestrians, fording through the slush, hurry round him. It began to snow, but now it's stopped.

* * *

Silvia is aggrieved. She's sick and tired of Rácz. She won't go back to the Hotel Ambassador and, even if she does, then only after the stoker comes personally to beg her pardon. Naturally, she soon began to miss Rácz's money. She's still got her savings, but she doesn't want to fritter them away. She'll stay at home for a few days; a week, maybe two. Maybe three. Then she'll look for work. With a body like hers she's not afraid she'll have to walk the streets. Recently, quite a few private businesses have opened up and a dancer of Silvia's talent will always be in demand.

Until then she can rest. When she feels that she's been out of circulation too long, she can cruise the town at night and get a few punters. After all, the Ambassador is not the only hotel in the city. Silvia can have fun in the hotels Sartor, Acropolis, or even International.

Edita doesn't move an inch from her side. They live together. She doesn't go to the Ambassador any more, either. They spend a lot of the morning asleep. Edita wakes up first. She runs her tongue all over Silvia's body, parts her legs and puts her tongue into her crotch. She makes Silvia do the same to her. "Good morning." Then they get up and have breakfast. Any shopping is done in the supermarket across the street. They don't feel like going into town. It's cold, snowy and chilly. They undress, get into bed, and caress each other's long, slender bodies. Edita knows every freckle on Silvia's body, and Silvia likewise. That's how they entertain themselves for hours on end. They don't need anyone else. Silvia is certain that, as she and Edita feel so good together, she will reject Rácz's first attempt at reconciliation. And only then will she agree to go back — possibly. But Rácz does not come.

* * *

Rácz is sitting in the dark in a taxi taking him home to the hotel. It's a few minutes after midnight. Rácz is content. He got a taxi and called on the dot for Lenka. He introduced himself to Lenka's parents. "I am Rácz," he said. He brought Lenka's mother, a tiresome old witch, a bouquet. Not like the hundred orchids he had sent to Lenka, but still a beautiful bouquet. At Lenka's parents' invitation he took off his long black overcoat and narrow white scarf. He left his hat on the hat-stand and accepted the offer of coffee. He sat in an armchair and drank the coffee exactly as the restaurant manager had taught him that morning: saucer in one hand, cup in the other. He ate just one biscuit. He didn't dunk it in the coffee as he dunked his roll at breakfast in the hotel. He ate with his mouth closed and tried to move his jaws as inconspicuously and slowly as he could. Then came questions from Lenka's parents. "What was his profession?" Rácz said, "Businessman." The parents nodded their heads respectfully. Then Lenka's father, a typical intellectual parasite with glasses and a beard, asked where Rácz had studied. Rácz replied that he'd graduated from agricultural college. "You mean economics?" Rácz pondered. "Yes," he said after a moment. The father nodded, as if he knew but was just checking. "And what is the nature of your business?" he asked. "I'm mostly in the hotel branch," declared Rácz. "Meaning what?" asked the tiresome old witch. Rácz shrugged. It was hard to get the words out. Rácz would like to buy the Hotel Ambassador and the department store next door. Then he'd see. He took a sip of coffee, resisted temptation and declined a second biscuit.

Lenka's parents were dumbfounded. The intellectual parasite was able to control himself; you couldn't tell anything from his expression. But the old witch was impressed; otherwise her eyes would not have bulged so much.

Then Lenka appeared. In her gown and her evening make-up she was even more beautiful and tempting than he remembered her from the New Year's Eve party. He would have loved to rip that dress off her body and stick himself up her right there, in front of her parents, but once more he overcame his instincts. He got up and politely kissed her hand.

"Good evening, Lenka," he said. "Shall we go?"

They left the apartment and out of the corner of his eye Rácz could see Lenka's parents, sitting in their armchairs completely charmed, like fat flies stuck to the wall. If he were not so self-possessed, he'd have jumped for joy and burst into song.

The opera worked out well. Going upstairs, into the box. Horrid squawking. Screeching violins. Goggle-eyed singers performing various live tableaux on stage. Sporadically, each would sing alone, sometimes a pair, or even a trio, shaking comically and rolling their eyes at the ceiling. The main hero was a fat bearded man. He squawked much higher than the rest, burying his fat fingers into his lace-edged shirt. Rácz felt like roaring with laughter at the ridiculous clowns, but when he looked out of the box where he and Lenka were sitting, he saw that nobody was laughing. In the interval he went downstairs. He ordered two glasses of champagne. He would have drunk a bucket of sparkling wine by himself, but realised this was inappropriate. Lenka told him about French art and Parisian bohemians. She also told him about French impressionists. Rácz listened in silence. In the meantime he was thinking who in the hotel he could grab by the scruff of the neck and force to give him all the available information about these things. Rácz decided he'd take an interest in these things. Not too much, of course. Rácz would be happy to say, if Puccini was mentioned, "Yes, Puccini the painter." After the interval, going upstairs again. More squawking. One of the performers was dying of TB and expressed it in dark, bass tones. Then some died and others survived. The fat man, the main hero, survived. He sang the loudest. At the end they hurled flowers at him. They raised and lowered the curtain several times. The fat bearded man did not want to leave. He kept coming back forever. His soft white body shook comically under the lace-edged Bohemian shirt. Then going downstairs. Cloakroom, and taxi waiting at the entrance.

In the *Puszta* restaurant a waiter showed them to their table. There was a candlestick with a lighted candle. They sat down. They chose their dishes and wine. Rácz ate with a knife and fork. He drank wine in small sips. When the waiter came to flambé the meat in front of them, the stoker made Lenka laugh with his story about a waiter in the Ambassador restaurant suffering third degree burns while flambéing. They weren't content to do it with fake local rum, instead of Havana Club, said Rácz: they had to experiment with surgical spirit. Rácz laughed at the memory. The waiter was engulfed in flames, ran about the restaurant and set fire to several tables and the carpet.

Even the waiter doing the flambé smiled at the story, but his smile was forced. He took the burning meat off the ornamental sabre and put it on Lenka's and Rácz's plates. "Enjoy your meal," he said and left.

Rácz liked it there. He was glad that he'd ventured out of the hotel. He even regretted that he hadn't done so earlier. "We'll come here more often, what do you think?" he said to Lenka. Lenka smiled. Rácz happily nodded and loosened the bow tie that was strangling him. Maybe he'd buy this restaurant one day. They cook well. Rácz likes good food.

They finished dinner with a dessert and a bottle of Veuve Cliquot. Rácz paid. They went into the cold night. The taxi drove up. All evening it drove them, or waited for them.

"Next time we won't do it that way," said Rácz. He decided to buy a car. A better quality car, of course: a Mercedes, a BMW, or a Volvo. Nothing cheap! A big top-of-the-range saloon. Ďula will drive them. Rácz has a driver's licence, he used to drive a tractor and is not ashamed to admit it, but why drive if he has people to do it for him?

They stopped at Lenka's apartment building. Rácz got out and opened the door for Lenka. They entered the hall. Lenka did not turn the light on.

"When are we going see each other?" the stoker asked.

Lenka smiled in the dark. "I've got quite difficult exams at college now," she said. "But when I've got shot of them, I'll ring you."

Rácz called the lift down and held the door open for her. "Good night, Lenka," he said.

"Good night, Rácz," Lenka said, "and thank you for a lovely evening."

"You ain't seen nothing yet," thinks Rácz, returning to the street and the taxi. He is quiet all the way home. He constantly imagines penetrating

Lenka's virginal body and rolling together all over the bed, both moaning loudly.

At the Ambassador he asks the taxi driver, "Do you have a wife?"

The taxi driver is alarmed. "Yes," he says.

Rácz takes out a banknote and hands it to the taxi driver. "Take it," he says. "And don't work any more tonight. Go home, and keep your wife nice and warm."

When the taxi driver sees the banknote's denomination, he's flabbergasted. "I'm much obliged to you, sir," he murmurs. "Thank you very kindly, sir." He can say no more. Rácz has already slammed the door and crossed the snowy pavement to the hotel.

"Let's get the band over here!" he yells in the cabaret bar and stops at the steps leading to the cloakroom. "Ďula!" he shouts for his sidekick. "Let's drink! At the double!" He scans the room. He heads to the back of the room, where Video Urban is sitting with Wanda and Eva. "So you've joined forces," he tells Urban. But Rácz is all for it. "Women need looking after. They have to have an eye kept on them. They have to be protected, and so do a man's interests. That's how it has to be. Rácz invites them all to his table."

"And what are you celebrating?" asks Eva, clutching her handbag, as she prepares to join the stoker's table. Out of the corner of her eye she watches Urban, but he's not moving yet.

Rácz smiles. Rácz is simply celebrating being happy. He's in love and is going to get married. Yes, sir!

"Well, if that's how it is," says Urban, "we'll gladly accept Rácz's invitation." He's got nothing against the stoker. He's not jealous over Lenka. In fact, Urban is almost convinced that Rácz is exactly the sort of man that Lenka needs. At least he'll knock all the bullshit out of her head.

"You bet I will!" says Rácz. Urban can be quite sure that Rácz will put her right. She's young and silly. Rácz will tame her. You have to loosen the reins from time to time, and then tighten them again. That's the way Rácz sees it.

They sit at the table. The panting gypsy Stojka runs in with his violin, but Rácz sends him away. He bangs the table. "Champagne!" Ďula sits down, too. He eyes Wanda. He'd like to screw her, but ever since Urban started looking after these two sluts' business affairs, he hasn't a chance. Only westerners get a chance. Life's a bitch!

"Boss!" Ďula addresses the stoker.

"Well?" asks Rácz, "What do you want?"

Ďula lowers his voice to a confidential whisper. Ďula has new information about the black man.

"Later, later!" Rácz waves his hand. "Now sit and drink, damn and blast you."

They drink. Ďula is soon stupefied. He sits, looking straight ahead. He doesn't even blink. Rácz has turned him into an alcoholic.

Urban can hold his drink, but he isn't drinking much. He keeps an eye open, registering each new guest who enters. It's not long before he sends both girls to the bar. Let them find some punters. They don't feel like it and they'd like to get out of it. They don't feel like it tonight. Urban gives them a stern look. He doesn't know what they're going to live on. Are they going to skive for ever? Wanda protests: they feel best when they are with Urban. He's nice and considerate. He doesn't yell at them. If Urban gave them their share of the Swede's money and car, they could have at least a few days' rest. Urban shakes his head. Urban has put this money aside for them. They'd have squandered it in no time. This way they'll learn to be prudent with money. Work is what keeps a person going. Urban didn't invent their line of work. He's just making it easier for them. They don't pay rent. Urban took them out of cold, uncomfortable rented rooms. Now they can lounge in a spacious luxurious apartment near the centre. And what does he want for that? Nothing, would you believe it! What he does want from them from time to time is the same thing they want, too. And now they should stop bitching and move to the bar; there are so many Germans here, it looks like Stalingrad. "Be quick about it!"

When both prostitutes go off with long faces, Rácz murmurs with approval. "You've got to be tough with women: tighten the reins, loosen the reins." Rácz hopes that Urban is not angry with him. There's no reason: Lenka chose Rácz. But it is pointless analysing these things. Rácz is in love and is getting married. Full stop! Rácz wanted to talk about something else. He has a proposition for Urban.

"What kind of a proposition?"

Rácz lights a cigarette, pours Urban and himself a drink. They're alone at the table. Ďula doesn't count. He's frozen into a posture with head bent backwards and mouth open.

"Well?" Urban asks.

Rácz begins to explain. Rácz has had a lot on his hands lately. And he's on his own. Ďula is useless. He's a sidekick. A driver. He can be given small tasks, but can't be trusted to work on his own. He's too stupid. Besides, he doesn't have a mind of his own. Rácz can rely on him, but only within limits. Rácz needs more than a sidekick. He needs an independent, creative employee. The stoker blushes. He's used the word "creative" for the first time in his life and is not sure if Urban has noticed. He takes a drink and puffs on his Marlboro. Rácz needs a man who wouldn't have to agree with Rácz on everything, but who'd work for their mutual benefit. Rácz has big plans. Maybe Urban doesn't know, but Rácz would like to buy the Hotel Ambassador and perhaps even the department store. But that would only be a beginning. In time, Rácz would want to start up other operations. But he can't do it alone, or with one sidekick and a bunch of Albanians. Rácz falls silent.

Urban clears his throat. "That's all very well," he says. Urban is glad Rácz is thinking so far ahead. After all, the situation is changing at incredible speed. What was unthinkable just two or three months ago is now quite simple. But Urban can't understand where he comes into this.

The stoker offers Urban a cigarette and gives him a light. Rácz was thinking of Urban when he spoke about a creative employee. Ďula is an idiot. Rácz hates doing the rounds of government offices. And besides, quite frankly, he doesn't feel like it. And now's the time when you have to run round government offices. Rácz wants to buy the hotel. That has to be done somehow. He's got the money. Urban will be able to buy the whole government, if need be. Besides, Rácz believes that Urban has all the necessary charm and can express himself well. He can get access anywhere. And he'll never regret it. Rácz is offering him a good position. A salary he's never dreamt of. He can start immediately: unofficially, for the time being, as Rácz himself is still registered as a stoker. They'll sign a contract afterwards. Rácz is straight: he says what he thinks. "Well then?"

Urban shakes his head. He doesn't know if he's the right man for this kind of work. He will, of course, think Rácz's offer over. But he can't give him an answer off the cuff.

Rácz gets upset. His face goes red. "What?" He can't understand. A firm offer like this needs thinking over? Hasn't Rácz made himself clear? He is, after all, offering Urban a solid position in Rácz's future company. Urban will never have to hustle as a foreign currency dealer, or make videos of children's idiotic smiles, or pimp two whores. And if this isn't good enough, then Rácz really doesn't know what is!

Finally he wins Urban over. They drink to it. Rácz smiles contentedly. The two of them, Rácz and Urban, will show everybody. Nobody can hold a candle to them! Then there's another topic, more of a personal nature. Rácz ought to buy a good car. Not a Škoda, or cheap Mercedes that stupid butchers buy to pretend that they amount to something! Rácz wants something really luxurious. He has money, though not to throw about. But he'll pay good money for a good car. Does Urban know of anything suitable?

Urban has a good think. Yes, there is something he might know of. Khunt is selling a beautiful Volvo. It's a big luxury saloon. If Rácz likes, Urban will arrange it.

Rácz nods. He's interested. And the third thing, a more or less personal request: could Urban lend him a few books about art, culture, and so on? Rácz would like to read something about painters, writers, and that sort of thing. But not a big fat book. Rácz doesn't have the time for that. Something in a nutshell.

Urban bursts with suppressed laughter. Yes, Urban will look out for something. Certainly.

Rácz mutters approvingly. And to get back to the main thing: Urban must keep himself free for tomorrow. Dealing with the bureaucrats will have to begin. He'll have to find out what possibilities there are of buying the Hotel Ambassador. Rácz falls silent. "And now, let's drink to it." Then he adds, "To all of it!"

* * *

Mozoň is unhappy. Everything happened so quickly that he couldn't even use the anæsthetic injection, or give a signal to his two subordinates hanging around the snack bar in front of the hotel. He was listening at the door of Rácz's suite when the door opened, Rácz himself came out and, without bothering to explain himself, dragged Mozoň in by his hair. The first blow of Rácz's fist knocked out the former secret policeman's self-confidence, the next took away his ability to use the self-defence moves he'd been taught, and a mighty kick in the testicles finally forced him to whine and beg for mercy. "Mercy!" he whimpered. "Mercy!"

Rácz stands over him proudly, his fists clenched. Ďula kneels over Mozoň, finishing a tight knot. The secret policeman is trussed as tightly as a rolled ham.

"Well?" asks the stoker. "Why are you spying? What are you looking for here?"

Mozoň is silent. He reflects on what he's done wrong. Until now he's been sure that he was behaving circumspectly and vigilantly. Now he feels like a boy caught masturbating. Rácz bangs his fist on the little table.

"Answer!" he yells.

"Answer!" Ďula repeats and shakes their tied up captive.

Mozoň licks his dry lips. "I just happened to be passing. I heard talking. I couldn't resist…"

"Liar!" the stoker shouts at him. "We've been watching you for several days. You're as inconspicuous as a box of dynamite! I repeat: what are you doing here?"

Mozoň tries to collect some of his wits and says, "My name is Mugambia Bwawenu and I am a citizen of Mayoumbe!"

Rácz bursts out laughing. "Like fuck you are!" He walks up to the former secret policeman, spits on his hand and passes it over Mozoň's face. "Aha!" he says, smiling, showing his dirty hand to Mozoň. "I'll give you black man!"

Mozoň uses a momentary pause to invent an excuse. He clears his throat. "All right then," he says with feigned resignation. "I'll tell you everything."

"You bet you will!" Rácz says and brings his clenched fist close to Mozoň's nose: a fist clenched tightly like a stick of dynamite. "Smell it!" he orders.

Mozoň starts to talk. His name is Ščepán. He works as a bank clerk. He's here incognito. It's supposed to be a business trip. In fact, he came here to let off steam. He wanted to have a good time. You know, whores, and so on. He's saved up some money. Not much. He's put on the black man disguise because he's heard that our whores can't get enough of black men. But so far he hasn't managed to pick up a single whore. He doesn't seem to know how. But he does have money! Ščepán-Mozoň winks meaningfully, but Rácz's metallic gaze is hard and merciless. Not a trace of understanding.

The stoker asks, "So you came here for the whores?"

Ščepán swallows and nods feverishly. "Yes, that's it, actually." That's why Ščepán came. But, for God's sake, his wife mustn't find out. He never meant to spy on anyone. Never!

"Then why were you following me?" asks the stoker. "Why were you listening at the door?"

Ščepán, says Mozoň, wanted to contact the big man, Rácz. He wanted to ask if he'd take money to arrange a contact. Ščepán, knows that nothing happens without the big man Rácz's say-so. So he wanted to talk to him man to man. Ščepán is innocent and utterly at Rácz's mercy.

Rácz ponders. He doesn't believe a single word the fake black man is telling him. He knows that some strange web of intrigue is being spun around him. He's sure that the hotel lawyer is behind it. Ever since the lawyer refused Rácz's invitation to the New Year's Eve party, Rácz has had no illusions. He knows that he's got an enemy. But the enemy has no way of getting at him; if Rácz falls, so does he. That's why the lawyer is looking at various ways to get him. Rácz has heard rumours that the lawyer was aiming to become the manager of the hotel. It is also possible that the lawyer, on the other hand, knows of Rácz's plan to buy the hotel. The lawyer hasn't got the money to buy it, so he's certainly trying something else. But what? This disguised black man, now grimacing with fear in his bonds, could be a link in a chain meant to shackle Rácz so that he can be thrown overboard. Rácz has to get to the mind behind the plot, to the lawyer himself. Only when he destroys the lawyer will Rácz be able to sleep soundly. But he can't just make him disappear by locking him in the boiler-room. So he has to pretend that he believes Ščepán and has to let him go. Ščepán will lead him to the culprit. And when it turns out that the culprit really is the lawyer, Rácz will find a way of destroying him. And if it's someone else, Rácz will at least find out who else is undermining him. Rácz can't afford to be hot-tempered or impatient. His ambitions require a rather different stance: cunningly biding his time, swallowing his initial anger and delaying his relished vengeance until the very end, when it is more intense and exciting. So he overcomes his desire to yell at the fake black man he's trussed up, clench his fists and tear him to pieces. Quite the opposite; he smiles and condescendingly asks him, "Whores? Why didn't you tell me sooner? I'm the boss here! I'll organize everything right now. You'll be satisfied, Ščepán. And don't be cross with us."

With these words, the stoker begins to untie the knot on Mozoň's bonds. "And what are you staring at?" he shouts at Ďula, who gazes at him, arms drooping, eyes full of wonder. Rácz winks with his left eye at him. He discreetly taps his right temple. Ďula makes a move and helps to free Mozoň from the rope.

Mozoň has swallowed the bait of Rácz's feigned credulity. He's pleased to have pulled the wool over the stoker's and his sidekick's eyes so easily. He's happy. Mozoň will kill two birds with one stone. He will destroy Rácz and get a hundred thousand for it from the lawyer, and he will also sleep with a real whore for the first time in his life. Only divine intuition could have made him think of such an excuse! Ever since childhood Mozoň has had a lot of perverse ideas. He had day-dreamed in the greatest detail about the things he would do in favourable circumstances, which also occurred in his dreams, with willing women. But he could not do this with his wife. He had never even dared suggest anything of the sort to her. Mozoň's wife handed him out sex as a teacher gives her pupils sweets which are harmful to tooth enamel, but pretending that she is doing them a kindness. When Mozoň, at the beginning of their marital life, had suggested a slight change of position, she took offence. She wouldn't speak to him for two days. She treated him like a pervert. Since then she allowed him to have sex with her with a tragic expression on her face. Like Beethoven's *Fifth*. Mozoň, for example, has never seen her naked; he could not summon up courage to try anything with her in daylight and can't see anything at night. He's never dared turn on the light; he, too, is embarrassed by nakedness.

Now Mozoň has a wonderful opportunity to make up for lost time. It's a pity that he hasn't got on him the little notebook where he notes, in moments of boredom, his erotic ideas and inspirations. They come to him almost daily, particularly when sitting on the lavatory, or after eating spicy sausage. But the safe house is a long way away. Mozoň hopes that he can recall all the positions and situations that he has dreamt up in the boring and dreary afternoons at the villa. Now he'll be able to see if his fantasies are technically, but above all anatomically, feasible! Mozoň hopes that his face doesn't show the sudden impatience and excitement that has come over him. He gets up and rubs his wrists.

Nothing escapes Rácz. He knows that he has Ščepán in his hand. Once Rácz carries out his plan, then Ščepán will be his for good. Rácz sits in the armchair and sizes up the fake black man. "I do have a whore for you; a nice bit of skirt. She'll do anything you ask her. She has a friend who'll also do anything for you."

"Anything?" Mozoň is shaking with excitement. Growing sexual tension makes him yawn a few times.

"But it will cost you a bundle," the stoker warns him.

The excited ex-secret policeman just waves his hand. He has plenty of money, he says. Everything is going like clockwork, he thinks. He will combine the pleasant and the useful. For the first time in his life he will have sex with two women at the same time. And he will eventually render Rácz harmless. The next day. Or the day after tomorrow. And when he's in their cell, then he'll have to give Mozoň every last penny back. So that'll be a free fuck.

"When could it be arranged for?" Mozoň asks Rácz impatiently.

Rácz shrugs. "Maybe tonight," he says. "I hope they'll both be available."

Mozoň rubs his hands in anticipation and yawns with tension. "That would be excellent," he says. His brain fills with images of naked and twisted female bodies, interwoven limbs, and moist and sticky skin contact. "Ooo!" he thinks happily.

* * *

In the evening, Mozoň sits in the lobby, trying to read a newspaper. He occasionally trembles with nerves and impatience. He stifles a yawn. There's nothing in the papers. Mozoň is no longer black. Why bother? It's quite unnecessary now.

"The boss asked me to tell you that the girls have been arranged and are ready," Ďula comes up to Mozoň and says. "What time do you want them to come to your room?"

Mozoň raises his head and looks at Ďula. "They can come right away," he says impatiently, puts down the paper and gets up.

Ďula nods. "They'll be with you in half an hour."

Mozoň hurries to his room. He deserves a bit of entertainment and relaxation. For days he has been doing nothing but lie in wait for the stoker. The stoker can wait. The lawyer won't bloody mind. When Mozoň, and his underlings undertake anything, they succeed. One day plus or minus makes no difference. Mozoň enters his room. He looks out of the window. Šolik and Tupý have already gone home. So why can't he get a little rest and relaxation, too?

He undresses and takes a shower. Then he splashes himself with cologne; especially his scrotum and around his organ. The cologne burns him and brings tears to his eyes. He gets dressed. Somebody knocks. Two extravagantly dressed and made-up young women enter the room. Both are slender; one is strikingly tall.

"Good evening," says the tall one in a deep, velvety voice.

"Good evening," says Mozoň, his throat tight with tension.

"I'm Wanda," says the tall one, "and she's Eva." Eva smiles.

"I'm Karol," says Mozoň. "Sit down." He points to two armchairs.

The prostitutes sit down. They both cross their legs, revealing substantial parts of their thighs. One is wearing black stockings, the other white. They are silent. Mozoň clears his throat. He makes a few awkward movements and then sits down on the bed, as there is nowhere else to sit. He spreads his arms as if to say, "This is how things are…" The prostitutes smile a broad studied smile. Wanda absent-mindedly runs her hand over her black thigh. This makes a quiet rustle in the silence.

"Would you like a drink?" Mozoň says suddenly, jumping off the bed.

The girls look at each other.

"Red wine for me," says Eva.

"Same for me," Wanda joins in.

Mozoň nods and is about to rush out.

"Where are you going?" Wanda asks.

"To get the wine," says the bewildered secret policeman.

"Just sit here," says Eva. "Phone room service, they'll bring it."

When Mozoň phones for a bottle of red, he sits on the bed. He watches the prostitutes.

"Well?" Wanda says. "What have we come here for?" She gets up and begins to undress.

Eva follows her. Completely naked, except for stockings, they approach Mozoň, push him down on the bed and begin to take off his clothes. The secret policeman starts to take rapid breaths. His penis sticks up vertically. Wanda takes it into her mouth, while Eva serves him higher up. The secret policeman murmurs in excitement. He loves it.

Somebody knocks at the door. "Who is it?" Mozoň asks from the bed.

"Room service," says a voice behind the door.

Mozoň hides under the quilt and covers up both prostitutes, as well.

"Come in!" he says.

A waiter enters with a bottle of wine and three glasses. His face shows no surprise. He opens the bottle and pours a little wine into a glass. He offers it to Mozoň. Mozoň impatiently reaches for the glass. He uncovers himself a bit. The prostitutes throw the quilt onto the floor and grab the struggling policeman by his shoulders from both sides. They pose on the bed with their thighs spread wide. Urban runs in from the hall with his camera, capturing all the action. Behind him stands Ďula with a malicious smile. Mozoň tries to cover his face and his genitals at the same time. His purple penis droops and quivers. The waiter has stepped aside.

Filming is over. The waiter, Urban, and Ďula have left. The prostitutes hurriedly get dressed. A stony-faced Rácz enters the room. Mozoň is whimpering in a foetal position on the bed. He feels as if he has been raped. He tries to cover himself with the quilt, but Rácz's foot, elegantly shod in an Italian shoe, steps on it.

"The comedy's over! Time for the bill!"

Wanda and Eva have both got dressed and left. In his nakedness Mozoň is humiliated by the immaculately dressed stoker. He grabs the quilt and tries to cover himself. Rácz bends down, rips the quilt out of his hands and throws it into the corner.

"What's this all about?" the secret policeman asks querulously. He has pulled himself together a little. "That wasn't the deal," he adds.

"No, that wasn't the deal," Rácz agrees. "Rácz doesn't do deals with crooks," he says firmly. Rácz raises a hand. He is holding a videocassette. "You're in it," he says maliciously, "in all your beauty. Your wife will be very pleased."

The secret policeman goes pale. "My wife! Not my wife!" He licks his lips. "What do you want from me?" he asks hoarsely.

Rácz lets him wait for an answer. "Tell me the truth!" he roars. "Who are you and what are you looking for here? Who sent you? I know you're a cop. I'll make copies of the cassette and send it to where you work. You might as well hang yourself. Well?" Rácz rattles the cassette.

"I'll tell you everything!" Mozoň shouts in desperation. "Everything!" Mozoň says his name's not really Ščepán. He's not a cop. He's unemployed. He was sacked. He used to work for State Security.

"Oh yes?" says Rácz.

Mozoň continues his confession. Mozoň now works as a sort of private detective. The lawyer hired him for this job. He was supposed to render Rácz harmless. Mozoň admits he's been defeated, but assures him that it's not his fault. The lawyer's to blame for everything. The lawyer is evil and stupid; Mozoň, on the other hand, is a good person. He's been given a job to do, so he has to do it. He lives from hand to mouth. He's unemployed. And if he doesn't want to starve to death, he has to do something. So that's what he did. The lawyer promised him a hundred thousand to help liquidate Rácz. Mozoň has a narrow-minded wife. Of course, he loves her a lot. If Rácz sends her the cassette, it will kill her. It would kill him, too. Rácz must reconsider and save two young lives and not make their children orphans.

Rácz laughs. "So it was the lawyer!" he says, but his smile vanishes in a flash, as if he'd torn a mask off his face. "Lawyer!" he adds with hatred.

In his nakedness Mozoň crawls out of the bed and kneels down before Rácz. Mozoň respects Rácz. He was becoming more and more aware that to side with the lawyer against Rácz was madness. It would be better to side with Rácz against the lawyer, and so on. Mozoň asks Rácz to pardon him. Yes, he was led astray. But he realises now where his place is. And Rácz needn't think that he is entering his service with eff-all to show! He's well equipped: he has two reliable subordinates who do whatever he tells them to. If he tells them to kill, they kill. They were trained in Moscow; they had the electric shock treatment. What's more, they have a beautiful safe house, a villa overlooking the city, by the castle. It has a beautiful, romantic panoramic view of the city. And there are several concrete cells in the basement. Mozoň and his two subordinates are well versed in undercover operations. They could be useful to him.

Rácz is silent; he is standing with his feet apart and his fists clenched. His teeth are clenched, too. He seems not to be listening to the secret policeman's offer. "So it was the lawyer!" he repeats, and his eyes seem to bulge from his head. Then he comes to. "A cell? You have concrete cells, you say?"

Mozoň nods eagerly. Mozoň never had anything against Rácz. It was the evil lawyer. If Mozoň had known how powerful Rácz really was, he'd never have let the lawyer talk him into this. He pauses full of insecurity, but of hope, too. With a look of doggish devotion, he watches Rácz raging over him.

Rácz stares at him with his malevolent steel-grey eyes. "Don't loll about naked like a bloody rent-boy!" he shouts at him. "Get dressed, quick!"

Mozoň jumps up. "Yes, boss," he says.

Rácz puts the videocassette in the pocket of his elegant jacket and turns to the door. "Come with me," he orders the secret policeman.

"Yes, boss," Mozoň nods obediently. He quickly gets dressed. His balls hurt, but he ignores it.

Rácz nervously stands by the door, tapping a foot. "Ready?" he asks when the secret policeman takes up a servile posture by him. They go to Rácz's apartment. Ďula joins them on the way. He has been keeping watch outside the secret policeman's room.

"The lawyer has to disappear, understand?" the stoker orders, sitting behind the desk.

"Yes, boss," says Mozoň.

Rácz murmurs in approval. The lawyer has to be punished severely! Rácz doesn't care how Ščepán does it. Rácz doesn't want to hear about it.

"Disappear?" Mozoň asks. "You mean…" Mozoň's hands make a violent twisting gesture. He looks enquiringly at the stoker.

The stoker raises both hands in denial. Rácz has said what he wanted. He doesn't want to hear or know about anything. Rácz's people are trained to work on their own initiative. Everyone has a share of responsibility. They share out the results of the joint work collectively.

Rácz reaches into the drawer and takes out a metal casket. He unlocks it and takes out a thick wad of banknotes. He throws them on the table. With a nod he tells Ščepán to come and take the money. "Here's the hundred thousand you would have got from the lawyer," says Rácz. He pronounces the word "lawyer" as if he were spitting. Ščepán takes the wad. Rácz puts his hand in the casket again and throws another wad, just as thick, on the table. "And here is another hundred thousand from Rácz," he says. "You know what for," he adds.

Ščepán reaches for the second wad of banknotes, but Rácz adroitly swipes him over the fingers with a metal ruler that he was holding in the other hand. The secret policeman screams with pain and sticks his throbbing fingers into his mouth. Rácz smiles. "I'll keep this money for the time being, he says. When we get rid of the lawyer, you'll get it. Until then, I'll keep it here." The stoker takes the money off the table and puts it in the casket, locks it up, and places it in the desk. "Everything clear?" he asks Mozoň.

Mozoň nods. "Yes, boss," he says.

Rácz gets up and approaches the ex-secret policeman. He lifts his right hand as if to look at his watch. He proffers it to Ščepán. The ex-secret policeman takes it in his hand and kisses it. The stoker accepts this gesture with lips grimly pursed and head held proudly high. The diamond glitters in his ear. "You can go," he says, and waves his hand contemptuously, as if chasing a fly away. "Keep me informed," he shouts at Ščepán, who bows as he shuts the door behind him.

"And what now, boss?" Ďula asks, after Ščepán has left.

Rácz bangs the table. "What now? Now we'll all have a nice supper. We've earned it. Find Urban and his two sluts and tell them Rácz is inviting them to the restaurant! We have to enjoy ourselves as well, right?" Rácz slaps Ďula's back. He sends him on his way with a friendly kick up the backside.

* * *

D-day has arrived: all morning the manager has been sure of that. He got up at daybreak and made a fire for the last time. He warmed himself up and cooked a nourishing soup from vegetable peelings, bacon rind and chicken guts he'd found in the skip in the yard. When the morning's work began in and around the hotel, the fire was already out, and the window that let the smoke out was closed again. Some of the dogs were growling restlessly, some were dozing; others were still straining in harnesses fashioned from old inner tubes and tyres.

The manager had planned everything thoroughly. He's quite certain that he doesn't stand a chance here in the hotel. Or anywhere else. He has no skills. His wife has taken a lover. The lover has grown the manager's moustache and she's happy with him. His father-in-law is in prison and won't get out soon. Any new amnesty is unlikely. The manager has nowhere to go. In the hotel, he lives at the stoker's mercy. He has nothing to eat. He hasn't, and won't have, any money for decent nourishing food. It's getting harder and harder to catch small animals near the waste bins.

Far, far away, in the north, beyond the Arctic Circle, live people among whom he would feel at home. They are stocky, rotund, with simple faces and slanting eyes and they wear the furs of animals they hunt. They can spend hours patiently waiting near a hole in the ice until a seal pokes its head out of the cold, blue-grey water. They are as simple as the manager, hospitable and cheerful. They like to sing songs; they often talk to themselves, as does the manager.

He knows them well. His favourite childhood book was *Daybreak Over Chukotka*. It was there that he got to know the good wise hunter Vaamcho, his courageous girlfriend Tygrena, the old one-eyed Lok, the cunning trader Alitet and his father, the shrewd shaman Korauge. The manager is certain that these characters may still be alive. He has proved to himself and others that he has every right to consider himself one of them. He has managed to survive in the inhospitable conditions of his office. He hasn't frozen or starved to death. He is an excellent hunter. His arrow never misses its target.

Yes, the manager has made up his mind. He is setting off north, beyond the Arctic Circle. No, he has no map. He doesn't need one. He will steer his dog pack straight north, always due north. He can't go wrong; he can't get lost: due north. The dogs will run for nights on end, never wavering. Daytime will be spent hiding somewhere. They'll camp and wait until dark. It gets dark soon now. When it gets dark, he'll drive his pack further. No matter how long it takes, the manager is sure to get there. He has to get there eventually.

"The hour is at hand," says the manager. He yells at his dogs. The dogs squat, howl, and gnash their teeth. The manager gets up and moves towards them. He harnesses them one by one to the sledge he stole from the little girl in the yellow windcheater. All that he possesses is on this sledge: a tent, bows and arrows, blankets, his accordion, a sleeping bag, the furs of animals caught around the Hotel Ambassador, and long thin strips of dried meat. The dogs are nervous; they tug at their harnesses and yap impatiently. They sit in a semicircle, their heads turned to the manager. They vent their nervousness in prolonged howling and gnashing of teeth. The manager takes from a string over the fireplace the last few strips of dried meat. He breaks them into small pieces and throws them to the dogs. The dogs catch their food in the air and their muzzles glisten hungrily. The manager pauses. He sits down for a moment. You need a rest before a long journey.

Then the manager gets up. He pulls on a long furry parka that he's made from dog and cat fur. He puts a furry hat on. He once caught a Persian cat. It must have run away from home. Now it will reach the Arctic Circle as a hat. The manager gets onto the sledge. He grabs a whip he made from a car tyre. "Mush!" he shouts at the dog team. "Mush!" He cracks his whip. The dogs begin to run, the sledge speeds over the bare cement floor, left after the manager pulled up and burned all the parquet. The team smashes through the office door, runs into the hall and drags and bangs the sledge, with the manager ensconced, down the stairs. "Mush!" the manager shouts, his face flushed with excitement.

The receptionist has just returned from outside. He'd gone to see if it was still snowing or not. "It's snowing again, bugger it," he remarks to the porter Torontál. Torontál is sitting by the reception desk, gripping the marble counter. From a distance he looks like a mummy an absent-minded traveller had left in the lobby. Close up, even more so. He hasn't got the strength to go to the cloakroom, let alone home. He stays by the reception desk day and night. He neither eats nor drinks. He doesn't need to go to the lavatory. The receptionists alternate shifts; Torontál stays. Occasionally they lift one of his eyelids and put a mirror to his mouth. They find he's still alive and pay no more attention to him. As far as they are concerned, he can croak. But Torontál is still very much alive. He saves his energy for a new guest to appear in the revolving door. Then he comes alive. First his left eye, then his right open up. His bony wrinkled hands begin to tremble with impatience and greed. They move independently of each other like two large crabs. Waggling his fingers, Torontál gets off his chair and resolutely minces towards the client. But there are no clients at night. Torontál stays at the ready, like a crane which has been switched off and left in mid-swing. The receptionist has also settled down on his raised chair behind the desk. The keys hang on the wall behind him and gleam softly in the dark. He opens the paper to read what's happening in the world. Suddenly he is alerted.

The enormous dark hall comes alive with the racket. At first the sound is muffled, but then gets louder. Some of the noise is the wild barking of a score of dogs. The receptionist can't believe his ears. He puts down his newspaper and gets off his chair. "What the hell…" he says.

From the stairwell at the back, a team of dogs pulling a sledge flies past the reception desk at breakneck speed. On the sledge sits a figure wrapped up in furs. "Mush!" yells the figure, cracking a whip. That's all the receptionist sees, as the sledge flies like the wind over the stone floor, sending a trail of sparks. The dog team flies into the glass door. The entrance glass shatters loudly, and dogs and sledge fly out into the darkness.

The receptionist stands there numb, mouth agape. He looks at Torontál, but the latter is like a mummified corpse. The receptionist goes up to the smashed and dislocated revolving door. A cold wind and the wet smell of the blizzard blow into the vestibule. "Bugger me," the receptionist says. He peeps out of the door. The dog team is at the end of the street. The traffic lights at the crossroads flash orange in the distance. Two parallel tracks in the fresh snow still glisten, but gradually fade as fresh snow covers them. At the crossroads, the dog team turns right, up to the north. The receptionist awakes from his stupor. He shakes his fist at the disappearing dog team. The dogs' restless barking becomes fainter. Finally, the racket, overlaid by the wind's rustling and the wet, heavy snowfall, dies out. "Bugger me," the receptionist repeats and returns to the vestibule to tot up the damage. If only he had a witness! Nobody's going to believe him. The receptionist is numb. He realises he'll have to pay out of his own pocket for the damage.

"Bugger me," he says for the third time.

The sledge pulled by the dog team hurtles up the sleepy street. The manager sings merrily. His cheeks are red. He joyfully cracks his whip. What a good sledge! Fast as a reindeer! Keep heading north! The manager's sitting pretty; he's comfortable. Just keep heading north, up the hill. He'll get there eventually. By daybreak, he'll have covered at least ten kilometres! His hunter's soul sings a joyful tune. Holding the reins in one hand, the manager pulls from his bosom a piece of dry meat. "Mush!" he yells when he senses the dogs easing off the furious pace. Snowflakes as sharp as needles cheerfully prick his face.

* * *

Zdravko G. arrives in the city early in the morning. "Damn it," he curses in Serbian when he finds out that he can't park his orange Opel banger in the usual car park. The lot is surrounded on all sides by giant concrete cubes filled with earth. Zdravko G. vainly tries to push one of these flower tubs aside. Out of breath from excessive exertion, he gets back into his car and decides that the distance between the tubs is sufficient to squeeze through. This decision costs him a torn left bumper and a dented and jammed driver's door. "*Jebem ti krv krvavu!* Fuck this bloody shit!" he says to relieve the tension, finally leaving the car parked by the pavement near the hotel. He gets out by the passenger door and has a look at the damage. Then he spits, waves his arm dismissively, and enters the lobby. The smashed entrance shocks him. The receptionist is standing there like a martyr. Torontál opens his left eye, but soon closes it. Zdravko G. stuffs a twenty-crown note in this desiccated corpse's greedy palm and then ignores him. "Can I have room number thirteen?" he asks the receptionist. The receptionist registers him and gives him his room key. "That's my lucky number, you see," says Zdravko G., jingling the keys.

Zdravko G. has a shower, changes his clothes and goes down to the bar. "Where's Silvia?" he asks the headwaiter. The waiter pauses. "Do you know her?" he asks. "She's a blonde. She used to work in the Cabaret... a dancer, you know?" Zdravko performs a little pantomime of a strip show to music. "Does she still work here?"

The headwaiter shakes his head. "No, Silvia no longer works here; she left the cabaret some time ago."

"Doesn't she?" Zdravko G. is surprised. "You know, I'm a friend of hers. *Freund.* I'd like to meet her. I haven't been here for some time. Do you know her address? *Wohnung?*"

The waiter accepts the hundred-schilling note as a matter of course. "I don't know where she lives, but if you wait a moment, I'll find out." He's back in no time. "Here it is," he tells Zdravko G., handing him a note with an address scribbled on it. "But be careful," he warns Zdravko, "it's not a good idea to mention her name in this hotel."

"What name?" Zdravko G. doesn't understand, but the headwaiter is now busy with other guests. Zdravko puts the note in his pocket. He's happy. He hasn't seen Silvia for a long time. He believes she'll agree to his plan. It's attractive. What woman would reject it? He's pleased as he leaves the bar.

* * *

The lawyer wakes up with a headache. He feels knocked out. He moves. His shoulder hurts. Oh yes, now he remembers. Mozoň had entered his office and he managed only to ask why Mozoň had washed the black paint off his face, when the latter took a disposable syringe out of his pocket. The lawyer remembered the syringe: the secret policeman had shown it to him when he visited the safe house. Mozoň had suggested using it to knock Rácz out.

"My name isn't Mozoň," Mozoň had said. His name was Ščepán and nothing else. Then he circled the syringe over the lawyer's head and stuck it in his shoulder.

"What are you doing?" said the stupefied lawyer. He was still conscious when Šolik and Tupý ran into the room and all three secret policemen dragged him down the corridor and downstairs to the yard, where they stuffed him into the hotel's Renault minibus, which was waiting there, with the engine running and Ďula at the wheel. By then, the lawyer had begun to feel the effect of the injection. He was laughing senselessly and his head was slumping. He let them bundle him into the vehicle like a piece of luggage. That's all he remembered.

It's cold in the cell. The concrete floor is damp. With a great effort, using the wall for support, the lawyer gets up. The barred window is high, out of reach. The cell is sparsely furnished: a wooden plank serves as a spartan bed; there's a hole-in-the-ground lavatory in the far corner. The lawyer looks at this with a numb expression. His head aches. He swallows. His mouth tastes as if he had a hangover. His head clears slowly. He has been locked up in the safe house. That means that the ex-secret policemen, Mozoň and his two subordinates, have imprisoned him. Does that mean that they've deserted him for Rácz?

A key rattles in the lock. The door opens and Mozoň enters. His face is blank. Šolik and Tupý follow. Tupý is carrying a bucket.

"What's the meaning of this?" the lawyer asks, his mouth dry. Mozoň shrugs. He nods to Tupý. Tupý puts the bucket in the middle of the room. "What's that," asks the lawyer, pointing to the bucket.

"It's a bucket," says Ščepán.

"And what's in it?" The lawyer is puzzled.

"Water from the Danube, you lawyer pig!" Ščepán suddenly shouts at him.

The lawyer goes up to the bucket and looks down. The water is muddy and foul. He asks, "Why do you need Danube water?"

The ex-secret policemen look at each other with amusement. "Because we don't want them finding tap water in your lungs when they fish you out of the Danube," Ščepán explains.

On his command, Tupý and Šolik grab the lawyer and violently bend him down towards the bucket. They force him to his knees and push his head under the dirty water. The lawyer fights back. Ščepán has to come and help his subordinates.

"He'th thtrong, chief," says Tupý with a hint of admiration.

"Keep pushing and don't fucking talk!" Ščepán rebukes him sharply.

The lawyer is struggling and making bubbles in the bucket. In a desperate move, he grabs Šolik by the sleeve and rips a piece of his shirt off. Soon his movements weaken. The ex-secret policemen are all wet.

"Shit!" says Šolik. "A six-hundred-crown shirt!"

The lawyer's head is in the bucket and has stopped moving. There are no more bubbles. The secret policemen take him out and lay him on the plank.

"Now we've earned a hundred thousand," says Ščepán solemnly.

The men are wet with perspiration and exhausted. It's cold in the cell. Šolik is upset. "A six-hundred-crown shirt!"

Ščepán snaps at him. "Shut your mouth! For that kind of money you can buy five hundred shirts."

Šolik stubbornly shakes his head. "No, no, he says, I'll never find another one like this. They only got them in the shop once and then they were sold out."

They drag the lawyer up to the ground floor. They are out of breath. The stairs are steep and narrow. The drowned man keeps sliding down, Ščepán curses and Šolik is aggrieved. He mutters unhappily.

* * *

Silvia and Edita look like beauty queens. They grin sardonically and show all their teeth. Their eyes are made up to look radiant. They know that their entire future depends on looking young and fresh. They are in Zdravko's orange Opel. Zdravko G. nervously taps the steering wheel, and then puts the car into gear and moves ahead in a column of vehicles inching towards customs control.

"Are they really interested in us?" Edita asks impatiently, as if she wanted to enjoy hearing the good news again and again.

"Yes, yes," says Zdravko G. "For sure!" he adds. He's arranged a lucrative engagement in a Viennese nightclub, where they will dance. They'll make fabulous money: up to twenty thousand schillings a month. Zdravko G. likes them. He's a doctor, he has no interests in the entertainment business, but he does have contacts.

The Opel moves a few more metres ahead. Zdravko G. turns off the engine and goes on. "There's just one more thing. The owner of the club doesn't want problems with the union head office, so Zdravko has to take them to the owner's country residence. They'll stay there until all the formalities are sorted out.

Silvia and Edita agree. Of course, they'll fit in with local ways. They've always dreamt of a chance like this. In a few months they'll look down on their former colleagues at the Ambassador. Silvia is particularly happy that she will be able to look down on that barbarian Rácz.

The customs and passport check goes smoothly. Zdravko G. starts his orange Opel and sets off into the Austrian hinterland. Silvia and Edita smile radiantly. Their eyes shine unnaturally. They know this shows them at their best.

After a few miles, Zdravko G. turns off into a copse and stops the car. The prostitutes exchange glances. Zdravko unzips his trousers and takes out his long, swarthy member. He puts the seats down and waits for Silvia and Edita to undress. He undresses, too. The girls have to satisfy him several times in succession. They are surprised by his potency and the quantity of hot liquid squirting from his member. The car shakes, the suspension creaks. Zdravko utters a deep contented murmur. The prostitutes are covered in perspiration.

Then they drive on. Soon it gets dark. They turn off before Vienna. They stop at a service station and eat. Like a gentleman, Zdravko G. pays for both prostitutes.

Silvia is content. She has said goodbye to the idea of dancing a black swan on theatre boards that once meant the world to her. Her last link with the ballet is her slender, but muscular figure. She knows that once she gets an engagement in a Western nightclub, she'll find it easier to realise her dream of a good marriage. He'll be either a very wealthy Austrian, German, or, ideally, an American. Silvia knows exactly how this encounter will happen. She'll be dancing on stage. Stripping. When she finishes undressing to music, she'll take a bow, collect her clothes, and leave for her dressing room. A huge bouquet will be waiting for her. There'll be a business card in the bouquet with a long name, full of titles before and after it. On the back will be a message written in an energetic hand. Silvia know a few words of German, but these expressions are connected with her profession: *"normal"*, *"französisch"*, *"griechisch"*, *"goldene Dusche"*, *"Natursekt"*, *"Wasserspiele"*, *"wichsen"* (straight, French, Greek, golden showers, sparkling wine, water games, wanking), and so on. The note on the card might say, for example: "Your performance has enchanted me. But I suspect you can do even better. Anyway, I shall be waiting for you outside the cabaret after the show. Respectfully yours in admiration, Rainer, Fürst von... and so on." Silvia will meet him. She will listen to compliments, all the more attractive for being old-fashioned. She will smile her big toothy smile full of eagerness.

Her face will be made up to show a fresh girl's face with wide, rather naïve eyes that suggest education and intelligence, but only a little bit. Men don't like very intelligent women. Besides, Silvia couldn't pretend all that much. She'll portray herself as a girl of good family who, as a result of an unhappy love affair, has fallen on hard times. She will have to arouse his protective instincts, a desire to defend a fragile being. "Ah, Silvia," he will say with feeling, "you don't realise how unbearably I suffer every minute you have to spend on stage in front of that mob. It seems you show them shamelessly, to the accompaniment of such lascivious and invasive music, parts of your body that should belong only to me." To which Silvia will answer, in pure German, of course: "Ah, Duke! I hear the words of a man who has never had to fight for his bread." Silvia will say this with a radiant smile painted on her lips, in a quiet, gentle voice, implying: "Look, I am a beautiful woman, a beautiful person! I can bend my body and limbs into various positions, but if my soul wishes, my body will stay pure. It will remain pure no matter what." And at the same time, Silvia will say: "Yes, Duke, that's how it is. And as for those parts of my body, those you seem to care for so much, I shall show them to anyone who pays to see them. But should it happen that I show these parts to one and only one man in the world, then it will be to my husband and you can be certain of that, Duke." At this point, the duke clasps her in his arms and never lets her go. Silvia becomes a duchess and lives in wealth and luxury until she dies.

Edita can't imagine a new environment. She knows Zdravko G. only fleetingly; she had sex with him a couple of times when Silvia was busy. But he's a serious man, a medical doctor who wants to help both Silvia and her. Twenty thousand schillings is more than seventy thousand crowns. That's what she was making in the Ambassador, but at what cost? Edita has made a decision: she is not going to allow the punters to screw her. She will only dance. After all, Edita is not a whore. She used to dance in a folk ensemble. They made it to the final round in Vychodna, the great Slovak folk music festival. She got into the Ambassador cabaret with the help of the hotel lawyer. Of course, she had to let him screw her, but then, who doesn't get screwed nowadays? If this works out, Edita won't touch a man with a barge pole. She'll dance and train herself to perfection. When she's saved enough money, she might open a dance studio. She'll teach young boys, but mostly girls, modern stage dancing. The girls will see her as an older friend. They'll trustingly let her touch them round the waist, thighs, and breasts. Maybe one of them will appreciate her gentle touch and then a gorgeous and deep relationship will blossom. It will be full of the tenderness that only a woman can show another woman. Later on, Edita will perhaps marry a wealthy man. He'll be experienced, a modern man without prejudices. He won't mind if his wife, Edita, occasionally gives in to temptation with her own sex. On the contrary, he will consider it an interesting enhancement of their marital life. He'll enjoy watching and will sometimes join in.

Zdravko G. is also happy. He will get more money for both whores than he's ever seen in his life. And that's only the beginning! Soon he'll go back to Bratislava to persuade Wanda the Trucker and Dripsy Eva to come with him to Austria for the bright future they'll find over there. However, neither long-legged Wanda, nor slender Eva is a dancer. Zdravko will have to come up with some other story. For example, he can tell them that he's found them well-paid engagements in a luxury brothel, a respectable institution where they'll soon manage to save enough for a life with no worries. Zdravko will think up something like that.

It is only a short distance to Woeningen, a village near Vienna, just a few more miles to go. Zdravko is so satisfied with his catch that he gets excited again. He turns off onto a dirt track. By the time he stops in a dark snowbound forest, both prostitutes are already undressed. They satisfy him cheerfully, as they are so grateful to him. When they think about it, he's plucked them from the boredom of everyday life and bought them a ticket to a happier world and a more beautiful and meaningful future. Afterwards, Zdravko watches Silvia and Edita make love to each other. The car is small. The suspension creaks. All three of them are panting.

After a moment, they continue their journey. Zdravko points to a sign: WILKOMMEN IN WOENINGEN.

"This is where my friend's house is," he tells the girls.

He slows down and enters a street. Haslauer's *Pervers Club* is behind the shopping centre. Zdravko G. knows what will happen next. He'll deliver the whores to Haslauer. He doesn't have to worry about anything else. Haslauer's wife will be very sweet to them. She'll take their passports away; she has to arrange their work permits, and so on. Then they'll put them in a room and keep them under lock and key. They'll start to ply them with drugs, gradually. Occasionally, they'll give them a slapping. Just so that they realise they have no alternative but to do as they're told. Zdravko has no idea what this means in the *Pervers Club*, nor does he care to know. He's not a client of those establishments. He knows about anal sex, but everybody does that nowadays. Zdravko is no pervert! After the girls have spent long enough in Haslauer's establishment, they'll let them go. They'll give back their passports, pay them the money they've made and that Haslauer's put away for them. Austrians are decent people; they have a sense of fair play. Haslauer would never rob the whores who've worn themselves out in his business. What they've been through entitles them to a big reward. But this works two ways. First Haslauer deducts the cost of accommodation, food, drugs (without drugs, it's impossible to work in his *Pervers Club* without the risk of going mad), sexy lingerie and various aids and items made of rubber and leather. What the whore has left over after these deductions is enough for a good dinner in the Vienna Hilton and a first class train ticket from Vienna to Bratislava via Marchegg and Devínska Nová Ves. And, of course, also her vast experience. A Slovak whore has to be thankful to Haslauer for that: used properly in Bratislava, that experience can make the whore a millionairess in one year. Zdravko has no pangs of conscience. If that's what people want, you have to help them get it. Haslauer hired Zdravko because the latter, in his opinion, knows a lot about Slovak whores. Zdravko does his best. He hopes that Haslauer is pleased with the first delivery, Silvia and Edita. Maybe for his next trip he'll let him use his brand-new white Porsche. That would be something! Then Zdravko will be able to bring him amateurs, as well: students, divorcees, jilted fiancées and young chicks. Haslauer told him clients prefer amateurs. He offered him ten times over the odds for a virgin. Ten times more!

The village is snowbound. There's not a soul in the street. They stop near a tall house in a residential area. Zdravko honks the horn. A light comes on. "So, girls," Zdravko says animatedly, "we have to get out. *Aussteigen!*"

After their last sexual bout with Zdravko, Silvia and Edita have now repainted their exhausted faces and are sporting radiant energetic grimaces. They are pleased with themselves. They boldly step towards the well-lit villa in tight knitted miniskirts, short, but expensive fur coats, and boots that end high above their knees.

Zdravko hurries behind them. He walks fast but carefully, so as not to slip in his expensive shoes. He, too, is pleased with himself. He's moved up in the world. He's no longer a dirty unemployed *Gastarbeiter*. He almost feels like laughing when he imagines that with a little less luck he'd be sitting on a rocky hill in Kosovo, herding stubborn, stupid donkeys.

* * *

When the woman from town council came to the snack bar on the old parking lot outside the Hotel Ambassador, only two drunks were drinking mulled wine there. A third one was sleeping in a snowdrift, half covered by the snow, his hat still on his head. The snack bar operator is angry. The Christmas Market is over, drinking bouts before and after the New Year are over as well and now the snack bar will be deserted for days on end.

"I've brought a decision from the town council," the clerk tells the snack bar operator and shows him a document. He invites her in. The clerk kicks the snow off her boots and enters the overheated wooden booth. Everybody has crowded in: two bartenders, two cooks, and someone to clean up after the messy customers. They have nothing to do. Yesterday they fried three pork steaks, warmed up two sausages, sold two packs of cigarettes and brewed eight coffees. Seven of those were for the staff. They sit around the table, playing cards.

"Well, what have you brought us?" asks the man in charge. The clerk opens the document with the council decision. There will be a car park outside the Hotel Ambassador again. There've been complaints from motorists after a major parking lot down outside the department store was closed, and so on. The booths have to be dismantled, and so has the concrete barrier. The lot has to be brought back to its original state. From the first of the month, the space will be leased again to Alfred Mešťanek, the lot's original leaseholder.

The snack bar people sigh with relief. At last! Things were getting unbearable. No business. Who'd come here in this cold? They all nod in agreement. The snack bar operator has to admit he had high expectations at first. Now he can see he was wrong. Who'd come here in this cold? People like winter if they can look at it from the comfort of a heated room.

The clerk is happy they've taken it so positively. "I'll leave this here," she says and puts the document on the table. "Now tell me where can I find Alfred Mešťanek, the car park attendant," she asks.

"Who?" the cook asks in surprise.

The snack bar operator hurriedly explains. "They must mean Freddy Piggybank! Holy Freddy!" Then he turns to the clerk. "Yes, that's what they call him here. Freddy, I mean Alfred Mešťanek, lives here, near the hotel. You're sure to find him in his trailer." The operator unties his white apron. If she likes, the council clerk can come with him. He'll take her to Freddy.

They all tumble out of the booth. They walk to the attendant's trailer. They pass by a drunk stubbornly lying in the snow with his hat on. They stop in front of Piggybank's trailer. Freddy seems to have heard them coming. He jerks the door open and stands on the threshold, long-haired as a savage, emaciated, dressed in sackcloth. Angry, bloodshot eyes burn in his face. He lifts up a bony hand.

"Stop, sinners!" he shouts. "Not a step further!" The clerk and the snack bar people stop. "What have you come for?" the hermit shouts at them. "Has your conscience moved you? Have you crawled here begging for pardon? There is no more pardon! The end is near. The sky will darken and the earth will begin to crack. Babylon will be burned, every last bit. Nobody shall survive the destruction. The evil seed of Babylon will be annihilated."

The snack bar operator and his people are used to the madman's moralizing and smile with amusement.

The inexperienced council clerk, however, tries to shout louder than Freddy and with a pretence of dignity, "Mr. Mešťanek, Mr. Mešťanek! May I say something, too?"

But Mr. Mešťanek is evidently engrossed in his sermon, in the sins of the world. "You are all from Babylon," he shouts, outraged. "You come from sin, from money! Terrible retribution will be meted out to you. You will be burned, hanged, quartered, and stoned! Babylonian harlots will be impaled! In your blindness and greed you cannot see the signs of the approaching end." Freddy lifts a warning finger. "The only way out is to abandon everything: money, property, passion! But not even that can help you now. God is stern and he punishes sinners."

The snack bar people clutch their bellies, laughing. The clerk is a young and inexperienced woman. She has no idea that she is dealing with a madman. Blushing, she insists on having her say. "Mr. Mešťanek! Mr. Mešťanek! HAVE YOU FINISHED? Let ME say something, too!"

Her faltering voice expresses a desire to sound authoritative and decisive and it surprises the holy man so much that he pauses just half a second for breath. The clerk uses her chance to take out of her briefcase a document and read it. "The town council has decided to renew from the first of February of this year its contract with Alfred Mešťanek for the lease of the car park. Do you understand? Here it is!" She hands the paper to the man of God.

Freddy takes a breath as if about to say something, but stunned, he reaches for the paper. The clerk shuts her briefcase. She has done her job and there is nothing else to keep her here. She turns round and leaves.

Holy Freddy holds the council's decision carefully, with two fingers.

"See, Freddy?" the snack bar manager tells him amiably. "You've been bitching so much, cursing us so often, and now you're rid of us." He slaps his back jovially.

A cloud of dust and insects rises from the sackcloth. The hermit still can't understand.

"It will all be yours again from February," says the snack bar operator. "That's in a few days. And we, gentlemen," he turns to his employees, "can start packing. We needn't even open tomorrow." He turns around and walks to the booths. His employees follow him.

Freddy remains standing there, stunned. He brings the document closer to his eyes. Then he lowers his hands. Somewhere, in the darkest recess of his consciousness, a device is switched on. His eyes glaze over. He sees himself walking contentedly between two rows of parked vehicles. He smiles. He holds on happily to his red bag, stuffed full of coins, resting on his voluminous belly. "Good morning! How long? Two hours? That will be four crowns, please: a crown for half an hour, four for two hours, and ten for three hours. Each additional hour ten crowns, please. Yes, please: turn round, you'll find a space free between the yellow Mercedes and the white Škoda."

The holy man crawls back to his burrow in the trailer. He has a massive headache. He presses his head with both hands as if about to rip out his long greasy hair. His eyes bulge. He opens and closes his mouth. He chomps his jaws. He gasps for air like a Christmas carp. Whimpering sounds escape from his lips, quiet at first, but louder a moment later. If anyone had stood behind the fibreboard wall of Piggybank's trailer, he would have heard inarticulate groans alternating with expressions like "Thank you kindly," "Much obliged," "Yes, ten, please," "How may I help you?" "Grateful indeed, Sir," and so on. And so it goes on all night. Around midnight, dull blows resound from the trailer. The car park attendant is banging his head in a regular rhythm on the trailer walls. The banging dies down by daybreak. Exhausted, Freddy Piggybank sinks into a deep, dreamless, but refreshing and energizing sleep.

* * *

The lawyer is retching. He vomits another portion of dirty water. Tupý observes him with growing amazement. He gets up and jumps to his feet.

"Chief, chief!" he cries. "He'th coming back to life!"

Ščepán and Šolik in his torn shirt run into the room. The lawyer moves.

"We'll have to drown him again," Tupý states.

Ščepán gives them a look meaning "no". "You've drowned him once," he says reproachfully, "and look how it's ended." Ščepán's nerves won't take it. He reflects. "Take him," he finally decides, "to his cell. We'll have to think it over before we do anything." Ščepán shakes with disgust. "We're not drowning him any more."

Ščepán's subordinates obey. They grab the uncomprehending and feebly resisting drowned man and take him to the basement.

"And what now, chief?" they ask when they return.

Ščepán is smiling. He keeps them guessing on purpose. "What now?" he asks significantly. "Now we go to the Ambassador. For new instructions. We won't be short of work, you'll see!" Ščepán claps his hands a few times and then rubs them. "Don't worry," he tells his subordinates, "stick with me, and you'll be fine."

They take the trolleybus into town. The stoker is waiting for them in the café. He's in a good mood.

Rácz did well to invite Video Urban to work for him. The lad is smart and knows how to deal with people. Privatization is looming at great speed but, thanks to Urban, Rácz has made sure that the Hotel Ambassador will not be auctioned off. They have to register a limited company quickly, as Urban advised. Then do a deal. Rácz asked him to do all the necessary preliminaries, but Urban shook his head. He'd be glad to, but he didn't know how. "You'll need to get hold of a lawyer," he advised Rácz. "He'd come in handy." Rácz smiled. "I have one like that," he told Urban. "And is he any good?" Urban asked. "He's good," nodded Rácz. "A real big swine. For the time being, I keep him behind bars, in the safe house, you know, to soften him up." Rácz extended a hand. "He'll be eating out of my hand. Like this," he demonstrated to Urban.

Rácz is content now, and in a good mood. Things are going his way. Whatever he touches turns to gold. That's true of Lenka, too. Nobody from his village ever had a girl like that; they'd never even set eyes on one. They saw actresses and models only on television. Yes, Lenka is exactly what Rácz needs. And she loves him, she does! And her parents? Her parents lick his arse at every opportunity. Typical intellectuals: when they have nobody's arse to lick, they get sick. An intellectual always bows down to wealth and wealthy people; especially intellectuals who have nothing but bookshelves full of books with nothing but shit in them. They put on ridiculous airs, but when they get to know someone who simply orders, pays for, and sends a hundred white orchids they just shit themselves. Rácz can figure them out as easily as he can a bloated goat. He knows that if Lenka were to decide in the future not to marry him, her own parents would kill her. And that is why Rácz is happy, because he is certain that Lenka is his and nobody else's. It's all a question of time.

Now he has more important problems to think about. They are connected with Rácz's future and Lenka's, too.

"Well, gentlemen?" A self-satisfied Rácz welcomes the three ex-secret policemen. He asks them to sit down. Ščepán and his two subordinates sit down politely, with half an arse, and put their hands on their thighs. "What will you have?" asks Rácz.

"Just mineral water, thank you," says Ščepán for all of them.

"I'll have mulled wine," says Tupý, but his superior gives him a look that goes right through him, and the intimidated Tupý squints and smoothes out the tablecloth.

"Actually, we don't drink," Ščepán remarks. "And if we do, never when we're on duty," he adds with an apologetic smile.

Rácz nods. He likes that. "With Rácz you'll always be on duty. But you'll be making money, too. Name a sum and Rácz will give you three times as much." He smiles, noting the ex-secret policemen's stares. The waiter comes and ceremoniously puts the drinks on the table. Ščepán, Šolik, and Tupý get mineral water and Rácz will have *Heevash Reygahl* and coffee. After the waiter has gone, the stoker continues. Rácz wants to tell them something in confidence: it won't be long before this hotel belongs to him. He will need reliable protection. Hotel police. He will need people with experience and dedication, capable of anything. Rácz raises his glass of Chivas Regal for a toast.

Ščepán clears his throat. "If Rácz is talking about dedicated people capable of anything, he's got them here," he says solemnly. And they do have experience. If Rácz tells them to kill, they kill. That's how they are, Ščepán and his two subordinates. Ščepán sips his mineral water. That reminds Ščepán of an idea. He says, "The lawyer."

Rácz is now all ears. Yes, he's curious, says Rácz. "How did it go with the lawyer?"

Šolik opens his big mouth. "A six-hundred-crown shirt! They had them only once in the shop! The next day the shirts were gone!" They tried to drown him in a bucket of Danube water. He fought like mad. Šolik was holding him tight, pushing his head into the bucket. "Six hundred crowns! Anyway, he finally stopped struggling and swallowed the water." Šolik bursts out laughing. "Ha, ha, ha!"

Rácz stares at him. "You killed him?" He's dumbfounded. He feels like throwing up. "You... killed him?" He blinks in disbelief and drinks his whisky. Then he collects himself. His eyes pop out of his dark face and he bangs his fist on the table. All the glasses jump. "You idiots!" he yells. I said, "Put him out of the way for some time! PUT HIM OUT OF

THE WAY! Now we're all in the shit! We can't get off a murder charge so easily." Rácz bores right through the ex-secret policemen with his wild, metallic grey stare. He now sees that all his plans have to be changed. He'll have to find another lawyer. Too bad, this one would have been perfect. He was a cunning scoundrel. He won't find another one like that anywhere. All he needed was his wings clipped a bit. For some reason Rácz remembered he had, a long time ago, in his native village, clipped his hens' wings to stop them flying over the fence to the neighbours' yard. Afterwards, the hens would sit in their coop, sadly looking into space. But they laid their eggs for Rácz.

Ščepán interrupts Rácz's rant. "No, no!" he tells Rácz. "The lawyer's alive! I swear to God, he's alive! We just clipped his wings a bit, drowned him a little bit, so he's more cooperative and pliant! We drowned him a little bit and then put him in a cell. That's how we did it."

Rácz is reassured. He gives a nod of appreciation. "That might work. The lawyer has to be frightened," he suggests. "You have to keep him in his cell and take him out every day to be executed, you see? Pretend you're going to drown him, hang him, and so on. And at the last moment, call it off. But don't go too far," warns Rácz. "I don't want him made completely nuts. He's going to be useful to us."

Ščepán shakes his head. If he may say so, he has a different opinion. Fake executions derange a person being worked over. If he could suggest something, it would be better to make night and day the same for him. The light has to be on at all times. He has to be woken up every hour and told to report, "Prisoner number so and so, cell number such and such, number of prisoners one, I report that nothing out of the ordinary has happened." And the same in an hour's time. Does Rácz see what he means?

Rácz smiles contentedly. He likes it.

Ščepán assures him, "He'll be done in two weeks. Then you come in and be all upset. Pretend, you understand, just pretending. You scream, 'What are you doing to this man? How dare you? Release him this instant! Right now! What sort of mediæval methods are you using here?' And so on. The person we've worked over will fall in love with you and will follow you like a little doggie." Ščepán smiles. He has a lot of experience. He remembers interrogating people who are in power now. That was a long time ago. It's hard to believe now. Would Rácz like to hear spicy details about subversives and enemies of the state they used to work over? "We wouldn't let our state be attacked." And today they're high up in government, in parliament. Oh, Ščepán could tell you a lot about them.

Rácz shrugs. He's not interested in politics. His politics is right here. But he's happy to be dealing with professionals. And now down to business. Here's the money he promised. The stoker gives Sčepán a package of thousand-crown banknotes. The lawyer will be having company. Rácz needs Sčepán and his people to take out of circulation a few inconvenient people. Rácz thought at first that he could do a deal with them, but now he realises that it can't be done the easy way. They only understand the hard way. They have to be caught one by one and put in the cells. Sčepán and his people have three days to do it. Rácz will let them use the minibus. Can any of them drive? Yes? Then everything is fine. They'll have to kidnap and lock up all the gypsies from around the Ambassador. "And then do the same to the Albanians, particularly the leaders. There are three of them: Bekim Bahmuci, Ahmet Sočila, and Enver Murcijča. They're easy to spot: they're all as dark as coal and expensively dressed. That's all. Then we'll see." Rácz finishes his *Heevash Reygahl* and waves to the waiter. "My secretary has the keys to the minibus," he tells the ex-secret policemen as they leave. "You know him from the last job: he's called Ďula. And now I have to go; I've got work to do."

Rácz lets the secret policemen think about their new mission. He's going to wait for Lenka. She sat her examinations successfully; she has time for Rácz now. He's invited her to his suite for lunch. The meals will be brought from a nearby Asian restaurant. He's very busy; he can't afford to leave the hotel.

Rácz looks at his watch. He still has time. He could use it somehow, but before every date with Lenka he is exhausted, no good for anything, but turned on by her, unable to concentrate. He would rather spend the time in the bath, up to his neck in hot, perfumed water; with a member that has not been satisfied for a long time, and that gets an erection after any accidental touch.

* * *

Freddy Piggybank got up early, while it was still dark. Soon daybreak came and with it objects took on blurred, slimy contours. A low grey sky did not promise a nice day. A thaw was setting in; the day started with tinkling in the gutters. The pavements and the parking lot are slippery. Here and there under the trees remain dirty piles of snow, awaiting their end. All the dirt and mess hidden under a thick layer of snow has risen to the surface. The drunk with the hat is not lying on the car park any more. As soon as the snack bar people and their slummy booths were removed,

Freddy decided to clean up, to dispose of the paper, paper cups and plastic trays in the rubbish bin. He was unable to awaken the drunk, so he waited until nightfall and dragged him off to the hotel yard, where he hid him under a thick layer of snow. Freddy does not need complications. Now all he wants is to start up the car park again. He has to forget the bad times. Whatever happened, happened. He can't remember what happened to him when the snack bar booths were there, anyway. The drunk had to disappear and that was that.

The car park in front of the hotel is still empty. It is light outside the window of the trailer. Freddy is awake and is eating sausages and beans from a tin he has quickly heated up. He knows that he won't be able to finish his meal in peace, but that's fine by him. Business is business. Through the window he sees the first car enter the lot. Freddy quickly wipes his mouth, jumps up and throws down his spoon. He grabs his red bag, slings its leather strap over his right shoulder and resolutely sets out into the miserable daylight.

* * *

"Yes, Hokusai," Rácz says, putting his chopsticks aside, having learned how to use them just to please Lenka. He lifts the tiny bowl of unsweetened green tea to his lips. He hates unsweetened tea. He drinks tea only when he has a cold and then he makes himself a quart of sweet rose hip tea with local rum. But what won't a great man do for the love of his life?

"Divine Hokusai," he adds dreamily and then falls silent again. He lets Lenka talk as much as she wants. He'd rather think about something else. He's decided: he'll screw her today. Taking this decision makes his mouth dry and the food tasteless. He hasn't had a woman for a long time, ever since he kicked Silvia out. Lenka has to realise that she's got to sleep with him eventually. Rácz is very happy that he had the idea of lunch with her in his own suite. He looks at the Chinese waiter standing straight by the wall. "Leave the bottle of that… that fruit juice of yours here," he tells him. "Then you can go." The waiter bows and puts the bottle of plum wine in a heater.

Rácz feels his member slowly swelling. Lenka looks especially lovely today.

"Lenka," he says, when the waiter vanishes from the room. He lifts a glass of sweet, lilac-coloured liquid. "I love you," he proclaims. Lenka raises her glass. They toast each other with the hot liquid. Rácz takes her hand with the glass and makes her put her glass down on the table. He takes out of his pocket a neatly wrapped little box and hands it to her.

Lenka's eyes widen in anticipation. "What is it?" she whispers in astonishment.

Rácz smiles. "Take a look," he says.

It's a gold ring with a diamond the size of a pea.

"I ordered it from Oppenheimer's in Vienna," says Rácz.

"I can't accept it," says Lenka. "It's gorgeous," she adds immediately.

Rácz embraces and kisses her. Lenka's lips are inexperienced. At the last moment she can't help moving her head away to avoid Rácz's moist fleshy lips, swollen with lust.

"Do you know why diamonds are so beautiful and precious?" she asks and gently pushes the stoker's probing fingers away. "Because a diamond hides the mystery of the entire universe. In its structure you can find everything that you need to know about the origins of our planet."

"And how about us? You and me?" asks the stoker, red-hot with desire and the heated plum wine.

Lenka does not answer. Lost in thought, with an Egyptian statue's mysterious smile, she twirls the precious ring around her finger.

Rácz targets her lips and savagely forces his tongue between them. At first he encounters the ramparts of her white teeth, but after squeezing her and bending her waist back like a blade of grass, he makes her mouth open in a suppressed sigh. Lenka's tongue is also inexperienced, but Rácz brings it to life with his caresses. For a second, Lenka manages to free herself from Rácz's devastating embrace.

"No…" she cries, but Rácz silences her with a kiss.

Rácz is now unstoppable. He picks Lenka up in his arms and carries her to the bedroom. He kicks the double doors open, walks over to the bed with Lenka in his arms, and throws her onto the eiderdown, plunging after her. He wildly kisses her body all over, while his fingers wrestle with the little buttons, hooks, and zippers of Lenka's clothing.

"I love you!" he shouts, his voice choked and rasping with excitement. He is impatient; the hooks and little buttons resist him. Rácz tears her clothes off. Buttons fly in all directions like sparks from New Year's Eve fireworks.

Lenka does not shout, she merely weeps and vainly tries to cover herself with the longer bits of her blouse and skirt. "Don't! Don't!" she begs, sobbing.

Rácz tears off his jacket and shirt and hurls them into a corner. Then he takes off his trousers and underpants. His violet-coloured member has swollen to inhuman size and pulsates wildly. He throws himself at Lenka with insatiable mouth, eyes, hands, tongue, ears, and teeth. "I love you!" he shouts and starts to force himself into the virginal Lenka. "Good thing I got her drunk," thinks Rácz. "If she hadn't drunk so much Chinese fruit juice, she wouldn't have been so easy to get into." Laughing, Rácz overcomes the resistance of her slender arms pushing against his hairy muscular chest and squeezes her tight, body to body. "It had to come to this one day," he thinks. He moves violently, like a steam-driven ram. He mutters excitedly and rhythmically. Lenka has now surrendered. She lies there with her eyes closed.

The wedding will be in March, Rácz decides, as his insides begin to contract in a mighty and liberating gush.

* * *

Every day a vehicle leaves the yard of the Hotel Ambassador with a load of cooking pots and boxes of bread and rolls. These are leftovers from the kitchen. The cooks give them to Ďula, thinking he uses them to feed a pig or two. They don't care. They're glad to get rid of the leftovers. They know that Ďula is Rácz's man and who'd want to argue with Rácz?

The loaded Renault leaves the hotel yard, drives down the street, turns right after the lights and, passing the plethora of side-streets, turns uphill to climb above the city, to the villa quarter.

Ďula stops in front of a luxury villa, gets out and rings the bell. Tupý or Šolik look out of the window, depending which of Sčepán's men is on duty at the time. Soon the secret policeman comes to the gate to the gravel path leading to the villa. He clears his throat, spitting and jingling the keys. Together they move the pots and boxes from the van to the villa.

The prisoners locked in the cells in the basement of the safe house know they are getting food. They shout nervously and bang their spoons on their mess pots. They are hungry. They don't like being in jug.

"How many are there?" asks Ďula.

"Šolik stops to think. "Twenty-eight," he says finally. "Twenty-one gypsies and seven Albanians," he adds.

"And the lawyer?" Ďula asks.

"I didn't count the lawyer," says the ex-secret policeman. "He's in solitary. He makes twenty-nine. If you like, you can take a look at him."

They go down to the basement to a corridor with cells. It's cold and dark here. The ex-secret policeman unlocks the door to the lawyer's cell.

"Come out!" he shouts at the lawyer.

The lawyer comes out into the corridor. He's unshaven and his clothes are dirty. His eyes blink uncertainly. His face twitches.

"Here are the food pots and here are the boxes of bread," Šolik orders. "Distribute the food to the prisoners!"

Šolik reaches into his pocket and takes out cigarettes. He offers one to Ďula and then lights them both. As they smoke, they watch the lawyer open hatches on the doors of the individual cells, take the mess pots the prisoners poke out at him and, after ladling out food, return them with bread. Šolik stubs out his cigarette and shivers with cold.

"Listen," he tells the lawyer. "When you've finished with the food, wash the pots and the ladle, understand?"

The lawyer looks like a broken man. He nods humbly. "How much longer will you let me live?" he asks, full of hope.

Šolik smiles contentedly. He hasn't yet forgiven the lawyer for the torn shirtsleeve. "We'll see about that," he says. "If you do your duties as you've done so far, you might live a few days longer. Understand?" From the cells comes the noise of slurping and quick chomping. The scraping of spoons against mess pots is almost unbearable.

"It's a bore," Šolik admits. "I'm looking forward to tomorrow, when it's Tupý's turn to be on duty and I take the hotel shift. Do you know how long Rácz plans to keep them here?" he asks Ďula.

Ďula shrugs. The boss doesn't confide in anyone about his plans. That includes Ďula. Despite Ďula being the closest to him, he stresses. He's been Rácz's right-hand man from the start. Ďula could tell you things.

They both go back to the ground floor. The ex-secret policeman helps Ďula load the pots and boxes into the Renault and then goes back to the villa and locks himself in. Ďula starts the minibus and drives down the steep little streets to the city hidden under a cover of low grey fog.

* * *

Rácz has a new toy. A beautiful white Volvo 940. He bought it from Khunt and is very satisfied with it. It's just the kind of car Rácz needed. He's driven it a few times, but only around the hotel in a small circuit: from the Hotel Ambassador straight, then right, near the Hotel Forum right again, near the Cafe Olympia right again, then round the petrol station near the Blumenthal church, then right again, and back to the Ambassador. The car runs like clockwork.

At first Lenka's crotch hurt, but that passed after a few days. Now she's happy and up to her ears in love with Rácz, giving herself to him at every possible opportunity. Her university girlfriends envy her. Which of them wouldn't trade places with her? What do they expect from life? Rácz comes from a world where he need not move without a car, where nothing seems to be a problem, where he can afford to blow in one evening as much money as a family of four's monthly budget, and so on. All the girls envy and hate her. But Lenka won't give up her Rácz. She loves him, and her parents love him even more.

Video Urban does what he can. He devotes all his time to the paperwork for the hotel. Wanda and Eva still live with him. After an exhausting day spent running around the offices, he falls into bed, and they are both with him, massaging him with their sensitive hands. He doesn't even ask them why they're at home instead of the Ambassador bar. They keep him going. They love him. They want to be absolutely faithful to him. Urban wouldn't mind if they were occasionally unfaithful to him with some wealthy customer so he didn't have to support them all by himself, but he says nothing. He daren't say anything, knowing that any insensitive remark might cause weeping and gnashing of teeth. Finally, after a trying day full of senseless negotiations and wrestling with stupid bureaucracy, Urban needs relaxation to put him back on his feet. So Urban keeps quiet and doesn't send them out to work. He doesn't know what he'd do without them.

The prisoners in the safe house don't know who's had them locked up, but they guess that the stoker may have something to do with it. They were brought to prison in a deep sleep caused by the injection. They don't know where they are. They want to smoke and drink. They're cold. Luckily, they are crowded in their small cells. That keeps them warm.

* * *

And then comes a day when Urban rings the bell of the safe house. Behind him stands Rácz's Volvo and in it sits Rácz. Ščepán runs round the big car to open the door so that Rácz can leave the car with dignity.

Tupý opens the gate. This time, Šolik is on duty in the hotel. Tupý is quite beside himself. What a visitor! He's overcome by humility and servility. He doesn't know to whom he should be more servile: his superior Ščepán, or his ultimate and final boss, Rácz.

Rácz gets out of the car and steps briskly toward the villa. He is well dressed. A brown leather jacket emphasizes his strong wide-shouldered figure; his black hair is carefully oiled, combed back and tied with a red elastic band. He wears dark glasses. He's chewing gum. An earring shines in his ear.

"Take us to the basement!" Rácz orders through clenched lips and rolls ahead like a stocky, perfumed and impatient tidal wave. Tupý obeys. He takes a ring of keys off the hook and leads the visitor to the steps leading to the basement.

"Which is the lawyer's cell?" Rácz asks.

"The very first one," says Tupý.

"I want to talk to him," Rácz decides.

"But, boss..." Ščepán has reservations.

"Well? What is it?" Rácz asks, his curiosity tinged with menace. Ščepán nods to his underling. Tupý goes up to the cell and unlocks it.

Rácz enters. The lawyer is sitting on a wooden plank, dirty and unshaven. He looks ahead, lost in thought.

"Well, how goes it?" Rácz addresses him. The lawyer is startled.

"Have you come to kill me?" he asks stoically.

"Maybe," Rácz says. "You'd deserve it." Then he overcomes his distaste and sits down next to the lawyer.

"What are they doing there?" Urban asks Ščepán, who is peering into the cell through the hatch in the door.

"Nothing," says Ščepán. "They're talking. Now the boss is getting up. The lawyer's on his knees begging him for something. The boss is giving him his hand and the lawyer is kissing it. Oh no!" Ščepán looks closer. "The boss is giving him his penknife," Ščepán says with astonishment. "He's giving him his knife."

"No!" says Urban in disbelief; he pushes the secret policeman aside and looks for himself. Rácz and the lawyer are now sitting together at the table. The lawyer is holding Rácz's penknife in his hand, cutting something. Urban looks closer. The lawyer is cutting off his left little finger. Pale as chalk, he saws it off with the knife. He wraps the severed finger in a dirty handkerchief and passes it to Rácz with a solemn expression on his face. Then he gets up and bangs the cell door.

"Hey!" he shouts. "Let us out!"

Rácz and the lawyer come out into the corridor. The lawyer is pale and sweating. His mutilated hand is bleeding. The prisoners in the neighbouring cells have discovered that Rácz has arrived, and everywhere swearing and cursing in Romany, Albanian, Croatian and broken Slovak break out. They all wish the stoker a slow death, illnesses, and accidents. But Rácz smiles.

"No food for two days!" he decides. "That'll teach them." Then he looks at his people. "We're taking the lawyer along with us to the hotel," he says. "There won't be any more problems with him," he adds. "From now on, he's one of us. He admits that you can't piss into the wind." Rácz addresses this to everyone, but his metallic and penetrating gaze is focussed on the lawyer. "He'll be cooperative. People have to be paid," he adds after a while.

When they're on the ground floor, someone digs out a first aid box. The lawyer doesn't want treatment, but Rácz forces him. Ščepán and Tupý hold him down in a chair, while Urban clumsily and amateurishly disinfects the stump of the lawyer's little finger. No one asks questions.

On the way down to the city, still in the car, the lawyer asks for the documents for the planned acquisition of the hotel. He browses through the documents for setting up a limited company and murmurs to himself. Finally he raises his eyes. "This is good work," he compliments them.

"He did it," Rácz points to Urban. Urban is driving, but smiles proudly.

The lawyer says, "If, God forbid, we have to go to auction, we can drag it out until they all drop out."

Rácz makes an unhappy face. "That won't work. We'd need to have cash and we don't. I've invested in building land."

The lawyer closes his eyes for a moment and then, covered in cold sweat, opens them. "That's all right," he says. "First of all, I need a bath and then a good meal." He looks at Rácz. "You don't look after your prisoners well, boss," he says.

"If I did, then nobody would want to work for me and everybody would want to stay in prison," says Rácz, making a joke of it. "But what did you mean about the auction?" he asks impatiently. The lawyer feels the thick bandage on his left hand. "It's simple," he says. "In an auction we go to any sum, just to get the Ambassador. Then we draft the purchase contract and at the same time apply for a delay in payment. A few days should be enough and nobody will find it strange at all. With the signed contract we go to Austria and get a loan from the first bank we find. I'm talking mortgages, you see?" The lawyer forces himself to smile. "We'll mortgage the Hotel Ambassador," he says. "As proof of ownership, we'll show them the sales contract. Then we take the money and pay the price. The hotel will be ours. That is, it will belong to the bank to begin with, but we'll soon pay it off. Anyway, in these unsettled times debts are the best and safest investment."

Rácz eyes his subordinates proudly and yet respectfully, as if to say, "How about that? Don't I have a good nose?"

"But that doesn't mean an auction has to be held," says Urban. "The hotel could be privatized by the sale of vouchers, in a major privatization."

The lawyer nods. "In that case, we have to buy as many vouchers as possible in the first round. And later we try to buy as many vouchers as we can from small investors, at any price. It will always pay off. But it'd be best to have an auction. My ex-wife's father works at the National Property Fund. He's a corrupt swine. I'll try and lobby him to transfer the hotel to minor privatization by auction."

By now the car has reached the hotel. Rácz, the lawyer and Ščepán get out.

"Take it to the garage," Rácz tells Urban, "and then join us in the restaurant."

Rácz enters the Hotel. It will soon be his, he thinks. He will be a hotelier, the owner of a hotel. But that will only be the beginning. He laughs. He overcomes a sudden urge to clap his hands together and rubs them instead. He has a perfect grasp of what the lawyer meant. It's a brilliant idea! If it works with the hotel, Rácz will try to use it elsewhere. He will be able to buy anything he wants without a penny in his pocket! Rácz has it all figured out. You only have to surround yourself with competent people. And you need to pay the competent people well.

Rácz feels a gargantuan hunger. As always when he's in a good mood.

"Let's go and eat!" he says. It's his treat.

He enters the restaurant, faithfully followed by his people.

* * *

Freddy Piggybank radiates happiness. It seems that all the good gypsies around the Hotel Ambassador have disappeared somewhere. There's no one to come and extort money from him for protection from bad gypsies. Freddy's mood improved once he realised this. He looks better every day. His cheeks have filled out; the skin on his face and hands is taut and shiny. The traces of the torments he endured are definitely disappearing. All is fine at home, too: his stingy parents had a change of heart and have accepted him back into the family. But Freddy goes back as rarely as ever; usually he sleeps in his white trailer, which is once again supplied by power from the hotel. In the pleasant warmth and the soporific ammonia-hydrogen sulphide smell of his socks and work boots, Freddy Piggy-bank lies down on the narrow bed and, pleasantly exhausted, closes his eyes to sleep. He used to listen out and be woken from his slumbers by any suspicious noise, but now he sleeps undisturbed. There are no gypsies. The pavements in front of the Ambassador and the glazed mall between the hotel and the department store are clear. Freddy is happy, but at the same time also curious about the gypsies' fate. His imagination thinks up the most outlandish possibilities: a contagious disease that killed them all off, a stroke that felled all their obese bodies, or mass poisoning. "Go and kick the bucket!" Freddy Piggybank wished them every time he calculated how much money his swarthy fellow-citizens had extorted from him. Maybe his God-fearing desire was fulfilled, he thought. What-ever had happened, a smile had returned to Freddy's round face, and joy to his eyes, Life is really beautiful, after all!

* * *

Rácz is getting the hang of his position of a future hotelier and big busi-nessman. He has had at least a dozen suits made to measure from top-quality fabrics, bought ten pairs of soft shoes, twenty handmade ties and five new long elegant coats. He gave away his Benson & Hedges cigarettes to his employees: for some time he's been smoking only cigars. He prefers above all Cohibas, though he won't say no to Punch, or Romeo y Julieta. On his head he wears his favourite toy: a broad soft felt hat. He has about a dozen of them, of various colours. He wears them inside as well, even when he dines. Of course, he doesn't wear them in Lenka's or her parents' presence. Only when he's with his employees: at meetings, working breakfasts, lunches, or dinners.

Rácz's people don't dress like slum dwellers, either. Rácz insists on them dressing properly. "You're paid bloody well," he tells them at every opportunity. "So go and dress well! You don't expect me to buy you clothes, do you?"

He has even sent Urban home to change. That was before a business meeting at the headquarters of International Hotels, when Urban showed up at the car in the morning in leather jacket and baggy jeans. While Urban was changing, dead silence reigned inside the white Volvo. Rácz was sitting with his attaché case on his knees, pretending to be engrossed in the documents he had on top of the case. Ďula in the driver's seat and Ščepán sitting next to him were such small fish that they dared not say anything. The lawyer looked out of the window and kept silent, too. When he took a breath to say something, Rácz interrupted him, as if he'd been thinking about it the whole time.

"If Rácz can strangle himself in a tie the whole bloody day, why can't that brat?" Rácz tapped the documents on the attaché case. "People who work for Rácz are not second-rate currency hustlers running round in jeans! Rácz and his men are entrepreneurs, businessmen: everyone kindly remember that!" At long last, Urban's figure flashed by the misted up side window and Rácz opened the door from inside to let Urban into the spacious heated interior of his car. "You can wear jeans when you take your two whores to the pictures or an ice-cream parlour, understand?" said Rácz.

"Yes, boss," answered Urban. "You're right, but maybe this isn't such a big deal."

Rácz looked at his watch. "Not a big deal." He nodded to Ďula to start the car. "Rácz's people are well groomed," he said firmly.

Lenka appreciates the change in Rácz's appearance. The stoker has had a haircut. The gold earring with a diamond is banished to the jewellery box. Only rarely will Rácz remember the times when "he too" used to wear long hair and an earring. He has bought a few jewels for Lenka, too. She buys her own dresses, but with Rácz's money. She's a young girl and everything looks good on her. She's not as extravagant as Silvia used to be. After all, shopping's not her only interest.

Rácz would like her to move into his hotel suite. Lenka doesn't want to; she has everything she wants at home: books, lecture notes and all the peace and quiet she needs. "OK, don't get your knickers in a twist," thinks Rácz. But even as a student, she often spends two or three days a week in the Ambassador. At those times Rácz is a different man. He lets Urban and the lawyer take over the running of the business. Ščepán and one of his men see to it that no competition comes onto their turf. Those who can take a hint get a word in their ear. If that isn't enough, they get frightened off with the sight of a police warrant card. Ščepán's other man in the meantime guards the imprisoned currency dealers. Ďula, ever the sidekick, acts as a messenger, chauffeur and confidant. Rácz spends all his time with his fiancée. Ever since she got a taste for male genitalia, she makes Rácz do it to her anywhere and any time. She vents her feelings during sex with high-pitched moans that modulate smoothly from a delicate pianissimo to a forte that makes all the windowpanes in Rácz's suite vibrate. Rácz doesn't mind. He'll do it for her as much as three times in a row, though the third time he is actually masturbating.

Lenka likes to go for walks. She drags Rácz to museums, galleries, and tows him around exhibitions. There, in some shady corner, she gets him to make love to her. The risk that someone might come across them at any moment arouses an animal thrill in her. She bites her lips and stops her mouth with her hand, so that only a sort of muffled whining escapes her clenched teeth. Rácz likes that, too. He is in love and Lenka's every whim is dear to him.

Once he does it to her on the steps that twist up towards the castle above the city. Lenka holds onto the rail and Rácz enters her from behind so forcefully that both of them begin to shout with pleasure. Soon a group of tourists passes by on the way up, but that doesn't bother Rácz and his fiancée. They move deeper into the bushes by the side of the steps and continue their vigorous love-making. Sometimes they copulate in the lift taking them up to Rácz's suite. By the time they get there, they've come. It is pleasant to remember such things. The more common memories they accumulate, the closer they become to each other.

Rácz is familiar with all the galleries and exhibition rooms in the city. He's walked through them silently; Lenka kept talking and talking. She'd like him to be a well-informed civilized man with wide interests. Rácz is in agreement; he wants that as well. He sits in front of the television, trying to copy various gestures: the way men smoke cigars, adjust their ties or look at their watches in films and commercials.

Of late, they have enjoyed frequenting the Castle Restaurant. Its windows have a gorgeous view of the city at the bottom of the hill. Rácz loves that view. After all, this city brought him success, love, and happiness. Whether having lunch or dinner, Rácz can't tear his eyes away from that view. He has no problem recognizing the Hotel Ambassador building, drowned in a sea of roofs, and he gives it a lingering, longing, but resolute look. The hotel will be Rácz's property.

"Shall we go for a walk?" Rácz asks one night, after they've paid the bill and left, shown out by the bowing staff. The evening is cool, but the air heralds an insistent spring. Rácz does not wait for an answer. He takes Lenka by her hand and they set out. The streets are empty. Round the corner hums a trolleybus, the trolleys rattle and in a moment Lenka and Rácz are lit up in its headlights. The trolleybus is half-empty. Lenka stops and looks at it. Rácz draws her to him. Lenka stops him.

"Do you love me?" she asks.

Rácz nods. "Certainly," he says.

"And how do you love me?" Lenka asks.

"Well," Rácz says, "... nicely," just to say something.

They stop by a spacious villa standing in a walled garden among old trees. The villa's windows are dark. The wall is made of sandstone blocks, half-overgrown by ivy.

"Do you like it?" Rácz asks Lenka

"Do I like what?" Lenka doesn't understand.

Without a word, Rácz points a finger at the villa. Lenka looks over the wall. "Do you know what style this villa is built in?" she can't help asking.

Rácz is quiet, he's thinking about something else.

"Cubism," Lenka informs him.

Rácz nods absent-mindedly. "Would you like to live in a house like that?" he asks her.

Lenka laughs. "Who wouldn't? Of course I would!" she adds.

Rácz is silent, as if reflecting whether to speak or not. "If you're nice to me," he finally says, "you'll have it from me as a wedding present. It belongs to me," he adds, when he sees Lenka making an ironic and doubtful face in the dark. "It's mine," he says, upset that he's failed to convince her.

"So let's go and take a closer look," Lenka suggests, heading for the gate. Rácz shakes his head. "Not yet." He smiles. "It's in a mess. Besides, Rácz hasn't brought his keys with him. Lenka will see it later," Rácz promises, dragging her away by the hand from the house.

"I still don't believe you," remarks Lenka, when they're sitting in Rácz's car and the stoker drives off carefully, like any new driver with an expensive car, towards the city centre, to the Hotel Ambassador. "Who'd want to get rid of a villa and try to sell it in times like these?" She doesn't understand.

Rácz smiles under his moustache. He is not impatient in this sort of business. He has no desire to prove to her at all costs that he is right. Lenka will find out and then recognize that she was wrong. She still underestimates Rácz's abilities.

Back at the Ambassador, they each follow their own interests. Lenka is in her armchair, reading lecture notes, or a novel. Rácz watches a video. He loves sadistic horror movies and while he watches them, comments loudly, with satisfaction. Above all he looks out for horror movies with action in space, with monsters and aliens. But he won't say no to a good massacre. His favourite heroes are Freddy Krueger, crazy Mike Myers with a white mask on his face and the immortal monster Jason Vorsteed, wearing a hockey goalkeeper's mask. Later, he shows their moves and gestures to Ďula, though not as often as he used to. First of all, he now has a dignified, hotelier-entrepreneur style; secondly, sudden attacks on the unsuspecting sidekick don't arouse the same side-splitting hilarity in Lenka as they used to in Silvia. Rácz doesn't mind watching a good western, particularly if there are no women in it, and he also likes historic battle films: the bigger the swords, the better.

Recently, new private shops have been springing up. Rácz is interested in every one of them. Of course, he's choosy. Each day he wants to see in his suite a list of newly opened small businesses in the centre and hear detailed reports about them. Apart from their shifts in the safe house, Ščepán and his men do nothing but monitor small businesses. Rácz listens, sometimes while still in bed, with his eyes closed. His face has a stony expression: his sharp hard features do not react to mentions of a luxurious entrance, extravagant and expensive décor, colourful advertisements, and the number of customers gawking at the full shop windows. No reaction either to the supplementary information about expensive ads in the papers. But that's only a mask. No matter what is involved: private art gallery, café, vegetarian restaurant, electronics shop, cosmetics shop, boutique, or grocery store, Rácz is interested.

When the report is finished, Rácz reflects and very soon issues instructions in a concise dry voice. Ščepán and his men listen to the instructions and then leave to implement them. They start to visit owners selected by Rácz.

For example, they stop in front of *Sandra* boutique, near the Ambassador. First, they take a good look round. Cheerful and colourful children's clothing in the shop window, obviously designed to transform any child into mobile kitsch, is of no interest to them. Nor do they pay attention to the breathtakingly extortionate prices. However, as experienced specialists in the lives of strangers, they note an expensive Mercedes parked outside the boutique. It has a Bratislava licence plate and is parked where it can easily be seen from inside the shop. The ex-secret policemen exchange glances and enter the boutique.

"Please, come in," says a respectable lady in her forties, coming towards them. Her voice is tinged with a polite, but audible warning. It is aimed at anyone who is not a potential buyer and who can therefore be thrown out shortly after entering. She speaks firmly, but the experienced policemen detect a note of hysteria in her voice. They have no doubt that this lady in her forties has not spent most of her life on the wrong side of a shop counter, but was stuck in an office. They look at each other, inspired by special police telepathy. "This will be an easy job," say their eyes.

"Good morning," says Ščepán. "Could we speak to the manager?"

"I am the manageress," says the lady, cut to the quick.

"Excellent," says Ščepán. "We need to speak to you. Will you invite us into the office for a moment?"

The manageress swallows a couple of times dryly.

"Are you from the security police?" she asks.

Ščepán smiles mysteriously, as if hinting that this is possible.

"Sandra," says Ščepán in the office. "Sandra Boutique," he repeats thoughtfully.

Šolik pushes aside the curtain and looks outside. He sees a grey courtyard surrounded by blocks of flats, with a row of rubbish bins lined up like soldiers against the wall.

"Nice name," Ščepán comments and sits down on the chair.

"Thank you," says the manageress ironically and also sits down.

"Is that your name?" asks Ščepán.

"What do you mean?" says the manageress, puzzled.

"Well, Sandra," says Ščepán.

"No, says the manageress, "it's a business name. My name is Agnes. Is that what you came to ask me?"

Ščepán smiles. Šolik by the window smiles, too.

"To tell you the truth, no," Ščepán admits, looking like a man who would regret such a thing. "We've come to inform you of two important facts. One is good and positive. The other is worrying and not so good. Which would you like to hear first?"

"Do they concern me personally in any way?" the manageress asks dismissively.

"Unfortunately, they do," Ščepán admits. "And at the same time, thank God they do," he adds with a smile.

"Well then, let's start with the bad news," the lady in her forties concedes.

Ščepán begins his speech. "Small businesses are flourishing in the city. Thankfully, they are now widely approved of. Just last week, four new cafés and two boutiques opened. Right here, in the city centre. But this also has its bad side. Several criminal gangs are operating in the city. They're not afraid of anything. They rob businesses at night and then, to cover their tracks, they set fire to them. By the time the firemen arrive, enormous damage is done. What's more, most business owners start up to their ears in debt, so they don't have any money left for expensive insurance or a new start-up." Ščepán says this with a tragic mask on his face and with moist eyes, as if he were touched by the fate of each and every destitute businessman. "You also get another kind of nastiness:

teenage hooligans throw a smoke bomb, a stink bomb, or a teargas grenade into a restaurant or a shop. Devil knows where they get the stuff! And they don't spare business people's cars: characters with grudges won't leave them alone, especially the better cars that businessmen prefer. They scratch them with keys, spray them with paint, and slash their tyres." Ščepán pauses dramatically. The manageress fiddles with a pencil and says nothing.

"Fortunately," says Ščepán, there is a private service that he, Mr. 'Silent' (as he introduces himself) happens to represent. "It is designed for business people in the city centre and immediate surroundings. For a ridiculously modest fee compared to the sum that you'd have to pay to rebuild a burnt-out business, or for lost business after repeated attacks with stink bombs or tear gas, for this modest fee this private service, Sekuritatia, will ensure they can sleep peacefully at night and their businesses can flourish." Ščepán stops. His throat is dry.

The manageress is quiet. She is reflecting. "Sekuritatia?" she asks.

"Yes, Madam," Ščepán confirms.

"The name reminds me of something," says the manageress.

Ščepán spreads his arms, and suggests a subtle bow, as if to say, "You know, it can't be helped."

The manageress continues, "I don't think I'll need your services. I pay my taxes. Part of that money goes to finance the police. I can't see why I should pay twice over. Maybe I'm naïve, but I still believe that when I need them, the police will protect me from thieves, teenage hooligans, characters with grudges and, not least, extortionate speculators who'd like to live off us small business people under various pretences." The manageress gets up and opens the door defiantly.

"You said, 'When you need someone'?" Ščepán asks, still seated. He smiles. "My dear lady, when you need someone, it's too late. We in the private company Sekuritatia deal above all in prevention. We're not interested in running after an arsonist after he's started a fire, even though I'm not saying that sometimes we can't be very firm."

"I believe that I've made myself clear, gentlemen," says the manageress and with a smooth gesture points to the open door. "In any case, I'll mention your proposition to my friend, a major in the police," she adds. "He'll certainly advise and help me."

"You need to believe that," says Ščepán, shrugging. He nods to Šolik and the latter finally moves away from the window overlooking the yard.

"You're a very clever woman, aren't you?" says Šolik says, in an offended tone.

"Yes," says the manageress, "I had a very good education." Her facial expression suggests that she's pleased that everything has finally been made clear by Šolik's remark.

"That was a tough bitch!" Ščepán says outside, almost with admiration.

"So what?" Šolik remarks contemptuously. "An ordinary intellectual cunt," he lets fly, cut to the quick.

"Don't worry; we'll get her," says Ščepán. He opens his notebook and makes a little note.

"And now?" asks Šolik. "Where to, chief?"

Ščepán reflects. He looks in his notebook. "Let's go just round the corner from here, to Oravec and Debnar, the electronics shop," he says. "They're sure to pay up," he concludes, full of hope. "Just remember," he says to the depressed Šolik, "in the end, they all pay, and with interest backdated. After all: who are we? We're Rácz's men; that's who we are!"

Thus encouraged, the men resolutely set off.

* * *

Rácz is paying from his own pocket to renovate the office the manager abandoned; it will all belong to him, anyway. The tradesmen work frantically; Rácz pays handsomely.

Finally, all is finished. Rácz enters the comfortably furnished office and sits down in a leather swivel chair behind a giant kidney-shaped table. On his glass-covered work desk is a light blue screen.

"What gadget is that?" asks Rácz asks, pointing to the screen.

"It's a computer," says the lawyer, who was personally responsible for renovating the vanished manager's office.

Rácz looks round the room. His eye rests on the elegant blue paintwork covering the black, smoke-damaged walls. "What do we need a computer for?" he asks. "Rácz can calculate anything, anyway," he declares.

The lawyer clears his throat. "That's right, I know. But the computer is no ordinary calculator. Its memory holds the whole future financial dealings of the hotel and other affiliated businesses. We'll also be able to keep tabs on the people working in our protection service. And all this will be done without paperwork."

Rácz nods. "That's different. Rácz hates pushing papers, bureaucracy. Well, fine, we'll have to move with the times. The computer can stay for the time being. But have it turned off, the flashing screen gets on Rácz's nerves. Besides, his memory still serves him well. Rácz knows very well who's paid and who hasn't for protection services. Ščepán can sort it out at the double. Rácz has given him a free hand! Nobody plays games with Rácz." Rácz looks the lawyer over with a steady gaze filled with icy steel flashes.

"Now we're here," he says, "we're staying! Anyone who wants to do business in this city has to deal with us! Nobody will even fart without our permission, is that clear?"

The lawyer rubs his hands with enthusiasm. Whatever made him even think he could fight a genius like Rácz?

"Quite right, boss! You're right, as always! Without us, without our support, nobody will be able to do a thing! Nobody!"

Rácz sits back. He stretches out his arms. He's wearing an impeccably tailored suit. His eyes radiate energy. He picks up the phone. "Give me my fiancée, please," he says. "Three-eight-three, one-six-one. Listen, young lady, could you possibly make an effort to remember this number? Is that really too much to ask of you? Fine, I accept that." Rácz puts on a conciliatory self-satisfied expression. "But I don't want to repeat this in future," he says patronizingly. "Rácz's secretary has to know more than Rácz himself."

The lawyer backs towards the door. Rácz halts him with a gesture. "Get me a list of Austrian credit institutions," says Rácz, covering the receiver with a hand. Find out all that's necessary. If need be, you and Urban will go to Vienna even before the auction. We have to be ready. You can go now!"

"Good morning, Mama!" Rácz says, when Lenka's mother answers the phone. She insists on being called Mama. Rácz has to call Lenka's father Karol. "She's at the university?" He's disappointed. "When will she be back, in the evening? I'll call her then, and no, I won't be able to join you for dinner, I'm too busy. Yes, we're working on it. Auction? Perhaps next week. Thank you very much! But we'll see each other before then. I hope you're right! Of course, I'll do everything I can."

Ščepán knocks at the door and enters. He clears his throat. Rácz has just finished his phone call. His calls don't take long; he's brief and to the point. He sizes up the ex-secret policeman. "Well, how do you like your job? Is working for Rácz good, or bad? Is Rácz mean?"

Ščepán deflects the very possibility of such rhetorical questions with equally rhetorical gestures. "No, no, boss," he protests decisively, but respectfully. "All of us, my men and myself, are very grateful to you and will serve you to our last breath."

Rácz nods happily. Rácz has plans. They may be a bit grandiose, but that doesn't change a thing. Rácz is accustomed to achieving everything he attempts. He is planning to build a big security organization. A private security firm. The police will be nothing by comparison. It will happen soon. The nucleus of this powerful force will be Ščepán and his two people, Šolik and Tupý. This organization will take care of security at the Hotel Ambassador and other sites that Rácz will eventually buy. Similarly, as Ščepán can imagine, it will take care of the security of all small businessmen who ask Rácz for protection.

Ščepán listens attentively and unwittingly stands to attention. Rácz pauses. Why go rabbiting on? Everything's quite clear! Rácz gets up and walks up to the ex-secret policeman. He looks straight into his eyes. Rácz wants to know if a certain issue has been resolved. There were apparently problems with a boutique nearby.

Ščepán smiles, proud and content. As far as the *Sandra* boutique is concerned, the boss needn't worry at all. A few days ago somebody threw a stink bomb into the shop. A day later, unknown evildoers flattened and slashed the owner's car tyres. Now the owner is ready to pay the sum requested for protection.

Rácz nods. That's how he thought it would go. Rácz takes a wooden cigar box from the table and offers it to Ščepán. Ščepán takes a cigar and holds it reverently with two fingers, waiting for Rácz to light his own, and then Ščepán's, cigar. A light blush covers his face: he would have given his life for Rácz at that moment.

Rácz takes a few puffs and becomes chatty. He is quite sure that the time is ripe. Soon the prisoners will have to be released. There are several reasons. Firstly, they can't be held forever. Most of them have families and after a few months' absence, the families might panic and go to the police. At the moment, Rácz doesn't need that. Secondly, prolonged imprisonment has changed them, reformed them. Now they know there's no point standing up to Rácz!

Ščepán agrees wholeheartedly. Yes, indeed, that's how it is! To stand up to the big man Rácz is the same, one could say, as pissing into the wind! Or even better, as barking at the moon! And to put it really expressively, it would be like quarrelling with God Almighty!

Rácz looks at him without moving a muscle: in Rácz's opinion, Ščepán couldn't have put it better. He knows that Ščepán is speaking from personal experience. Ščepán was once on the wrong side of the barricade. Now he's on the right side. The same goes for the lawyer. None of them now regret serving Rácz. He's sure that prolonged isolation in a small space, cold, thirst and hunger have changed the minds of the Albanians, as well as the gypsies. They will be released. From now on, they will serve Rácz. And those who don't want to, will have to leave town one way or another. His organization will not tolerate competition. That means there are only two possibilities: they either work for him, or they get out. It is important for Rácz that here, in the centre, everything has to be under his control. And he means everything: currency dealers, whores, gambling, sales of smuggled cigarettes and alcohol, protection racket, and in general, business as such. There is no other way. As far as Rácz is concerned, there is no longer any reason to keep prisoners. Here, in the centre, everyone is needed! Anyone willing to work for the common good has an assured position in Sekuritatia.

Rácz, lost in thought, nibbles the end of his cigar.

As for the villa, Rácz has a plan. As soon as the last prisoner is released, they will send a good architect there; they'll hire a good team of the best tradesmen who will turn the neglected building into an impressive mansion. Rácz's impressive mansion with an indoor pool, and so on!

Ščepán comes to life. "Is the boss suggesting that he'll personally reside in the villa?"

"Yes, exactly that!" says Rácz. The villa is spacious and comfortable. Does Ščepán know what style of architecture it is? No? It's cubical style. Ščepán should remember that. Cubical. Rácz unwittingly taps his forehead. You have to read a book or two sometimes! But to continue: there's a beautiful view of the city from the villa. Rácz will get married and move into the villa. He's had enough of living in a hotel and eating in restaurants. Rácz wants a home of his own!

Despite Ščepán's enthusiastic agreement, Rácz pauses and puffs on his cigar. Why on earth is he sharing personal information with this sidekick? Sidekicks surround Rácz. They watch his face to catch the smallest hint of Rácz's mood of the moment. He puffs on his cigar and sits down at his desk. Actually, he finds it both pleasant and unpleasant.

* * *

The stump of the severed little finger heals quickly. Above the office desk hangs a battered mess pot. It's hanging there on Rácz's orders, to remind him of his imprisonment.

The lawyer has sincerely repented his actions. Without any falsity or treachery he has admitted he wronged Rácz. He doesn't know what got into him. He can only regret that he did not think of joining the mighty stoker earlier. The lawyer should have realised that this was not just anybody, but somebody aiming for the heights! Had he sensed it earlier, he could have had a much better position. At present, he has to be content with being Rácz's second deputy. The first deputy is that show-off bisexual Urban. And Urban got there despite having nothing, no education, except a shitty College of Applied Arts. But still, the lawyer has to give him his due: Urban is smart and proactive. As Rácz's deputy, Urban has visited all the important people in the city, leaving behind generous gifts from the stoker, memories of his radiant smile and a slowly dissipating aroma of manly Fahrenheit perfume. Rácz has never had to poke his nose out of the Hotel Ambassador and yet, thanks to Urban, he's become a popular person and a man everyone has to reckon with if they want to amount to anything in the city.

The lawyer advises the following. As soon as Rácz becomes the owner of the Hotel Ambassador on paper as well as in reality, he has to contact representatives of the most influential political parties. He has to invite them one by one to the Hotel, best to a working breakfast — it's fashionable and doesn't take up so much time.

Rácz agrees, but is a bit embarrassed. He doesn't see what he's going to talk about with the bearded leaders of social democrats, national democrats, people's democrats and who knows what other democrats. Rácz says he doesn't give a shit about politics. He thinks everybody should take care of his own shit.

The lawyer explains that Rácz won't have to say anything: he's a rich hotelier and businessman. Let the political leaders blether on: it's they who will want Rácz's help with their election campaigns. Rácz only wants to have breakfast. He has the advantage.

Rácz has mixed feelings. He's suspicious and dubious. Of course, he can sit straight and keep a poker face, his metallic grey eyes looking straight ahead, but the lawyer has learned how to read him. Clenched fists and a slightly jutting lower jaw are sure signs of a struggle inside Rácz.

"We'll promise to help all of them," advises the lawyer. "And we'll help them all," he adds.

Rácz fixes his eyes on him. "All of them?" he murmurs unhappily.

"All those with chances of good seats in the elections," the lawyer corrects himself. "We'll give something to the Left and something to the Right; something to the Catholics, and something to the Atheists. Let's not forget the Ecologists either, or the Nationalists."

"What about the Hungarians?" Rácz asks menacingly.

"We'll give them something, too," the lawyer answers hastily. "We'll get it back after the elections. Whoever wins does so with our help. That help will be repaid a hundredfold. No man is an island," he says.

Rácz listens without comment. He's stubborn, but doesn't fight new ideas. "Do you think that would be clever?" he asks, reflecting.

The lawyer smiles politely. "You can't even fart without politicians nowadays," he says. "And if you think that you can run away from politics, politics will find you," he adds sagely.

Rácz smiles. He likes the lawyer's idea. He'd never before even thought of concerning himself with politics. Politics is the roguery of the rich, he's known that from childhood. But now he's rich, he realises, once and for all. He stands up abruptly and lights a cigar that went out during his sustained reflection. Yes, he decides: from now on, politics and hotelier Rácz will be inseparable partners!

* * *

The long awaited auction of the Hotel Ambassador is happening semi-legally in a small meeting room of the Town Hall. It's one of the smallest rooms, thanks to the means the lawyer appropriately selected to motivate the miserably paid city officials. The lawyer is now sitting in the first row, together with Rácz and Urban, his arms crossed and looking confident. The employees of Sekuritatia hired by Ščepán are placed all around the room. They are wearing civilian clothes, but their shaven heads and broad shoulders without any intervening necks suggest dangerous vitality and silent menace. Anyone who knows something about the functioning of the city centre is aware that this will be Rácz's one-man show.

Rácz absent-mindedly browses the auction catalogue. Besides the Hotel Ambassador, the neighbouring department store, a big food palace named CentroGourmand, the luxurious Restaurant Savarin and a few smaller restaurants will have their fates decided. Rácz looks at the lawyer. Words are unnecessary. This is their day. They'll have to take it all. If the Austrians lend them money for one site, they'll lend them money for all of them.

There are few interested parties. Almost none. Not only because they've managed to keep the auction almost secret, but mostly because everyone in the city knows that Ambassador belongs to Rácz. There were only two other potential buyers, from outside the city. They learned of the auction by some mysterious act of fate, and so they came.

"They might have a man in the Fund," the lawyer explains to allay Rácz's worries.

Fortunately, the two cheerful vegetable growers from the Danube Island are happy to learn that it would be much appreciated if they would be spectators this morning, and they would get a small sum in compensation. Rácz knows how to appreciate a favour.

The auction begins at nine sharp. At first the small sites in the city centre are auctioned off. Rácz is not interested and magnanimously leaves them to the vegetable growers. When the Hotel Ambassador lot comes up, he gets nervous. He doesn't let on. He sits relaxed, not moving, one leg crossed over the other, and his metallic eyes hypnotize the auctioneer.

The starting price is ten million. Nothing: no interested buyer comes forward. The auctioneer has to move to a Dutch auction after a while, lowering the price. Gradually, in a dramatic voice, he reduces the price of the hotel. In the end, Rácz buys the Ambassador for five million, five hundred thousand. He looks at his companions with satisfaction.

"We could pay for it with cash from the office safe," he tells Urban.

In the same way they acquire CentroGourmand and Savarin. Rácz's people are sitting calmly and well focused. The next item is the department store. Rácz has plans for it. He wants to hire an architect and turn the building into a hotel and office building. So there'd be two hotels next to each other, like twins. One would keep its original name, the Ambassador, and the other one would be called Hotel Rácz, what else? Or both would be called Ambassador-Rácz: One and Two. He would decide.

The department store also changes ownership by Dutch auction. A bribe to the National Property Fund worked. Rácz gets it for a paltry four million.

Rácz laughs. "This is a dream, damn and blast it!"

At the end of the auction, the stoker is as proud as any outright winner should be. It's all legal, in accordance with the law. He'll never go back to the boiler-room, or drive a tractor in the village. He realises this and unobtrusively wipes an involuntary tear from his cheek.

Contracts are drawn up and a copy of each goes into the lawyer's fine-leather case. Arranging a few days' delay in paying the final sum is no problem for the lawyer and Urban. Each important official will leave with a thick envelope, a financial gift, in his pocket. Everybody is happy, as well as Rácz. They managed to keep everything quiet and no journalist will be digging around.

Euphoria has overcome Rácz's companions, as if they'd drunk several glasses of sparkling wine. Their faces turn red; their staring eyes judge the surrounding world joyfully and with a merciful tolerance. The men have become noisy. The world has become elastic; it is both funny and joyful. They feel like doing nothing but celebrating and having fun. Only Rácz, happily smoking his cigar, brings them back to earth.

"We haven't won yet," he says and splashes a bucket of cold water on the merrily bubbling fountain of happiness. "The Hotel Ambassador is ours, we have enough money for that, but we are not masters of the other properties yet. What if they won't give us a mortgage in Vienna?" he asks almost reproachfully, looking gravely at the excited Lawyer who has been happily playing with his nine fingers: he was the architect of the coup.

"It's as good as done!" the Lawyer shouts. "It's in the bag! Don't you get it?"

Rácz shrugs: he is not so sure! It looks good, but it's not yet time to celebrate. However, when the hotelier notices that his men look a bit down in the mouth, he hastily reassures them. Rácz didn't mean to say that when everything is done, he's not going to organize a big blowout, the biggest blowout in the history of this bloody city.

Rácz spells out his instructions in the car. "We are going to *my* hotel, you'll let me out there, and continue directly to Vienna," he says. "You've got your passports? Good. When you get the mortgage, call me from Vienna. I'll be waiting. And call me even if you don't get it," the hotelier stresses. He'll be waiting for a phone call.

"But why don't you get yourself a passport, too, boss," asks Urban. "You could travel with us."

Rácz smiles. Rácz does not need to travel anywhere. He never travels anywhere. Rácz has people to do it for him.

They arrive at the Ambassador and park in the yard. All the employees are waiting, looking out of the windows. When Rácz enters the lobby, they all bow to him. They know already that Rácz is now their boss, legally as well as in reality. They all want to shake their employer's hand. They bring him bread and salt on a round tray. Rácz takes a piece of bread and, chewing it, he pinches a pretty waitress on the behind.

The lawyer claps and announces, "Mr. Rácz, the President of Rácz Ltd., a company that has today acquired the Hotel Ambassador, is grateful to you all for your welcome and asks you to go back to work. Our President would like everyone to know that nobody who works hard and responsibly need fear losing his job. And now, please, back to work!"

* * *

Rácz shortens the tormenting wait for a phone call that will set him free by sipping a drink in the bar. He has Ďula and the ex-secret policeman Ščepán for company. They, too, are glad: they will finally get proper work contracts. Ščepán was promised a small percentage share in Rácz's company. Nothing big compared with the percentages of Urban and the lawyer. They're real partners, though the majority owner is, of course, Rácz.

He's as tense as a taut string. He's irritable and relieves his impatience by drinking *Heevash Reygahl*. He checks his watch and thinks: Urban and the lawyer must be in Vienna by now. And now they're entering the bank. Maybe they're negotiating already: both speak German very well. Rácz downs another Scotch and wishes that he had got a passport after all, and could accompany them.

Ščepán and Ďula sense that Rácz is nervous, and say nothing. They drink silently, but because they can't take as much as the hotelier, they begin to reel on their chairs. Rácz ignores them, shrouded in the smoke of an expensive Cohiba cigar, and looks tensely and uncertainly at his nails. The blackness from the coal has long disappeared from the pores of Rácz's hands. The dirt has washed out and the constantly damaged nails and fingertips have turned pink. The rest is due to a manicure: Rácz is now proud of his sensitive gentleman's hands. Only their excessive size and his thick fingers tell a watchful observer that there once was a time when those hands worked to support their owner.

Both Urban's wives, Wanda and Eva, appear in the bar. Rácz invites them with a gesture to join in and sit down. He orders each a glass of Becherovka.

"Where's Urban?" asks Wanda.

"The boss has sent them to Vienna," says Ďula, who makes a grab for Wanda's knee, but Wanda pushes his hand off so vigorously, that even Rácz, roused from his thoughts, lifts his gaze from his hands.

Urban's lady-friends are silent. They don't feel like being pawed by Rácz's drunken sidekick. They no longer feel like whores; they are attached to, and very much in love with Urban and they want to be faithful to him. They cook for him, buy him clothes, and do whatever he wishes. They're not jealous of each other. They like and understand each other very much, like sisters. They want everyone to think of them as married women, as Urban's wives. But it is hard for the men from the hotel to do that, since they remember them as prostitutes. Rácz looks wildly at Ďula. Ďula begins to squint with fear and downs his glass of Chivas Regal. Not that he likes it; he drinks it only because of Rácz. Rácz doesn't care for it that much, either; he drinks it because it happens to be the most expensive whisky in the bar

"Fucking hell!" the hotelier shouts and bangs his fist on the table. "What's wrong with the phone?" He drinks. He's sure that Urban and the lawyer could have phoned a long time ago. "They're taking their bloody time!"

Finally comes the long-awaited phone call. The lawyer's voice sounds happy and excited. "Everything's in order, boss," he shouts, to drown out the noise and voices of other people's phone calls, audible in the receiver. "It's a done deal," he repeats. "We've got credit for everything. We've got a ten-year mortgage. We're on our way home."

Rácz collects himself. "Are you bringing the money?" he asks joyfully. "No, boss," shouts the lawyer. "Everything will be done by direct bank transfer. We won't see a single schilling."

Rácz nods, a little disappointed. "And how much have they lent us?" he asks.

"Exactly thirty-five million, boss," the lawyer says proudly.

Rácz feels vertigo. My God, when will Rácz finally pay it all off? So be it. He digs his heels in. He will start acting right away, tomorrow. The department store will be rebuilt as a hotel: no doubts there. Centro-Gourmand will be closed down and speedily converted to a fitness centre with a pool, exercise rooms and a sauna. Also included will be a Thai body massage parlour, and a bar. The Highlander Restaurant will stay, together with other small fast-food operations, or they will be converted to sex shops. Yes, that will be something new! Rácz is getting happier. "Move it, men!" he orders on the phone. "Get in the car and hurry here! You've done a great job!" he praises the lawyer.

* * *

When Urban and the lawyer return that evening, complete euphoria breaks out full. Rácz is already drunk, but still sitting upright. He lets his men tell him in detail they've seen and done. He is mostly interested in what happened in the bank. He calmly nods when he hears how warmly they were welcomed, how the bankers looked at the sales contracts and business reports for the last few years. It seems to have been a good business deal for the Austrians, too. They'd have liked to meet Herr Rácz in person and they voiced their regrets that he could not actually be present at the negotiations. Rácz is happy to hear that: they respect him. That's good. He'll invite them to come here, he decides.

The lawyer brags: the negotiation was so successful because both the lawyer and Urban made a very smooth, solid impression on them. Their Austrian partners were very hospitable; they were disappointed that Rácz's deputies had to return to their country the same day. They would have preferred to have them both stay for a working dinner. The credit manager, who led the negotiation for the bank, wanted to invite them to some *Pervers Club* not far from Vienna, saying they'd have had a very good time there.

Rácz praises their refusal of such entertainment. "Tomorrow we'll have our work cut out for us," he says. "And so everyone will get a good nightcap of *Heevash Reygahl* and good night and good-bye to all! We'll always find time for a big blowout," the hotelier decides. They drink up, finish their cigars and cigarettes and go to their homes. Urban takes his concubines in a taxi, Ďula drives the lawyer in the hotel Renault, and Rácz takes the lift to his suite. He can't get to sleep for a long time and keeps tossing and turning in bed. He doesn't know what to do first. There are so many things to do: renovating his villa overlooking the city, rebuilding the department store, building a fitness centre, his own wedding with Lenka, setting up sex shops, and as well as all that, there is the everyday routine work on hundreds of small, but important details.

Rácz gets up several times during the night. He drinks water from the carafe set out for him, then goes over to the window, lights a Havana and looks into the darkness. The line of light on the horizon over the river almost surprises him. He crawls back into bed, but no matter what, cannot get to sleep. Only just before dawn does he doze off and dream a brief flash of a dream, one of very few in his life.

None of the dream was true. Rácz was going home to his native village without a crown in his pocket. He was walking slowly and heavily, even though his bag was empty. Eržika had married proud Feri Bartaloš and Rácz couldn't even recall their faces. The road was wet and Rácz wandered through the village. Nobody recognized him and he couldn't even find the way to Kišš's house. He silently accepted hospitality from a stranger. The man's wife brought him out a bowl of bean soup and a thick slice of bread. Rácz chewed silently. He wanted to talk about the great wealth he once had, but the words wouldn't come out of his mouth. When he finally got them out, the man and woman listened to him with sad faces. They were sure he was lying, but they did not call him a liar. Even Rácz was not sure that he'd really been as wealthy as he tried to suggest to the hospitable peasants. He stopped chewing and thought about himself: was he only dreaming, or had he just invented it all? He started crying bitterly, moved by his own fate. He felt pity for himself and for the strange man that he had taken a liking to.

"Time to get up, boss!" Ďula's voice interrupts him, and Rácz wakes up. He is in bed in his suite and everything is intact. Ďula is standing over him and firmly, but respectfully shaking him by the shoulder. When he sees that the hotelier is awake, he gives an explanation. "You told me to wake you up at half past ten."

But Rácz is not at all angry. Quite the opposite, he is in a thoroughly good mood, though he's still sleepy. The bad feeling of the dream has vanished; Rácz jumps out of bed and runs to have a shower. He alternates cold and hot water. He exercises with resolute gestures. He puts on his trousers, shirt and a tie. Ďula snaps his fingers and a waiter quietly enters the room, pushing a breakfast trolley before him. Rácz lets him pour a cup of hot coffee and slurps it down, looking out of the window.

The city is empty. A dark, overcast and lead-coloured sky weighs heavily on the roofs of the buildings. There is no sun; it has been hidden by clouds for a long time. When it does peer out occasionally, it shines a cold, chalky colour. The river is muddy, black. The boats slowly fight the current. A shower of rain passes, drumming on the roofs of cars waiting for a green light at the crossroads.

"Nothing you can do about it," says Ďula, catching Rácz's eye. "It's March," he adds, as if apologizing.

* * *

What else is there to add?

In the next few days Rácz will take several important steps. He will order the release of the detained Albanians and gypsies. They will all have to swear an oath of loyalty until the grave. From now on, they'll work only for him.

Berki and Šípoš will be free as well. By now they have got so used to the boiler-room that they decide to stay in the hotel and work as stokers.

Nobody has heard any more about the unfortunate manager of the Hotel Ambassador. It may be that he did reach his goal, the Arctic Circle. And maybe he's still on his way there, hiding during the day from curious eyes and driving his pack of dogs at night over the snowbound plains, always heading due north. Those dogs that the manager left behind discovered Hurensson as soon as the snow melted. They dragged his bones all round the yard and the surroundings of the Hotel. A boy found Hurensson's skull; it was cleaned bare by the dogs, and he put it in a glass case. Until his father confiscates the skull, squeamishly wraps it in a newspaper, and discreetly takes it out in the dark to dump it in a skip, the Swede will go on obtusely baring his teeth behind glass.

The eventual fate of Silvia and Edita is also unknown to us. Their traces vanish after the Austrian border. So many beautiful women between the ages of thirteen and forty disappear each year from our country that two solitary prostitutes are like two drops in the ocean.

Of course, Rácz will keep the promise he gave Lenka in a moment of weakness. As soon as the tradesmen have restored the weathered, neglected, but attractive villa high above the city, turning it into a luxurious mansion, Rácz takes a giant bouquet and goes to ask for Lenka's hand. He is immediately accepted.

Rácz's wedding becomes the social event of the year. Rácz would not be the man he is if he did not use the occasion to turn it into a sort of representative and promotional event to which all the city's important personalities are invited. They all come; Rácz's name has been mentioned too often for too long. Rácz is happy. He keeps repeating that this is the greatest day of his life. The bride is beautiful. And the groom is manly and well dressed. And wealthy, very wealthy.

All those invited accept the invitation: politicians, businessmen, influential journalists, and even those clowns, the artists. The latter get drunk since they can drink for free; they agree with everything, nodding their bearded mugs, ready to kiss anyone's arse.

Soon after the wedding, the newly-weds move into the villa.

The lawyer's plan for Rácz to move into the politics turns out to be realistic and easily carried out. At his wedding, Rácz makes friends with all the invited government leaders and politicians. With the caution of a stubborn, ignorant peasant, he selects two of the many political parties that seek his favour. He places Video Urban in one of the parties. The party leader soon promotes Urban to the central coordinating committee as thanks for the latter's exceptional contribution to a successful election campaign. No wonder, as Rácz is generous with his money. Urban runs for the party in the communal elections. He wins and becomes a deputy to the city legislature. The party leader promises to let him run for parliament in two years.

Even the lawyer isn't left unrewarded by politics. Using generous financial contributions, Rácz pushes him into the other political party. Soon the lawyer gets into the Slovak National Assembly and becomes a member of various committees close to Dr. Renceš, the Mayor. Rácz is keen to push the lawyer even further, but he has to wait a bit. They can move only after faithful Ščepán produces a document that will be used as evidence of Dr. Renceš's alleged collaboration with communist State Security. After sensational disclosures, nothing will stop the lawyer being elected Mayor. It need not be stressed that the battered aluminium mess pot will take place of honour on the Mayor's office wall. Of course, the lawyer will never forget whom he has to thank for his career and will never forget to show his gratitude. The same goes for Urban.

Lenka becomes pregnant and after the end of the academic year she interrupts her studies indefinitely. She may resume them in the distant future.

Rácz will open his Fitness Centre in the summer. The formal opening will be graced by the presence of the new Mayor who will remain ensconced with the hotelier in mutually advantageous conversation on the topic of the development of private business in the city.

The luxury Hotel Ambassador-Rácz II will start operating in autumn. Rácz is up to his ears in debt, but he looks happy. He knows that these days debt is the best investment.

By the end of the year he has a son. His name will be Karol, after his father-in-law, Lenka's father. He will be baptized in the church where the wedding took place. In addition to permanent resident staff consisting of two maids, two butlers, a gardener, a chef, and, of course, Rácz's personal secretary, butler, chauffeur, and clown Ďula, they hire a governess.

* * *

As always, after a light, but delicious and nourishing dinner, Rácz goes out onto his terrace to smoke his cigar quietly under the twinkling stars. He looks down at the city below the hill. Each building belonging to Rácz Corporation carries on its roof a striking green light. Rácz counts them every night like shining pinheads stuck in a map. When he has finished counting, he is content to puff on his cigar and blow the thinning smoke into the indigo black sky.

This is what Rácz has achieved with these two hands and this head, he realises. The world belongs to smart people, he says to himself. Rácz got the chance and used it. The wind blows. The hotelier shivers in the chilly air. He puffs once more on the cigar and then, with his thumb and index finger, sends it flying down into the darkness. He does not wait for it to get colder or for the next gust of wind. He hurries inside, into his villa, and firmly closes the big glass door behind him.

* * *

Do you feel that we may have forgotten someone?

Do you sense we haven't ended the story of one of our heroes? You are not mistaken. But what can one say about the further destiny of Freddy Mešťanek, known as Piggybank? Unwillingly, but conscientiously, he pays the private service Sekuritatia for protection from bad gypsies, eats sausages and beans and has long ago put his weight back on.

Like an angry and choleric fanatic, he runs up and down the car park in front of the Hotel Ambassador-Rácz I, and he either explodes in anger at innocent customers, or ardently kisses their arses.

You don't believe me? Run and have a look! He might still be there.